An author of more than ninety books for children and adults with more than seventy-five for Mills & Boon, **Janice Kay Johnson** writes about love and family and pens books of gripping romantic suspense. A *USA TODAY* bestselling author and an eight-time finalist for the Romance Writers of America *RITA*® Award, she won a *RITA*® Award in 2008. A former librarian, Janice raised two daughters in a small town north of Seattle, Washington.

Justine Davis lives on Puget Sound in Washington State, watching big ships and the occasional submarine go by and sharing the neighbourhood with assorted wildlife, including a pair of bald eagles, deer, a bear or two, and a tailless raccoon. In the few hours when she's not planning, plotting or writing her next book, her favourite things are photography, knitting her way through a huge yarn stash and driving her restored 1967 Corvette roadster—top down, of course. Connect with Justine on her website, justinedavis.com, at Twitter.com/justine_d_davis or on Facebook at Facebook.com/justinedaredavis

Also by Janice Kay Johnson

Hide the Child
Trusting the Sheriff
Within Range
Brace for Impact
The Hunting Season
The Last Resort
Cold Case Flashbacks

Also by Justine Davis

Operation Midnight
Operation Reunion
Operation Blind Date
Operation Unleashed
Operation Power Play
Operation Homecoming
Operation Soldier Next Door
Operation Alpha
Operation Notorious
Operation Hero's Watch
Operation Second Chance
Operation Mountain Recovery

Discover more at millsandboon.co.uk

DEAD IN
THE WATER

JANICE KAY JOHNSON

COLTON K-9
TARGET

JUSTINE DAVIS

MILLS & BOON

First Published in Great Britain 2021
by Mills & Boon, an imprint of HarperCollins*Publishers* Ltd
1 London Bridge Street, London, SE1 9GF

www.harpercollins.co.uk

HarperCollins*Publishers*
1st Floor, Watermarque Building,
Ringsend Road, Dublin 4, Ireland

Dead in the Water © 2021 Janice Kay Johnson
Colton K-9 Target © 2021 Harlequin Books S.A.

Special thanks and acknowledgement are given to Justine Davis for her contribution to *The Coltons of Grave Gulch* series.

ISBN: 978-0-263-28351-8

0821

MIX
Paper from
responsible sources
FSC™ C007454

This book is produced from independently certified FSC™ paper to ensure responsible forest management.

For more information visit: www.harpercollins.co.uk/green

Printed and bound in Spain
by CPI, Barcelona

DEAD IN
THE WATER

JANICE KAY JOHNSON

Chapter One

Claire Holland cautiously separated the flaps of her tent to look out. At least there was no patter of rain, but after two cold, foggy days of paddling while battling ocean swells, she was ready for dry and warm.

She and her partner, Mike Maguire, had chosen to follow the western shore of Calvert Island off the coast of British Columbia, Canada, unshielded from the open Pacific Ocean, and it had been all the challenge any sea kayaker could wish. A brutal headwind had been followed by ten-foot-high ocean swells as they crossed Hakai Passage. Claire had been immensely grateful for last night's campsite above a beautiful sandy beach on Triquet Island.

She blinked at the view outside her tent. Sunshine, dazzling her eyes.

As was the case on most of the BC coast, the setting was glorious. The wooded arms of the inlet wrapped around them, and they could see a cluster of the small rocky islets that dotted the short stretches of water between these islands, creating a maze of narrow passages. The air was salty, but she could smell the sharp tang of the spruce and cedar trees a few feet away.

Mike crawled out of his own tent and grinned as he rose to his feet and stretched his lanky body. "Wow.

Maybe we should camp here for a week or two. We don't have to tell people we didn't really get to Goose Island."

She laughed. "What say we dawdle, at least?"

So that's what they did while they waited for high tide, which made launching a lot easier anyway. No hauling their heavily loaded kayaks—or their kayaks and then their gear—across the distance exposed by the low tide.

After a breakfast of oatmeal and coffee, Claire happily shed several layers of clothes to bask in almost-warm sunshine—this was only June, after all—while they waited for the tide to rise. She and Mike laid damp clothing and gear out to dry and indulged in an extra cup of coffee.

Today, all they planned to do anyway was wander. Both had paddled most of the Inside Passage from Washington State to Alaska before, although not together. For this trip, they'd agreed to check out some of the most scenic and less-traveled groups of islands on the coast, and catch the ferry home from Prince Rupert in Alaska, just over the border from Canada.

"Hate to say it, Claire," Mike said, nodding toward the shore.

She made a face at him. She'd already broken down her tent and rolled her sleeping bag, but still had to pack up the camp stove and minimal pans and dishes. Plus, they'd spread out more than usual.

They'd met at a kayaking class that she'd taken to strengthen her skills so that she could tackle more adventurous trips. Having been paired up for some drills, they'd gotten along well. After the class ended, they took day trips, then weekend explorations in the San Juan Islands and the Canadian gulf coast islands. Fortunately, Claire and Mike's wife, Shelby, hit it off right away. She was lucky Mike's wife let her "borrow" him, as Shelby put it. Shelby, who liked to sun herself on a beach in the Caribbean or Hawaii but hated getting cold or dirty, was perfectly willing to loan out her husband for the totally insane hobby he and Claire shared. As far as Claire could tell, Shelby had never had a moment of worry about the two of them together, isolated, off for weeks on this journey.

Claire wrinkled her nose at the thought. Gee, the fact that Shelby was stunningly beautiful and possessed eye-popping curves might have something to do with it. Mike was madly in love with his wife, too, or Claire wouldn't have agreed to this jaunt.

Thank goodness she no longer had to worry about what Devin—or any man, for that matter—thought.

Long practice allowed both to stuff their dry bags quickly, leaving air in them to increase buoyancy, and jam their possessions into their kayaks, lighter items at the stern and bow, heavier things like the tent, food bags and water close to the cockpit. The worst part, as far as she was concerned, was suiting up for another day on the water. She thought every time about the oft-used image of sticking your hand in a bucketful of worms. The inside of her wet suit was always clammy. And, even more fun, she had to squirm and contort to pull the stretchy neoprene over her body and get her arms inserted into the sleeves and her feet into the molded booties. With the day so pleasant and their plans so un-ambitious, she almost tucked away her gloves rather than wearing them, but then looked ruefully at her hands. She'd acquired a few blisters that had popped, and, gee, the rash from the devil's club she'd encoun-tered two days ago still burned.

Oh, fine. On with the gloves.

Once suited up, she reminded herself how happy she was on the water in her sleek blue Boréal Design Baffin Series kayak. She'd found much-needed peace and self-confidence in exploring the wilderness in her watercraft.

After she and Mike took turns slipping into the cold ocean, Claire looked around with pleasure. The water was almost completely still, a deceptive blue shimmer disguising the strength of tides and currents beneath. She barely had to dip her paddle in to send her kayak gliding forward. Those islets topped by stunted trees blocked much of the view ahead as they emerged from the long cove that sheltered last night's camp spot and zigzagged among the cluster of islands.

They hadn't seen another soul in days, only larger ships out on Queen Charlotte Sound and cabin cruisers and fishing boats at a distance when they crossed Hakai Passage, so it was a surprise twenty minutes later to hear voices carrying over the water. Probably, they came from one of those cabin cruisers or fishing boats whose skipper had chosen to anchor here. Larger boats kept their distance from the intricate maze of islands, inlets and passages in this part of the British Columbia Queens Sound, a small slice of the vast Queen Charlotte Sound that was cluttered with tiny islands on this western edge of the BC coast. Charts weren't always accurate.

Mike was ahead when he passed an islet almost large enough to classify as an island, although it was unlikely to have ever been named. She heard him say, "What the—"

Some instinct had her back paddling, although she'd already glided forward enough to see what had startled him: an older coastal freighter, probably no more than forty or fifty meters long but still wildly out of place. A crane on its forward deck was currently swinging a pallet of something heavy onto the smaller deck of a shining white yacht. Men were working aboard both yacht and freighter, neither of which would be able to linger here long with the tide already ebbing. And why they'd tucked themselves in among tiny islands— No, she thought slowly. They must want to be unseen. She'd read that smuggling was common across both the land and water borders between Canada and the US. People, drugs, who knew what else.

Mike's neon-red-and-orange kayak moved well into the open, even though he wasn't paddling. The frightened instinct telling her that neither ship belonged here kept Claire hovering in the shelter of the islet. Wispy branches of a twisted cedar hung low enough she was able to reach up and grab one to hold herself in place, her kayak bumping and scraping along the vertical rocks as the nearly unseen waves lifted and dropped. Through the feathery branch, she saw the moment someone on board the freighter noticed Mike.

The man shouted a name. Everyone visible on both the yacht and the small freighter turned to look.

Mike lifted a hand and called, "Hello!"

People tended to be friendly in these waters. Several times earlier in the trip, he and Claire had been invited to have dinner aboard one large cabin cruiser or another, most recently enjoying a wide-ranging conversation with a retired couple who said they spent most summers cruising between the San Juan Islands and Alaska.

But this—

Horror filled her chest when one of the men on the freighter lifted a rifle.

Mike saw, thrust his paddle into the water to push

backward. Stunned, Claire was still watching the guy with the rifle when a *crack, crack, crack* nearly deafened her, and something skimmed the water only a few feet from her kayak.

A bullet.

Events had become slow-motion. Mike jerked, then slumped sideways. His weight carried his kayak into a roll. To hide in the water, she prayed, but he didn't re-emerge. Untethered, his paddle drifted loose on the surface. Hull up, the kayak floated at the mercy of the tide.

Even as she whispered, "Please, please, please," Claire fumbled in her day hatch for the SPOT satellite tracker with the panic button that would bring help.

But not soon enough, not for Mike.

No, he'd only dropped his paddle and was snatching at something as he rolled. He'd freed himself from the cockpit and was swimming underwater, trying to reach the sanctuary of one of the islets. She'd hear a splash any minute.

Her hands felt clumsy. She couldn't look away from his overturned kayak.

Suddenly, she was juggling with the small electronic device. It slipped from her hand, bounced once off the glossy surface of the deck of her kayak and fell into the water. She grabbed for it, almost unbalancing the kayak, and missed. "Please" was supplanted by "Dear, God. Oh, Lord. Oh, no."

Claire lifted a terrified gaze to see that the crane had swung back into place on the freighter and the yacht was in motion. It turned in a tight circle to pass between two small islands and flee south. She couldn't make out the black letters on the bow. What was wrong with her vision?

Claire swiped angrily at her eyes, and realized she was crying.

RICK BECKMAN SPUN toward the shooter. "Why in the hell did you do that?"

Dwayne Peterson—although probably none of them used a real name—turned a scathing look on Rick. Dwayne cradled the Remington in his meaty arms. "We can't have a witness."

"A lone kayaker? Really? If we'd exchanged waves and a few friendly words with him, he'd have gone on his way without giving us a second thought. But what if some other boaters are in earshot? What happens when this guy is found?"

Dwayne's eyes narrowed. "Kayak's upside-down. He's dead. Probably fell out."

Rick didn't point out that, if the victim had released himself from the cockpit, his body was almost certainly now drifting on the surface, thanks to the flotation device kayakers all seemed to wear.

The *Seattle Flirt*, a pricey midsize yacht, was heading out of this cluster of islands to open water, putting distance between the two boats as fast as the pilot could manage without hitting a rock and grinding a hole in his hull. He was smarter than Dwayne, clearly.

Well aware of the five other men watching the confrontation—no help there—Rick kept his mouth shut, but he did shake his head.

"What?" Dwayne snarled.

Rick shrugged and raised his voice enough to be heard by everyone. "If any of us get arrested now, we'll go down for murder."

"I don't like your attitude."

Rick didn't take his eyes off his nominal boss, who was bristling as he always did at any hint at criticism. Still, Rick remained aware of the bright red hull of the long kayak floating aimlessly with the current. That poor bastard. Having a good time exploring this spectacular landscape, gets shot by a trigger-happy drug trafficker.

It had happened so fast, there hadn't been a damn thing Rick could do to prevent it.

"Nothin' to say?"

Shouldn't have opened his mouth. He balanced on the balls of his feet, staying deceptively relaxed, ready to move fast. But, damn, he wished he wore a Kevlar vest beneath his T-shirt and heavy sweater.

What was done was done. "Nope."

Dwayne started to walk away. He was halfway across the broad, flat deck when he turned back. "Well, I do. I've had it with you." He lifted the rifle and fired in one practiced movement.

The violent punch flung Rick backward. He crashed against the thigh-high metal curb. Flipped over it. Agony spread across his chest until he hit the icy water, when his entire body screamed in protest. Somehow, God knew how, he resisted the instinct to struggle in the water. He had to stay lax when he surfaced.

Had to play dead.

Odds were, hypothermia would ensure he *was* dead, but he couldn't let himself believe it.

CLAIRE STILL HUNG beneath the shelter of the cedar branch, whimpering, when she heard the next gunshot and saw a man topple backward off the freighter.

Terror and a stinging dose of common sense kept her frozen in place. If she was spotted, the next bullet would be the one that killed her. But, oh God, what if Mike was alive? Waiting for her to rescue him?

She knew better, she did. He'd been wearing his PFD. It wouldn't *allow* him to sink below the surface. If he'd managed to release himself from his kayak and was alive, she'd have seen him surface. Given the shock of the bitterly cold water, he wouldn't have been able to hold his breath long.

Her only salvation was that this storm-twisted tree had reached low enough to hide her and that her kayak was blue instead of a neon color like Mike's.

Tearing her eyes from the hull of Mike's kayak, she sought the *other* guy. The one who just went overboard. Him, she could see, floating on his back, unmoving. If he'd moved since he hit the water, she'd missed it.

A change in the sound of the freighter's engine jerked her gaze up. A moment later, men moved purposefully on deck, somebody securing the crane, others going into the squat building that filled the stern and was topped with a tiny wheelhouse and radar. She did her best to memorize what she saw. The hull of the ship was black with a faded red stripe and significant rust, the pilot house a scarred, stained white. She couldn't imagine the freighter still plied the Pacific Coast with any legitimate trade.

But it was moving, so slowly she first thought she was imagining it, but then it began a wide swing across the inlet to go the way of the yacht. Claire had no idea how much time had passed, but knew that with the tide falling the freighter had to reach deeper waters or risk being trapped or grounded.

She didn't move, didn't dare, even when it passed out of sight behind the islet that was her refuge. She waited, waited, until the sound of the engine receded and something like peace returned to the passage.

Then, she let go of her branch, dug deep with her paddle, and shot forward toward Mike's kayak.

The struggle to flip it was brief. It would have been

harder if he'd still been in the cockpit, but he wasn't. She swiveled frantically in place. He had to have lived long enough to release himself from the spray skirt that kept water out of the cockpit. A spot of yellow caught her eye. His PFD—

It floated alone. He had somehow shed that, too. A dying man thinking he was freeing himself from restraint?

And—dear God—he always kept a small day bag tucked in one of the mesh gear pockets on his deck where it would be accessible. The bag was missing, along with Mike himself.

His body.

She heard a splash, then another one. The man who'd been shot and fallen overboard was trying to swim, mostly with one arm. He was alive.

It might have been smart to hesitate, but she didn't. She snatched the PFD out of the water and laid it across her front deck, hanging it over the compass right in front of her, and then started paddling her kayak toward the only man she *could* save.

His already futile effort to swim had slowed to almost nothingness by the time she reached him. Somehow, he lifted his head and saw her. She had the impression of a bone-white face and seal-dark hair. Hypothermia would kill him in no time.

Bracing to hold her kayak a safe distance from him, she tossed the vest toward him. "Can you put this on?"

He grabbed it with one hand, but nothing else happened.

Rescuing him would be the most dangerous thing she'd ever done. A drowning man's instinct would be to lunge toward her kayak. He could sink her. Flip her.

He lifted a glassy-eyed look at her, and tried to dog-paddle toward her.

"Listen to me. Can you follow instructions? Do you understand what I'm saying?"

"Yes." His voice wasn't strong, but it sounded certain enough to make her think he was still aware.

"I'll back up to you. Climb up if you can and pull yourself to lie flat on my boat. Grab a hold of my cockpit. If you dump us over, neither of us will survive. Do you understand?"

She thought he nodded. This was worth a try. If he couldn't make it, she could go back for Mike's kayak, try to pour the water out, somehow help this guy get in…but he was fading fast. She thought he'd be past rescuing if this failed.

She used her paddle deftly, rotating the kayak in the water, backing up until his hand grasped the rear grab loop. Then she did her best to stay steady in the water as he somehow found the strength to heave himself upward and grip with one hand the rigging that criss-crossed the deck. The kayak rolled to the right; she dug in her paddle to brace it. Left, ditto. Then she heard a groan and dared to turn her head.

Somehow, he'd made it and lay sprawled the length of her stern, sinking it deeper than she'd like. The fingers of his one usable hand dug into the cockpit coaming behind her. Claire had practiced rescues like this a few times, but this man was bigger, heavier than anyone she'd tried it with.

The PFD… She looked around. Bumping against her hull. She grabbed it, knowing he might need it—if he survived the next hour or two.

The speed and liveliness Claire relied on from her kayak had turned into reluctance. It barely moved until she dug in to paddle as if she was crossing an open strait midstorm with whitecaps topping rolling waves, a powerful wind at her head.

She'd been thinking only one step at a time, but hadn't moved twenty feet before her mind cleared enough for her to realize she had no idea where she was going. Was there anything closer than last night's campsite? Besides, it didn't seem smart to go the same way the freighter had.

She and Mike had intended to reach Spider Island for the night, but they had notes about a couple of picnic stops where they could beach a kayak that were a lot closer. A chart formed in her mind, although with her current stress and desperation it wasn't easy to see the one-dimensional features in the cluster of rocky islands and unnamed islets in front of her.

I should take Mike's kayak with us, she thought with sudden clarity. Try to dump enough water out of it to allow her to tow it.

Her mind was working sluggishly now. Wait. She could call for help on the VHF radio, and rescue would come to them.

"No," a voice mumbled behind her. "They…could be monitoring for calls for help."

They? Fresh horror was answer enough. *Them*.

And…today, Mike had carried the VHF radio.

Thanks to her panic and clumsiness, the SPOT was gone…and seemingly the VHF, too.

Wait. He often stuck the radio in the pocket of his flotation vest. She paused with the paddle resting across the cockpit and reached forward to the PFD. One look told her the breast pocket was empty. She tried to remember seeing him shove the radio inside and snap the buckle closed this morning. Had he not bothered securing the pocket? Or somehow grabbed for both it and the day bag that held his SPOT?

With no answers, her mind clicked to the next problem as if she were watching a slide show. She'd have no dry clothes for her passenger without what Mike carried. Hers wouldn't do a large man any good. She *had* to reclaim Mike's kayak.

She explained what she was doing to the man behind her, hoping even inane chatter would prevent him from sinking into unconsciousness. He grunted a couple of times.

She wouldn't have had any choice but to abandon the plan if Mike's Tsunami had been carried very far away. Thank heavens the tide hadn't yet turned. Maneuvering her own already sluggish kayak the fifty or so yards to Mike's, she took out her towline and clipped it to the carrying toggle at the bow of his orange-and-red boat, fussed about where to attach the other end and finally chose rigging right in front of her.

With a struggle, she managed to roll it enough to dump out most of the water, but quickly found that towing another kayak, along with the deadweight behind her, shifted her normal sprightly skim over the surface of the water to a painful slog. If the waves had been any higher, they'd have been washing over the deck of her kayak, and over the wounded man clinging to life.

She focused grimly. If she were in the habit of giving up, she wouldn't have chosen a sport where the suffering often outweighed the triumphs.

She passed a rocky island on her starboard. But when she neared the slightly larger one ahead and to her port side, she spotted a hint of an opening. Really a crack in the steep rock. If there was nothing resembling a beach within it… Claire didn't let herself finish the thought. She'd go on, that's what she'd do. Her muscles burned.

"You still with me?" she called over her shoulder.

The fact that her passenger made a noise was a positive. If he was unconscious by the time they got out of the water…

Stop. One step at a time.

Chapter Two

Cold, so cold. With convulsive shivers rattling his body, Adam knew vaguely that he was alive. A woman was talking to him. Occasionally, something in the voice suggested she wanted an answer, so with a supreme effort he summoned a hoarse sound. He'd been shot before, so that part was familiar. Turning into an iceberg, he was sure that was new.

Who was she?

He tried to ponder that, but had no idea. The next bout of deep shudders wiped him clean of any curiosity.

He had to hold on. He knew that. Of course, he couldn't feel his fingers anymore, so he wasn't sure what they were doing, even if they were still attached to his body.

She breathed something in a prayerful voice. He tried to lift his head but failed.

Hold on.

Eventually, a scraping sound penetrated his consciousness. The angle he lay at tipped upward slightly. The surface beneath him—boat?—shifted side to side, him sliding with it.

Suddenly a face appeared before his hazy vision. "Can you move at all on your own?"

Move. Something else to think about.

"Don't know." He tried to form the words.

"All right. Um… I'm going to help you roll off the kayak. Okay?"

Not really, but he sensed she meant well, whoever she was.

This time, he tried to nod.

Next thing he knew, arms came around him and pulled him sideways. Either she'd uncurled his fingers, or he hadn't been holding on to anything after all.

He collapsed on his back, but she kept him rolling until he was on his face, cheek and nose pressed onto a cobblestone street. No, that wasn't right; these stones were smooth but loose.

"Let's get you up on your hands and knees."

Through all his confusion, Adam knew this was life-and-death. He dedicated what feeble remnants of strength he retained to doing what she asked of him. Once he was that far, swaying, he managed to get up to his feet, with her firmly wedged under his arm. On his good side.

"Too heavy," he mumbled.

Whatever she said, he couldn't parse. Not a good sign.

He put one foot in front of another, not easy with loose rocks as his footing. She swayed with him now, caught him a few times when he would have gone down.

He'd have thought this massive effort would have warmed him, but it didn't. They had to stop twice so that he could shiver until his teeth chattered.

At last, she said, "Here," and supported him until his knees touched the ground. When she let go, he toppled sideways and curled up in a tight ball, aware she was rushing away.

Either she'd come back, or she wouldn't.

CLAIRE HAD READ about the symptoms of hypothermia many times before, but always related them to herself. Shivering, subtle loss of coordination, confusion… those meant she had to get off the water, into warm, dry clothes and a sleeping bag.

But this man had passed way beyond the early warning signs. His face was ashen, his lips blue. What little he'd tried to say had been difficult to understand because of the slurred speech. That he'd been able to walk at all had to be from sheer willpower, because his muscles weren't very responsive.

Exhaustion—check. That he was still shivering was a good sign, she encouraged herself. Because that would be followed by muscle rigidity, unconsciousness and death.

And damned if she'd let him die after all this.

This beach was more of a nook than anyplace she would normally have considered for a campsite, but there was just room enough among the tree line to set up her tent, even if that meant flattening the undergrowth. First, though, she had to haul up all her gear, then root through Mike's dry bags for anything useful, then pull both kayaks above the high-water line and probably tie them to trees.

Maybe, she thought uneasily, she could get them under cover somehow. She wouldn't be that paranoid, no matter the deadly events of the day, except for what the man had mumbled.

No. They…monitoring…calls.

They likely had a motorized skiff or inflatable boat on board. Gotten nervous enough to anchor and send someone back to make sure both men really *were* dead.

The merest thought of Mike was inexpressibly painful. The delight on his face this morning as he stretched…

Grief had to wait.

She needed to concentrate on treating the stranger's hypothermia before she did anything else, and for that she needed stuff from both kayaks. She yanked open a hatch and carried several bags up to where he lay, holding himself tight but otherwise frighteningly still.

Thank heavens she'd dried her towel in the morning sunshine. She sank down, cross-legged, beside a man she'd already realized was formidably large. How she'd held him up, she didn't know.

She dried his hair briskly, then pulled a fleece hat over his head, low on his forehead and covering his ears. He didn't react.

"We have to get you out of those wet clothes," she told him.

Back to yank dry bags out of Mike's kayak and search them, tossing aside what she didn't want, finding wool socks, a sweatshirt and fleece vest, and fleece-lined running pants. Then she stumbled back up the beach.

She discovered as she started to peel off the man's clothes that he'd moved on to the next stage of hypothermia—rigid muscles—and, while he tried to help her, was only semiconscious.

The hardest part might have been getting his shirt and sweater off over his head. Only then did she see a ghastly, openmouthed wound on his back. Dear God, he'd been shot, and she'd forgotten.

This had to be the exit wound. Thanks to the bitterly cold water, it wasn't bleeding, but it would as she warmed him up. She draped Mike's sweatshirt over the stranger's bare back and then ran to her kayak for the first-aid kit.

She layered gauze pads over the exit wound, unwound the sticky vet wrap she always carried and pressed the end over the pads before she pulled it around his side. As stiff as he was, getting it under his arm was a trial. There was the chest wound, a smaller hole, blue against his marble-white flesh. No, he'd taken the bullet more in his shoulder than chest. Lucky for a lot of reasons, but she was glad his brown chest hair wouldn't get stuck in the wound. More pads. Cover them with wrap, then figure out how to roll him.

He wasn't quite unconscious. With her help, he almost reached his hands—well, hand—and knees again, swaying as she wrapped the sticky stuff around twice and called it good. Hypothermia was a greater danger right now than a bullet wound.

The Seattle Seahawks sweatshirt had been oversize on Mike, but seemed about right on this guy. After helping him lie down again, Claire tucked a pile of her extra clothes under his head, so his cheek didn't rest on the ground.

She tried very hard not to look too closely after pulling off his boots and socks followed by soggy, icily cold cargo pants and underwear. She used a flannel shirt of hers this time to dry more of him before getting the stretchy pants over his long feet—had to be a size twelve, at least—and rolling them up his legs. He managed to lift his hips a fraction of an inch so she could tug the pants up. They were too short, but once thick socks covered those fishy-white feet any gap was covered.

Exhausted, she bowed her head. What next?

Tent. Get him inside it and in the sleeping bag, laid out on top of the pad. Somewhere, she had one of those space blankets, too.

Once she was up, she found that and wrapped him in it before she decided to set up her tent as close to him as possible, while keeping it above the high-tide line. She had that part down to a fine art, and within minutes was able to lay out the pad and unzip the sleeping bag.

The tide gradually receded, stranding the kayaks. Before the last exertion of somehow getting him into that sleeping bag, she carried both kayaks up as far as the tree line and pushed them almost out of sight among the undergrowth.

That was the moment when it occurred to her that she hadn't checked for signs of bear presence. They weren't likely to appear on a tiny island like this, were they? She was almost too tired to care, but set out her bear spray.

Her stranger roused himself to crawl awkwardly, reminding her of a three-legged race—the few feet into the tent. Turning him around would have been harder than turning the sleeping bag so the head was at the back of the tent, so that's what she did. He collapsed onto the bag and she zipped him in, then used the space blanket again as a final layer.

"How do you feel?" she asked, her hand against his cheek. He wasn't warming up at all, as far as she could tell. He got his eyes open, but she doubted anyone was home. She wasn't even sure what color they were. Hazel, maybe?

As if it made the slightest difference whether he had brown eyes or blue.

Focus, she ordered herself.

Get out her cookstove and heat water? Would he be able to swallow if she made tea or coffee? Except, she had a vague memory that caffeine might not be good for him, and maybe not even hot liquid too soon. Warm might help…but she'd see whether she could warm him up using her own body heat first.

Belatedly, it occurred to her that she could have used Mike's camping pad, too. Damn. She could get Mike's sleeping bag to spread on top of them, and then she'd crawl in with the stranger who was no threat to her as long as he was so debilitated.

After unrolling the second sleeping bag, Claire stripped off the top layer she wore on the water, then the neoprene booties, skullcap and wet suit. Even in the near warmth of midafternoon, she shivered until she tugged on her own pair of fleece-lined running tights, a T-shirt, fleece top and socks.

Exhausted, she sat at the tent opening trying to decide if there was anything else she absolutely had to do before she could lie down.

Call for help came to mind, but she hadn't had cell phone coverage for days. She'd dig through Mike's kayak in hopes he'd stowed his SPOT or the radio somewhere besides his day bag or pocket, but she didn't believe it.

The jab of pain was fierce.

Worry later.

When she did squirm in beside the big man and wrap her arms around him, he moaned and burrowed his head against her neck. It was like cuddling a snowman.

Claire pulled the unzipped sleeping bag over their heads to warm the air they breathed, endured his cold face against her neck and shuddered when she lifted her shirt and placed the icicles that were his hands on her bare flesh.

That was not a good moment for her to flash back to the gunshots and him falling overboard. If the freighter had been off-loading illegal drugs, that made him a criminal, didn't it?

How safe would *she* be if he recovered?

Closing her eyes, Claire made the practical decision to push back this worry, too. If she couldn't get him warm, he wouldn't be any threat, would he?

All she'd have to do was figure out where to stash his body so the wildlife couldn't get at it until she could bring authorities back to retrieve him, and to search for Mike's body, too.

CLOTHES SEPARATED HIM from the woman in his arms, and he wished they didn't. The heat she radiated was most intense where he could touch her smooth skin. He pressed his face into her neck and the crook of her shoulder and tried to breathe in that warmth. He slid his tingling hands higher up her torso in search of her breasts, but stopped short. Since he didn't know who she was, that might not go so well. She was toasty enough to make him think about woodstoves, campfires, hot radiators, sunbaked adobe on the other side of the world.

Suddenly, his whole body shuddered so violently it felt as if his spine might snap. What *was* that? When the jaws released him, he sagged with a moan, but not ten seconds later, the jaws snapped closed again and shook him like prey. Was this what it felt like to die on the electric chair?

The woman held him tight, keeping him in one piece as his body quaked and his muscles screamed. She was talking, too, but he was lost in pain.

The first word he caught in one of the brief moments between shudders was *good*.

Good? Deeply offended, he gritted his teeth to keep from breaking a few when his jaws rattled together. He tasted blood and knew he'd bitten his tongue.

In the next surcease, he managed to mumble, "Not good."

Her lips brushed his ear. "Yes, it is. Shivering is how your body warms you."

Or, at least, he thought that's what she'd said.

Wracked by pain, he knew one thing: whatever was happening to him wasn't *shivering*. This was more like being torn limb from limb by an orca or a grizzly. Maybe that's what was happening.

Except it couldn't be, he thought confused, unless he was imagining her, too. Soft lips and voice, strong arms, *warm*.

He didn't remember the last time he'd prayed. He must have been a boy. But he prayed now.

Please, God, don't let me be imagining her.

CLAIRE STIFFENED. WAS that the distant sound of an outboard motor? Not a cabin cruiser, something smaller. Like the skiff sometimes carried as runabouts on large cabin cruisers?

It could easily be someone innocently exploring from a bigger boat anchored out in deeper waters. Still, she throttled any impulse to run outside and light a flare. She had to wait until the stranger could tell her what had been going on. Those certainly hadn't been good guys on the deck of *either* the small freighter or the yacht. If they were hunting this man, they wouldn't hesitate to kill her, too, if they found him. Just as they'd killed Mike, without a second thought.

If only this were Mike. If she'd found him floating, hypothermic but still *alive*. Tears in her eyes, she thought about having to apologize to Shelby for sharing a sleeping bag with her husband. Instead… Her face twisted and those tears rolled down her face. Instead, she'd have to tell Shelby that Mike was dead. Murdered. That she hadn't even been able to recover his body to bring him home.

The stranger lifted his head with what had to be a

monumental effort. Those eyes, green and gold and brown, devoured her face.

"Crying."

He still slurred the word, but she was pretty sure that's what he'd said. Then his teeth snapped together, and he had another vicious bout of shaking. No, that was too mild a word. *Convulsing* was closer to the reality.

"It's okay," she comforted him. "It'll be okay." She wished she had the slightest idea whether that had any possibility of being true.

Time passed. Hours, but she lost track of how many. Judging from the angle of the sun she saw through the open tent flap when she lifted her head, the sun was dropping in the sky. Given how long days were this far north in June, sunset was still hours away.

The shudders became mere shivers. Color was returning to his face. His hands...felt warm. He was the one to pull them from beneath her shirt.

"Burning," he muttered. "Feet, too."

Wincing, she told him, "That's...good, too."

The dark look he gave her stirred unease that reminded her—stranger. Criminal. Threat.

She kept forgetting as she cradled him, sharing her body heat to save his life. Staying afraid of a man you had shared this kind of intimacy with wasn't easy.

Maybe he could handle a cup of tea now. She really needed to slip behind a shrub or tree trunk to answer the call of nature, too.

Oh, Lord—what if he needed the same? Was he capable of walking yet? Mike might have some kind of urinal in his kayak...but if so, she'd never been aware of him using it. And...what if the stranger needed *help*?

Claire pushed the extra sleeping bag away so it no

longer covered their heads and began wriggling to reach the zip of her own bag so she could free herself.

A strong arm locked around her. "What are you doing?" he growled.

Ignoring the chill his gruff demand had awakened, she said, "I have to pee."

For a frightening moment, she wasn't sure he'd let her go, but then he withdrew the arm. "Oh."

"What about you?" she felt compelled to ask.

He blinked a few times and finally shook his head. "No."

"Good." She crawled out and zipped up the bag again, tugging up the extra layers to tuck him in like a child. "How do you feel?"

"Terrible." He gave a rough laugh. "But better."

"The water along this stretch of coast is likely below fifty degrees. You wouldn't have lasted long in it."

His brow creased in puzzlement, as if he wasn't sure what she was talking about.

And, of course, he hadn't exactly gone for a swim voluntarily. They had to talk, but peeing came first. Getting her camp stove set up, too, and having a bite to eat. Lunchtime had come and gone.

She didn't hear a peep from behind her as she got to her feet in front of the tent and walked away. Clearly, he was past the most frightening stage, which meant he'd live.

And meant he now posed a danger to *her*.

Did she have anything in her kayak that could serve as a weapon? Maybe the bear spray, which was really just pepper spray. Since she'd already set it out, she'd grab it when she got back. Turning, she studied the front of her tent from an angle and tried to remember whether she'd put it inside or just outside. She'd paid no attention as she crawled out.

If it had been outside…it wasn't there anymore.

Chapter Three

He hadn't lied to his rescuer; he felt like garbage. Muscles might as well be Jell-O. Man, his hands and feet especially still burned as if he'd taken a dip in a molten crater instead of the northern Pacific Ocean. Out of curiosity, he worked one hand up above his covers so he could see it.

Yeah, flaming red. Damn.

Beat being so cold he'd expected to die, though.

He pulled his hand back into the warm cocoon and listened for her return. He thought, once his brain worked again, however sluggishly, he would become intensely curious about her. Just now was the first real look he'd had of her face and then body.

Messy blond hair, long enough to be mostly captured in a braid that hung to the middle of her back. Blue eyes, vivid against a face that was as much red with sunburn as tan, and peeling in places, too. From behind, she was slender and strong, but with curves, too. Nobody could mistake her as a guy. After having her breasts pressed against his side for hours, he knew they were generous.

He lay there, rigid, listening for any sound but especially a voice. He didn't like having her out of his sight. What if she called for help? He'd tried to tell her not to, but wasn't sure she'd even heard him. They could use the VHF to call for help, just not on the channel all boaters monitored. Who knew? Her mobile phone might have enough bars to connect.

If she *had* issued a general call for help, their life spans would end shortly.

He should have followed her out, or insisted she give him custody of all electronic devices before she headed out on her own. He huffed. Sure, that would have worked. Given his condition, she could tip him over with a tap of one finger.

He didn't hear so much as a whisper until some small noises out front had him lifting his head.

Seated on what appeared to be a folding canvas-and-aluminum chair, she was setting up a stove at her feet. He could just see her face in profile.

"If you're awake," she said over her shoulder, "I'm going to boil water. I have tea, coffee and hot chocolate. Unless you hate chocolate, that might be the best choice. You could use some sugar."

He didn't have much of a sweet tooth, but she was right. "Hot chocolate."

She didn't comment, just put a pan on top of the flame, then rustled around in a vinyl bag. After a minute, she stood and walked away. When she came back, she had a tall mug in her hand.

From the dead man's kayak.

He labored for a minute over that realization. Was it her husband or boyfriend who'd been shot and killed? Whose clothes he was wearing? Almost had to be. And yet she'd collected herself enough to save the life of a complete stranger. Why would she?

He sat up and, still enclosed in the sleeping bag, scooted himself forward using only his left arm until he sat in the opening created by tent flaps tied back.

She didn't turn her head, but her shoulders and back stiffened, betraying her awareness that he was moving.

"What's your name?" he asked hoarsely.

Now she did look at him. "Claire Holland. What's yours?"

"Rick—" He shook his head. "Adam Taylor."

"Not Rick?"

"I've been calling myself that for a while. I…have to think of myself by that name."

She didn't so much as blink, seeming to look right through him. "Why the fake name?"

"I'm a federal agent. DEA. Those were drug smugglers."

"Why were you shot?"

"I objected to the kayaker getting shot." He hesitated. "You must have been together."

She tipped her head back and said in a tight voice, "We were."

"I'm sorry." He wasn't real good at sounding compassionate, but he tried. "Was he your husband?"

"No." She didn't want to look at him. "Friend. I'll have to tell his wife—" Her voice broke.

"I'm sorry," he repeated.

"Why kill him?" Tears rolled down her face when she let him see it again. "He wasn't any threat to them."

"No. That's what I said." He tried to flex his fingers, but they were reluctant. Swollen, he decided. Grimly, he added, "And that they'd now go down for murder as well as smuggling if they were caught."

"They didn't…guess that you were undercover?"

"I didn't think so, but now I have to wonder."

"Do you have ID?"

Her suspicion didn't surprise him. He had to say, "Never carry any undercover. All I had was a driver's license that shows me as Richard Beckman." He reached automatically toward his back pocket and realized he didn't have one. He'd known these weren't his clothes. His pants... He looked around and saw heaps of wet clothing scattered around. "I have a wallet."

"You *had* a wallet. Or...maybe." She rose with a lithe ease he envied and picked up a couple of pieces of clothing he didn't recognize until she found his dripping-wet cargo pants. After patting the various pockets, she shook her head. "Nope. I hope it didn't have anything important in it."

"A few bucks. Fake Alaska driver's license and insurance card."

"Okay." She returned to the camp stove.

Since she was occupying her hands by spooning hot chocolate mix into two mugs, followed by boiling water, he couldn't tell what she was thinking.

"How is it we didn't see you?" he asked abruptly.

"I was hidden behind that islet. The one Mike popped out from behind. I had a funny feeling when I saw two such big boats squeezed into a narrow passage between islands. It didn't make sense, unless... I've read about smuggling. Mike was too far ahead for me to stop him, but I back paddled and squeezed up next to the rock where I could see through some cedar branches."

"Smart."

"As it turned out, yes. Lucky for you, too."

"Yeah." That came out so gruffly, Adam cleared his throat. "I wasn't standing ten feet from the guy who shot your friend. Why did you rescue me?"

Her shoulders jerked. "You were alive. I knew Mike was gone. I couldn't just watch you drown."

"Thank you," he said after a moment.

She nodded and poured boiling water into the two

mugs before turning off the small flame and reaching out to hand his drink to him. "Can you hold it?"

"Don't know," he admitted.

He could only lift his left arm out of the sleeping bag. When Claire got a look at his hand, she shook her head. "Uh-uh. It's too hot to take a chance of you spilling it and burning yourself." She set it down on a reasonably flat rock. "Let's let it cool down a little."

He watched her. He thought she flushed, but couldn't be sure because of the sunburn.

"Did you just contact anybody?" Adam jerked his head toward the dense forest just behind the tent.

"No!" Her head came up. "Now I'm thinking maybe I should have."

"I won't hurt you." He hesitated. "I'd like to be able to tell you that you're safe with me, but you're not. You got mixed up in something dangerous."

Those vivid blue eyes widened. "You think I didn't notice?"

He grimaced. "No."

"You told me not to use the VHF radio."

"Did I? I...couldn't remember."

"You said they'd be monitoring any talk. But I don't understand. Why wouldn't they be long gone?"

"They might be." He wished his thinking didn't still feel so muddled. "But I'm afraid they might have gotten nervous. Wished they'd pumped a couple more bullets into me before they left."

"Surely they'd know how quickly water that cold would kill you, if you weren't already dead."

"These guys weren't as dumb as I expected them to be." The job hadn't been quite what he thought it would be, either. Adam shut down any temptation to tell her that part, not until doing so became absolutely essential. "Dwayne will be remembering the kayak floating not that far away," he added. "What if I got to it? He doesn't take chances."

"Thus, him shooting you."

Adam tried to touch the shoulder that hurt. "Guess so. Uh…did you wrap it?"

"Yes. I should take another look at it while it's still light. I have some antibiotic ointment, but I didn't think to put any on. The hypothermia was a greater danger then."

He grimaced. "Is the bullet still in there?"

Claire shook her head, sending her braid swinging. "No, there's a really big hole under your shoulder blade."

"That whole upper quadrant hurts like hell."

"I do have some painkillers. You can swallow them with the hot chocolate." She reached for a bright red square container marked clearly as a first-aid kit and unzipped it. "Aspirin…no, not when you're probably bleeding. Um, acetaminophen, or I have a few prescription-strength painkillers."

Adam thought about it. "Let's hold off on those. I may get worse before I get better."

She nodded, shook out a couple Tylenol tablets and set them in his outstretched hand before checking the tall mug, apparently deciding the contents had cooled off enough, and kneeling beside him.

He took a cautious sip when she lifted the mug to his lips, then tossed the pills in his mouth and took a lot longer drink, using his own hand to guide the angle of the mug. Damn, that tasted good, and the warmth flowing down his throat and spreading through his core felt even better.

"If you help me stick my fingers through the handle, I think I can do this," he suggested.

She did, then scooted away with what appeared to be relief. Gazing out toward the water, she sipped her own drink, her thoughts well hidden.

But finally she said, "I checked my cell phone. No coverage."

"Have you had any since you left…?"

"Anacortes. I'm from Seattle. And I've been able to make a couple of calls, but mostly my phone is dead."

He nodded. The small city on Fidalgo Island in Washington State was a frequent launching point for boaters heading up the Sunshine Coast and into the Inside Passage to Alaska. Washington State ferries that serviced the San Juan Islands and carried passengers and cars to Victoria on Vancouver Island launched from Anacortes, too.

Up this way, he'd seen Canadian ferries. Waving down one of those would be good, but he'd also seen the nautical chart currently displayed in the wheelhouse of the freighter and knew this current position was at least a few nautical miles from any strait large enough for that kind of traffic or the open ocean.

Then there was the fact that he wouldn't be paddling a kayak for at least a day or two. And *that* only after some lessons. He'd never been in a kayak, or even a canoe. Sending Claire Holland on her own was an option…but not one he liked. She'd be as vulnerable as her kayaking partner had been.

Unarmed, how much help would he be if he were with her?

"Have you heard or seen any other traffic since we got here?" he asked.

Her gaze skittered from his. "I…heard a motor while we were in the tent. Unless I was imagining it."

He waited.

"Something small. A skiff, maybe."

Adam swore under his breath.

"Did that freighter carry one?"

"Yeah, and a fancier inflatable boat, too, that has an outboard motor."

"And…the yacht?"

"Probably, but it's long gone." Unless the load hadn't been fully transferred. He'd expected to see them use a little extra care with the truly dangerous part of the cargo. Maybe it had happened while he was playing dead in the water…but maybe the captain of the yacht had panicked and fled with the exchange incomplete.

Might he still have a chance to keep the delivery from happening?

Not sitting on his butt on a rocky beach that was more of a sliver cut between the sheer rock walls of this island. The idea of endangering the courageous woman who had saved his life didn't sit well with him—but that cargo had the potential to kill thousands. Tens of thousands. Or more.

He needed to get word out, but he also had to live to do that.

"Damn," he exclaimed. "This campsite is visible from the water."

THE STRANGER—ADAM TAYLOR, if he was to be believed—faded fast after draining the mug of hot chocolate while cradling his hand around it as if it felt better than anything he remembered experiencing. He supervised while she used a knife to cut some branches to further disguise the kayaks—especially Mike's bright orange-and-red one—and the tent. Once the stove had cooled off, she moved it and her heap of dry bags to a rocky spot that was mostly shielded from the water by a boulder.

After dropping a couple of bags, she circled back to the tent to find his head nodding. When she gently disentangled his hand from the mug, he jerked back to awareness and conceded that this might be a good time to take a look under his bandages.

He wasn't quite handsome, she decided, but he had a strong-boned face with a nose that was slightly off-center—broken?—and a sexy mouth. And, boy, she was an idiot even *thinking* a word like that in connection with him. The odds were not good that he was really a US Drug Enforcement Administration undercover agent. Although it was a clever story, she had to give him that.

All that gave her hope was when he'd said, *I won't hurt you.* In that moment, she'd believed him.

Which made her stupidly credulous. Except…she couldn't have left him to die. She just couldn't. Right now, he needed her. Once he no longer did… She hoped she recognized that moment when it came.

Prepare first, she told herself practically. But not yet.

With him watching her sidelong, Claire felt way more self-conscious than she had even when she was stripping him naked the first time. Now all she had to do was lift the sweatshirt off over his head. She then unpeeled the vet wrap, trying to look dispassionate at having to grope his body.

If not for the puckered hole seeping blood—and a long, thin scar crossing the left side of his rib cage—his shoulders and chest were magnificent. Those shoulders were broad, and she was disconcertingly aware of the powerful muscles sliding beneath his skin and the mat of brown hair centered on his chest.

Yep, dispassionate, that was her.

And, no, she couldn't help letting her gaze lower to where the by-then-narrow trail of hair disappeared beneath the waistband of those too-tight thermal pants. Heat rising in her cheeks, she hoped he hadn't noticed.

After squeezing plenty of ointment in the hole, she placed the dressing over the wound.

"Can you hold this while I look at your back?"

He reached over with his left hand and complied.

Glad he couldn't see her once she shifted behind him, she admired a muscular back very briefly. Then she paid attention to the blood soaking the dressing. Not gushing, but…

"This might hurt when I unpeel the pads."

He craned his neck, but of course couldn't see the exit wound. All he said, flatly, was, "Do it."

They came fairly easily, but she hated looking at this hole torn in his skin and muscle. His wounds needed more help than her basic first-aid training could provide. Given her limited supplies, she cleaned this jagged hole, squeezed more ointment out of the tube, then made a thicker dressing before she renewed the vet wrap.

"Is that too tight?" she asked worriedly.

"No." He started to roll his shoulders, winced and reached for the sweatshirt.

Claire helped him ease it on.

"I think I need to lie down."

She urged him to eat a handful of almonds first, because it was the easiest, quickest thing she could think of.

Then he retreated back into the tent, but did some contortions that had to be painful, judging from the grunts and groans she heard, and turned so the head of the sleeping bag faced the opening.

"This can yours?"

She saw what he held out. Oh, thank God. She took it from him, aiming to appear casual. "Bear spray."

"A bear likely to come visiting?"

"Probably not." Claire didn't like the uncertainty she heard in her voice. "This is a really small island. But there are plenty of black bears around here."

"Grizzlies?"

"Only on the mainland, thank goodness. But any female black bears we encounter at this time of year will likely have cubs with them."

"Don't want to get between them."

"No, you definitely don't."

"Any chance you or your friend were carrying a gun?"

"This is Canada. Neither of us would have been anyway, but it's not legal."

"We had a steel deck panel that lifted to stash weapons if the coast guard boarded us."

"Too bad you didn't have a handgun stashed in one of your pockets," she said flippantly, while thinking, *Thank God he's unarmed.*

Well, except for all those muscles.

"Lousy planning," he grumbled.

"If your wallet disappeared, the gun probably would have, too," she pointed out. "I'll wake you in a couple of hours for dinner."

"Or if you hear any company coming."

Her heart jumped. "Yes. Okay."

He mumbled something else she couldn't hear and seemed to drop immediately into sleep—or possibly a coma. Claire only stared at him for a minute before turning away and going back to her minikitchen. She would have given a lot to take a walk, but thick vegetation crowded right up to the tiny, pebbled beach. Finding this spot had been a miracle; asking for a path perfect for stretching her legs was pushing it.

Besides, feeling jittery was her real problem. It was like having spiders crawling up her arms and legs. Some of the numbness must have worn off after the sugar boost.

All she could think was, *Now what?*

Load her kayak with the essentials, drag it back to the water and paddle away for all she was worth? Or stay to take care of the man she'd saved and trust that he really wouldn't hurt her?

Could she be so attracted to a real scumbag? Was she foolish to think she could read him, when he was either a criminal lacking any sense of morality or an undercover federal agent who had to be an Oscar-worthy actor?

She gazed at the green walls of the tent, as if she could see through the fabric and into the heart of a man who, whether he was a good guy or bad, had plenty of secrets.

Then she sighed. Getting away at all wasn't likely. Unless Rick aka Adam Taylor really was in a coma, he'd hear when she pulled her kayak from hiding and carried it down to the water—which was a lot farther away now than it had been when they got here. Yes, he was weak…but what if he summoned the strength to stop her?

That was the moment when the noise of a motor reached her—and this time, it sounded a lot closer.

Chapter Four

Feeling drugged, Adam blinked bleary eyes and stared up at the pitched green roof of a small tent. Light filtered through the fabric. The sight made no sense. Where was he? Why?

A hand shook his arm. "Are you awake?"

A cascade of memories returned. Shot. Dumped overboard. Breasts pressed to his chest, smooth belly melting the ice.

He turned his head slightly to see startling blue eyes set in a sunburnt face. "Yeah," he said hoarsely.

"I hear a small boat again, a lot closer this time."

He groaned, gave his head a hard shake and listened. Small engine, running a little rough.

"Damn." He lurched upright and, to his regret, her hand fell from his arm. Unzipping the bag, he growled, "Need to look."

"I don't know if you can without being seen. And if anyone is crawling out on the rocks, it's me."

"You wouldn't recognize the men." He scrambled through the opening made by tied-back flaps, having to hold his right arm up to his chest. His shoulder and back hurt horribly. Amidst his other miseries, he'd been able to ignore this one.

Once out of the tent, he assessed the setting. Yes,

they were hidden if someone nosed partway into the narrow inlet. If they were curious enough to follow it to its end, intruders could probably see the green of the tent that didn't quite fit in, or a glint of the gaudy paint job on the one kayak. That wouldn't happen right now, not after the tide had receded so much.

Aware of Claire next to him, not to mention the buzz of a small craft puttering somewhere within a half mile or so radius, he grabbed his still soggy boots and started to pull on the left one. Swearing under his breath, he had to ask, "Help?"

"This is stupid." She'd already knelt close enough to wrap her right arm over his thigh and between his legs so she could help pull. "Let me do the right one. But if you fall and hurt yourself worse—"

If Claire Holland was afraid of him, she wasn't about to let *him* know.

She also had a point.

But if this boater—or these boaters—were complete strangers, say, hearty-looking guys in their fifties, he could signal them. She surely carried flares. The boaters could notify the coast guard.

Feet protected from any sharp rocks, he rose to his full height, trying hard not to sway. "Do you have—"

Claire handed him a compact pair of binoculars.

He had to grin at her. "Don't suppose you have—"

She rolled her eyes. "A Remington rifle? AK-47? Or did you have in mind a nice T-bone to toss on the grill?"

"Any or all."

Man, his legs felt like noodles cooked al dente. Kind of there under him, but ready to fold up at the least excuse. The astonishing woman who had rescued him eased herself under his left arm and wrapped hers around his waist, ready to prop him up even if she was six inches shorter and at least eighty pounds lighter than his big body.

"We might be able to get a ways toward the open water." She pointed at jumbled rocks crowded with small twisted spruce and cedar trees, huckleberry bushes and more growing from cracks. The footing looked treacherous, assuming they could push themselves through the tangle.

Adam grunted and started forward.

They never made it to the rim of the island that would have given them a broad view. They did find a spot where they could crouch and get a slice of a view beyond the narrow passage.

The buzzing sound of the outboard motor was enough distance away, Adam felt safe in lifting the binoculars to his eyes. He was surprised by the crystal clear quality of the lenses when he focused across the water to other densely-green islands.

He saw a ripple in the water, followed by the appearance of a dark head, then a second one. Seals? Sea lions?

"There!" Claire said with sudden urgency.

He followed her pointing finger. Metal dinghy, running low in the water. Two passengers. One of the two bent over the engine, but Adam knew that jacket. The other was looking this general direction, using binoculars of his own.

Adam swore and let his drop, not wanting to take a chance of the sun glinting off the glass.

"Two of my shipmates," he said grimly.

"But…they've been searching all day? I mean, I don't have any way to check the exact time, but it has to be evening!"

"Unless you heard a different boat earlier. I don't like this persistence."

"Could they have found Mike's body?"

"And wondered why they didn't find mine?" He thought about it. "I'm guessing they're more worried about the missing kayak."

Or not. They'd worry about a witness, but he knew too much. Yeah, they'd be desperate to be sure he really was dead. Pretty slapdash of them, he thought wryly, to sail away without pausing to hold target practice, using his body.

He glanced at Claire to see her stricken expression. "I should have left the kayak. Except…"

"Except you needed clothes that would fit me, and probably other supplies." He kept his gaze on her face. "We'd have been trapped here without a second kayak."

Her eyes didn't quite meet his. "I could go for help. You're not in any shape to paddle anyway."

Adam jerked his head toward the dinghy, disappearing behind the arm of the island they hadn't been able to traverse. "And meet them?"

"I… No," she mumbled. "I didn't mean right away."

Never. But he only said a milder, "Let's get back to camp, and we can talk about our options."

Claire nodded and rose lithely to her feet. He climbed awkwardly to his own and then would have gone down if she hadn't immediately tucked herself up against him, demonstrating her strength when she bore a good deal of his weight.

"Thanks. Damn, I'm as weak as a kitten."

"Kittens are whirling dervishes. Haven't you ever seen one?"

His laugh was more of a rumble in his chest. "Yeah, now that you mention it."

They made their slow way back, Claire finding footing and then instructing him where to put his feet. Even so, he screwed up by taking a too hasty, incautious step, and felt a wrench on his ankle as his boot slid into a deep crack. She braced herself, patient and solid, while he recovered.

What would he do without her?

I'd be dead, that's what, he reminded himself.

THE STUBBORN MAN refused to take the only chair she'd set up, although admittedly, it was awfully low to the ground for such a tall man with long legs. Still, there was no place soft to sit without moving to the other side of the tent where they risked being spotted.

"I'll get Mike's."

"Don't bother. I'm fine—"

She spun. "You are not *fine*! You're shaky on your feet, you're hurt and you're stupidly macho!"

She stomped to the best of her ability to the bright red kayak and dug farther in the compartments, retrieving the second sleeping pad as well as the chair—and noting the extra paddle Mike had carried. She'd brought an extra, too, but a beginner was all too likely to capsize himself and potentially lose his.

These intricate passages between islands, so far from any civilization, were not recommended waters for a beginner to learn. He'd have only her, and that frightened her.

One more scary reality.

She returned, unfolded the chair and plunked it down. She had a bad feeling her cheeks were still red. "There."

He gingerly lowered himself, supported the last distance by her.

"You mad at me?" Adam asked.

She gave a distinctly unfeminine snort. "Why would you try to convince me you're A-okay? Unless you plan to take off on your own, you *need* me—and I need to know what you can and can't do."

Very smart. Give him a chance to lie about his intentions.

But he sat quiet for a minute, then gave her a crooked smile. "You're right. With the kind of undercover work I've been doing, I rarely have a partner. It's not smart to confess any weakness to the scumbags I investigate." His mouth quirked. "I'll...try to curb the tendency to be stupidly macho."

"Sometimes I don't know when to shut up." Speaking of confessions. When they first met, Devin had claimed to love her directness. He rapidly found it less charming. He belittled her in front of friends, always with an "I'm just kidding" air that fooled some people, but not all. Then he hit her.

She was almost glad he had. She'd put up with too much, started asking herself if he was right. She was happier single than she'd been having to watch every word out of her mouth. Being dominant in a relationship was too important to some men. She should be *celebrating* the fact that getting tangled with a guy like Devin hadn't left her timid.

As if to echo her thoughts, Adam Taylor was shaking his head. "I want you to speak out. Here, you're the expert. Except when it comes to dealing with criminals who are quick to turn violent."

"If you're the expert on that, how'd you get shot?" Claire challenged him, then resisted the instinct to cringe or apologize. Standing up for herself was one thing, rudeness another.

Amusement crinkled the skin beside Adam's eyes. "You can be really hard on my ego, you know."

She made a face. "I'm sorry. Your job must be dangerous."

"It is. But in this case…" He shrugged. "Speaking of not knowing when to shut up, I knew the minute I opened my mouth that I'd made a mistake. Then I should have groveled, but I didn't. I've seen more men killed than I want to remember, but they were always people involved in the drug trade. Or cops or federal agents, and at least we know the risk we take on. Seeing that creep just casually shoot a completely innocent man who wasn't a threat in any way was a shock."

A fist tightened around Claire's heart, and she bent her head in apparent contemplation of the unlit camp stove. "It was."

"Yeah." Adam's gravelly voice didn't do tender very well, but he seemed to be trying. "I'm sorry. I wish I could have prevented it."

She swallowed and looked up with eyes that burned with her need to cry. "I wish you had, too, except… was it even possible? There were a bunch of men on the freighter, and more on the yacht. You'd be dead if you had, I don't know, tried to jump the guy with the rifle, and then he or someone else would have just shot Mike anyway."

He cleared his throat. "It wasn't a good situation."

"I'm sure you have way blunter descriptions than that."

His smile twisted. "I do, but I throttle that kind of language when I'm dining with a nice woman."

Claire's chest seemed to unclog, and she laughed. "Well, we haven't chosen our entrées yet, but I admit, I'm hungry. What about you?"

"Starved. I could eat half a dozen steaks, but I guess that's not on the menu."

"Nope. Kayaking in British Columbia, I tend to go vegetarian, since I'd rather not attract any local meat eaters, if you know what I mean. Fishing is a really bad idea for the same reason. Mike—" her voice hitched. "He liked to live a little more dangerously and made things like chicken curry."

"You don't buy ready-made food?"

"Some kayakers do, but I cook extensively before a trip, and freeze-dry individual portions in packets. Mike's wife helped him with that, although he's—he *was*—actually a really good cook."

She wasn't ready to talk about Mike.

"In fact, let me go see what I can dig out from his stores. This is probably a safe place to eat meat." She hoped Adam didn't notice her uneasy glance at the forest behind them.

Fortunately, since she and Adam might be stuck here for a few days, she and Mike had packed more meals than they would usually carry because they wanted to take their time before a diminished larder forced them to divert to one of the scattered outposts of civilization along the coast to restock supplies. Both had mailed boxes filled with more homemade freeze-dried meals as well as candy bars, nuts, tea bags, toilet paper and more to Shearwater, where it would be held for pickup, a common arrangement for Inside Passage kayakers.

She found a chicken-with-wine-sauce entrée that she knew from experience was good, and brought two of the packets back to the "kitchen."

Adam watched her return with unnerving intensity and no real giveaway about his true thoughts. When she reached for a box of matches, he said, "Once you get that lit, we should talk."

"Now?"

"Why not?"

Because she didn't trust him? Hadn't decided yet what she should or shouldn't tell him? Good answers, but not ones she could share, so she only nodded.

BY THE TIME Claire put water on the stove and added the contents of both packets, she'd closed herself off. Adam could almost see her donning a mask. Not that he blamed her—she was too smart to have buried all doubts and bought into his claim to be a federal agent. That said, what was she hiding?

After setting clean dishes, forks and a big spoon within reach, she sat down. "I suppose we can't have a fire tonight."

"Not a chance."

"The gas tank for a motor that size must be small," she argued. "Even if they carry a couple of gas cans as backup, they'd be limited. Plus...would they keep searching after dark? That can be really dangerous. I mean, do they even have detailed charts for these islands?"

"The pilot was able to pinpoint where to meet up with the yacht. He insisted it had to be at high tide, and that they needed to bolt within an hour or two."

Claire looked dismayed. "I guess we can't rule it out, then."

"Them still prowling come twilight? No." He'd have to ask her if there were rocks hidden just beneath the surface that could split open the hull of a fragile dinghy. As for now...

She took a deep breath. "So. What are we going to talk about?"

"I need to know what electronic devices you have." Probably he sounded uncompromising. That's how he felt.

She blanked all emotion from her face and eyes, as if she'd had plenty of practice doing that. Why hadn't he asked what she did for a living? Could she possibly be a cop? She was tough enough.

"You think I'm hiding something so I can bring help you don't expect." She shook her head and rose to stir and check their dinner.

She didn't add, *Or is it help you don't want?* He heard her loud and clear anyway.

"I'm asking because we do need help." Right now, he was a very weak link. "We can't broadcast a general plea on the VHF radio, but we can make a call to someone who'll contact the Canadian Coast Guard for us."

"Well, here's the bad news. Because I apparently don't handle pressure well, the only device we have is my cell phone. Which might as well be a slab of marble right now."

She was lying. She had to be.

"You mentioned using the VHF to call for help."

"Before I remembered Mike had it today. We…sort of handed it back and forth." She closed her eyes. "I've read about how important it is to have multiple backups of anything important. I know better. I do."

"We have his kayak."

The open anguish that she let him see made him feel like a rat. "When I flipped it back over, the waterproof bag where he carried things he wanted within easy reach should have been in one of the mesh pockets just forward from the cockpit. My kayak has a day hatch, but it's the same concept. It's where we carry stuff like snacks, lip balm, suntan lotion…and emergency supplies and devices. He had a flare gun, too. He had to have lived long enough to grab that bag while he was freeing himself from the cockpit. Probably his last thought was to call for help."

"He wouldn't have had time," Adam said slowly.

"He…he never surfaced. The weird thing is that he also ripped off his PFD."

"Because it felt confining, or he thought he could swim underwater?" He shook his head. "A dying brain isn't rational."

"No." Claire bent her attention again to their meal, dishing up a portion into an aluminum bowl and handing it to him with a fork. She set the pan in front of her, apparently choosing not to dirty a second bowl, but didn't take a bite.

He waited a moment out of respect for her grief, but, damn, he was hungry, so finally he let himself start eating while keeping an eye on her. After a minute, she did the same.

They finished eating in silence. She sighed when she set the pan on a rock and leaned back again.

"We each carried a SPOT beacon. I don't know if you're familiar with them. They're what's called an emergency position indicator. You register it in your name, so if you have to push the button, the coast guard—or whoever—knows who they're supposed to rescue and, thanks to the GPS, where you are. You're only supposed to use it as a last resort." Claire paused. "Mike's would have been in that bag I told you about. I mean, I haven't searched, but that's where he always carried it except when we took a short hike or something like that."

Adam nodded.

"When…that guy shot Mike, I took out my SPOT, only I wasn't as careful as I should have been. I guess I was shocked, and I was wearing my gloves, and I think I didn't even look down. I was so transfixed by what was happening—"

"You dropped it. Overboard."

Shame burned on her cheeks. "They probably float, and eventually I looked for it, but not for very long. I didn't dare move, and I was watching you to see if there was any chance you were alive…"

"I understand," he made himself say, although their inability to summon help put them in more danger than she yet understood.

At last, her eyes met his. "I should have looked harder. It wasn't until I turned Mike's kayak over that I realized the bag was gone."

"I'd say we should have looked for anything that was floating when we went back to pick up the kayak, except…" He grimaced.

"You were in such bad shape. Getting you mostly out of the water wasn't enough to help, not when you were sopping wet and severely hypothermic. All I could think about was finding someplace to camp so I could get you warm."

"I thank you for your priorities." He'd have reached for her hand if he'd been close enough. "I thought I was dying."

"With water that might not even be fifty degrees, you would have died really quickly. Even so, if I'd taken just a few minutes longer—"

"What are the odds you'd have seen something as small as the SPOT? I'm assuming it's not a lot bigger than a cell phone."

"No."

"My philosophy is, what's done is done. It won't hurt to search everything your friend carried," Adam added, "just in case. We should probably inventory what he had anyway."

"He did carry an extra paddle, because the one he was using was gone, too. You can tether them to the kayak, but…neither of us did that." More shame etched her voice.

He nodded matter-of-factly. Kicking herself now did neither of them any good. "Okay."

"If you're bored, he always brought a few books along." She wrinkled her nose. "Just what we need most. I have some, too. We'd swap sometimes, except we didn't share the same tastes."

Adam found a smile. "I'll check out the library. I'm thinking we almost have to stay put for a day or two."

Her eyebrows rose. "You actually think you can paddle that soon?"

"Do you have a better idea?" he asked dryly.

She was quiet.

Chapter Five

Fortunately, bright daylight kept them from needing flashlights or a kerosene light. Sunset wasn't until something like nine forty-five, although the color of the sky would deepen with twilight up to an hour before that. Unless she was imagining it, Claire felt the chill of the oncoming night, though. Frowning, she looked more closely at Adam.

Arms tightly crossed, he'd lost color in his face. Claire wished anew that they could afford to have a fire. She wondered if his core temperature had ever reached normal.

After she heated water for tea, he accepted the cup gratefully. While he drank his, she collected Mike's bags that held clothing and miscellaneous things and set them next to her chair. After taking a few swallows of her own sweetened tea, she pulled everything out of the first bag.

To inventory it, in Adamspeak.

"I shouldn't have let you put those wet boots back on," she muttered. "I wish Mike's feet weren't so much smaller. Ah. His parka."

He looked up when she carried it to him. "You can tell I'm cold?"

Was there a faint slur in his words again? She was probably imagining it. "Of course I can."

He obediently held out his arm, but it quickly became apparent that they'd never get it on the injured arm. It was just plain too small to stretch across his broad back.

After a moment's thought, Claire fetched the sleeping bag that had been their top cover and brought it out as a replacement for the parka to wrap around Adam, creating a hood and making sure he could hold it closed with one hand. Then she tugged off the wet, cold boots and the fleece socks that had absorbed moisture.

"I think he has a second pair..." She went back to rooting through bags, finding what she sought and sliding them over Adam Taylor's feet. Then, with a sense of unreality, she sank back on her heels and assessed him. Here she was handling him as if she had a right to dress him and touch him as she pleased.

The circumstances that had made her so bold must feel as odd to him as they did to her.

I saved his life, she thought in astonishment. For all that she'd seriously practiced rescue techniques, she'd never imagined using them beyond helping someone back into a kayak after a failed roll.

He was watching her, even as she watched him. *Stranger. Remember?*

Right now, his eyes were deeply shadowed. The color was rich and bright, but changeable as the light and his mood shifted. They were beautiful eyes, set in a lean dark face. She was reassured, given her first sight of him, when she'd thought of his face as bone white. He was chilly, not freezing. Somehow, his brown stubble only emphasized the strength of his bone structure.

"You must have shaved this morning."

He lifted a hand from the sleeping bag as if to test his whisker growth but winced. "Damn shoulder."

"Normally I'd suggest icing it, but, well…"

"Yeah, no thanks."

Claire sighed. "I wish there were something we could *do*, instead of sitting here like, um…"

He lifted one eyebrow. "Sitting ducks?"

She made a face at him, almost hoping he'd smile.

He didn't. Instead, the lines in his face deepened, aging him. "I'd give a lot to be armed."

Guns made her uncomfortable. No one she knew well carried one, but she shared that wish anyway.

Whatever else she thought about this man, she did believe he wouldn't hurt her. Steal all the paddles and leave her stranded, maybe—but he'd send help for her before he slid back into his sleazy underworld, wherever that was.

Fine, then.

"NORMALLY I GO to bed long before sunset, because getting on the water early is usually best. We don't have to plan for that, but even if we wanted to keep late hours, we have only a couple of flashlights and one kerosene lantern."

With quick alarm, Adam said, "We have to be careful not to show light."

"I kind of guessed you'd say that. Which is why I'm going to stow everything and then use the facilities."

Surprised, he glanced up at the sky, which seemed to have acquired a violet tint. "There's no indication it'll rain."

"You mean, why am I putting stuff away?" She was doing exactly that, starting with the clothes she'd pulled out of her partner's bags. "You'll totally understand if you once have raccoons visit during the night. They can do some damage, and make an awful mess."

He didn't think much about his childhood, but a memory came to him. "My—" Foster father. No, he had no desire to get into that. "We had raccoons knock over the garbage cans a few times."

"Bears can be just as bad. They're usually just curious, but they don't see any need to handle strange objects with delicacy."

Adam laughed, feeling better for it. On top of all his other reactions to this brave, capable woman, he was finding that he *liked* her. She made him laugh, and he hadn't done much of that in years.

"Anyway, we don't want to store food any closer to the tent than we have to. These bear vaults theoretically seal in the smell and can't be broken into, but I'd rather not have a bear trying to crack it open only a few feet from where I'm trapped in a sleeping bag."

Even as she talked, she put on a smaller quantity of water to heat and produced a small plastic bottle that must hold dish soap. A dish towel came from the same plastic ziplock bag. In minutes, she'd washed the few dishes and pan they'd used and stacked them efficiently into very little space.

He should offer to help, but felt very little inclination to move. He'd have to use the facilities, as she put it, but wasn't eager to stagger even ten feet deeper into the trees. Crawling into the tent was more appealing, except that he'd *really* hate having to get up in the middle of the night and drag himself outside to take a piss because he'd put it off.

"Here's a bag of Mike's toiletries," she said. "He might've brought a second toothbrush, but even if he didn't…"

Using a secondhand toothbrush wouldn't kill him, although it would feel wrong when the original owner hadn't been dead even a day. Still, Claire was probably hinting that she didn't want to share close quarters in the tent with someone who had bad breath.

"He did bring a shaver," she continued, "but usually only bothered to use it when we stopped somewhere with running water. *Hot* running water, and a shower. Partly because we carry our drinkable water, and it's wasteful to use it if we don't know when or where we can get more. And, in case you haven't noticed, this campsite has a tiny problem."

"No stream," he realized.

"Right."

"So plan to grow a beard."

She tipped her head to one side. "Have you ever had one?"

"A beard?" Adam was finding it harder to make out her face than it had been, which meant it must be getting on toward nine thirty. "Yeah, for the job." He hated even wearing stubble for more than a day or two; he always itched like crazy.

"If you'll excuse me." She had a roll of toilet paper in one hand, a plastic bag in the other. "I'll be back in a minute."

She seemed to disappear. Night had found them.

He hastily groped his way through the dead guy's toiletries, finding an unopened toothbrush, to his relief, and a small, half-used tube of toothpaste. Claire had left him a cup with less than an inch of water in it, which he made use of.

By the time she reappeared, he'd zipped the bag back up and given some thought to standing up.

"Let me help."

He flinched at the cold when she unwrapped him and tossed the sleeping bag into the tent before coming back to serve as a crutch. Once on his feet, he wavered for a moment, not liking his weakness and dangerous vulnerability. At the same time, he appreciated Claire's matter-of-fact brand of assistance.

Yeah, he liked her. He more than liked the feel of her curvy body pressed against his side. And then there was the fact that she was as strong as she was feminine.

He made himself say, "You can let go."

"You can make it by yourself?"

"Don't have to go far."

"Since you don't have shoes on, step carefully. Oh, um, do you need the toilet paper?"

He grinned at her delicate inquiry. "Not right now, thank you."

Of course, she was blushing.

What he wanted to know was whether she'd opt for her own sleeping bag tonight, or decide he still needed her body heat.

She waited for him to return from his little excursion, presumably so she could pick him up if he'd done a face-plant, but when he appeared, Claire slipped into the tent ahead of him.

Adam paused, first to listen for any indication other people were near—or even existed—and then to look up at the sky. Sailing the Pacific Coast, whatever his objective, he'd enjoyed standing out on deck and gazing up at the night sky. The splash of stars was astonishing, the faint glow of more distant ones visible in a way they never were in a good part of the lower forty-eight. Humanity had forgotten what they'd lost in their dependence on electricity.

Tonight, he needed to stretch out and not move for ten hours or so.

He lowered himself carefully to a crouch and then crawled into the small tent. A dark shape only, Claire reached out a hand to touch him.

"Are you warm enough? We can share a sleeping bag for the night if…you worry about holding on to your body heat."

She sounded endearingly shy, in contrast to her usual boldness.

Adam said, "I'd probably survive, but I'd prefer sharing."

Quiet for a moment, she said finally, "Okay, but only for warmth."

"I'll be good." He doubted he was in any physical shape to take his attraction to her anywhere.

"May I touch your forehead?"

Her hand still rested on his arm. He lifted it gently, uncurled her fingers and bent forward to give her access.

"You feel warm," she murmured.

"I did say—"

"I'm worrying that you might develop a fever."

"Oh." That made sense, except—"Wouldn't the salt water have cleaned out the wound adequately?"

"Probably. Never mind. I'm a worrier."

They were alike in that, then. Worrying, planning, staying wary, kept a man alive.

Sounding brisk, she suggested he remove a few layers of clothing, and offered to help when he needed it. He felt damn shaky by the time they were done, and he was able to lie down. Cold, too, but that was remedied when Claire climbed in with him and zipped up, closing out the night air.

Tonight, she'd even provided a pillow. He patted it, realizing it was one of those bags full of clothes.

She squirmed next to him, pulling up the second sleeping bag to provide additional warmth, then lay completely still. There couldn't be more than an inch separating them, given the tight quarters, but she was trying to stay separate.

He reached out his left arm in an invitation. "Isn't cuddling the idea?"

"I…guess so." She scooted closer.

Smiling at her stiff concession, Adam discovered that, while drowsiness was taking shape, he wasn't quite ready to sink into a deep slumber yet. Although Claire had laid her head on his good shoulder, she was far from relaxed.

"Will you tell me about yourself?" he asked to offer a distraction to the uncomfortable situation. "What do you do for a living?"

"I work in human resources. Not very exciting, I know." She told him the name of the good-sized manufacturing company. "I started at Boeing, worked for a hotel chain, then made this latest jump for a more senior position."

"How'd you get into that?"

"I majored in psychology. I couldn't really afford to go on for an advanced degree and wasn't sure I wanted to do counseling, so I looked out there to see what the degree was good for. What I learned in the psych classes actually does give me some insight I use for hiring and solving problems with existing employees."

"I bet." Adam thought about a couple of fellow agents who had major issues that most people shrugged off.

"What about you?"

Her breath whispered over the bare skin on his neck, momentarily sidetracking his brain.

"Chemistry. That's what I majored in. I went to work for the DEA as a chemist. The agency isn't all about illegal drugs. I got bored fast, and when I saw a chance to shift to becoming an agent, I jumped at it."

"Is it everything you thought it would be?"

Not a good time to confront his recent unease. "Sure. I liked action. I even liked playing roles. Did I mention that I acted regularly in theater productions during college?" Hoping she didn't notice his use of the past tense, he shut up.

"Undercover work must be hard on relationships," she observed thoughtfully.

Talking like this in the increasing darkness, unable to see expressions, was different.

"Yeah," he agreed. "I come back from being under for a couple of months, find friends have moved, fellow agents have been transferred. *I* get transferred." He frowned. "Fine by me. I'm a loner by nature."

Yet, he'd taken to wondering whether that was true. A lonely childhood had left him used to being alone, but did that mean it was his nature? Or had he just lost the chance to learn how to form or maintain lasting ties to anyone? All he felt was suspicion when he saw outwardly happy families.

Why the hell was he indulging in soul searching?

"Let's get to sleep," he said brusquely.

When she didn't say a word, Adam realized he wasn't quite ready to end the conversation.

"Are you involved with someone?" he heard himself ask.

"I thought you didn't want to talk anymore."

"Question just struck me." He hadn't wanted to lie,

but he wasn't going to tell her that he'd been wondering from the moment he'd warmed up in her arms.

"I...was engaged," she said softly. "Broke it off about a year ago. Among other problems, he hated my kayaking. If he wasn't interested in a sport or hobby, *we* couldn't to do it."

He liked her wryness even as he suspected it hid lingering hurt. "Good thing you didn't go so far as marry the jackass."

Her chuckle raised goose bumps.

The small electrical charge blended with his increasing relaxation.

What kind of idiot would let her go? Adam didn't trust easily—or at all—but with this woman... He came suddenly alert. Sure, she'd surprised him. Astonished him, really, with her guts, strength and persistence, all in aid of a man she didn't even know. She'd never quit on someone she loved.

But she neither loved nor trusted him. And he shouldn't need the reminder. Speaking of idiots.

It was a long time until he surrendered to sleep, and she was still tense beside him when he checked out.

CLAIRE WAS FIRST aware of blissful warmth, then of a large hand wrapped around her side, securing her against a muscular body. His slow, deep breaths stirred her hair. She couldn't quite hear his heartbeats, but felt the rise and fall of his chest.

The stranger.

Abruptly awake, she realized how closely entwined they were. He'd stayed on his back, probably the only comfortable position for him given the shoulder injury. She'd flung one of her legs across his sometime during the night.

Time to retreat. She shouldn't have even offered to share a sleeping bag with him last night. Then, the idea of holding each other felt comforting, even necessary. Now *dumb* was the word that came to mind.

She couldn't forget that she really didn't know him.

Chemistry major? Maybe. It's not like she could even ask casual questions to confirm he had basic knowledge. She'd hated the class in high school, and let any short-term knowledge go once she'd received a passing grade.

First, she very slowly lifted her leg off his, then squirmed backward. His arm tightened around her, but then relaxed and fell away. She saw no sign he was waking up. Unzipping the sleeping bag took some gymnastics, but she made her escape.

Morning or not, this wasn't sunbathing weather, so she dressed hastily and crawled out of the tent. One last peek found him still breathing deeply through parted lips. Definitely asleep.

They'd survived yesterday, but her nerves crawled at what today would bring.

Take advantage of the privacy for a quick trip to the woods, she decided, then a cup of coffee. When Adam appeared, she'd make breakfast, which usually consisted of oatmeal with dried fruit and sugar or honey.

Finish searching Mike's kayak. Who knew what he might have stashed away? Pray she found his SPOT. He might have dropped it into a bag, comfortable with the knowledge that he had the VHF radio at hand, right?

Not convinced, Claire grabbed the toilet paper and made her absolutely necessary trip. Returning, she let herself enjoy the weak sun on her face.

The tide was on its way in. She ached to pack up and

ready her kayak for departure. When the tide turned to go out again would be the perfect time to launch.

South to Haikai Passage would be the most direct way to find help, but they—she—would risk encountering the freighter. It had to be hovering at the first deep anchorage beyond the string of islands. But where?

Knowing how close Fitz Hugh Sound and the town of Namu were, as a crow flies, frustrated her. They wouldn't even have to reach the town, because they were certain to encounter heavy marine traffic on Fitz Hugh Sound, or before that when they got near a fishing camp. Getting there from here was the trick, though.

She continued to worry away at the problem.

West into Queen Charlotte Sound was too risky unless she left Adam behind. Dodging among islands had risks, too, but any weather change could mean swells or worse out on the open ocean. And, in her experience, the weather *would* change. There'd been more rainy or foggy days than sunny so far on this trip.

North seemed most logical, then, toward Hunter Channel and the Indigenous settlement of Bella Bella—assuming they didn't meet up with friendly fishermen or vacationers in a cabin cruiser on the way.

Maybe, given Adam's inexperience and injury, the best they could do for a day or two was sneak around islands and gain some distance from the searchers.

Unless she deserted Adam, they didn't dare go anywhere today, though. Tomorrow, however, they almost had to, because they'd run out of drinkable water.

She and Mike—

The stab of pain forced her to bend forward. It wasn't as if she hadn't thought about him, but now, everything she'd suppressed hit her. The first wrenching sob took her completely by surprise. She clapped her hand over her mouth to keep it silent, but nothing could stop the onslaught of grief that had chosen its time.

Chapter Six

Adam came awake with a rush, knowing instantly that something was missing.

Someone.

He surged to a sitting position, listening and not hearing a peep. As hyperalert as he always was, even in sleep he never let himself be unaware of any movement or sound from a woman in his bed, or men he bunked with. If Claire had decided she knew best and left, he'd—

Do what? he asked himself, angry. Dive into the freezing water and swim after her? That'd probably be faster than he'd move in a kayak, especially given the fierce pain in his right chest and back. At least the water would numb the pain if he dove in.

Swearing under his breath, he unzipped the bag and reached for the borrowed pants. For an almost-summer day, it was a lot colder than he liked. Not knowing the time increased his sense of being cut off from the world.

Dressed in the borrowed layers, he scrambled out, pulling the extra sleeping bag around him.

The minute he emerged from the tent, he saw her, sitting in her low-to-the-ground folding chair, nursing a hot cup of something in her hands. The relief was almost painful, although he noticed immediately that her eyes looked red and puffy.

She held a shushing finger to her lips, then pointed toward the trees. He went still, his gaze following hers.

A bald eagle sat on a branch not twenty-five feet from them. He clutched a fish in his talons, presumably breakfast. He also glared at them with savage disdain. They weren't supposed to be here.

"Friendly-looking guy," Adam murmured.

Claire smiled. "There's something almost reptilian in their eyes."

He'd seen bald eagles before; they were everywhere in western Washington, British Columbia and Alaska. Never this close, though. Never looked at one of the magnificent birds and known it was looking back.

After a moment, it spread broad wings and lifted off, fish still dangling, limp, from sharp talons.

Claire leaned forward to light the stove again. "Didn't want to have breakfast with us."

"Guess not."

"Coffee? Tea? Cocoa?"

He'd caught the fragrance of her roast. "Coffee."

First he made a detour, just as glad to have an excuse to gather himself before facing her scrutiny.

She averted her face when he returned and took his own seat. After a minute, he asked, "You okay?"

Claire lifted one shoulder in a tentative shrug. "Sure. It just hit me, that's all."

"Not helped by my presence, wearing your friend's clothes and using his toothbrush."

"No, that part doesn't bother me. I'm glad I could save someone. You know?"

He knew, although the ghosts of those he'd failed

seemed more populous than the people he'd been able to pull out of bad situations. Still, he nodded.

"How do *you* feel?" she asked.

Now that the adrenaline was subsiding, he could evaluate his condition. "Better," he decided. "I felt steady walking. My brain isn't foggy."

"Good. You're due for some painkillers. After breakfast, let me take a look at your wounds."

He grimaced. "Do I have to take my shirt off?"

She laughed.

As she poured his coffee, he said, "The drug trade is thriving in the Caribbean, but it's warm there. I should have resisted the last transfer."

"But it's more beautiful here, right?"

He waggled a hand, and she laughed again.

He bet she'd enjoy kayaking in the vivid blue waters off Belize, say. He'd done some diving there, just for fun. *Fun* didn't play much part in his life, which might be why the memory was so vivid.

"You mind oatmeal?"

"As opposed to scrambled eggs and bacon?"

Nose wrinkled, she admitted, "Oats are all that's on the menu."

"I'll take it." Adam turned his gaze toward the water advancing between the sharp cut of rocks, white fingers reaching forward. Kelp had been deposited on the tiny pebble beach last night, but would likely be pulled out by the next low tide. As hidden as this spot was, the fact that Claire had found it was downright miraculous.

"Hear any motors this morning?"

"Nope. They could be circling different islands and still not be far away, though."

She declined his offer to help her clean up after breakfast, and he didn't blame her. She had it down to a fine art. Still, he watched carefully, not enjoying the experience of being a burden instead of useful.

Once Claire was done, she fetched the first-aid kit, and he reluctantly shed his sweatshirt. Her hands were gentle as she removed the wrappings and gauze. He could tell she was trying to be dispassionate, but this was nothing like an examination in a hospital or clinic. He was too aware of her, and her rising color betrayed equal consciousness of him even if she was careful not to meet his eyes.

Adam twisted his neck to see the bullet wound in front. He'd had them before, and this one looked clean to him. Claire seemed to agree, because all she did was apply more antibiotic ointment and cover it with gauze.

Once she'd moved behind him, she said, "This is going to leave a heck of a scar."

"Not my first one."

"No."

He didn't have a lot of sensation where he'd been slashed by a knife on his back, but he'd swear he felt her fingertips skim along the trajectory of the scar.

"Ever think you might be getting down to your last of nine lives?"

He'd never thought about it that way, but she might have a point.

Once she rewrapped him, he eased the sweatshirt back on.

Again, Claire didn't quite look at him as she retreated to her chair. Too much close contact?

"So." She sounded stiff. "I've been doing some thinking."

He waited.

"Mostly, about our route when we do make a move." Without waiting for a response, she laid out charts in front of him. Bending over, he studied them as she calmly told him her conclusions about their options.

He didn't disagree, although he said, "We're having a streak of good weather."

"Have you spent much time on this coast?"

"One previous trip in May on that rust bucket out of Juneau. Ended farther north than this, somewhere off the McNaughton islands. I can't claim to be an expert."

"Well, boaters in general check the weather every evening on the VHF radio, because it's so changeable. A large ship can handle a twenty-foot swell, but kayaks are relatively frail. You need to know whether it's safe to launch, given the route you plan for the day. It makes me nervous not having access to weather reports. A sunny sky when you launch at dawn doesn't mean it could be pouring rain four hours later, or high winds won't coincide with a rising tide. As it is…" She shrugged. "We'll have to judge from our limited viewpoint. In general, mornings are calm, but the winds rise in the afternoon. That's one reason we aim for early departures. Speaking of…"

He looked at her.

"Are the men looking for us likely to be out at dawn?"

Depended on how desperate they were getting, he thought. "If we can't paddle in the dark, as early as possible seems the safest to me."

She nodded. "Once the tide's all the way in, we'll have a lesson in kayaking. I can at least demonstrate some basics."

Paddling was not going to feel good. Adam had worked through pain before, but he was having too much time to anticipate the agony. Still, she was right. If nothing else, running out of drinking water would be a critical problem.

He traced the route she suggested with his finger. Convoluted, relatively speaking, but as long as they weren't spotted by his shipmates, they could escape the net they were trying to cast.

She slipped the charts back into the plastic that protected them from water damage, her gaze on him thoughtful.

Damn. She'd been working herself up to something. Adam tensed.

Her chin lifted. "I don't understand why they're so determined. They head back to Alaska, who can even prove they were ever here? I didn't see a name or registration number on the freighter, and I couldn't make out the name on the yacht. Plus, they didn't see me."

"You're hundred percent sure?"

Her forehead crinkled, but she said, "They wouldn't have left if they had."

"Look at it from their point of view. Say they didn't see you, but they decided to send someone back to make sure I was dead. What did they find? My body? Nope. The empty kayak, floating hull up? Not that, either. Maybe some debris, like the paddle, but probably not much, because the smaller stuff would have dispersed fast."

"Your body could have become submerged."

"But I was floating when they last saw me."

"And…and currents among these islands aren't as straightforward as the tide they deal with out on the open water."

"Kayak wasn't going to sink, though. And it's gaudy as hell."

Claire wanted to be stubborn, but her usually sky blue eyes had darkened with worry.

She went with stubborn. "They could be back in Juneau by now, but they're not. The drugs they transferred to the yacht are well on their way to a warehouse, ready for distribution. You're one man. You didn't have anything on you. No camera, no flash drive, no phone. Unless you have something stashed in Juneau, wherever you were staying, you can't prove anything. So why are they so worried?"

ADAM COULD WISH she weren't so logical, except she was his only backup. Reality was, the other agents involved in the overall investigation wouldn't start worrying about him for days, unless the freighter docked and he didn't check in. If that rusty old tub didn't reappear, they'd know he had no way to call, and would assume that something unexpected had come up and he was just keeping his head down. Doing his job.

That left Claire.

In a tight situation, he'd appreciate her brains as well as her astonishing strength. Right now, he wished she hadn't followed that train of logic quite so far down the line.

"I was there to nail them for drug trafficking. They've been transporting a steady stream of top-quality product to the US. I hadn't gotten even a hint of anything else, so no, I don't have anything useful stashed back in Juneau. I've passed on what I've learned." He paused. "I was back on board the ship when I overheard something not meant for my ears."

"Because your boss already distrusted you?"

"Because this wasn't something anyone high up in the organization wanted the grunts to know. Most of us on that ship were grunts." He hesitated again, his instincts always to hold what he knew close. But he did need her, and if he had to scare her to make her more cautious, he'd do that. "This time," he said bluntly, "they'd been persuaded to carry something extra. I'm sure they were paid well, but it wouldn't surprise me if everyone who knew about the extra cargo isn't eliminated as soon as they show their faces back in Alaska."

"Weapons?" she whispered.

"Close enough."

Her eyes narrowed, and he caught himself twitching at her piercing scrutiny. She saw a lot deeper than he liked...or was damn good at faking it. He knew he wouldn't want to face her in a job interview if he were hiding part of his past.

Suddenly, she stood and crossed her arms, looking down at him. "Which makes it important you get the word out as soon as possible." Not a question.

He inclined his head in agreement.

"There wasn't anyone else on that ship or in port who can do that."

"No."

"Let me ask this."

He knew where she was going.

"What if they catch up with us and you get shot, but I make my getaway? What if I survive and you don't?" She bent toward him, with her slim body not as good at looming as she probably imagined, but she was making her point, all right. "Shouldn't I know who to contact and what to tell that person?"

Adam closed his eyes and scrubbed a hand through his hair, stiff from the salt water. "Yeah," he said hoarsely. This went against all his training, but she was right. Hell, he might die by making a beginner's mistake in the kayak she'd already described as frail. Or because he was injured, far from his peak health and strength.

"Well, then?"

He wanted to stand and pace. He needed to expend some of his fear. Aware of his weakness, he made himself stay put.

"Uranium. Terrorists convinced a couple of dumb-ass traffickers to carry the makings for a nuclear bomb—or several, who knows? All they saw was the bucks." He rubbed his thumb and forefingers together. "Worse thing is, I don't know what group is behind this, or who is waiting for the delivery." In his intensity, he leaned forward. "Passing on the name and registration number for the yacht is critical."

Claire stared at him, unblinking.

AFTER DROPPING HIS BOMBSHELL—bad pun—Adam made her memorize the information as well as the phone number to reach his boss.

Somehow, Claire stayed calm. Or managed to look calm anyway. She had a suspicion it would all hit her at some unexpected moment, just as grief for Mike had earlier. After everything she'd seen and learned in the past twenty-four hours, it took a lot to stir her out of her state of numbness.

Why was this happening to her? The biggest drama in her life had been the final months with Devin followed by their breakup. Right now, the Devin situation was receding fast in her rearview mirror. A jerk, so what. A real crisis? Terrorists getting their hands on the critical ingredient to manufacture a nuclear bomb… No comparison.

While brooding silently, she removed the evergreen branches hiding her kayak. Then she did her best to shove the huge, scary problems into a compartment in her brain that had a really sturdy door, focusing instead on carrying the kayak down to the water while slip-sliding on the rounded rocks that made up the beach. A careless trip could leave her injured, too.

Plus, it was easier to think about the next step than the big picture.

When Adam saw what she was doing, he scowled and shot reflexively to his feet. "Let me help—"

"I carry it all the time. You don't need to be lifting anything yet."

His lips tightened and he relented. Claire had already noticed he didn't like to feel weaker than her. Of course, in his case, a need to be tough was probably a professional requirement.

He did watch in grim silence as she suited up, just in case she took a dunking. That got her thinking. Yes, he'd clearly hated letting her do the heavy work, but was that really because he needed to swagger in front of a woman? He'd been a lot more open to her suggestions and even orders than Devin ever would have been, even in a life-and-death situation. She'd like to think Adam just had old-fashioned good manners, or maybe tended to be protective. Being protective would come naturally to anyone in law enforcement, she assumed.

On the other hand, it was still open to question who he was. Maybe he'd cooked up this latest story to remove her doubts. It was certainly a good one. He'd hardly taken his eyes off her since his revelation about the contraband on the ship, as if he was assessing the effectiveness. Did she buy it? Didn't she?

Next step, she reminded herself.

"I'll help you pack and load your kayak tomorrow morning," she told him, "so we won't worry about any of that. Um…why don't you bring your chair down to the waterline instead of having to stand?"

She read a flicker in his eyes as frustration rather

than annoyance at her continued coddling. Without a word, he picked up the lightweight chair and carried it down, picking his way carefully. His boots probably weren't entirely dry, but cold and clammy had to be an improvement on soggy. His own pants, sweater—with holes torn by the bullet front and back—socks and briefs were still draped over a huckleberry bush, probably dry.

Wow, would he be able to get into Mike's wet suit? Aghast, she wondered why she hadn't thought of this latest problem already. Damn.

Next step.

She shoved this new worry onto the pile.

Once she started her demonstration and found herself stumbling over her own tongue, Claire discovered how self-conscious Adam Taylor made her feel with his attention one hundred percent on her.

Of course, part of it was her awareness of his tall, strong body and what it looked like beneath his clothes. She knew the pattern of brown hair on his chest and had no trouble at all picturing his hard belly and strong thighs. She'd even saved a mental screenshot of him naked, despite pretending to herself that she wasn't looking.

By that time she had to be beet red, a step up from the sunburn she could never seem to avoid on these trips, given her extremely fair skin.

If Adam looked quizzical, who could blame him?

He watched intently as she showed him how to hold the superlight carbon fiber paddle. Mike had used a different style of paddle, so she used her own spare paddle for Adam to practice the grip.

She had him study the interior of the cockpit, with the seat and back cushions, the foam thigh braces and

foot braces. The rudder... No, too much, she decided.
It turned out he knew how to read the compass.

As she cinched up her spray skirt around her waist,
Claire hoped Mike's wasn't too tight for Adam's more
muscled torso. As a beginner, he was unlikely to do any
rolling maneuvers, but without a spray skirt, even mod-
erate waves would start filling the compartment with
water. He'd be ankle deep or more in no time. Given the
temperature of the water, he'd get cold. The risk would
be even higher if he couldn't use the wet suit.

She stayed close, demonstrating forward and back
strokes, the sweep stroke for turning, braces for stabil-
ity. Then she returned to shore, pulled the kayak up and
answered questions.

They ought to be holding this lesson in a swimming
pool, or maybe a placid lake. She shouldn't be having
to condense even basic techniques and knowledge into
an hour exhibition. Even if he magically achieved mas-
tery of the strokes, he'd still lack seamanship, the understanding of weather, tides, the subtle changes, what
it took not to make a fatal mistake.

But finally, she said, "We need to figure out whether
you can get into Mike's wet suit. As long as the weather
stays nice, it's not as important—the fleece pants you're
wearing will be okay. At least now you have some dry
pants to change into at the end of the day. But there's
no guarantee about weather, and if you get really wet it
could trigger another bout with hypothermia."

He listened with an odd expression on his face.
When she was finished, one side of his mouth turned
up in a smile she could only think was tender. Her heart
cramped hard.

"You're doing your best, you know," he said in his gravelly voice. "That's all you can do. Don't beat yourself up."

They stood close enough, she could have taken one step forward and leaned on him. Rested her forehead against his broad chest.

Even the temptation scared her. Instead, Claire snapped, "The better you plan, the more chance of success. You must know that."

"I do," he said quietly, that same quizzical look in his eyes, the same tilt to his mouth.

She turned her back to start to lift her kayak. Almost immediately, some of the weight vanished. Adam had grabbed the toggle at the stern with his left hand, and all she had to do was lift from the bow.

Weight shared.

Chapter Seven

Adam was all but twitching with his need to do *some-thing*. Anything. Get on with tomorrow's plans, whether he was ready or not. Scramble through that damn tangle of vegetation to a point where he could watch surrounding waters through the binoculars while wishing they were a rifle scope.

Have sex.

That wasn't an option for a lot of reasons, starting with the fact that Claire Holland was a nice woman who'd risked her own life to save his. He'd known her for twenty-four hours—and that was generous, given that he'd been semiconscious for a good part of that time. There was plenty he still didn't know about her, but he'd bet she wasn't the kind of woman who had brief hookups with men, even if she felt the stirrings of attraction. So as fast as that ephemeral thought crossed his mind, he banished it.

He thought about suggesting they take the kayaks out far enough to get a peek but knew that was not possible. He wouldn't be ready tomorrow, but he *really* wasn't ready right now.

The tentative warmth of the day felt good, if he'd been in the mood to lean back and relax.

Claire had picked up an electronic reader, told him

that no, it wasn't displaying the time because it couldn't connect to the internet any more than her cell phone could. "I want to finish the book I'm reading," she'd announced, "and after that it'll be dead until I have a chance to charge it."

If she had a chance.

She had to be thinking that. He'd give anything to ensure she survived the coming days. Almost anything, Adam amended—he needed to get to someplace he could make a phone call. The bomb, depending on its size, could kill thousands to hundreds of thousands of people. That had to come first. Maybe it was fortunate that he needed *her* to get him to that phone. He wouldn't have to make a hard choice.

She abruptly set down her reader, stood and marched over to pick up a bag and carry it back to her chair. She dug inside and came up with a pile of tattered paperbacks that she held out to him.

"You're making me crazy. You can read, right?"

With all the hairs that had escaped the braid or broken off around her face, she made him think of a ruffled owl.

"You're peeling," he commented.

"Gee, I didn't notice." She waggled the books, and he accepted them.

Then she plunked down in her chair hard enough she was lucky not to bend the aluminum frame.

So, she didn't like him staring at her. He got that, but suspected she was as antsy as he was. They had the whole day to get through, and days were too damn long at this latitude. The two of them would have to go to bed well before the sun set if they were to make a really early start.

What in the hell were they supposed to *do* all day?

He bent his head to look at the book on top of the pile. A thriller, which wasn't likely to be pleasant recreational reading at the moment.

"Listen," Claire said suddenly.

Adam cocked his head. There it was, distant but audible. An outboard motor. That was no cabin cruiser or fishing boat.

His body went rigid.

Voice as tense as he felt, she said, "The tide's far enough out they can't get close enough to see us."

"I'm going out to where *I* can see them." He rose to his feet. "Do you have flares, in case we get lucky and spot some innocent boaters?"

"Yes. Should we bring one?"

"Let's hold off. We don't dare set off a flare if there's any chance the skiff is nearby. Where are the binoculars?"

"You're not going without me," Claire insisted, just as she had yesterday.

She'd kept the binoculars close at hand. He was glad to have her given the difficulty of the trek. If he fell and did further damage to his shoulder, he was screwed. Likewise, if he sprained or broke an ankle or ribs. Or if she hurt herself. In fact, he had to grab her once when her boot became wedged under roots crisscrossing a crack between rocks, and she returned the favor a few minutes later.

The distant hum of the motor continued as background noise that rasped his nerve endings. If only he had a rifle.

No, better not to take a shot even if he'd had one. Unless he succeeded in killing both men in the boat, or punching enough holes in the aluminum hull to sink the thing, all he'd have done was pinpoint their current location.

Thinking about weapons gave him an idea, though. He'd check to see how many flares were available between the two kayaks. They could potentially be used as weapons, and he'd be especially happy to find a flare gun. In the event the two of them got cornered and were under attack, flares might draw attention his former buddies wouldn't like.

Today, Claire and he pushed farther out toward the rim of the island, although they paid the price of a sore ankle—in his case—and a wealth of scratches on both their faces and hands.

Once they had a good view, they hunkered down behind the scrappy vegetation and rounded granite.

After two or three minutes of waiting, Claire burst out, "It's like…the whine of black flies or mosquitoes!"

"I'd like to swat this one," he agreed.

The reflection off the water was bright enough, he had to blink frequently. "Did Mike have dark glasses?" he asked.

She gave him a startled glance. "Yes. Unless they were in—" Her voice became smaller. "I think he might have been wearing them."

Oh, well. Protection for his eyes would be a luxury, not an essential.

Once again, she spotted the boat before he did, making him think she had exceptionally sharp eyes. "There. Only…it's not the same boat."

He trained the binoculars on the gray-green inflatable boat, and immediately confirmed the identities of the two men in it. "Son of a—" he muttered under his breath. "The skiff ran really low in the water with both of them aboard. This is newer and larger." Motor didn't sound any more powerful, though.

"Do you suppose they have a map showing potential campsites?" Claire asked.

He took his eyes off the boat. "I don't know. Do you?"

"Yes. I've been worrying that the campsites everyone knows about might not be safe for us."

Adam handed her the binoculars. If she ended up alone, she had to know the bad guys when she saw them. "Take a look. Memorize their faces."

She didn't look happy about the directive, but adjusted the binoculars and stared through them for a long minute.

"Those campsites," Adam said. "Who is likely to stay at them?"

Lowering the binoculars, she answered, "Other kayakers, mostly."

"Who'd be carrying a VHF radio or satellite tracker."

"Yes, but…"

He kept an eye on the inflatable, which was gradually growing closer, but also watched her.

"Well, would help come fast enough if *they* see us? And…would we be endangering other people?"

Given a new worry, he quit listening and took back the binoculars. Unless the path of the boat changed, the two men wouldn't be able to miss seeing the almost-hidden entrance through the crack in the sculpted rock wall of the island. All they'd have to do was come back once the tide was high again.

Adam and Claire wouldn't have any defense against being strafed with bullets from semiautomatic weapons.

Lunch consisted of rehydrated soup, dried fruit and a candy bar each.

Adam was never chatty, and Claire had been so frightened by the near disaster that she still felt shaky.

Something had distracted those men. The one sitting in the bow had pointed northeast, and the pilot had steered them into a curve leading away from Adam's and her hideout.

Thank God.

Adam had kept a sharp eye on her for a while, but finally started reading one of the books from the pile. He'd tossed aside a couple of them—Mike had really liked thrillers—in favor of an older science fiction novel, *The Mote in God's Eye*, that even Claire had read and enjoyed once upon a time, although she didn't remember much about it. Even as he appeared to be engrossed in the story, she suspected his attention was as divided as hers was.

She'd let herself feel almost safe here. Illusion obliterated, she started at every tiny sound, from a flurry of wings as a flock of ravens came to rest in the taller trees behind her, to the cries of gulls and terns. The ravens especially disturbed her. Northwest Coast First Nations legend had it that ravens perching on a house meant a death would come.

Once they heard a powerful marine engine, but too far in the distance. If anyone on board saw a flare, they'd come looking, but as Adam had pointed out, someone closer could find them first.

At a loud splash, she must have jumped a foot, but the new arrival was a black oystercatcher, a foot-and-a-half-tall bird with distinctive red markings that paddled into sight and, ignoring them, poked in the tidal pools to one side of their miniature beach.

If a black bear had waddled into sight, Claire probably would have had a heart attack.

"I doubt they'll be back today." Adam didn't even look up from his book, but he'd read her anxiety just fine.

"I know."

His faint smile annoyed her.

She stared at the lit screen of her electronic reader and discovered she was on the last page of the book. She hadn't a clue what had happened in the previous two chapters and didn't care. Only a sliver of battery life remained. She closed the cover but still clutched the reader in a tight grip. She could grab her remaining paperback, or sort through Mike's, but reading was futile.

With the bad guys apparently gone for now, maybe she and Adam should pack up and make a run for it. Claire almost opened her mouth to suggest it, but then she took a good look at his face.

The flesh seemed to have evaporated, leaving skin stretched tight from sharp cheekbones to the bony line of his jaw. If anything, the stubble enhanced the gaunt effect. Creases marred his forehead, and his eyes… She waited for him to lift his head.

When he did, she sucked in a breath. "You hurt."

"Nothing I can't handle," he said shortly.

"Why would you suffer when you don't have to?" She gave her head an exasperated shake. "You've been wounded before. Surely a few doctors along the way have given you the lecture about the benefits of staying on top of the pain?" Her voice had been steadily rising. "As in, you'll heal faster?"

"I did intend to ask for some more Tylenol," he admitted.

"I think you should go for the heavy-duty stuff. Maybe even take a nap." Except she'd be left alone out here, afraid to miss a single sound.

"No nap. I'll take the meds, though."

So he hurt even more than she'd guessed. Shaking her head, Claire poured water into a cup and handed it to him with two of the pills. He gulped them down and gave her back the cup.

"I don't like admitting to weaknesses," he said after a minute.

An apology, she suspected.

"It's not a weakness to feel the normal symptoms from a wound. I mean, a bullet went *through* you."

"Yeah. I've had a lot of practice at hiding what I'm feeling."

"Because of your job?"

He rubbed his hand through his hair, which had to be stiff with dried salt. She kept watching him, and finally he said, "I'm guessing you grew up feeling secure."

"I did. My parents split up when I was fourteen, but…yeah. I knew Mom and I'd be staying in the house. I'd keep going to the same school. It was just weird with Dad not there. I was ashamed for friends to find out."

"Did he stay in touch?"

"Sure. He didn't always show up when he'd promised to, but he mostly paid the child support, and my mother encouraged me to understand he was having a hard time."

"In what way?"

None of this was his business, but he was a good listener, and they had to do *something* while they waited for nightfall.

"He was drinking heavily. After a couple of DUIs, he spent months in jail. It took him a couple of years to get himself together, but too late for Mom."

"He'd broken her trust."

"I guess so." He'd broken hers, too, but he stayed

sober the days he took her out for lunch or to do something fun, like ride the ferry or go to the Puyallup Fair, so she'd been able to continue loving him, and knew he loved her. Still, she'd felt abandoned, which might explain why she'd stubbornly stayed with Devin despite all the warning signs.

What an unexpected conversation.

"Did your father walk out on you and your mom?"

"Before I was born." Long pause. "My mother had her own problems. She worked as a waitress or in a bar, from what I remember. I was four when she didn't pick me up at this home day care. I went into the system. Never saw her again."

"That's awful." Claire knew she couldn't let him think she felt pity. He'd close up tight. Tighter than he already was, that is. He was talking, but not giving away much emotion. "Did she... Were her problems with drugs?"

Their eyes met, and he made a rough sound. "Guess I'm obvious. Yeah, I have a few memories of watching her shooting up. When she couldn't afford her next hit—" He shook his head.

Claire didn't even like to think about what he hadn't said.

"Did you look for either of your parents later?"

"Mother. Found out she'd died a couple of years later. My father...no. Why would I?"

She understood. She wouldn't have, either.

He stayed quiet for what had to be several minutes, not reading, just frowning. At last he shook himself. "I don't usually talk about my past."

"We're spending a lot of time together." No TV, tablets or phones to distract them. And...she had shared more than she'd have expected with him, too.

Adam grunted what could have been a laugh. "Sunbathing and dining together. You've started introducing me to your favorite sport."

Sleeping together, too, she couldn't help thinking.

"Right." She smiled. "Nothing but fun."

"Might be, under other circumstances."

The painkillers must be having an effect, because Adam's eyelids grew heavy. He lapsed into silence for a few minutes again, Claire not breaking it. A raven cawed and, to her relief, they all took wing. Spreading their blessings elsewhere? Adam's gaze appeared unfocused. He really should take a nap.

His voice startled her. "Look."

"What?" She tipped her head back to see the sky, the endless blue marked by a long vapor trail. Claire felt a strange pang. There was proof they weren't alone in the world, but they might as well be.

"You like your job?" Adam asked unexpectedly.

Still gazing at the vapor trail, she had to think about that. "Most of the time, but…it's a job, not a passion. You know. I suppose I wouldn't miss it, but I'm satisfied. I make a good living, and I can put it out of my mind when I leave the office." She realized how that sounded. "I guess you can't do the same, can you?"

"Ya think?"

"I don't think I'd enjoy a job where I got *shot* on an average day in the office," she said honestly.

That earned her one of his hoarse laughs. "Yesterday wasn't an average day."

"You have an awful lot of scars."

"Yeah." He fell back to brooding.

It was all she could do not to fiddle, or chatter brightly about some inane topic. Desperate at last, she said, "Would you like some hot chocolate? Or coffee? Or…"

His eyes, now bloodshot, met hers. "Can we spare the water?"

"We can't let ourselves get dehydrated."

"Hot chocolate."

Heating the water and preparing the drinks kept her busy for a few minutes. Once she handed over his, she worried when she saw the way he cradled the mug and breathed in the steam. She certainly hadn't stripped to her T-shirt, but the day wasn't *cold*. If he started to shiver…

But he took a sip and lifted his head to study her. "Why'd you break up with the fiancé?"

Nosy, but she'd been dying to ask if he'd been—or was currently—married or living with someone.

Anyway, why not answer? Once they reached safety, she doubted she and Adam would ever see each other again.

"He didn't like being challenged, not even in little ways. If he told me his opinion about some issue and I mentioned an article I'd read that included facts that didn't support what he was saying, he'd be cutting. He'd say I was credulous, believing everything I read no matter what the source. He hated that I made more money than he did. It got so he was constantly putting me down, both in private and in front of our friends. He seemed so confident when we first met." Claire felt her face twist. "Maybe I'm a know-it-all—"

Adam made a derisive sound. "Sounds like he wanted a submissive partner whose goal in life was to make him feel big." His eyes narrowed. "Did he get abusive?"

"You mean, did he hit me?" She clenched her jaw.

It was an effort to say the rest. "Yes. Once. That was the end."

"Did he grovel afterward and tell you he wouldn't do anything like that again?"

She nodded. "I told him he needed counseling, went to spend the night at a friend's house—" Mike and Shelby's, of course "—and told Devin to be out by the time I got home from work the next day."

"Your place? Bet that rubbed him the wrong way."

Of course it had, but he liked living above his income. "He had an apartment—I own a nice condo."

She hadn't been surprised to come home to find him still there. He'd packed, but he had also cooked a fancy dinner and set a candlelit table. He'd uncorked a bottle of wine to breathe.

Fortunately, she'd had the forethought to ask Mike to go with her. Devin screamed ugly accusations and obscenities at her as he handed over his key and left.

After she was done crying, she and Mike had planned this trip but had to wait until they'd both saved enough vacation from their jobs to take it.

He'd given her the gift of anticipation, even hope, and what had his kindness and friendship given him? A senseless death.

She started to cry and had to cover her face with her hands to try to hide it. The next thing she knew, Adam was kneeling by her chair and embracing her. She let herself cry against his shoulder for a minute, that was all, then lifted her head to give him a shaky smile and to lay her hand lightly over his heart.

"Thanks."

"That son of a bitch."

Surprised, she said, "I wasn't crying about Devin. It was…"

She didn't have to explain, it was for Mike…and Shelby. He retreated to his chair and stayed silent for so long.

"Are you married?"

His head turned sharply. "God, no!"

Well, that was telling her. Not that she was foolish enough to be thinking of him in that context.

"Not a fan of the institution?" she asked.

"It's not that." He frowned. "I don't know many people who've made a success of marriage, though."

"You don't run in the best circles," she pointed out.

Adam shrugged a concession. "I know agents who've been divorced two or even three times. There's a flaw in the 'absence makes the heart grow fonder' theory."

"It would be hard. But if you love someone enough, and that person loves what they are doing…"

"Nice idea, but then you have children, and you're trying to be both parents, hold down a job, make decisions you resent having to make on your own, while they are off doing God knows what, and what if your partner is having an affair while away from home? Or what if they come home with yet another bullet hole?"

"You can't tell me there aren't spouses tough enough to take it."

His eyes, unblinking, held hers longer than was comfortable. Then he growled, "Let's talk about something else."

And what exactly would that be?

Chapter Eight

Bedtime rolled around at last, thank God. Adam swore he wouldn't ask Claire to share the sleeping bag with him, but, damn, he wanted to. Her curves fit him just right. She didn't have to worry that he'd expect anything but a warm body to hold. He'd been deluded earlier, thinking about having sex.

"Strange trying to sleep when the sun is still high," he grumbled, crawling first into the tent. It was dim inside here, but far from dark.

"Didn't you on that boat?"

"We had bunks inside."

"Oh. Well, if it really bothers you, I can throw a space blanket over the tent. That would help."

"I'll be fine." Especially if he could clutch her to him like a gently worn teddy bear—or the lover he'd like her to be, when he regained his strength. When they were both safe.

"Okay."

He couldn't quite see what she was doing, but thought when her head turned that she was taking a last scan to be sure everything was securely stowed. Then she crawled in, too, and let the flaps fall closed.

"You never zip those," he commented.

"Huh? Oh. I like to be able to see what's coming without fumbling for the zipper."

There was a thought.

He'd taken some more of the hard-hitting painkillers in hopes they'd give him both a good night's sleep and a boost in healing. They hadn't quite taken effect yet, though, so he groaned and swore a couple of times while inserting himself in the sleeping bag.

He closed his eyes as she stripped off most of her clothes, although he heard the rustles and sighs just fine. Pain or not, his body was responding to the images that filled his head.

"Let me feel your forehead," she said softly. A moment later, her palm settled on his brow. "No fever." She sounded as if she was talking to herself.

He lay tense, wishing he could think of a good excuse to ask her to join him.

"I suppose I should, um, sleep in my own bag tonight. In Mike's actually, since you're in mine, but—" Sounding flustered, she broke off.

"Either way is fine." He made sure she could tell he was okay either way. "But I liked sleeping with you."

After a very long pause, she said, "I liked sleeping with you, too. It was...comforting."

He didn't say anything.

"Why not?" she decided, and a moment later she squirmed her way in with him, tugged up the zipper, shook out the second sleeping bag into a cozy layer and unerringly found the hollow below his shoulder to pillow her head.

He tugged her closer, wrapped his arm around her and smiled up at the peaked roof of the tent. Now he was too relaxed to waste the energy thinking about morning, and the risky run from danger.7

CLAIRE FLOATED TEN or fifteen feet off to Adam's left, looking as if she and the kayak were one. He felt as awkward as a big man perched in a first grader's chair, pretending he was comfortable. His knees weren't quite up to his nose, but that was only because they were trapped beneath the deck of the kayak.

Didn't help that he was humiliatingly aware that he required frequent critiquing.

"You're trying to do it all with your arms," she said just then. "Use your torso." She demonstrated a stroke that had her upper body twisting side to side as she paddled. Her kayak shot ahead as if a flick of a fishtail propelled it.

He tried what she suggested and found she was right—this was easier and put slightly less strain on his painful right upper quadrant. Which wasn't saying much.

The sky had still been pearly when they left their campsite, having to carry the kayaks over the long, narrow stretch of smooth, slimy cobblestones bared after the tide went out, but once afloat they emerged from between the wave-sculpted cliffs to find themselves alone. Or so it seemed. With the multitude of islands and rocky islets topped by wind-twisted trees, another boat could be hiding just out of sight, as Claire had been when her partner was shot. She'd been right that the air was still, the morning utterly quiet. Eerie wisps of fog hovered, not quite touching the water nor reaching as high as the trees. From time to time, she'd become oddly indistinct, until he reached the same band of fog and then glided through it.

They had chosen the northerly route, winding between islands, planning to hug the east coast of Spider Island. There were a couple of designated campsites there. He'd argued they circle to the west side of the biggest island in this immediate area because he feared Spider Channel would be too open, exposing them to watching eyes.

Claire had nixed that, pointing out that in the channel, they would be sheltered. On the west coast they'd be exposed to open ocean with powerful tidal currents and swells that could reach ten feet high even if the weather remained fair.

"You're a raw beginner," she reminded him, as if he'd forgotten, "and injured besides. I hate the idea of us losing sight of each other even briefly as we dip between swells and climb over them."

"You're the expert," he had said simply.

Now as they glided past yet another island, Claire suddenly back paddled and said sharply, "Look!"

The pain already crippling Adam more than he'd anticipated; he was grateful to let his paddle rest across the cockpit while he squinted to see what she had.

That didn't take much effort, since the bright red kayak stood out in this blue-and-green-and-pale-gray landscape. Hope of finding a fellow traveler who had a radio or SPOT didn't even have a chance to catch hold, because it was immediately obvious that there was no paddler.

"Somebody may be in the water!" she cried and shot forward at a speed he couldn't equal.

"Claire!"

But if she heard him, she didn't stop.

He dug in to catch her, but his kayak immediately felt unstable, the rocking making him afraid he might capsize. And he was no longer going straight after her, either; clearly, he was favoring his right arm. Adam made himself slow down and regain the steady pace he'd so far maintained.

For the, what, fifteen minutes they'd been on the water?

He didn't hear the sound of any engine. Trouble was only this single kayak, bobbing on the lift of the waves.

Claire reached it well before he did, and immediately began to cast in increasing circles around it. He glided up to the empty kayak and back paddled until he could lay a hand on it.

Half expecting to see streaks of blood or bullet holes in the hull, he found nothing alarming—except for the missing kayaker.

Claire came back to join him. "It might have floated out of reach when someone was launching, or if they didn't tie it up last night." The anxiety in her eyes told him she didn't believe her own explanation.

"From where?" he asked.

She looked around. "There's a picnic spot, maybe good for emergency camping, not far from here. Let's check there."

She gave him a comprehensive look that probably saw through his stoic veneer.

He said, "Why don't we look in the day hatch first?"

"You're right." She snapped it open, and he saw a water bottle, snacks, lip ointment, suntan lotion, a flare and some other miscellaneous items. Claire lifted a broad-brimmed foldable hat. "A cell phone."

They hovered over it from opposite sides of the empty kayak. Unsurprisingly, its charge was either gone or it could only be activated by a fingerprint.

"Damn," he muttered. "Wouldn't anyone kayaking out here have at least a VHF radio?"

"Yes, but he might have it in the vest pocket." She patted hers. "I carried the SPOT in there."

Frustrated, Adam watched as Claire snapped a towline on a loop at the bow and started paddling. She'd only left a short line, and Adam followed like a duckling.

He didn't like this. The empty kayak wasn't quite the same color as the one he was paddling, nor the same shape—it was shorter by a couple of feet, too—but it *was* red. Would Dwayne and the others have noticed the orange shading into red on this one? It wouldn't have been until later that they started worrying about the combined absence of his body and the kayak.

No, he seriously doubted they'd have paid attention to any subtleties.

Claire had them circling an island with the ocean-hewn rock walls washed pale and oddly smooth in a way that was typical. She was moving faster than she had earlier, driven to find the missing person. Adam labored to keep up.

An inlet opened, and he groaned in relief, knowing she wouldn't hear him.

He heard her half-whimpered "Oh, God," followed by a tremulous, "Mike?"

Within moments, he came abreast of her and saw the body bumping against the rocks.

He had no idea what her friend had worn when he was shot, but knew he'd shed his yellow flotation vest. This body still wore his.

"It can't be Mike," he said flatly. "Let me closer."

Sunburned or no, her face had blanched. She did something complicated with her paddle that enabled her to edge out of the way. The empty kayak bumped against Adam's and almost forced him into the wall, but he pushed away with his paddle. When he reached the body, he snagged it by the vest.

"Watch out!"

Hell. He'd almost gone over. "Help me get him across my deck."

She scooted over so that she could stabilize his kayak with their paddles lying across both decks as he bent over again. A man's weight coupled with the soaking-wet garments was almost too much for his one-handed grip, but he forced himself to use his right hand, too, and heaved upward.

He didn't see the face, but with the body draped right in front of him he couldn't miss the several holes left by bullets punching through the puffy yellow PFD.

Claire's shocked stare told him she understood what had happened to this poor bastard—and why it had happened.

THEY DIDN'T HAVE a lot of choice but to land on the small, gravel beach.

Claire released herself from her cockpit and then her spray skirt before pulling her own kayak a few feet higher on the beach and reeling in the towline so she could capture the empty kayak.

"Do we dare stay here even for a little while?" she asked. They hadn't made half a mile yet.

But then she saw Adam's face as he stumbled climbing out of his own kayak. His face looked almost as bad as it had when she saw him surface after he'd been shot. White lines of pain bracketed his mouth.

"You hurt yourself pulling the body on board."

He glanced up. "No. Already hurt. Damn. Help me get this guy up to dry ground."

"Yes. Okay." She had to swallow some bile as she

looked at the body sprawled over Adam's kayak. This wasn't Mike; she knew it wasn't, but...his body would look as bad.

Worse, she thought, after being in the water for two extra days.

Adam mumbled something profane as he looked around them. Then he scrubbed a hand over his face. "Can you tell if he camped here last night?"

"Let me look."

It didn't take her long to find a rectangle of flattened vegetation where a tent must have been pitched—although it wouldn't have been comfortable to sleep in, given the ridge of a tree root that ran the length of it—and some scuffed moss.

"Somebody did," she said. A furrow in the gravel added to the tale. "One kayak."

"Okay. I have to think. While I do that, let's search the kayak and the body for anything useful."

"Why don't we both think?" she suggested a little tartly, despite the horror she had trouble moving past.

He grimaced. "Right. I didn't mean to imply— Sorry. I'm just used to being on my own. What we need to decide is what to do with the body and the kayak, and whether we'd be safer hunkering down here for the night or going on."

She came close to shouldering him out of the way so she could take most of the weight, but needed Adam's strength. Now she knew where the term *deadweight* came from. The body flopped onto the beach, the head coming to rest so that the man stared up at the blue sky.

Having gotten to know a lot of people in the Seattle area who were into sea kayaking, she'd been afraid she might recognize the victim, but he was a stranger. His brown hair was mostly contained in a short ponytail.

Otherwise, he had brown eyes and a stubbled jaw and was a big guy.

She and Adam wrestled the PFD off the body, but found the pocket empty. A pat down came up empty.

The two of them divided up the hatches on the kayak for a thorough hunt for identification, a SPOT or VHF radio and food, water and clothes that might fit Adam. She hated the idea of stripping the wet suit from the victim, but knew she'd have to. Adam might need it. He hadn't been able to squeeze into Mike's. If they hit rough or substantially colder weather, it would be critical.

"This'll solve one of our problems," Adam said after a minute.

She took a step to peek into the hatch right behind the cockpit, seeing three bags of drinking water. One ten-liter, two six.

"Yes." She gestured at the open deck hatch. "I took another look in here, but unless you like his brand of suntan lotion better than what Mike and I were carrying, there's nothing useful."

Adam's mouth tightened. "I'd hoped those SOBs might have been careless."

Claire didn't say anything.

She found two bags filled with clothing and set them aside. From the clanking sound behind her, she could tell Adam was digging through a bag with dishes and pans.

"Keep an eye out for any extra fuel canisters for the stove," she said over her shoulder.

"What about the food?"

"I don't know. Let me look at it while you go through these clothes."

Adam's expression was almost as grim as she felt when they changed places.

She saw right away that he'd set aside a knife with a six-inch blade. She had one, too, but the more the merrier, right? She guessed that depended on perspective. Adam's main goal in this search had probably been weapons. He'd found a flare gun, too, although she wasn't sure that qualified as a weapon, despite appearances.

Most of the contents of the bag holding kitchen gear were duplicates of things she and Mike had carried. She repacked it with unnecessary care, then evaluated the foodstuffs, deciding on some that would supplement what they already had.

Adam straightened, although he was still kneeling. "Here's a small bag that has…a wallet." One by one, he set items aside. "Canadian passport, wristwatch, sunglasses."

A lump formed in her throat. "What's his name?" Her gaze was drawn to the body.

"Kyle Sheppard." Adam sounded completely unemotional. "Twenty-eight years old. He's from Winnipeg."

Only twenty-eight. Claire shivered, unable to take her eyes off the young man's face. "Lots of lakes there. That's probably where he started kayaking."

When she finally glanced at Adam, she saw him rifling through the contents of the wallet.

"Credit cards, Canadian money, phone card, what looks like a car key," he said after a minute. "And a photo."

She didn't ask; she couldn't.

Adam rolled his shoulders and closed the wallet, dropped it on the small pile, then went back to his task of digging through the bag.

Claire returned each dry bag to one hatch after another once she'd looked through it. They almost had to put the kayak back into the water, and wouldn't want a cursory inspection to reveal that the contents had been searched.

Adam salvaged a fair pile of clothes. Without consulting her, he pulled bags from his kayak and pulled out Mike's clothes that didn't fit him, filling the bags with this new stuff that did. He even sat down and tried on a pair of sturdy sandals before adding them to the "keep" pile.

Claire spoke up. "When you're done, I'll tow the kayak out a little ways and turn it loose again."

He frowned at her. "You won't go far?"

"I won't need to. With the tide going out, it'll carry the kayak away."

He nodded. "Next question is, should we stay here under the assumption they've already been and have no reason to come back?"

"We haven't come very far this morning—" To put it mildly. "I'm thinking we're a couple of hours paddling away from the campsite I had in mind."

Adam didn't noticeably react. Finally, he said, "I can make it if I have to."

All she had to do was remember the expression on his face when they first landed to know how much he'd suffer if they went on. They'd been too optimistic—or was *desperate* a better word?—in thinking Adam would be ready to paddle a kayak so soon, after such a serious injury. Would another night's rest give him enough chance to heal to make a difference?

Tomorrow would have to be better than today. Only…

She had to say this. "The body will attract any wildlife on the island."

"Oh, hell."

The idea of putting the body—no, a dead young man named Kyle Sheppard—back into the water at the mercy of the tides and sea life horrified her. How would they be able to tell Kyle's family what they'd done? She hadn't been able to recover Mike's body, and that would haunt her. But this…

With short, angry movements, Adam restuffed the bags he'd had open and carried them to the kayak. "Let's start by getting rid of this," he said.

Feeling sick at their choices, Claire nodded.

Chapter Nine

Having Claire even momentarily out of his sight didn't sit well with Adam. He should have used the time to strip the body of the wet suit he knew he needed, but that would have taken concentration he couldn't summon. Instead, despite the pain ripping through his shoulder, chest and arm and the weakness that had taken him so aback once they launched this morning, he paced the width of the beach repeatedly, tripping twice because his eyes were trained on the water rather than the ground in front of him.

He hated knowing *he* was the one holding them up, endangering her because he was incapable of completing a distance on the water that a kid probably could.

When she reappeared, gliding toward shore, he wanted to yell at her for taking too long—but when he glanced at the wristwatch he'd appropriated it was to see that only fifteen minutes had passed.

Claire climbed out of her kayak and began pulling it ashore. Her eyes met his then shied away. Yeah, he hadn't hidden his emotions as well as he'd have liked.

"I had an idea," she said hesitantly. "If you think staying here is a good idea."

"What's that?"

"We could weigh his body down in the water someplace accessible, then recover it in the morning and, I don't know, hang it over a tree limb or something like that. I can mark this beach on my chart so rescuers will know where to come for him."

Adam's relief surprised him. He didn't need to point out that they had no way of guaranteeing that something wouldn't get to the body in the water, weighed down or no, but it was a more palatable solution than just dumping it. He'd been bothered by the photo in the wallet of a nice older couple with warm smiles. A young guy like Kyle Sheppard probably kept most photographs on his phone, but he'd carried a printed one, too. His parents meant a whole lot to him. Adam knew he'd gotten hardened, to an extent, and since he lacked family, a wife, even a girlfriend, he could have lived knowing the guy's body would never be found to hand over to family. But that would be harder for Claire, and even he... Hell. Maybe it was knowing her that made him squeamish.

"Let's do that," he agreed. "Although I'd like to get our camp and kayaks out of sight from the water if we possibly can. What if we don't set up a tent?"

"That'd be fine unless the weather turns this afternoon. Or if we get swarmed by mosquitoes or flies. Let's hold off and see."

They hauled the kayaks up and unloaded what they expected to need, Claire doing more of the work than Adam liked, then got them out of sight behind dense evergreen branches. Neither said a word as they took the wet suit, gloves and neoprene booties off the body before looking around for suitable rocks to weigh down the cadaver.

The tide had withdrawn to reveal a pool that was deep enough for their purposes. Recovering the body in the morning, with the higher tide, would be more of a challenge.

Back to where the wet suit lay on the gravel, Claire said, "Let's rinse this out," and began methodically to turn it inside out and dip it in the water. Adam hadn't loved the idea of donning garments taken right off a dead guy, especially ones that couldn't be aired out like those made of breathable fabric.

Lucky the sun still shone today, giving the suit time to dry out.

He'd gotten his boots and the calves of his cargo pants wet, so he blanked out the source of his new wardrobe and changed into a pair of similar chinos that were only a little tight in the waist—Kyle had been thinner than Adam—and into dry socks and the sandals.

Claire pushed aside branches and found a wide enough spot beneath the dense canopy to lay out their sleeping bags, the tent pieces beside them, the camp stove just a few feet away.

"I'm going to heat some of this extra water and give myself a sponge bath," she announced.

Adam was startled by the sound of her voice, only then realizing how little she'd spoken after they made the important decisions. Of course, he immediately got to thinking about her peeling off clothes and washing. Probably she just wanted to be clean, but she'd also been handling a corpse. Yeah, she might be hoping soap and water could scrub away that experience.

It wouldn't, but she'd find that out soon enough.

"I wouldn't mind doing the same," he admitted. After the past few days, and especially today, he wasn't likely to smell very good.

Once the first water had warmed, Claire produced a skimpy towel, a washcloth and soap, collected a clean set of clothes and disappeared behind a sizable tree trunk. He sat down with his back to her, but he heard her garments dropping, squeaks a couple of times, branches swaying. When she gave a happy hum, he gritted his teeth and looked ruefully down at the bulge that made the pants even tighter.

Damn, he wanted to see her naked. Touch her, kiss her, hear another hum like that when he made love— no, damn it—*pleasured* her.

Love had nothing to do with it.

The rustle of fabrics told him she was getting dressed again. Adam made himself think about their grisly tasks of this morning, and the perilous days ahead.

His body grudgingly accepted his changed mood, but at least he was able to stand up when she returned, to take the saucepan from her and fill it with water on the stove.

EVEN AS SHE pretended to read, all Claire could think about was the dead man when they had pushed him underwater and lowered rocks on top of him. Adam had gently closed Kyle's eyes before they picked him up, but she kept imagining him staring up through the water at her.

It didn't help that the next thing she'd done was inspect Adam's wounds before covering them again and pulling the vet wrap around his chest again. She thought they were healing; neither hole had turned flaming red or seeped pus, but they were still gruesome. Between the gunshot wound and the cold water, he'd come so close to dying. She kept sneaking peeks at him, picturing him laid out on the beach, marble pale as she'd first seen his face, utterly still, beyond reach.

Adam appeared to be reading, close to finishing *The*

Mote in God's Eye. She made a point of turning a page regularly, hoping he hadn't noticed her occasional shudder. If he was really concentrating on the story, he must have better vision than she did. The light was really lousy. It almost felt as if they were in a cave, surrounded on every side by vegetation. What sunlight did reach them had been filtered through the overreaching spruce and firs that turned it green. If only her electronic reader hadn't reached the end of its charge...

"You've got to think about something else," Adam said gruffly, breaking the lengthy silence. "We made the best decision we could."

She bobbed her head. "I know." And she did, but— "I've never seen anyone dead before."

His surprise was obvious. "Really? Not a grandparent, or—"

"Mike." Wow, the memory of her last glimpse of him made her teeth want to clank together. "I guess I saw him dead."

"He had to have still been aware enough to release himself from the spray skirt and grab things from that deck pocket after he rolled."

She lifted one shoulder. "Okay, almost dead." Wasn't this a macabre topic. Of course, it had been that kind of day. "Does it...get any easier?"

New tension on his face had her shaking her head. "Forget I asked. You can't possibly want to talk about this."

In the ensuing silence, she didn't look at him.

But then he said haltingly, "I...usually don't."

"I suppose you don't have to with other agents." She hesitated, focusing on a delicate spiderweb strung between two fern fronds. "Assuming you really are a DEA agent. Don't worry—even if you're not, I'll do whatever I can to get us to safety. Then you can just…disappear."

"Claire." He spoke softly, only a little gravel remaining in his voice.

She had to meet his eyes.

"I really am with the DEA. The sooner we can connect with Canadian law enforcement, the better."

That had to be honesty in his eyes. If it wasn't… well, she'd feel really dumb, wouldn't she? But right now, she only nodded.

"As for the dead…" He ran his fingers through his hair. "You're right. We don't talk about it. Mostly, the bodies I've come across were scumbags in real life. Traffickers or muscle sent to intimidate." His shoulders moved. "Users who died from an overdose. Once—" He shook himself. "You don't need to hear about that."

"If you want to talk about it…"

"I don't," he said shortly. "Mostly, in my job you do get inured to it. I've shot and killed four men. Our goal is to arrest them, but things happen."

Like it did on the deck of that freighter, she realized. Undercover, Adam must walk on an edge, knowing his cover could be blown at any minute. Claire couldn't imagine the stress.

"It's not the kind of thing you forget," he continued.

She might be imagining that he was thinking the same she was. That neither of them would forget her friend's death, or Kyle Sheppard's.

When she nodded and stayed silent, he finally went back to his book. Claire went back to pretending.

It wasn't quite dusk when she raised her head. "Listen."

"What?" Adam started to rise to his feet, then stopped. "What the hell?"

"Do you recognize the sound?" She was smiling for the first time since this ordeal had started.

He'd turned toward the beach they could barely see through the heavy screen of vegetation. "Whales?"

"Yep. Probably orcas. Let's see if they pass in front of us."

She pushed through the branches with him right behind her. From this beach, they had a broader view of the inlet than they'd had at their former campsite. Tinted purple, the sky had deepened the color of the water, too. Looking east, they couldn't see the setting sun.

But she heard again the noisy exhalation made by a whale surfacing for breath, followed by another, and another. As many times as she'd seen orcas, she always got excited. They were magnificent, with their patterns of white against black, the sharp jut of fins and the grace of their massive bodies arching above the water.

Seeing the first one appear, she whispered, "Oh!"

Keeping his voice low, too, as if the creatures would pay the least notice to the humans standing on land, Adam said, "We saw some in the distance on my earlier trip on the freighter. Otherwise, I've never seen an orca."

Soon half a dozen of the pod were visible; others were presumably submerged. They were moving fast, led by the largest, probably a male. By the time she saw the last arching back, the sky had noticeably darkened. A few more exhalations drifted to them, and finally quiet returned with the advent of night.

"They're magnificent," Adam murmured.

She wrinkled her nose. "It's a little unnerving when one surfaces near your kayak."

"A *little*?"

Still smiling, she said, "Ready for dinner?"

THE BIG MINUS, as far as Adam was concerned, was that last night, Claire had laid out her own sleeping bag and pad a foot from his at bedtime, and without saying a word to him. His sleeping bag felt cold and unwelcoming with just him in it. The tree root stretched alongside the edge of his pad kept him from spreading out. He had a feeling she hadn't fallen asleep any faster than he had.

Both of them were quieter than usual over their morning oatmeal and coffee. She made a couple of brief suggestions as they packed up.

On the positive side, Adam didn't have to get wet when he and Claire removed the rocks weighing down the body and hauled Kyle Sheppard from his temporary watery grave. Adam tried not to think about the fact that he was wearing the wet suit he'd appropriated. He'd never robbed the dead before.

And, damn it, he didn't know why he was giving sentiment any room in his head. It wasn't like him. Practicality was a big component in surviving the dangers of working undercover.

Claire won the argument about who'd climb the cedar tree they chose. It made sense, given that she was less likely to have a limb break under her, and his injury left him debilitated. She went ahead, working her way up as high as she could by stepping from one branch to another and stabilizing herself with a hand on the trunk. Then she tossed an end of a towline they'd tied to a fist-sized rock up and over her chosen limb of the cedar. "Is that high enough?" she called down.

He evaluated the branch. It wasn't twenty feet off the ground, but he didn't see how they could do better. "Yeah. Can you reach the rock?"

"Sure."

She lowered herself carefully, Adam hovering below

prepared to catch her, although he hoped she didn't notice. The feathery branches of the cedar shook until she had her feet solidly on the ground.

Adam tied one end of the towline to the dead man's ankles, and then both of them hauled on the other end until the body wedged to a stop. They weren't going to be able to maneuver it over the branch the way Adam had hoped. Making do, he tied the line as securely as possible to a sturdy limb close to the ground. When he stepped back, the body didn't plummet back down.

Good enough.

Claire stared up for a long minute. He saw her throat move, and wondered if she was praying.

They'd already loaded their kayaks and were ready to shove off. Claire hesitated.

"Do you think there's any chance they've given up?"

They hadn't heard the outboard motor yesterday or so far this morning—but yesterday they didn't hear the gunshots, either.

"I want to think so."

She gave a small nod, hearing his doubt, gave her kayak a gentle push and then stepped into the cockpit.

Adam did the same, not looking forward to the day. Claire had insisted on trying something she hoped would help with his shoulder pain, though; using a good-sized book, the BC atlas, and a cutting board, she'd created a stiff cocoon around his shoulder that would accomplish something of the same effect as a plaster cast. Limiting his movement, mostly, forcing him to use his full body to paddle rather than his shoulders. He'd also taken Tylenol, but refused the heavy-duty painkillers in case he needed a clear head.

A moment later, they glided out into a morning he suspected was unusually still. With no breeze, the low-lying fog hadn't broken up into shreds. Claire had a compass mounted to her kayak deck. Without that, Adam couldn't even guess how she'd have navigated. They headed north, their goal a campsite on Spider Island, the largest island in the group.

Even he knew that was a joke. A half-hour outing for a serious kayaker. Another day, he'd asked Claire how far she typically planned to go in a day. Roughly twenty miles, she'd admitted, but she could—and had—exceeded that. The plan for today was two miles, tops. Okay, maybe a little farther than that, given their winding route.

In fact, at the moment, they completed a half circle between smaller islands and the rocky islets that reared from the fog and disappeared as suddenly.

"Stay close," she said one time.

He had no intention of letting her out of his sight. How would he ever find her again? He heard the lap of water against the hull of his kayak, an occasional cry or caw that must be some bird or other overhead. Once a dark head came out of the water so close to him, he could have touched it. An inquisitive face with dark eyes and long whiskers studied him.

A sea otter.

Claire momentarily vanished into the mist, her blue kayak far less visible than his red one. He could see how she'd been able to hide the day her friend was shot. Her neoprene suit was gray and blue, her skullcap navy blue. With her blond hair tucked out of sight, only her yellow flotation vest stood out, and it had either faded or was dirty enough to subdue the bright color.

Adam clung to that thought. She might be able to slip away unseen if he was spotted.

He dug in his paddle to shoot forward and retain his visual on her.

The silence was almost eerie, making him feel as if he wore earmuffs. He started to itch between his shoulder blades, familiar prickles climbing his spine. No reason, he told himself; the fog cloaked them, and they couldn't be tracked by sound. Yet he hated not being able to see more than ten feet in any direction, and kept wondering how much the fog would muffle the noise of a boat motor.

He also began wondering whether the two men he'd seen hunting him—Lee Boyden and Curt Gibbons—were returning to the freighter at night, or making camp somewhere nearby. What if they weren't alone? Another man or two could be taking out the skiff.

How was Dwayne justifying this all-out manhunt to his crew? Adam doubted many, if any of the crew, knew what was at stake.

Adam considered himself damn lucky that the meet had been set up amidst the cluster of islands. The intricate passages were what made this escape possible.

He realized suddenly that Claire must have put on the brakes, because his kayak had glided up beside hers.

"How are you?" she asked.

He had to take a moment to think about it. The pain hadn't immediately hampered him the way it had yesterday.

"Better. Stronger," he decided. He grinned at her. "I think your jury-rigged shoulder harness works."

She laughed. "That's because I'm so smart."

"Has to be," he agreed not quite solemnly.

"I think the fog is starting to lift," she said.

He turned his head. "How can you tell?"

She pointed with her paddle. "See? It's thinner off that way."

"Damn. I like being invisible."

"Well, Spider Island lies off our port side. We'll hug it until we see the inlet where I know there's a campsite."

Adam would have rather aimed for a stop that wasn't listed in maritime guidebooks, but what glimpses he caught of any land seemed to be buttressed by those rock walls rearing from the water. There was nowhere they could pull a kayak ashore.

He cursed his own weakness again.

On that thought, he realized he felt more resistance against his paddle. The tide was still ebbing, but he had no idea what effect that had in a north-south ocean passage between islands. Adam dug in the paddle with more effort and stayed a few feet off the stern of Claire's kayak. She was right—the fog was tearing into long shreds. One moment, the world was gray, the next almost too bright, with glimpses of the blue sky and sun.

They'd been on their way for a couple of hours, at a guess—he'd dropped the wrist watch into the deck hatch to keep it from getting soaked—when he heard a low growling sound.

Swearing, he shot forward again just as Claire's head turned, too.

"That's close," she exclaimed.

"Too damn close. Watch for anyplace we can get out of sight."

She looked scared. "The channel is pretty open here. I don't think we'll be that lucky."

"They may go right by without seeing us."

She gave a sturdy nod and kept paddling, Adam

matching her speed even though he was starting to feel as if a spike had been driven through his shoulder.

A shout behind them carried across the water. They'd been seen, and Claire was right—there was no place for them to hide.

Chapter Ten

"Go!" Adam called to Claire. "Don't wait for me!"

Fog again closed around them, all-encompassing gray. He paddled as fast and hard as he could, and hoped she was doing the same. To his frustration, he could still see her. Why wasn't she pulling ahead? Hadn't she taken him seriously?

When they next emerged from the mist, he cast a look over his shoulder. He couldn't see the boat, but the volume of the outboard motor grew. What he'd give for a gun. If they were being pursued by the inflatable, he could capsize it with a few well-placed shots.

His muscles screamed but he didn't ease up. There had to be something he could do to delay these bastards enough for her, at least, to slip away.

Grabbing the flare gun he'd taken from Kyle Sheppard's kayak would require him to quit paddling, if only momentarily. The pocket of his PFD had seemed handy enough, but he'd been wrong.

Using the flare gun—that would mean he had to be within two or three hundred feet, and he had to be able to see the boat. He'd get only one shot, too, so it had to be a good one. If he was in range to use it, they'd sure as hell be in range to shoot him, too, with their far deadlier firearms.

Some distance had opened at last between his kayak and Claire's. She disappeared in fog while he was still in the open, but she yelled something back at him. He couldn't make it out.

He shot into the band of fog and she yelled again. The buzzing from behind grew ever closer, but he heard something else, too. An odd sound. Another boat approaching from the north?

Then she called out again, and this time he heard her. *Orcas.*

That's what he'd heard: the explosive exhalation of an orca. The same pod they'd seen yesterday evening, now turned around to head south?

It came again. A gun fired, too. He was low in the water, which made him a less-than-ideal target. God. What happened if bullets passed through the hull of the kayak? Would he sink? Get dumped back in the bitterly cold water, where he'd wait for death from another bullet…or death from hypothermia if they didn't see him—or felt especially sadistic?

But he was still moving forward, his level in the water no lower. He rotated his body the way Claire had taught him, going for maximum speed, praying she'd achieved even more.

A bullet skimmed the water to his left even as he heard the report from the gun. Not easy to be accurate when shooting at a moving target from a small craft on the water, he thought, in that remote part of his mind making calculations.

And then water and sound exploded into the air not ten feet to his right, just as a massive black-and-white body leaped out of the water. His rhythm broke. Would one of them come up right *under* him? As close as he and Claire had been on the shore, he hadn't understood how huge these animals were. Would his kayak pass for a seal or whatever these particular orcas hunted?

Or would one come up right under an inflatable boat with a color that would be hard to distinguish from water?

More likely, he thought grimly, the orcas would choose to pass wide around the boat because of the rumble of the motor.

Go, go, go, he ordered himself, not daring to look back. Another back rose a few feet farther away; another spout of water shot into the air. More, more. A couple of the whales passed to his left. They were splitting to go around him.

The shouts behind him now had a different tone. He hoped Boyden and Gibbons were scared by the killer whales. He hoped this pod was huge.

Instead of pausing to go for the flare gun, he concentrated on paddling for his life. White-hot pain consumed him, but it was a small part of the whole.

Go.

He caught a glimpse ahead of Claire, pausing in her strokes to take a look over her shoulder.

Another orca rose so close by, his kayak rocked and the spout rained on him. He couldn't hear the outboard motor behind him anymore, and finally dared to risk a look back himself. Mist swirled; he saw nothing but whales, beautiful and almost ghostly rising from the water, their spouts joining the mist, the sound of their breaths a powerful symphony.

Adam looked down at the butt of the flare gun, but instead of reaching for it, he resumed paddling.

ADAM'S PROGRESS WAS no longer smooth. Checking frequently behind her, Claire saw that he'd begun a subtle zigzag, inevitably pushed out toward the middle of the passage. Scared, she realized they had to stop, and soon.

The last of the orcas had passed Claire a few minutes ago. She could still hear them, that mysterious, deep blowing that sounded primeval. What she *couldn't* hear was the outboard motor. In their panic, the men might have choked the motor, they might have turned around and fled or the boat might have been overturned by the wave created by a rising or diving orca.

She so wished the last was true, but doubted it would happen. An inflatable boat the size she'd seen would be especially hard to tip.

Even as she paddled for all she was worth, she wished desperately that she'd chosen a different route. This was her fault; the Spider Channel was too open. She'd hoped they would encounter other boaters, but all she'd done was leave Adam and her vulnerable to the men hunting them. Men who could move faster because their boat was motorized.

Maybe they should have gone directly east, except they'd have been even more exposed there, crossing the same anchorage where the freighter and the yacht had met to exchange cargo.

Hurricane Channel would have been good, narrow as it was, with rocks lurking beneath the water at high tide and reputedly choked in with kelp where waters were shallow—except she and Adam would have had to paddle east across Spider Anchorage to reach it.

Same problem.

She strained to hear the motor behind them, but it didn't come. They *had* to get off the water and pray their hunters didn't see the inlet.

There'd been a radar station on Spider Island during World War II, one of a string of them along the Pacific Coast. She'd read that a wooden boardwalk had led from a dock on the west coast of the island to the station, set at a high point. In recent years, the station and boardwalk alike had been overgrown to the point of disappearing. The inlet she was aiming for was now on private land, according to the books she'd read when planning the trip, but right now, she didn't care. They'd be *lucky* if the projected fishing resort had been built. If not—trespassing was the least of their worries.

She kept stealing looks over her shoulder. Adam was falling back, but had her in sight. The water grew rougher as they neared the north end of the island, losing its protection from the open ocean currents and weather patterns. What if they crossed the channel, took a chance that there'd be someplace to pull their kayaks out of the water on Spitfire Island?

Even if their progress was frustratingly slow, she knew better. Adam needed time to recover. They couldn't go on now.

She saw a cove of sorts and turned toward it. If a fishing resort was under construction, it wasn't here. This was no hidden inlet, either, nor even a beach, but surely they could haul their kayaks and gear over the rocks and hide in the forest.

She waved a paddle. Adam waved back. She still didn't hear any pursuit.

THEY MOVED FAST once they'd managed to beach the kayaks on low-lying slabs of ocean-sculpted rock. Pull out necessary gear, get it above the high-tide line, keep it out of sight in the vegetation. Back for the kayaks, one at a time. Claire slipped on the rocks and would have given in to the injury and exhaustion except they couldn't afford time for whining. She held up her end of Adam's kayak and kept moving.

Once they, the kayaks and their gear were out of sight from the water, Claire collapsed on a rotting log that was probably full of creepy-crawly things, but she was past caring. Adam lowered himself more carefully beside her.

That's when she noticed what looked like the butt of a pistol sticking out of the pocket of his PFD.

Her eyes must have widened.

His gaze followed hers. "Flare gun. Kyle Sheppard's. Remember?"

"Yes. It's just…it looks so much like a gun."

"It *is* a gun. Unfortunately, it shoots a flare instead of a bullet, and has to be reloaded before it can be used again."

"Oh." Of course he was carrying it for its potential as a weapon. "At least it's legal." Heat singed her cheeks. "That's a dumb thing to say. Like that matters." She usually carried one. That, in an effort to lighten her load, she'd figured one flare gun between two people was good enough was just another example of her complacency.

His lips firmed. "If it comes down to us or them, I don't give a damn about the legalities. I feel pretty sure that using it to shoot someone isn't legal."

She'd swear it hadn't been in his pocket when they set out this morning. "That's what you have in mind."

"If need be." His voice and expression both were implacable.

Claire imagined what a flare fired at high speed would do to a human being, but she couldn't work up the horror she should probably feel. Those men had not only shot Adam, they'd been trying to shoot him again today. With bullets. And their guns probably had magazines that allowed for multiple shots before needing to be swapped out.

"What if you shot the boat?" she asked.

"I saw it on the freighter. Didn't look closely, but I doubt it's like the rafts people buy for their kids. You know, the ones that sink after one puncture, or even a little wear and tear. I'm betting an inflatable like this one has compartments. One gets punctured, the boat still floats."

"You're right. I didn't pay that much attention, but I heard a few people talking who had inflatable kayaks. The fabric is really tough, and I think they have multiple valves and separate chambers for air." She frowned. "That means one shot might not even slow them down."

"Right. Although it's possible a flare would penetrate deep enough to do some real damage. Still, I doubt the accuracy is the same as a serious handgun, either." He sounded regretful. "I'd need to be fairly close to take someone out."

"And there are two of them."

He tipped his head but didn't say anything.

"If only I had one, too." *If only* were about the most useless words in the English language.

Eventually, they poked around until they found a relatively flat spot to lay out their sleeping bags or set up a tent, and moved their gear. Adam asked for help removing the makeshift body cast, and after that, they began to unpack what they needed.

Her ankle hurt and she had a bad feeling it was swollen, but she could ignore it, along with the scratches she'd just acquired pushing through branches not eager to give way. There wasn't much she could do about the ankle, for sure, and fortunately, Adam didn't seem to have noticed her favoring that leg. Anyway, if she hurt, he had to be in agony.

They didn't have much view through the dense growth of trees, but they'd hear a motor, and Claire felt sure they'd see anyone dragging a boat up onto the smooth slabs of rock.

Not until she had water on to boil on the small stove did she say, "They have to know more or less where we are."

"Possibly," he said slowly. "That depends what they did when the orcas scared them. They could have tried to get off the water and failed, turned around to run for the ship, or actually suffered enough of a mishap to have a motor that's dead or some other damage to the boat."

She had to say this. "It's my fault we were so out in the open. We can't go back now, but… I've changed my mind about our route."

Furrows deepened in his forehead and between his nose and mouth. He spoke slowly in contrast to what she'd blurted out.

"If we make it out into Queens Sound, you seemed confident there'd be enough traffic, we wouldn't have any trouble waving someone down."

When kayaking up the Inside Passage, she'd gone two or three days at a time without seeing other people, although in those better-traveled waters, she'd had frequent sightings of passing ferries or other large boats in the distance.

She and Mike had chosen to come on this trip early in the season partly because of their jobs, but mostly in hopes of being able to enjoy the beauty of these islands without constant company. By July, there'd be a lot more cabin cruisers, fishing boats and other kayakers. This surprisingly complete solitude…well, she'd have appreciated it in other circumstances.

"Why not go ahead?" Adam asked, after she failed to respond to the last thing he'd said. He'd studied the charts carefully.

Claire took a deep breath. "Because the freighter could be anchored there. As we've been chased north, it would have made sense for your former boss to putter along in the same direction to wait for us. Also, we'd have no place to hide if we're spotted out in the open like that."

"So what are you thinking?"

"Let me grab my charts."

"Water's boiling," he remarked, and they agreed to eat first. This was early for dinner, but they hadn't had lunch. They could snack closer to bedtime.

She took some ibuprofen, as did he—his a double dose.

When she was able to show him what she had in mind, he leaned forward and traced a fingertip along the narrow, twisting channel that headed east and then sharply south, cutting between several of the larger islands in the area.

"That'll let us out not far from where we started," he said slowly. "What's the point of that?"

"I think it would be unexpected. They've followed us this far. Would they expect us to circle around?"

"You think they can't follow us?"

"I imagine they can, but from what I remember reading, the Spitfire Channel is tricky. It's really narrow at one point, has dangerous submerged rocks, kelp beds that could tangle around the propeller." She hesitated. "There are two problems with going that way."

"Besides going in a circle?"

Claire ignored his comment. "One is that I have no idea whether there are any places at all where we could beach the kayaks until we come out on the other side, and I think that's too far for you to paddle in one day. There almost has to be a possible campsite somewhere, but we'll need to keep a sharp eye or miss our chance."

"And the other problem?"

"Crossing the open water unseen to get to the channel."

He gazed down at the chart for a minute. "What about crossing the channel, then heading north along the shore of this Hunter Island?"

"That's the logical route. They'll think we're running for Bella Bella."

"I take it that's the closest thing to civilization on this part of the coast?"

"Yes, which makes that direction too obvious. We need to do something they won't expect. Just…disappear."

He frowned over the chart for a minute, then nodded. "They didn't spot us for a couple of hours this morning. They may not be early starters."

"No, but I'm more worried because they have to guess we've gone to ground somewhere in this vicinity."

"Then we launch at first light," he said grimly. "Or even earlier."

He was right; they could cross the open channel in the murky, purple light before the sun actually topped the horizon, given the lack of other boat traffic. That meant setting out between four thirty and five o'clock.

"You expect to see more boat traffic in this Kildidt Sound?" he asked.

Claire nodded. "Once we aren't dodging between tiny islands." When he didn't comment, she set aside the charts and put more water on to heat to wash their dishes.

Watching out of the corner of her eye as Adam brooded, she decided not to mention another issue: Hunter and Hurricane Islands must boast plentiful wildlife, including the bears and wolves smart campers avoided.

IN THE LATE AFTERNOON, a cloud of insects found them.

They'd been incredibly lucky so far not to have to crouch under netting to keep from being eaten alive.

"Son of a bitch," Adam growled, hearing the first whine. "I hate mosquitoes."

"They're not alone. I think those are midges, too. Their bites are even more irritating."

Claire dug hurriedly in a bag and came up with some netting and a baseball cap. "You take this. Wrap the netting around your head."

Adam clapped the baseball cap on his head. "What about you?"

"I have another one." She found it, and a pair of thin gloves. "Look through your bag. Mike carried these, too. They're actually glove liners."

Momentarily protected with no skin exposed, he still swatted irritably at the cloud of bugs swarming them. He swore he itched even if he hadn't been bitten. "Don't you have some repellent?"

"No, it can melt synthetic material. Plus, the smell attracts bears."

"Great."

"We'll have to set up the tent. It has netting."

He hadn't noticed, but was glad to hear it.

"We might as well do that now." She stood suddenly. "I'll be back in a minute."

She'd already pushed her way through the evergreen branches and lower-growing bushes that blocked them from the beach before he could get to his feet. Surprised and uneasy, Adam followed her.

Head tipped back, she was looking at the sky. When he did the same, he saw that it was no longer clear the way it had been. The air felt different, too, he realized. Damp.

"Can we take off in the morning if it's raining?"

"It'll depend."

About to ask on what, he stiffened. "Hear that?"

"Oh, no," she whispered.

"You have the binoculars handy?"

She ducked back the way she'd come and handed them to him. They both crouched behind a veil of low cedar limbs and waited.

That damn inflatable boat appeared, moving slowly along the shoreline. Adam lifted his netting to use the binoculars. It had come almost abreast of them when he realized he'd left the flare gun at the campsite.

Don't look this way.

Damn, he wished for twilight.

The boat kept going until it was out of sight. Not sure he'd taken a breath, Adam pulled in a deep one and yanked the netting down.

Neither he nor Claire moved, both listening to the receding sound of the motor. They heard it for a while, continuing north, until it either faded away or was cut off.

He swore. "Is there another campsite up there?"

"I think there must be." She was almost whispering. "I was aiming for one that has to be better than landing on rocks. You think…?"

"You know as much as I do," he said shortly, immediately regretting his tone when she stood up and pushed her way back toward their camp.

By the time he got there, she was packing away the pan, stove and dishes for the night, so practiced at it he didn't bother to offer to help.

Damn. He hated feeling completely inept. He'd been stuck in some tight places before, but he'd never been so outside his areas of expertise. Yeah, he was getting better with the kayak, but he didn't kid himself for a minute that he could handle anything but the placid seas they'd so far traversed, and that in slo-mo. If his kayak rolled, he'd hang there head down until he drowned.

He knew nothing about navigating or about the dangers in this wild part of the world. Babe in the woods, that was him.

Which left him utterly dependent on the gutsy woman who'd saved his life and was serving as his guide, trusting him even though she had no reason to believe a word he'd said.

The woman he would do anything at all to protect from the consequences of her courageous act. He'd like to think that was out of gratitude and because it was part of his job as a federal law enforcement officer, but knew better.

This woman had gotten to him in a short time, as he'd never allowed anyone to do. These feelings baffled and alarmed him, but he had to acknowledge them. The sooner he got away from her, the better...but he'd like to hold her in his arms every one of the remaining nights before he had to let her go back to her formerly safe life.

His mouth twisted. Too bad he knew what she'd say if he suggested sharing a sleeping bag again.

Smart woman.

Chapter Eleven

They went to work raising the tent. As irritating as the swarming insects were, Adam was about ready to crawl into it, however cramped the quarters, zip the flap closed and huddle there until morning.

This task was another one he had to leave mostly to Claire, exacerbating his mood. As little as he'd paddled, he was developing some blisters. Probably gripping the paddle too tightly, a mistake that could have several unpleasant consequences. They had yet to camp anywhere Claire could drive stakes; instead, the tent had to be secured by lines tied to nearby tree limbs. Given the lack of mobility in his right arm and the blisters, he was lousy at dealing with the thin cord.

Yeah, he could have done it, but would have taken twice as long. One more source of frustration.

Given their relative sizes, he gave up and let her crawl inside and lay out the pads and sleeping bags, too. She didn't suggest they head right to bed, though, only crawled back out.

Apparently, she wasn't any readier to drop into peaceful slumber than he was, and didn't favor squatting in the tent until she was.

Net masking his face, Adam sat down on that too-low-to-the-ground chair and resumed brooding.

"What are you thinking?" Claire asked at last.

"Wishing we could have holed up at either of our previous campsites," he said honestly. "Someone would have come along eventually. And yeah, I know that wasn't possible."

They'd come too close once to being discovered at the first campsite. If the boat had circled closer, one of the men would have seen the break in the rock guarding the island. No matter what, the diminishing supply of drinking water would have forced them to move on.

He slapped a mosquito that had settled on a strip of skin between his cuff and glove.

Lingering at the inlet where they found Sheppard's body would have been too risky, too. It would have been logical for Adam's former shipmates to revisit it. Adam wasn't crazy about tonight's, either, even if they were hidden in the woods. What they weren't was in a good position to put a kayak in the water fast to intercept a passing boat they could be sure had no connection to the freighter or the yacht.

What ate at him was how many days had gone by. Had the yacht slunk back to finish taking on the remaining cargo? Or was he wrong, and it had already loaded the important and dangerous part?

"Damn, I wish we knew if they'd set up camp," he said aloud. "The flare gun isn't much use, but I could slash that damn boat with a knife and make sure they couldn't ever launch it again."

She turned her head to stare at him, alarm in her eyes. "Just tiptoe up and start poking holes?"

"Something like that."

"You don't think the air rushing out wouldn't make noise? Sort of like the orcas exhaling?"

He unclenched his teeth. "It might. Wouldn't take me long, though."

"I wish I thought you were just dreaming."

"I have trouble believing they're going back to the freighter every night. The smaller boat coming and going might draw unwelcome attention. A rusty old tub like that is in danger of catching the eye of the coast guard as it is. If they see it twice…why is it just sitting there?"

"Good reason for them to be moving around, except they almost have to be staying out in deeper waters most of the time." She sounded thoughtful. "They might have anchored in Fulton Passage, but if they're really following us north, they'd have had to follow the western shore of Spider Island."

"The two guys we've seen—" he told her their names, not sure he had before "—must have radio contact with the freighter, but they might be afraid to go back in person and admit to Dwayne that they can't seem to find us. Or, now, that they did, but let us get away."

"Because a bunch of orcas got in the way."

Adam grinned, knowing the expression wasn't a nice one. "Dwayne wouldn't have much patience if they make up stories like that."

"It was sort of surreal."

"Yeah. That's the word I was trying to think of. Between the fog and the gunshots following us, their appearance seemed…" He hesitated.

Claire supplied a word. "Magical."

Adam couldn't argue with her, although that wasn't a word that had ever crossed his lips.

"Well, right now, you have no idea where those guys are camped for the night," she said briskly. "So you can put out of your mind any fantasies of slashing their boat to ribbons. I'm not volunteering to head back out on the water to look for them."

"I wouldn't take you if you did."

He didn't have to see her to know she was glaring at him. His very silence let her know she'd won this argument. No, he wasn't stupid enough to set out as dark gathered hoping to see the light of a campfire or kerosene lantern.

That didn't mean he put the idea out of his head.

CLAIRE CRAWLED INTO her sleeping bag, lay still for about ten seconds, then squirmed in search of a more comfortable position. The loamy soil had seemed to pad the spot where she'd positioned the tent, but she should have realized how many tree roots reached and tangled beneath the surface. She might as well be stretched out on crisscrossing iron bars. This was like an ancient sleeper sofa with about a two-inch thick mattress, except she couldn't seem to find anywhere to settle her butt and shoulder simultaneously *between* roots.

"You okay?" Adam's gritty voice came out of the darkness.

"Sure. Just... There's a tree root right under me." Or two or three—or ten. She shifted to her left, then tried to scrunch herself up against the back wall of the tent.

"Scoot over closer to me," he suggested.

She wanted to, so much she knew it wasn't a good idea. But she wouldn't be sleeping at all if she didn't get more comfortable. So she rolled once, sleeping bag and all, until she came up against a hard body. Claire held still for a long moment.

"Better?"

"I think so. I'm afraid to move."

His low chuckle might be the sexiest sound she'd ever heard.

"Here." After some rustling, a long arm wrapped around her and pulled her even closer. She could rest her head on his shoulder, and would have been able to lay an arm across his chest and a leg over his, if the bulk of two sleeping bags hadn't separated them. She suddenly regretted that barrier.

"Warm enough?" His breath tickled her hair.

"Uh-huh." Too warm, which was his fault.

"Sleep tight, sweetheart."

She froze, and thought he'd gone completely still, too. She'd swear he had quit breathing. Had that just slipped out?

If so, he'd surprised himself, and not in a good way.

But he didn't say anything, and she didn't move. Eventually she did drop off to sleep, although she felt like it wasn't that long before she woke up again. Apparently she'd moved enough to find a new lump. She had to squirm some, waking him, although all he did was mumble, "Wha's wrong?"

"Nothing. Just..." Turning over? No, she couldn't do that. She wriggled a little, fell back asleep. Woke up again, tried rolling away from Adam, but had to go back where she'd started from.

The next time she woke up, it was because she heard rustling accompanied by heavy breathing outside the tent. Even in the dark, she saw the side push in as something leaned against it.

Claire became aware that Adam's entire body was rigid. "What the...?" he murmured.

"Bear," she whispered in his ear. "I think."

Snuffling noises and a grunt confirmed her fear. She

grabbed the can of bear spray, but once she had it in hand, she continued to lie still, glad Adam did the same.

Neither of them had spilled any food, had they? Was the smell of their dinner lingering in the air? It had been vegetarian, thank goodness, nothing that should have attracted any particular attention. They'd set the food vaults a fair distance away.

Another grunt, more rustling…and silence. Claire listened for all she was worth, but couldn't hear anything except…

"Is that rain?" Adam asked quietly.

"I think so." It was a little hard to tell for sure, because they were protected by such dense forest. Instead of pattering onto the tent—or hammering—they were getting the drips filtered through multiple layers of tree branches. "Oh, joy."

"Good thing we set up the tent," Adam commented. "For more than one reason."

He was right; she definitely wouldn't have wanted to wake up to a curious bear snuffling in her face.

Even thinking about water falling from the sky caused her bladder to suggest that she make a trip outside, but she'd have had to be a lot more desperate to obey. As Adam said, for more than one reason.

Somehow, she fell asleep again, and he must have, too, because she was half lying on top of him when she opened her eyes again to gray light and a strong neck and throat.

Dark stubble was becoming a beard. Would it be wiry or soft? She was suddenly breathing a little faster. If she lifted her head from his shoulder the tiniest bit, she could press her lips to his neck…

She'd either shocked herself, or come completely

awake, because her next, more coherent thought was, so much for that early departure.

And now she *really* needed to put some clothes on and get out of the tent so she could pee.

He protested when she rolled off him and started squirming into the garments she'd kept in the sleeping bag with her so they wouldn't be miserably cold this morning.

"Gotta get up," she told him, pulling a fleece top over her shirt.

He groaned. "I wish you hadn't said that."

As she scooted out of the tent, she heard him scrambling into clothes behind her.

Ugh. Straightening in the clearing, she felt as if she were breathing water. Yes, it was still raining, and every branch and fern frond dripped. She heard movement up above, too: the wind that had been absent for most of the past week.

Claire pushed her way through the soggy vegetation to find a spot to crouch, then made her way back. No Adam, so she stepped out of the trees to find choppy waves not far from her feet. This had *not* been an ideal place to stop and set up camp.

Looking out at the channel, she knew there was no way they could set out today. On her own, she'd have hesitated. For an inexperienced kayaker, it was impossible.

Her first awareness that Adam had joined her was his growled profanity, followed by, "We're stuck."

"We've been lucky with the weather so far," she pointed out.

"What if this lasts for days?"

Droplets clung to his dark hair and dampened his

face. Muscles flexed in his jaw as he stared out at the choppy waters.

"What do you think? We sit here. We have enough food and drinking water, and could catch some rain if need be."

Boredom and this unwanted sexual attraction would be the biggest threats, she thought.

Still glowering at the channel, he said, "Damn!"

"We have a couple of tarps we can tie over the campsite so at least we don't get any wetter than we already are," she offered.

He growled, "That'll be cozy."

Finally getting mad, Claire punched his upper arm and snapped, "Suck it up."

ADAM FOLLOWED HER to the kayaks and delved into the hatches on his own kayak while she did the same on hers. He should be grateful that he still had plenty of dry garments, he told himself. A day resting up wouldn't be the end of the world.

Immediately, he wished he'd chosen a better way to phrase the thought. No, the uranium being smuggled wasn't enough to end the world, but it could blast a significant part of it. A military base? A city? He'd give a lot to know the target of the terrorists who could, even now, be assembling their bomb.

He had to remind himself that, even if he knew more, there wasn't a damn thing he could do about it. What they'd needed was some early intelligence so they could have prevented the freighter ever leaving the harbor.

All he could do now was dial down his disagreeable mood, however justified it was, and accept that he was no superhero. Nature had given him a slap to remind him of her supremacy.

He wondered how stormy the seas were out in the open ocean. The picture of the freighter rising and sliding down twenty-foot-high swells gave him some pleasure. Everyone on board violently seasick. Anything on deck washed overboard.

Except maybe for the uranium. He wasn't sure what would happen with it sitting on the ocean floor. It might be an environmental disaster.

He and Claire hung the three big tarps they'd located over the tent and the rest of the campsite, using cords and even a towline through grommets to tie the corners to branches.

Neither of them said much while she cooked up a pan of their usual oatmeal, adding dried cranberries to it this morning instead of the usual raisins or nuts. Only when she handed him a mug of coffee did he say, "I'm sorry for the whining."

She raised her eyebrows. "Is that what it was?" Then she relented. "I understand your sense of urgency."

"You know any prayers for good weather? Or what about a dance?"

Her chuckle brightened her face and his mood both. "Nothing I've ever tried has worked. Sorry." She chewed on her lower lip for a minute, watching him without quite meeting his eyes. "You know, I've gotten caught out on more turbulent water than this and lived to tell about it. I could make a run for it while you—"

"Not a chance," he interrupted. Coffee splashed onto his hand as he glowered at her. "Do you seriously think I'll let you lay your life on the line while I hunker down here…doing what? Catching up on my reading?"

"But every day counts," she said quietly.

She was right. He remembered thinking that he could end up having to sacrifice her to save the hundreds to thousands of people that damn bomb would kill. Collateral damage, a concept he'd had to consider before while working undercover. What might have been thinkable on day one had become a hell, no.

"It would take you longer to get results," he said, still looming over her. "If I'm there, things will move faster."

"A whole day faster?"

No, but he felt sick at the idea of seeing her paddling away, the frail kayak tossing on waves capable of flipping it. Her disappearing in the rain; him not knowing whether she'd made it. Given the weather, what were the odds she'd meet up with other boaters? Even large cabin cruisers or fishing boats would surely stay anchored in sheltered inlets. Struggling on her own, how long would it take her to pop out in Kildidt Sound, somehow signal as big a boat as possible to stop in the gray, slanting rain and wait for a representative of the Canadian Coast Guard or Navy?

Or *she* could go north and strike boldly out into Queens Sound. Where, lacking any electronic devices, she'd have only flares for signaling for help. If the pilot of a large ship miscalculated the origin of the flare, that ship could just as well run right over the top of her—especially if the ocean and sky were both still gray, swells sometimes hiding her kayak.

No.

CLAIRE WASN'T ABOUT to tell him how grateful she was that he'd nixed her suggestion. So, okay, she was scared, but she still thought splitting up might be the smart thing to do. Even if the two men from the freighter came upon her, why would they do anything but exchange the time of day with her and ask if she'd seen a guy in a red kayak?

Unless they saw her yesterday paddling hard not that far ahead of Adam.

Yes, but would they go out in such miserable weather? A lot of people, even sailors, got seasick when such a small boat was tossed around.

Adam obviously considered the argument over. He dug in one of the dry bags and produced the short stack of books. He didn't seem excited by any of them, but finally started reading. Claire followed suit, although it was hard to concentrate on her last unread book, a British procedural mystery. So what if she wasn't in the mood for it?

Thanks to the addition of poor Kyle Sheppard's stash, they had meals aplenty, enough that she heated a vegetarian chili for lunch instead of the cold alternatives.

Adam accepted a bowl from her and inhaled the spicy scent. "This isn't an invitation to last night's visitor?"

"No meat. I doubt chili pepper and cumin smell appealing to a black bear."

"That was a bear."

"Yes. There might be wolves on the island, but they don't snuffle and grunt."

"Think it'll be back?"

She waggled a hand. "I imagine it stumbled on us, but it didn't find anything appealing."

He grimaced.

For some reason, Claire smiled at his expression. "I take it you're not into nature?"

"No. City all the way."

The mood changed as he haltingly told her more about his background. Claire learned that he'd grown up in Dallas, which admittedly felt like a world away from this wild, rainy edge of North America. His voice sounded rusty as he talked about his childhood and eventually how he'd ended up in law enforcement. He gazed more at the stove, as if it was a crackling blaze, than he did at her.

He admitted to half a dozen foster homes. With the last, he got lucky. The foster father was a Texas marshal.

"Not…fatherly, but he pushed me toward college. Helped me find scholarships. I don't know if he saw something in me. I wanted to think so. I tried some classes in criminology. Took enough for a minor." He flicked a glance at her. "Majored in chemistry."

He'd mentioned starting as a chemist.

"Did you stay in touch with your foster dad?" she asked gently.

"First year." There was a long pause. "Then he started sounding impatient. He and his wife were fostering a brother and sister they'd taken in after I was out of the house." He shrugged. "I took the hint."

"Are you sure that's what it was?"

Seeing the look on his face, she was immediately sorry she'd pushed.

"He never called again."

Struck by the way he'd said, *his wife*, Claire wondered what kind of relationship Adam had with her. Not much of one, if she had to guess.

"So you went to the DEA."

"Yeah. It seemed like a good fit."

Chemistry and criminology. Of course it was.

"You've never been married?"

Deepened furrows on his forehead made her wonder what he was thinking. But then he said, "With my history, I've…had a hard time imagining it. Never met the right woman, anyway, which was probably just as well considering what I do for a living."

She couldn't be surprised by his attitude. Saddened, maybe. She couldn't tell him that in so few days, he was responsible for her being able to dismiss even the smallest regret about Devin.

Adam's profession didn't overshadow all the qualities she'd seen in him: determination, reliability, kindness, patience, a sense of humor. Would he ever recognize how much he had to offer a woman?

Probably not.

A secret part of her remembered how desperate he'd been yesterday for *her* to escape, even if those creeps caught up to him.

Because she could carry his message to the proper authorities?

Yes, but he'd seemed curious about her, too, and hadn't been anything but kind and thoughtful. Even... tender, although that had to be her imagination.

Wow, there were a lot more important things for her to be thinking about than this ridiculous attraction to him. Even if they were spending the day in close proximity, and she'd have no choice but to sleep pressed up against him.

She went back to listening for any sounds that didn't belong and pretending she didn't notice the thoughtful way he was now watching her. Finally, Claire picked up her book and did her absolute best to be gripped by adventures that paled by comparison with everything that had happened to *her* in the past few days.

Chapter Twelve

If they'd been exploring the islands for fun, the day might have been relaxing. Say, if this were Claire and her buddy. They'd obviously been good enough friends, with enough history, to enjoy hanging out and talking. Under the circumstances, would she have slept cuddled up to her partner Mike instead of to Adam?

Adam was immediately ashamed of himself, considering that her friend was dead, his body adrift. Murdered because he'd inadvertently stepped into the middle of Adam's investigation.

He frowned. That wasn't quite true. If the DEA had never succeeded in inserting an agent on that boat, Dwayne would have shot the poor guy anyway.

Unless he was on edge more than usual because he'd begun to suspect I wasn't what I appeared.

Adam told himself to knock it off. The nature of his job was that anything could happen, and he couldn't take responsibility for all of it. He mixed with suspicious, volatile, violent people who lacked any semblance of empathy.

Unfortunately, his thoughts circled back to how much he wanted Claire. *You can't have her. Live with it.*

Several times during the night, he'd surfaced to find himself holding her, her breath tickling his neck, and he'd been thrown back to remembering the nights when they'd shared a sleeping bag and he'd been aware of all her curves pressed against him. When he could so easily have—

He slammed that door shut. No, he couldn't have, not given what bad shape he was in then, not given his awareness that this woman had saved his life at great peril to herself. Even more important, she was grieving for her friend, and had to be a lot more scared than she let him see.

This was not the time and place for what he'd been thinking.

The way she looked at him sometimes, though...

He shook his head, then hoped she hadn't noticed. If he could just go for a long walk. Have a hard workout. Anything to take his mind off her, give his restlessness an outlet. Instead, they were trapped in a space that wasn't more than ten square feet that encompassed bedroom, kitchen and sitting room. They were almost always close enough to each other to touch, if they chose.

If she asked him what he was thinking right now, he didn't know what he'd do. Kiss her, he was afraid, and not gently.

They read again that afternoon. If anything, the rain had picked up, although the tide did recede so their home-away-from-home wasn't quite so alarmingly waterfront.

Bored with his book, he asked if she carried any games.

"I'm afraid not," she said regretfully. "That might have been smart. My other trips with Mike were shorter, and usually it was all we could do to set up camp, have a meal and get to bed early enough to set out at the crack of dawn the next day. If Mike had cell phone coverage, he'd call his wife. The two of us are—" she choked on that "—we *were* both big readers, so…" Claire let that trail off.

"Just a thought. You know his wife pretty well?"

"Yes. I met Mike in a kayaking class, and once he introduced me to Shelby, we hit it off. We're…really good friends. I'm so dreading—" She didn't want to finish that sentence, either.

"She must know by now that something is wrong," he said quietly.

Claire's mouth twisted. "Maybe. His SPOT is being pulled around by the tide and currents, you know. Either…with his body, or not. The signal might be moving weirdly, or showing up out in the ocean farther from land than we should be, but she knows we intended to take our time and wander. She could still be telling herself that he's out of cell phone range. That happens."

"We *are* out of cell phone range." Adam had seen her check her phone twice today. He hadn't had to tell her that the weather probably wasn't helping.

"What's Shelby like?" he asked, not sure why he wanted to know. Except he did know; if Claire had been his wife, he wouldn't have been okay with her heading off for a couple of weeks' trip to the back of beyond with another man.

"She's wonderful." Claire visibly relaxed. "Dramatic, funny, smart. Gorgeous, too. The first time I met her, I felt squat and plain in comparison, but Shelby isn't constantly aware of herself the way I might expect someone with her beauty to be. She's a redhead with masses of wild, curly hair and an hourglass figure. And not a single freckle."

His eyebrows rose. "Because she stays out of the sun?"

"Probably. She's not the outdoorsy type, that's for

sure. Well, that isn't true. Last winter, she and Mike went to Barbados for two weeks and sounded like they had a fabulous time. Somehow, she came home without more than a hint of a tan and still with *no freckles*."

Adam laughed. "Don't like your own freckles much?"

She crinkled her nose. "I'm resigned. You can probably tell I don't tan at all—I just burn no matter how much suntan lotion I plaster on. Which also doesn't keep me from getting freckles."

He grinned at her. "I can barely see them through the sunburn. When you peel, do the freckles go, too?"

"Nope." She laughed at herself. "I don't actually care if I have them or not. I don't love slathering myself with suntan lotion and then aloe vera, so I'm greasy all the time, and still knowing I'll go through that awful peeling and itching phase. Plus…" She hesitated.

"You need to start thinking about skin cancer."

He hadn't meant to sound so stern, earning a startled look from her.

After a minute, she said, "I don't know if sea kayaking will ever give me the same joy again. Although, I do love being in the middle of nature instead of concrete. You know?"

He'd never thought about it before, but this experience seemed to be altering his perspective. If he and Claire were lovers, paddling between the islands for fun, marveling at sights like the pod of orcas, sharing life stories and the small touches that would lead well into nighttime passion… Yeah, he thought he could be happy.

He couldn't offhand remember the last time he had been.

"You'll remember the good times," he said, as if he

were spouting the pat lines from a greeting card, "and let go of the grief."

She snorted. "You mean, seeing what a bullet does to a man's head? I don't think so."

"I'm sorry you got caught up in this."

The filtered green light here under the trees altered the vivid blue of her eyes. The eyes that held his. "That, I don't regret. If I hadn't been here, *you'd* be dead, too."

Staggered, he didn't move. She almost sounded as if his death would have hit her as hard as her friend's. Harder.

She wouldn't have known me, he reminded himself.

Adam had a little trouble remembering how he'd felt before *he* met *her*.

On a scrabble of panic, he picked up his book again, opened it and stared sightlessly at the page.

So much for relaxation.

As far as Claire was concerned, the day had been interminable. She was grateful for the distraction of preparing dinner and cleaning up afterward. She and Adam returned to the rocky shore, only to find an angry tide devouring the rocks, but the rainfall seeming lighter.

"Maybe there's hope," Adam growled, and left her standing there.

His mood had been up and down all day; he'd go from friendly to withdrawn within seconds. It had to be intense frustration and impatience, nothing to do with her, but she didn't like it. She wished she thought she could sneak away in the morning, but knew better.

She also seriously considered finding a softer piece of ground where she could spread out her mat and sleeping bag, rain or no rain, but remembering the visitor last night cured her of that foolishness. A curious bear was liable to wander by again to see what these strange creatures were up to. And then there were the bugs.

With a sigh, she turned to follow Adam.

He had the wristwatch in his hands. She didn't want to ask, but couldn't help herself.

"What time is it?"

"Eight. If we're going to get up at—what?—four in the morning, we should probably hit the sack."

She'd almost gotten used to going to bed in bright daylight. The tent was a big help, dimming the light enough to fool her circadian rhythms. Most nights on a trip like this, she was exhausted by a long day on the water and the work of setting up camp. She hadn't just *sat* all day.

"I'll keep the watch close along with the flashlight," Adam said. "I wish I could set an alarm, but I'm usually pretty good at setting an internal one. Last night… wasn't like me. If there's any chance it quits raining, we can get that early start."

"Fine." If that sounded snippy, so be it.

She set about heating water, and carried the pan and a washcloth, soap and towel behind the tent, where she could take what Mike had called a sponge bath. A hasty one, given the insect life. When she came back, Adam said, "Good idea."

He took the saucepan from her hand, filled it with water and pulled out his own bathing supplies.

He wasn't really out of sight behind the tent, but he didn't strip down any more than she had. While he scrubbed his underarms, Claire brushed her teeth and hung the dry bag with her toiletries from a high branch. Not that she thought bears would like the smell of soap—a bar that was citrus scented—or toothpaste, but they could be nosy and she didn't want her possessions scattered. Or a claw through her toothpaste tube.

Maybe if she hustled, she could move her sleeping bag onto his mat and vice versa, and be sound asleep before he decided to go to bed.

Or pretend to be.

But she had no doubt he'd be right on her heels, so instead she stayed on her hands and knees and tried to find a corner in the tent where she might be able to wedge herself to sleep.

"You know," he said right behind her, "if we shared a sleeping bag again, we could put both mats and the extra sleeping bag beneath us. We might actually be comfortable."

"No."

"Was it that bad?"

Of course not. But that was then, this was now.

"The stress is getting to me." His voice was a note lower, a quiet rumble. "I know I've snapped at you a few times today."

Claire swiveled and plopped her butt down so she could see him. Adam was crouched just inside the tent opening, his elbows braced on his thighs. The position stretched the fabric of his cargo pants taut over long muscles and made her very aware of his hands dangling between his thighs.

"I don't mind the snapping," she said honestly. "I don't like doors slammed in my face."

He didn't so much as blink for a minute. "I…didn't realize I was doing that."

"It's not like I can take my toys and go home."

Furrows deepened on his forehead. "I'd hate it if you did that. I'm…grateful for your company even if I wish all this hadn't put you at risk, too."

She sighed. "We shouldn't share a sleeping bag."

He let his head drop forward. "I want you."

Electrified by a zing of shock, she stared at him. He'd come right out and said what she'd guessed even as she doubted herself. "This…isn't good timing," she said, barely above a whisper.

When he lifted his head, his eyes burned into hers. "I know that. Believe me. I wouldn't push you. I won't." One side of his mouth tipped up in an almost smile. "Whichever one of us was on the bottom would probably end up with a few broken vertebrae anyway."

She frowned at him to cover the continuing shock and startling arousal. "I thought your mat was laid out on flat ground."

A flash of humor made her heart clench.

"Are you kidding? I'm just used to…shutting out discomfort." He shrugged.

Claire laughed despite everything. "Gee, your suggestion that I sleep with you is even more irresistible."

"You could sleep on top of me," he said roughly.

She almost whimpered. "I sort of did last night," she admitted.

"I know."

That gritty admission sent her into a meltdown she absolutely could not afford. She didn't really *know* this man. Even if he was all he professed to be, that meant he was a loner, damaged by a childhood lacking in love and security, a guy with a dangerous job that would have him gone for weeks or months at a time, and that was assuming he worked out of Seattle and not… She didn't know. Anchorage? San Francisco? Miami?

And, okay, she had some vanity issues. Despite what she could do with a washcloth, she needed a hot shower or bath to shave her legs and underarms. Not how she'd want him to see—or feel—her the first time.

"I think I'd better stay in my own sleeping bag," she said, her voice huskier than usual.

The heat in his eyes didn't diminish, but after a moment he nodded. "I'll give you a few minutes of privacy."

"Thanks."

He backed out, leaving her alone.

ADAM DETERMINED TO keep the bear spray close that night. Turned out, he didn't have to look for either; Claire had placed both in easy reach for either of them.

And no, she couldn't be asleep, but she stayed absolutely still as he slipped into his sleeping bag beside her. He lay there wondering if the spray was any more useful than pepper spray that was known to just enrage a human assailant. Not that he and Claire had any other weapons or deterrents to chase a bear away. From what he'd read, not even a handgun was an answer. Grizzlies, at least, were hard to bring down. Bullets from a pistol might be the equivalent of a few bee stings.

He forced himself to think about tomorrow. His shoulder had ached less than he'd expected from yesterday's exertions. Of course, they hadn't been on the water long at all, but he'd sure as hell tried to hurry, forgetting any of the technique that Claire had tried to drum into him.

He told himself he shouldn't have any trouble paddling across the channel to the island on the other side and finding a campsite. He'd like to think it would be that easy, but Boyden and Gibbons had popped up every time he and Claire made a move. If they'd camped versus returning to the freighter, they couldn't be that far away. Adam would give a lot to know where they were.

He and Claire at least had the advantage that the kayaks were silent and low enough in the water to make spotting them more difficult. Too bad they couldn't summon the pod of orcas again.

It took a while, but he finally thought he could sleep. He hoped so; he'd been trying not to move around despite the ridges digging into his back, butt and even calves. Claire remained so damn still, he knew she wasn't asleep, either. Adam had hoped she would drop off so he could relax, but maybe it had to work in reverse. His wounded body probably required more sleep than usual to heal, too.

When his eyes snapped open, full night had fallen. He'd heard something…

It almost sounded like a voice, deep throated and demanding. Hell. He started to sit up, reaching automatically for the weapon that should be under his pillow, but Claire's hand gripped his arm.

"Bear," she whispered.

The sounds continued. Then she said something a lot more alarming. "Bears."

Plural.

Scrabbling sounds followed. Claws digging into bark?

Adam seized the spray bottle. It was like facing off with a guy carrying a semiautomatic when all you had was a starter's pistol. Feeling completely vulnerable did not sit well with him.

Scuffling, the shaking of vegetation, and something crashed into the side of the tent, pushing it inward. Low, not high like a full-grown bear's rump bumping the fabric wall. It wasn't trying to dig them out, was it?

More vocalization. He heard sounds coming from in front of the tent and off to the side.

Claire leaned so close her lips tickled his ear. Her voice was almost soundless. "I think that's a mom and cubs."

Cubs that might have been wrestling and rolled against the tent wall. Hell. Mom had to know he and Claire were right here. Didn't bears have poor vision and rely instead on a powerful sense of smell?

Claire still leaned on him, her fingertips biting into his forearm. Okay by him. His heart slammed against his rib cage. This form of danger was way out of Adam's frame of reference. Maybe they should start shouting and make a racket to try to scare the bears away, but he trusted Claire's knowledge of local wildlife. The decision was hers.

More snuffles, grunts and something that was almost a squeak. Mother bear giving orders that were being protested?

He and Claire remained absolutely still. If she was breathing, he couldn't hear it. Adam had done plenty of stakeouts, but he didn't remember ever staying so rigid for such a length of time.

A branch cracked under pressure. Others swished back and forth. Eventually, there was silence. Even then he didn't move, straining for the slightest sound.

"Oh, my God." Claire let go of him and collapsed back onto her mat.

Adam groaned. He had no idea how much time had passed since he'd opened his eyes, but he was betting it had been fifteen minutes or more.

"That was scary," Claire suggested.

He looked down at her, tracking her voice, because he sure couldn't see her.

"Damn right."

Suddenly, she was giggling.

He couldn't help himself. He bent over her, succeeded despite the darkness in finding her mouth. He had to kiss her. His tension had built for days, and now that band had snapped. Rebounded.

He wasn't as gentle as he should have been. When her lips parted, he dove in, his tongue plunging into the soft depths of her mouth. His hands clamped to each side of her head before one slid beneath her neck to squeeze the muscles. Incoherent sounds broke from her, and she'd grabbed hold of him, too, a hand squeezing his upper arm, the other finding the muscle that ran from his neck to his shoulder.

He'd have given damn near anything to be able to *see* her, but they grappled in complete darkness. He rolled to his shoulder and took her with him. She said his name before stinging his lip with her teeth. When he shoved down her sleeping bag and found her breast, she moaned and arched her back to press into his touch.

Adam was on fire, desperate to escape the confines of his sleeping bag, to bring her feminine body into contact with his. He finally had to pull back to fumble with the zipper and wrench it down.

On hearing the sound, Claire froze against him.

"What are we *doing*?"

Hearing the cry of panic, he made himself go still, too. "Claire?"

"I can't!" Her hands fell from his body and she tried to scramble away as much as her sleeping bag would allow.

"Stop." He'd never been in such an agony of desire, but he managed to sound almost calm. "You said no. I heard you. Please don't be afraid of me."

He waited until she said, very softly, "I'm not afraid of you. More...of myself."

His eyes closed as he battled himself. "We kissed, Claire. That's all."

"We..."

Came so close to making love, his body throbbed. But he could stop. She'd made her feelings plain earlier. He hadn't meant for this to happen.

"Let's...try to go back to sleep," he said after a minute. And then, "I don't hear any rain."

"No." She moved, but he couldn't tell if she'd shrugged, hunched, what. "Okay." After a pause, she added, "I'm—"

He interrupted, "Don't even think about saying you're sorry."

Chapter Thirteen

It was still dark when Claire woke up, and she guessed immediately that Adam had moved, or his breathing had changed, or something. With her head resting on his shoulder, her forehead pressed to the side of his neck, she was in a position to know. The rest of her… Yep, she'd managed to squirm partway on top of him, only the bulk of two sleeping bags thwarting her.

She tried to ease herself back, but discovered his arm wrapped her and his hand spanned her waist. When he felt her resistance, he lowered the arm. He must have been cold, having much of his chest, shoulder and arm outside the sleeping bag, but it appeared she hadn't given him much choice.

"Let me check the time," he murmured. "Close your eyes."

She did as he asked, but she still saw stars when he turned on the flashlight.

"Three forty-five. Up and at 'em." His satisfaction was plain. Apparently, he *could* set an internal alarm.

Too bad she felt no enthusiasm at all for shedding the sleeping bag and getting dressed, never mind launching in the near dark. But he was right—even an hour lead on their pursuers might allow them to reach the narrow channel unseen, especially if they could be well on their way before full sunrise just after five o'clock.

"Ugh," she mumbled, and got herself into action.

The rain had definitely stopped, and when they pushed their way to the shore and Adam shone the flashlight toward the water, it appeared less choppy than yesterday.

Neither said another word until they sat hunched over their bowls of oatmeal. Then she asked, "How's your shoulder today?"

As if it hadn't occurred to him to wonder, he rotated his arm. "Good," he said, sounding surprised. "A lot better."

She only nodded. Being that the sky hadn't begun even to subtly lighten, he probably didn't see her.

"Last night," Adam said abruptly. "I want you to know I didn't plan that. You don't have to be afraid."

"Apparently I'm not," she said dryly. "I practically climbed on top of you to get comfy."

"I noticed." A smile could be heard in his voice.

"Anyway." Claire was determined to be fair. "It's not like I wasn't…participating."

"I noticed that, too."

"I'm not sure I'd have thought of birth control, and I'm not on any, so it's a good thing we stopped."

"I have condoms," he said.

"*What?* How could you?" He hadn't even had a wallet when she rescued him!

Adam interrupted, "Kyle. I found them in his toiletry bag."

Her mouth opened and closed a few times as if she were a fish. Had Adam had her in mind when he decided to hold on to the condoms? Or was it just a waste-not, want-not thing?

She knew better than that, but wasn't prepared to think about it right now. So she said briskly, "Let's just put what happened behind us. Are you done eating? I'll wash up the dishes if you'll roll the sleeping bags and mats."

Without comment, Adam rose.

Did he have the condoms in his pocket *right now*?

No, no. Not thinking about it.

The packing up went so smoothly, she was forced to realize how adept he'd become at everything but the kind of maneuvers in the kayak and strokes she hoped he wouldn't be called on to perform.

Let this work.

The hardest part was carrying the kayaks and gear across the wet, slimy slabs of rock to the water. No waiting for daylight and the turn of the tide for them. Even with each using a flashlight to allow them to see where to put their feet, they both skidded a few times, and once Adam swore.

"Did you hurt yourself?"

"Stepped in a damn tide pool."

"Oh. I hope you didn't—" Claire cut herself off before she could make him feel guilty if he'd smashed a sea urchin or star or... She rolled her eyes and ordered herself to get her priorities straight.

It didn't take them long to load their kayaks. They'd used enough drinking water that both would be a little lighter.

After lowering herself into the cockpit and snapping the spray skirt into place, she used the paddle to nudge herself forward and into a long glide. Moments later, Adam joined her.

Only a few minutes later, he said, "The tide is still coming in, isn't it?"

"I'm afraid so." Slack was best, when the tide was hesitating before changing direction. "Since we can't wait, this morning we'll be paddling against it for a couple of hours unless we want it to carry us back down the channel."

"I'd like us to hug this side of the island for a little ways before we start across," he said. "We might spot their camp."

Alarm leaped in her as if he'd stamped down on a gas pedal. "The idea is to avoid them."

"I'd be happier to sabotage their boat."

Adam sounded so reasonable, as if his suggestion was matter-of-fact. As it probably was for him. If *he'd* been the healthy one and an expert kayaker, *he* wouldn't have hesitated to leave her and strike out on his own. She had the appalling realization that what to her was extraordinary or terrifying was his normal.

"I *hate* that idea."

"If we do see their boat, I don't expect you to come with me. In fact, all you should do is loiter somewhere you can hide if worse comes to worst—"

If he was killed.

"Or join me when I appear again."

"May I remind you that it's still dark and we need to stay well off the shore so we don't split open the hull of one of our kayaks on a big rock?"

"Let's just stay close enough to spot a kerosene lantern or a flashlight. Or an obvious inlet or beach."

Claire swallowed further arguments. She'd expressed her feelings about this stupid idea, but wasn't entirely sure he'd follow her if she ignored him and struck out directly east.

As she turned to go northeast along the coastline, her stomach churned. If she'd known what he had in mind, she wouldn't have eaten the oatmeal that now felt like a load of sand in her stomach.

THIS WAS STUPID. Claire was right, damn it. They needed to use the darkness to run, not go on the attack.

Adam recognized his problem. He craved the feeling of control. Needed to take action, not to continue as a passive victim.

A flicker of light caught his eye.

He pointed to it with his paddle, hoping Claire would see.

She'd quit paddling. Oh, yeah, she saw.

Adam edged his kayak to come up beside hers. "I want to take a closer look. I won't go ashore. You're right—it's too risky. But we could get really lucky and find this is some other kayakers who could call for help."

"Oh! Yes."

He led this time, trying to ensure his paddle slipped quietly in and out of the water without a splash. The campsite, if that's what this was, came closer with startling speed.

The tide going in, the pull carrying them toward the shore. He had to watch it.

At that thought, he quit paddling and reached for the binoculars he'd hung around his neck. Through them, he saw the light brighten. Someone was turning up a lantern. In that flare, he spotted a bulky shape between the light and the water.

Adam swore under his breath. "It's them. We need to get out of here."

This time, she took the lead, taking a rounded turn. Sometime in the next hour, they'd see the sun rise directly in front of them.

They hadn't been underway ten minutes when he heard a motor coming from the north. Circling the island, maybe? Strange, this early in the morning. Then he heard it cough, unlike the smooth running of the newer outboard motor on the inflatable. Was this the aluminum skiff, joining up Boyden and Gibbons? Say, to plan a pincer scheme intended to crack him and Claire like a walnut in a nutcracker? Or maybe only to split up with the idea of blocking more options they might have for escape?

Didn't matter.

Adam cursed himself for delaying their crossing even by the fifteen minutes or so they'd lost.

Thank God they'd left so early.

He fixed his eyes on the darker-on-dark shape of Claire and her kayak, and paddled for all he was worth.

CLAIRE WORRIED THE entire way across. The tug of the current trying to pull them south kept them working hard, but that wasn't all. Out toward the middle of the channel, choppy waves got rougher, then became white-caps and even minor swells. She was terrified of losing sight of Adam, but he did well sticking close to her stern.

At one point she was sure she heard an outboard motor again, although it was impossible to pinpoint from which direction. How much experience did their pursuers have in rough conditions, or boating at all? She'd paddled in more dangerous conditions—the day she and Mike had followed the ocean coast of Calvert Island was one—but just because these guys knew how to start a motor and maybe had trawled for fish on a lake a few times didn't mean they wouldn't be scared out here. The swells made it a lot harder for anyone to spot kayakers, too, given their low profile.

As the light grew brighter to the east, Claire almost wished for rain. It would be miserable, but would also make visibility so bad, one of those boats could pass thirty feet from her and Adam without seeing them.

No such luck, she saw, as a pale gray sky revealed itself.

Go, go, go.

She kept an eye on her compass, and felt confident that they were heading directly toward the opening into Spitfire Channel. Unfortunately, that opening was wide enough that they wouldn't immediately vanish from sight, as she wished they could.

The chart had showed an hourglass-shaped inlet on her port side close to the opening, but the marks indicated it was usually choked with kelp. It would be a trap, anyway, with no outlet but back into the channel. A deeper inlet lay farther along; she felt sure that, even a few weeks from now, other boats would be anchored in it. At the moment? She had no idea.

As her mind circled desperately, she cursed herself for not having made a different choice early on. Truthfully, this channel slicing between myriad islands wouldn't let them out *that* close to where they'd started, but if she hadn't been so afraid of crossing the deep anchorage east of their first two campsites, they could have been hidden in the islands in the Kittyhawk group until they saw a boat to approach.

Too late.

Keep paddling. Her arms and shoulders ached. She was pushing harder than she had at any time on this trip. After all, she and Mike hadn't been in any particular hurry. Every time she stole a look over her shoul-

der, though, there was the red-and-orange kayak, Adam
paddling as hard as she was. What glimpses she saw of
his face showed him to be grimly focused. He wasn't
giving away how much pain he had to feel.

The blackish-green hump of Spitfire Island grew
ahead and to her right, as did what she knew to be the
much larger Hunter Island that formed the northern
shore of the Spitfire Channel. Neither looked...hospi-
table. All she saw was rock and the deep green of im-
penetrable forest.

The paddling became briefly easier despite the wind-
ruffled water and ocean swells. Then, it abruptly became way harder. The tide had turned, and was rushing
out of Spitfire Channel.

Their timing couldn't have been worse.

They could *try* ducking into the kelp-choked inlet.

No. Trap, remember?

A jutting finger of Hunter Island suddenly reared to
her left, which meant they were entering the narrower
channel. She expected the first half of it to be easy to
traverse—except, of course, for the battle against the
outgoing tide. If only they could reach the neck where it
was almost choked off, and only a fathom deep. Tricky
for most boats, but both the inflatable and the aluminum skiff would have a shallow draft.

Now, *that*, it occurred to her, would be a good place
to set up an ambush—although only if she and Adam
could beach the kayaks and be able to set foot on land.

If they could find a place to stop at any time, the two
boats hunting them might go right on by.

Yes, but wouldn't it be worse to know the enemy was
ahead of them, and could be lying in wait anywhere? Say,
setting up an ambush at the narrowest place in the channel?

Keep paddling.

SOMEBODY WAS DRIVING a stake through his shoulder again, and damn, his muscles were screaming. Adam discovered that he'd kidded himself that his workouts kept him in prime condition. He'd barely glanced at rowing machines in his usual gym, and was now thinking twice about that.

He'd studied the charts that Claire had laid out, and hoped like hell she would find a place to stop. He wasn't a quitter, but he didn't think he'd make it all the way through to Kildidt Sound.

This was the toughest paddling yet, with the tide one hundred percent against them. Still, they kept on, and on. He fixed his eyes on Claire and fell into a mind—but not muscle or nerve—numbing rhythm.

The land to each side seemed forbidding. In different circumstances, beautiful, but he wasn't in a mindset to appreciate it.

His relief was huge when they passed the opening for yet another channel, this one going straight south and separating Spitfire Island from Hurricane Island. Claire ignored it, looked over her shoulder at him and passed the wide mouth of what he thought was a dead-end lagoon to their left.

A little later, it looked like Spitfire Channel itself turned directly south. Ahead…he couldn't tell.

This time, Claire turned to follow the densely forested shore. Did she know where she was going?

This coastline wandered. They reached an end, where he was able to lay his paddle across the deck, bend forward and groan.

Claire deftly maneuvered her kayak beside his. He lifted his head to find her looking anxiously at him.

"How are you?" she asked.

"Beat," he admitted, "but I can go on."

"You may have to. I thought we might find a place to put into shore in this lagoon, even if it's only for a break. Otherwise, we'll be going through that narrow bottleneck, and I'd like to do that at slack tide if we can."

"Okay. I haven't heard a motor since we entered the channel."

"No, I haven't, either. The trouble is, they can explore all day looking for us. If we're going to stop, we have to get completely out of sight again."

Why say the obvious?

Because she hadn't seen any possibilities, he assumed.

"We'd better not hang around here," he said.

Claire bit her lip and nodded.

As her kayak shot away from his, he glanced up. Unless he was imagining things, the thin gray cloud cover had darkened. Could be good. Could be very bad. He of all people knew how horrible it was to be drenched and cold, without any way to dry off or get warm.

He thrust his paddle into the water and followed Claire.

To his surprise, she swung suddenly to the right, straight toward a stretch of shore that looked as unwelcoming as all the land had since they launched this morning.

For the first time, he had to skirt a patch of kelp. Strange stuff. The only kelp he'd seen was on beaches, dried or still slimy and stinking. In this quantity, it could be a field blooming with some strange flower.

On the back side of it, Claire must see something, because she kept going. And then he saw it, too: a tiny cove with a gravel beach of sorts. Drift logs were stacked at the back of the beach, the forest looming just beyond. Would it be possible to get over the pile of driftwood?

Claire nosed her kayak onto the gravel and climbed out to pull it higher. His ground to a stop, but he didn't get out.

"I need to explore a little," she said. "Wait here."

Fine by him. Once the spasms in his shoulder relented, he'd stand up. Stretching would be good.

Claire tried to clamber over what appeared to be wet logs, gave up and walked as far left as she could go, then right. After a moment, he lost sight of her.

Adam climbed out of the cockpit so fast, he caught a foot and almost went down. Regaining his balance, he grabbed the forward carrying toggle and hoisted the kayak high enough he could be sure it wouldn't be pulled away by a wave.

By the time he reached the end of the wall of driftwood, Claire popped back out.

"This should work. We'll have to carry the kayaks farther than usual, but I found a flat spot above the high-tide line."

He reached for her, lifted her off her feet and swung her in a circle. She laughed at him the entire time, until he set her down again, his hands still on her waist.

Adam went for light. "Saving me again." His voice came out gritty, though, and she'd gone solemn, searching his eyes.

He didn't know what she found, but her smile bloomed again.

Her hair had to be stiff with salt spray, her cheeks and nose glowed red, her lips were chapped and all he could think was how beautiful she was.

He was in deep trouble. Had been since that first day when she warmed him so generously with her own body. His cautious nature kept waiting for her to show herself as something less than the foolishly brave, thoughtful, compassionate woman he'd discovered so unexpectedly.

Wasn't going to happen today.

And tomorrow...tomorrow they should make it out to Kildidt Sound, where there had to be other boat traffic.

Beyond that, he couldn't see.

Chapter Fourteen

Late afternoon, Claire stiffened at the sound of an outboard motor.

Adam was already moving, pushing toward the driftwood logs where he could crouch to see through a gap to
the small beach. Claire followed and knelt beside him.

"Won't they ever give up?"

He shook his head. "I'm beginning to think they
still have the on board. If the yacht owner is unwilling
to chance setting up another meet, Dwayne must feel
like he's up a creek."

"Without a paddle," she murmured, her eyes fixed
on the gray water of the inlet. The brown mat of kelp,
rooted on the seabed, bobbed on the rising and falling
surface, pulled by the currents. In this backwater, in
kayaks they could have cut through it, but Claire was
glad they'd been able to find a way around.

"Yeah," Adam agreed in response to her comment,
which was almost a pun. But not a funny one. "Bad
enough if Dwayne has to go back to Juneau and admit
he wasn't able to complete the job, but if he also admits
there's a possibility a witness got away, he's a dead man,
and he has to know it."

Claire absorbed that. She'd assumed that Adam's
sense of urgency had to do with what would happen to

the uranium once it reached Seattle, or whatever port at which the yacht had taken refuge. With all the days that had passed now, the door had probably closed to the possibility of keeping the uranium out of the hands of the buyers, whoever they were—unless it was still on the freighter. That would be better for US security, not so good for her and Adam.

"So they never will stop."

His head turned and his eyes met hers. "You didn't ask for any of this. Maybe I should have told you to leave me once I was back on my feet and had the kayak."

"And maybe they'd have shot me if our paths had crossed."

"Your kayak isn't red." He closed his eyes for a moment, his mouth tight. "I don't know. There was no good reason for Dwayne to shoot your friend."

She only nodded. Both of them went back to the too-familiar need to watch for their enemy. With the sound of the motor growing louder, Adam lifted the binoculars to his eyes.

Almost immediately, he growled an obscenity. "They're across the inlet from us." He handed over the binoculars.

She had to adjust them, but not by much. The inflatable boat came into sharp focus. She'd gotten to hate the sight of it.

"They're searching the shore. How can they possibly know we turned in here and didn't go on through the channel?"

"They don't," he said flatly. "They're being thorough. They know they're faster than we are, and don't want to chance missing us."

She made a small sound that might have been a moan. Adam's big hand gripped her forearm and squeezed.

Claire took a deep breath before she asked, "What do we do if they turn in here on their way back?"

He kept staring, she suspected unseeingly, out at the restless water. The inflatable boat had disappeared from their limited view, although they could still hear it.

Then he said the words she'd dreaded. "Ambush them."

No, HE DIDN'T love the idea of killing Boyden, especially, or even Curt Gibbons. Neither was the sharpest knife in the drawer, and he felt sure they didn't know about that extra cargo. But it was obvious they'd been willing to murder a complete stranger because he was in a kayak that was the right color…and had no qualms about killing Adam when they caught him. What enraged Adam most was that they wouldn't hesitate to also murder the gutsy woman who'd done nothing wrong except save Adam's life.

Maybe their fear of Dwayne drove them, but the hunt had been unrelenting. So, yeah, if he had a chance to knock out either or both, he had to take it.

"Under these circumstances, there's no need to bother disabling the boat," he said. "In fact, we could take it."

"You mean, if…"

He killed the two men. Yeah.

The question was, how could he do that when his only two weapons were a knife and a flare gun?

Knowing they didn't have long, he set Claire up behind the driftwood logs, not far from their camp. He found a solid branch—not driftwood, those were too lightweight—and told her if either of the men made it over the barricade, she should swing for the son of a bitch's head with everything she had.

"Can you do that?" he asked, not sure if her answer mattered. Even determined people often couldn't pull the trigger when the moment arrived.

She swallowed, firmed her jaw and nodded. She had more steel in her backbone than most people, he'd long since realized. Seeing her good friend shot right in front of her had to be strong motivation, too.

"I'll take one of them out with the flare gun." Depending on whether he could aim it with any accuracy. "And hope I have time to reload it."

He'd practiced during some of their downtime.

If the flare missed... Adam didn't let himself contemplate it for long. Boyden and Gibbons would both be carrying semiautomatic handguns. They'd strafe him with bullets.

His plan was lousy, but if there was a feasible plan B, he couldn't see it. Thinking about leaving Claire on her own felt like a knife blade to his chest.

The sound of the motor had diminished as they talked, but now grew again in volume.

He kissed Claire gently, gazed into her astonishingly blue eyes for a moment that stretched, then turned away to jog to his own hideout.

The wait couldn't have been longer than ten minutes, but felt interminable. His habit was to think of everything that could go wrong and figure out how to shift the odds. Today, the odds were so damn bad, he had trouble envisioning how this could go right—but he'd been in tough places before, and survived.

He'd kept the binoculars with him, but didn't even lift them. When the inflatable appeared, it was so close he could make out the men's faces. They idled on the other side of the field of kelp, Boyden, seated at the stern with the outboard motor, talking and gesturing.

Right then, the motor died.

Some swearing went on, Adam able to hear every agitated word.

Boyden leaned over the back, then gesticulated some more. He raised the rotors from the water, and even Adam was able to see that kelp tangled them, slick and topped by brown bulbs. Meanwhile, the boat bobbed at the mercy of the tide and currents that pushed it farther into the broad bed of kelp.

Adam debated shooting the flare gun at them while they were distracted. The range was farther than he liked, given that he'd never fired the thing. He'd undoubtedly have time to dive back behind drift logs and reload, though.

He kept watching as the two men broke out some oars and clumsily attempted to back out of the trap they were being sucked into. Boyden finally concentrated on cutting the kelp from the propeller, although that left Gibbons to single-handedly wield the oar.

God, what Adam would have given for a gun.

Gradually he relaxed, as what had been impending battle and potential bloodshed became farce. If he hadn't guessed that Claire would find no humor whatsoever in watching those two idiots struggle, he might have enjoyed himself.

He didn't forget that they might yet break free of the field of kelp and decide to take the narrow path free of entanglements to the beach.

Except he noticed something he hadn't earlier. The tide had turned again, leaving wet gravel…and rocks. The kayaks had floated right over them, but they hadn't been exposed then.

No, the beach was no longer accessible. Pray to God those two didn't realize that it ever had been.

PREPARING DINNER A couple of hours later, Claire couldn't help thinking that this could be her last night with Adam. If all went well and they made it the rest of the way through Spitfire Channel tomorrow, they might immediately encounter a boat they could stop. They could be separated from the minute the Canadian Coast Guard responded, or maybe taken to Shearwater or Bella Bella—communities right across the bay from each other—to stay until ferries docked. She would be on one going south, Adam on one going north, or so she assumed.

No, he might stay on a coast guard vessel, it occurred to her.

Not looking at him, she asked, "Are you based out of Alaska?"

He shook his head. "No DEA office in Alaska. I'm currently working out of San Diego. That's where we caught the first whiffs of this particular drug trafficking operation."

"I've never been there."

"It's a nice city. Beaches are great. With the border so close, we're busy."

"I'll bet." She concentrated on dishing up the vegetarian chili she'd served before and that he'd seemed to like. It seemed safest, since she guessed Hurricane Island was plenty large enough to have active wildlife. With the memory of the previous night, Adam hadn't suggested a steak, even tongue in cheek.

"We…tend to get transferred regularly," he commented, after swallowing a bite. "There is a Seattle office."

"Oh." Was he hinting that he might request it?

Sure. Jumping to conclusions, are you?

"My mom is down in Arizona now," Claire heard herself say. "She likes the dry heat." As if he cared.

"Your father?"

"They're divorced. Did I say that? He's remarried and in South Carolina. He works for Boeing," she added, seeing that he knew the company had a plant there.

"That's why you started at Boeing?" Adam surprised her by asking.

Claire made a face at him. "Of course. Dad knew someone. Once I had experience, I moved on. Boeing is just so huge. Plus, I liked getting a job on my own." She almost tacked on a *You know?* but remembered in time that he'd had no parent to help him get a first job.

"So you've always lived in the Seattle area?"

"Yes. I've sometimes considered venturing farther afield, but… I don't know. The idea is a little scary."

"Scarier than this vacation?" he said with wry humor.

Despite the ache inside, Claire laughed. "My perspective has changed a little."

"On what's fun?"

She loved the smile playing with his lips, but answered seriously. "No, mostly on what I'm capable of doing. I thought I was being brave taking up sea kayaking. Testing myself against nature." She rolled her eyes. "Now I've been stretched beyond anything I thought I could do." She tried to smile, but knew she wasn't successfully. "Like, say, bashing a man's head in with a tree branch."

"I'm glad you didn't have to," he said with sudden intensity. "I hope you never have to do anything like that. Killing a man, even when it's justified, isn't easy to live with."

She scraped the sides of the pan with her spoon by

feel, her gaze on his hard face. "These guys are trying to kill *us*."

"They are," he said after a moment. "Even so, I worked with them for over a month. Went out for a beer with one of them. I doubt either had killed before, although I could be wrong about that. They apparently didn't hesitate when they came on Kyle Sheppard, which surprises me. I'd have said they're muscle-on-the-hoof who don't mind breaking the law, but that's not the same as going out on a search-and-destroy mission." He shook his head. "I doubt they know what's really at stake."

Disturbed, she said, "I wanted to hate them."

"I shouldn't have said any of that." He set down his bowl with a sharp movement and reached up with his good hand to knead the back of his neck. "Better you do hate them. I'm afraid now we'll find them lying in wait for us."

"I know." And oh, she didn't want to think about an attack coming out of nowhere. Of straining tomorrow to see anything that didn't fit, listening for the rumble of an outboard motor. Knowing that along most of the way they had yet to paddle, they'd be in a narrow chute between rock shoulders with very few coves shallow enough to offer any chance of letting them get off the water or hide.

If only she'd made a different decision early on, she thought for what had to be the twenty or thirtieth time.

But if she had, they would have been completely exposed in Spider Anchorage. And…could Adam have paddled across that distance the first day they set out? Or even the second day?

She didn't think so. Plus, she didn't believe even Adam had expected a hunt quite so relentless.

"We can't leave until the tide is in," he said out of the blue.

"No. You saw the rocks?"

"Did you know they were there?"

Claire shook her head. "It's actually a miracle one of us didn't scrape our hull."

"What happens if you do?"

She shrugged. "Most often, just a scar. I carry a kit to mend anything more serious, but it's a nuisance."

"Under the circumstances, more than a nuisance," he said dryly.

"One hole won't sink a kayak, any more than it would that raft. Kayaks are designed with bulkheads and multiple air compartments, too, you know."

"Accessed by the different hatches," he murmured in a tone of enlightenment. "I should have realized."

Now she could smile. "Have you been worrying about sinking like a rock?"

His grin changed his face in a way that always startled her, and made her heart do gymnastics. "It's crossed my mind."

"I never thought to ask how well you swim."

"I'm no Michael Phelps, but I can get up and back a few times in the swimming pool. In these waters, does it matter?"

"Well…only to be sure you can hold out until another kayaker comes to your rescue."

He smiled again. "I did that."

"You did." She couldn't help smiling back. But the grin faded when she said, "We can't launch in the dark tomorrow."

"No, I can see why. But early."

Claire nodded. What else was there to say?

Rᴀɪɴ ᴀɢᴀɪɴ, ᴡʜɪᴄʜ Adam told himself was a good thing. It gave them a better chance of passing unseen.

Of course, it also limited their visibility, which he hated.

Both he and Claire wore their wet suits and wide-brimmed hats to fend off the rain. Since the rain seemed to be coming down at a slant, the hats weren't as helpful as he'd have liked. At his suggestion, they had also donned rain slickers over, rather than under, their too-bright yellow life vests. With the knife he had taken to carrying, he slit the rain slicker so that he could easily reach the flare gun he again carried in the vest pocket.

They had set out when the sky was barely tinted gray. The tide had just turned, meaning the rocks were once again submerged enough for the kayaks to skim right over them. Paddling out of the inlet was fine, the tide giving them a smooth ride. The moment they turned east, back into the channel, that changed.

Yesterday, he'd seen how narrow it became, but he liked it even less once they were in it. If one boat waited ahead for them, and another came up behind, they were dead.

But how could their pursuers know for sure where they were? Adam had studied the map and charts Claire carried long enough to doubt Boyden and Gibbons could feel any certainty. The waterways were too complex, lace studded with islands and the dark humps of rocky islets. He and Claire could have gone any number of ways. Even using the skiff, too, it wouldn't be possible to watch every route they might have taken.

He especially hoped they weren't watching this one.

His shoulder felt stronger yet today. He wasn't having any trouble keeping up with Claire, even as he searched the shoreline to each side. His gaze lingered on a small cove choked with what had to be kelp, although the veil of rain let him see only a dark mat.

They wound between fingers of rock, abutments that offered no place to beach even if they'd wanted to. Everything around them was painted in shades of gray, from pale to almost black. Wind sighed through the trees and ruffled the water. The rainfall was steady but soft. He had to blink away droplets now and again.

They'd gone a surprising distance, the channel having widened, when it swung south. Claire slowed once and gestured with her paddle toward a cluster of lower rocks on the shore—and the bear and cub both peering into what he guessed were tide pools. Mama swiped a giant paw in one, a silvery fish wriggling from her claws when she pulled the paw out. She flipped it onto the rock slab, then lifted her head and stared at the kayaks.

Adam saw dark shapes in the water that could have been seals or sea lions a few times—probably too big to be otters, like the one he'd seen close-up the one day. If he hadn't been paddling, he'd have been getting chilled despite the multiple layers he wore, he realized.

Claire stayed in what appeared to be the middle of the channel. Maybe she'd paid more attention than he had to the depth. Stood to reason.

He split from her path to round a small islet, partly to take a better look at what appeared to be a cove or inlet to his right. *Starboard*, he corrected himself. He was about to turn his head to look for Claire when his attention was snagged by a shape that didn't quite fit on what might be a gravel beach, or simply smooth slabs of rock tilting into the water. A pile of snoozing sea lions?

Damn. Could that be the inflatable?

He didn't see any movement around it. Nothing that looked like a tent—but he doubted there'd been a small tent available in the freighter's stores. A little grimly, he hoped Gibbons and Boyden had spent a miserable night huddled under a tarp. If they were lucky enough to have one of those.

He used his paddle to come to a near stop, and waited until Claire reappeared, her head turned anxiously. Then he gestured for her to come closer.

When he pointed, she stared.

"They won't see us going by."

"This is my chance to cripple them. I can beach twenty yards or so away, do some damage to the boat and take off."

For all the sunburn, her face looked pale, her eyes dark in the gray surroundings.

"You hover just past their camp."

"I can help."

Adam shook his head. "If things go wrong, get the hell out of here. Do not put yourself in danger by thinking you can help me."

She nodded.

"We're not far from Kildidt Sound, are we?"

"No. Wait! Even if you slow them down, they must carry a VHF radio, which means they can pinpoint our location."

"That's a downside, but you saw how inadequate the skiff is for any serious pursuit. It ran dangerously low in the water carrying two men. This will give us a jump start."

Adam could tell she wasn't happy, but she dipped her head and said, "Be careful."

He lifted the paddle in a casual response, then dug it in to glide away from her, not letting himself look back. He couldn't be sure whether he was doing the smart thing or not, but if he could eliminate these two, he and Claire might actually have a chance of not only stopping Dwayne and his crew, but also of coming out of this alive.

The alive part wasn't usually something he let himself think much about, but this time…something had shifted in him.

Adam shook his head. He had to get in the frame of mind to do this job and get out. He couldn't afford anything else.

Chapter Fifteen

The sole of Adam's boot skidded on rock that was both wet and slimy with seaweed. Twisting, he barely kept his footing. Damn, damn, damn.

He took a moment to regain his composure before gingerly reaching for the carrying toggle at the stern of his kayak and lifting, taking several careful steps until he was sure he had the kayak far enough out of the water that it wouldn't go adrift. It had taken a few minutes to turn it around, but he wanted to be able to jump in and take off with maximum speed.

The flare gun stayed in the vest pocket, but the butt protruded so he could lay his hand on it in an instant. The knife he held in his left hand as he made his way along the shore.

A snort sounded, and he froze. *Not a bear. Please, not a bear.*

But there were no crashing sounds, and nothing moved except overhead branches and the eternal rise and fall of the sea.

At twenty yards he saw lumps beneath a blue tarp. If the sleepers hadn't gotten soaked last night, they were lucky, he thought dispassionately. Hard to be sure, given the rain, but high tide had to have come close to lapping at them. Tying the boat to a tree trunk was smarter than he'd have given them credit for being.

Quiet. Quiet.

He crouched beside the boat and studied what had been left in it. No guns that he could see. He rose to his feet and carefully opened a canvas bag before sticking his arm in it. Almost immediately, he traced the shape of what felt like an aluminum pot. Some energy bars, a jar that might hold…coffee.

Apparently, they'd kept their weapons at their sides.

Okay. He flexed the fingers of his right hand a few times to be sure his grip would be strong, then switched the knife to that hand.

Another snort was followed by a ripple of the tarp. He held his breath. One of the men waking up? Or just rolling over?

If the tide *had* reached them, an unwelcome surprise, they'd have had to stumble up and relocate during the night. No wonder they weren't up with the dawn.

Nothing else happened. The rain kept coming down. He rolled his shoulders, suspecting Claire had been right. If he slashed the fabric, air would escape with a rush. Probably a loud rush. Too bad the wind wasn't blowing harder—except if it had been, he and Claire might not have been able to launch.

What if he only pierced a few compartments? Would the air seepage be slow enough they'd make it onto the water before the boat began to sink?

Slash, he decided, and make it fast. It would take them a minute to wake up enough to realize what they were hearing and fight their way free from under the tarp.

Slash, and then shoot. He might disable at least one of them.

Adam took a few slow breaths, lifted the knife—and stabbed the blade into the side, wrenching it toward him before yanking it out. Escaping air was as explosive as a whale expelling a breath. He moved fast, gashing, moving a few feet, doing it again.

Shouts came from beneath the tarp as the men thrashed. Looking at the damage he'd done, Adam tucked the knife away and raised the flare gun. Just as one end of the tarp lifted, he fired.

The flare whistled as it sped faster than his eye could follow. Adam didn't wait to see the result, but heard the screams as light flared in an orange-white cascade. He bent over as he jogged away as fast as he dared over the slick rocks.

Vicious profanities reached his ears. Then a shouted, "Beckman? You're dead."

Almost there.

The buzz sounded like a wasp, but he knew better. He dropped almost to his belly for a minute, then threw himself to his feet again. A bullet stung his arm and he reeled before pushing the kayak downward into the water and leaping into the cockpit.

The bow almost submerged but then bounced upward. Adam began to paddle, heading northeast, wanting to put as much distance from the gunman as he could. The sting in his arm became a burn, but he was able to ignore it beyond cursing the fact that the wound was in his good arm. More bullets skimmed over the water too close to the kayak.

Gibbons—he thought that had been his voice—kept shooting until he emptied his magazine. Adam gambled that he was now out of sight and turned gradually to rejoin Claire. He hoped she hadn't panicked, hearing the gunshots.

WHAT IF HE was dead? Oh, dear God.

Claire's fingernails bit into her palms. Her instincts all but screamed at her to go back. To see what had happened. There had to be *something* she could do.

There was. She could follow Adam's instructions. Save the world—or at least some people—from the possibility of a rogue consortium of nutcases with a nuclear bomb.

She couldn't abandon him.

She had to, if he didn't show up soon.

Was that even remotely possible? Considering the number of gunshots she'd heard, how could he be able to get back in his kayak and paddle away?

He can't, she thought in despair, but braced her paddle against the pull of the tide to stay where she was. He hadn't said how long she should wait—and he hadn't thought to give her the watch, anyway—but she didn't dare linger too long, not if he'd failed in his mission. If the inflatable boat was still seaworthy—

Movement through the sheets of rain had her straining to see. She prayed. *Please, please.*

"Claire?" His gritty voice, even kept low, carried.

"Adam?" she whispered. He wouldn't hear her. "Adam?" she repeated.

The bright kayak appeared, altering course until it came straight at her. Claire was terribly afraid tears were running down her cheeks, but she consoled herself he wouldn't be able to tell, as wet as her face was anyway.

He came abreast of her, and laid his paddle across her forward deck where she could grab it. She did the same, the two paddles forming a bridge to turn the side-by-side kayaks into a raft.

"I heard shooting," she managed to say.

"Yeah, I think I got winged." He sounded unconcerned. "They won't be able to follow us."

"You did enough damage to the boat?"

"Yeah."

"What about the men?"

"I think one of them is dead. Badly hurt, at least."

Claire saw grief on his face, grief he was trying to hide. Any tiny bit of reservation about the truth of his original story dissolved in that moment. She was also afraid she fell the rest of the way in love with him.

He continued, "Gibbons probably got burned, but he was in good enough shape to pull the trigger a few times."

A few times. It had sounded like a fusillade to her.

"He recognized me." His eyes met hers from beneath the dripping brim of his hat. "Let's hope the radio was damaged."

Claire swallowed and nodded. She had to do her best to match his near stoicism. She wouldn't tell him how terrified she'd been when she heard those gunshots.

THEY SEPARATED AND went back to paddling. Claire started worrying about what he'd said about being *winged*. That meant shot, right? In his case, shot *again*. Surely he'd have the sense to suggest a quick stop to bandage his arm if he thought it was seriously bleeding.

The rain let up enough she'd call it a mist. Thank goodness for her spray skirt, mostly keeping water out of her cockpit. Otherwise, she'd be sloshing. She hoped Adam's was working, and that he wouldn't forget the hand-operated bilge pump he carried.

The neoprene booties he wore would keep his feet reasonable comfortable, no matter what, but enough water sloshing around in the cockpit could make its response sluggish.

Maybe another hour on their way, he signaled toward what the generous might call a beach. One that would quickly disappear once the tide started coming back in, Claire realized, but adequate for a quick stop.

A soaking-wet log provided seating once she spread a tarp on it. Adam reluctantly peeled off the rain slicker—which looked as if it had been sliced by a knife on the upper left sleeve—and let her see the bloody garments beneath. No, he wasn't hemorrhaging or anything like that, but when she separated the fabrics, she found a significant gash cut through skin into the muscle.

Peering down at it, he said, "I can ignore it until we stop for the night. Look, it's clotting."

Claire gave him a stern look. "Let me wrap it over your shirt. I'll just cut up an old T instead of digging for the first-aid supplies. But at least it'll be covered. The rain soaking in probably doesn't hurt anything, but the water might be a lot rougher out in Kildidt Sound, and *salt* in an open wound wouldn't feel good."

Looking chastened, he handed over the knife he'd been carrying and waited semipatiently while she cut and ripped until she had a couple of strips of reasonably clean cotton fabric. Once she tied it off, she helped him slide his arm back into the sleeve of the rain slicker.

Then they ate cold foods they had on hand: almonds, dried fruit and granola topped off with candy bars. He swallowed more ibuprofen, restocked from poor Kyle Sheppard's supplies.

The picture of Kyle's body dangling awkwardly over the tree branch flickered in Claire's mind's eye. She did her best to push it back down into whatever recess it had been staying. Forgetting… No, she'd never forget, either the sight of his body or the things they'd had to do to it.

After she and Adam bundled the remains of lunch back into their kayaks, they sat down again. She had an awful disinclination to move. Now that the most immediate enemy had been vanquished, she wanted them to have won. For rescue to be immediately at hand.

She wanted a hot shower, damn it! A real bed. The knowledge that the authorities were on the job, and the threat of nuclear attack was no longer a burden only she and Adam carried.

Instead, gray mist made her feel chilled however warmly she was dressed, and it worried her that Adam didn't look any more excited about getting a move on than she was.

"Are you all right?" she asked at last.

Predictably, he nodded. But then, after a pause, he added, "Wrenched my back a little, and this, uh…"

"GSW?" she supplied tartly, remembering the acronym for a gunshot wound from some mystery or thriller she'd read. Probably one of Mike's.

"Yeah." Adam's eyes smiled more than his mouth did. "Now that we've stopped, my arm has stiffened up some. And the wound does burn."

"There's a shocker."

He laughed. "Are you mad at me?"

Yes! "No. I understand you were doing your job. Waiting for you, hearing the shots when I knew you didn't have a gun, that was…" Claire found she didn't want to put into words what that had been like. She was too close to doing what she'd sworn she wouldn't.

Any humor on his face had gone, leaving his expression… She couldn't decide. He was troubled, certainly.

By the reminder of what he'd had to do? Or because of what, in his view, he'd put her through?

He had to be a remarkably strong man to do a job this hard, one that had to have left him with internal scars to go with the ones on his body. And yet, *he* hadn't hardened so much as to lose his sense of empathy and compassion, felt even for men like their pursuers.

When she studied him again, she saw that he'd taken care of whatever emotion she'd so briefly seen. Sounding brisk, he asked, "You haven't changed your mind about our route?"

"No. This is still our best bet."

They'd discussed this earlier. If they didn't see any boats right away close enough to stop, they'd head southwest across the sound, aiming for Nalau Passage, which they could follow to Fitz Hugh Sound. That being one of the major inside passages, they could wave down a cruise ship or ferry. Claire didn't expect them to get that far, though; Nalau Island and Passage were popular with fishermen. She'd read there were even a couple of lodges aimed at sportfishermen.

Adam nodded. "A nice big fishing boat would suit us just fine."

She made a face. "If I just hadn't dropped my SPOT—"

He gripped her forearm and looked steadily into her eyes. "You had every reason to be shaken by what you'd just seen. Hardly anyone would have had steady hands in the middle of something like that."

"No, but—"

He interrupted her again. "Even the best-planned operations often go off the rails. That's the way it is. You've more than made up for letting the damn thing slip out of your hands by saving my life, and guiding us through these past few days. If you hadn't had the courage to put yourself out there to rescue me, I'd be dead. No question."

"I couldn't just paddle away," she protested.

"No." This smile was crooked, deepening the lines between his nose and mouth, warming his eyes. "You'd never have done that."

He was right, she decided; she'd screwed up the one thing, but done a lot right since then. It was time, once and for all, to ditch the inner critic exacerbated by a desire to head off Devin's constant discontent with her. In fact, she could just plain quit thinking about a guy so inadequate, he had to put other people down to make himself feel better.

Besides, as for her most recent fussing…it wasn't as if she'd had any experience being on the run with a federal agent from murderous smugglers.

"You're smiling."

She grinned at him. "Thank you for making me feel better. Now, I suggest we actually do get our butts back in the kayaks and move on."

Before she could stand, he wrapped her with his newly injured arm, pulled her close and kissed her forehead. She held entirely still, breath caught in her throat, and reveled in the moment.

As he seemed to be doing.

ENERGIZED BY THE hope of being able to contact the coast guard, Adam felt strong enough to go on.

The gray-green bulk of what Claire had informed him was Hurricane Island reared ahead. Tiny, tree-topped lumps of rock appeared from the mist. None were big enough to qualify as islands. This whole area was a maze.

As she'd warned him, the more open the water, the more it felt like real ocean, swells replacing swirls of currents. He was able to keep her in sight, and the waves weren't large enough to challenge his limited kayaking skills, but he was having to work harder. The new injury had progressed from burning to a deep ache that felt as if the bone had been cracked. He knew that wasn't so, but muscles and ligaments in his upper arm *were* attached to the humerus, the long bone. And some of them had to be damaged.

The older, more serious wound had woken up in the last hour, too. This pain was deep in his shoulder and torso, and diffuse. Nothing he couldn't ignore, but he'd really like to see a gill-netting fishing boat any minute.

Like now.

A curiously even line of those islets, these bigger than some, stretched ahead, north to south. Claire was staying well away from them, and something about the turmoil of the surrounding seas made him wonder if there weren't more rocks that lurked just beneath the water.

Adam had been studying the islets, but he heard something that snapped his attention back to Claire.

She'd come to a virtual stop, and was trying to turn around, sliding sideways on a long swell. What the hell…?

The bulk of a ship appeared against the gray seas. The silhouette wasn't one Adam had ever wanted to see again, unless he was in a helicopter with a dozen members of the Canadian Coast Guard or Navy. He reached for the binoculars and, despite the droplets that immediately blurred the lenses, confirmed his fear.

That rusty old tub was sitting out here waiting for them.

Chapter Sixteen

If anyone aboard the freighter was standing watch, it would be hard to miss the two kayakers heading straight for them. Especially him in this electric-orange-and-red kayak.

He struggled to turn, too, just as Claire reached him.

"Do you see it?" she called. "Is it them?"

"Yes," he roared, "and let's get the hell out of here."

"If we can drop behind the Mosquito Islets—"

"Damn it." He'd been craning his neck. "They're doing something." Then he knew. "Lowering the skiff down to the water."

The skiff wasn't much, but it did have an outboard motor. Even a single man in it could strafe them with bullets.

At that moment, the sound of an engine reached him, throaty and deep. Multiple engines. He turned his head sharply and saw a snow-white sharp-prowed boat cutting in front of them not half a mile ahead. Thirty to forty feet long, maybe, with a big cabin and what might be radar equipment topside. He'd seen plenty of sport-fishing boats like this when he'd been based in Miami.

What scared Adam was wondering whether Dwayne and company would think twice about killing half a dozen more people.

He took a hand from the paddle to pull out the flare gun. Adam closed his eyes, but only for an instant.

This was a risk, but what choice did they have?

He pointed the gun at the sky and pulled the trigger.

Not thirty seconds later, the flare shot high into the air, a vivid, sparkling, universal call for help. Damn. Had the fishing boat gone far enough past them, people in the cabin wouldn't have seen the flare? He fumbled for the plastic bottle that held more flares and extracted one to reload, but first he twisted to look back. If the skiff was in the water, he couldn't see it, no surprise considering it was aluminum against the gray-on-gray landscape.

He pivoted back to see the fishing boat slowing, beginning a turn. Kicking up waves of its own and a frothing white wake. After shoving the flare gun into his PFD pocket, he dug in his paddle, saw Claire doing the same and wished they were in the US where there might have been a chance in hell one of the boaters would be armed.

He started paddling again, Claire doing the same. God help them, they couldn't outrun any boat with a motor, but the much larger fishing boat approached them a lot faster than the skiff could.

A putt-putt behind them reached his ears. Adam didn't bother looking back. A shot. The sportfishing boat closed the distance. A quarter mile, a few hundred yards. He pinned his gaze on it, paddling for all he was worth even as he veered to fall in behind Claire. Maybe the shooter would be content to kill him and would let her go. Or maybe, paddling just a little bit ahead, she'd be able to slide out of sight behind the larger boat in time.

People crouched on the narrow walkway at the prow,

waving and calling, although he couldn't hear what they were saying. A man midway back had binoculars trained on something beyond the kayaks.

Water kicked up less than a foot from the port side of Adam's hull. The muffled crack of a rifle shot came after it. He had a minute then while he slid down the back side of a swell high enough to hide him.

One of the men in the boat ahead bellowed through a bullhorn. "Stop firing a gun! We've called for the coast guard. You're committing a crime—"

Adam's kayak jerked sideways. It had been hit.

Afraid you'll sink like a rock? Claire had asked.

Here was his chance to find out what really would happen.

The next thin line of water shooting above the waves was close to Claire's kayak. Damn. The men on board the sportfishing boat were retreating from the prow and railing, alarm evidence.

Then one of them shouted and pointed. Adam couldn't see what they did, but a moment later a new flare shot into the air. Claire's kayak sped by the prow of their rescuers and tucked in behind it. Adam fought to keep his kayak lurching ahead.

Another shot, another. A spray of bullets surrounded him. One could have struck him, and Adam wasn't sure if he'd have noticed. He saw a man on the fishing boat drop out of sight suddenly.

But then another, similar boat approached, and Adam saw a third one speeding toward them from the south. Every skipper who'd seen the flare was responding.

He bumped into the side of the first boat, his hull scraping it. Nobody reached down toward him or hung over the thwarts, but the next thing he heard was music to his ears.

"It's turning around! It's running away!"

With a groan, Adam slumped forward, head almost touching the deck. The kayak was still gliding forward—until a paddle was thrust toward him and he was able to grab it. Claire held firm until the two kayaks once again lay side by side, and he could clumsily hold an arm out to her.

He thought she said, "We made it."

"ONCE WE SAW that someone was shooting, we called for the coast guard," said the red-faced man who looked like a former football player who was thickening around the middle.

Adam asked, "Did one of you get shot?"

"Tony Vargas." The guy jerked his head toward what appeared to be the steps leading down to the cabin. "We moved him right away." His expression was grim, as were those of the four other men surrounding them. "What the hell is this about?"

They'd hauled Claire and Adam as well as their kayaks up onto the first boat. The other, similar boats stayed close.

Claire asked anxiously, "Is he badly hurt?"

"Not good. Gut shot," one of the men said.

She saw Adam and that man lock gazes for a moment, but couldn't know what they shared.

Beside her, Adam exhaled a long breath. "Long story. Are you Americans or Canadians?"

"American." That was the first speaker. He nodded toward the boat closest to them. "They're Canadians. I think the others are Americans, too. They're putting up at the same camp we are."

"I'm Claire Holland," she offered. "From Seattle.

I was…sea kayaking with a friend when all of this started. He was shot…"

"Adam Taylor. I'm with the US Drug Enforcement Administration. Things went wrong during an operation. I was undercover with drug smugglers." He hesitated. "Some of what happened, and that I know, needs to wait for the coast guard. But the immediate story is that Claire and her friend chanced on the ship I was on while it was transferring illegal cargo."

He told the bare bones of the story: her dead friend, getting shot himself, her rescue, their discovery that they were being hunted.

She gestured north. "We popped out of the Spitfire Channel to find the freighter that was carrying the drugs anchored where they saw us immediately. They lowered a skiff into the water and that's what was pursuing us."

"We're sitting in deep water," one of the men said uneasily. "Any chance this freighter will show up any minute?"

She saw the expression on Adam's face just before he donned his mask, something he did so well. Yes, he thought that was conceivable.

What he said was, "I doubt it. Three boats here, others that will come running if we shoot off another flare. They have to know at this point that someone will already have been in contact with the authorities. The smartest thing they can do is run. What I don't know is whether they'll continue south or go back north to Alaska. I want that ship boarded before it can dock."

The apparent skipper on this boat had been listening from the doorway into the wheelhouse. Now he nodded toward something behind him—probably a radio. "Sounds like the coast guard cutter will be here in fifteen, twenty minutes. They were tied up at Shearwater. A helicopter is on the way, too. Vargas needs to get medical care fast."

Claire, for one, would be very glad when that coast guard ship appeared. Right now, she felt dazed. Was this even real? Believing she and Adam had actually made it, that they would survive, didn't come easily.

Reassurance came from the rocking motion of the boat bobbing on the waves, and from her feeling so chilled. And the sight of Adam, dirty, wearing a week-old beard that didn't quite hide the furrows on his face that were so much more deeply carved than they'd been the first time she saw him.

He kept glancing at her, checking to be sure she was okay the same way she was doing with him. The minute she'd been helped to a seat, he'd chosen the one beside her. Their arms brushed. She needed to stay connected to him.

And how long will that last? she asked herself.

She already knew the answer. Not for long.

Authorities would want to hear her description of events. After that, their next concern would be figuring out how to get her home. But Adam, he'd have to keep doing his job. Their closeness felt more real than anything else that was happening, but it was the illusion, not these kind men surrounding them. Or the *whap whap* of helicopter rotors she heard.

They all turned their heads, looked up. A red-and-white-painted helicopter swooped toward them. Several of the men on this boat stood and waved their arms over their heads.

Within minutes, a medic had dropped down to the boat deck from the helicopter, bringing a stretcher with him. With the help of a couple of the fishermen, Tony

Vargas was strapped to the stretcher. He was in so much pain, Claire wanted to look away from his face but didn't let herself. He was another victim of these monstrous criminals, just as Mike had been, and then Kyle Sheppard.

Oh, God, she thought. If she didn't have cell phone coverage, she could surely borrow a VHF radio to call Shelby and tell her Mike was dead.

She'd never had to bring that kind of news to anyone, and didn't want to start now. But it had to be her, not some impersonal police officer asked to do the notification by Canadian authorities.

"What are you thinking?" Adam asked, as the stretcher swung into the air, being winched to the open door of the helicopter hovering above.

"That I should call Mike's wife."

He took her hand in his, the warmth more comforting than it should have been. "Why don't you wait until we talk to the people from the coast guard? We don't want your friend's wife—"

"Shelby."

He nodded. "Shelby calling friends or family to tell them, or posting what she knows about his death on social media, until investigators are ready to release the information."

She wriggled her hand, but he didn't release it. "You mean, you?" Claire asked.

"I'm one of them." His expression was gentle, his voice less so. "Most of it will be taken out of my hands from here on out."

"I'm glad." Seeing his raised eyebrows, Claire said, "You need to go to a hospital and have your wounds checked out."

A smile appearing in his eyes, he rotated his right

arm. "Now you're telling me you didn't know what you were doing when you patched me up?"

She wrinkled her nose. "You know I didn't."

He dipped his head toward her, speaking too softly for any of the other men to hear. "I think you did." His breath tickled her ear. "Turns out, you're a lot more capable than you knew you were."

After a moment, she straightened. He was right. She'd proved herself over and over this week. The challenge she'd believed she and Mike were facing was nothing in comparison. She'd have gone home feeling good about their adventure, but now...

I'm more than I knew I was.

But she couldn't forget the cost. She'd miss Mike, although that was nothing to what Shelby would have to endure. Kyle Sheppard must have had friends and family who would be plunged into shock and grief. Tony Vargas, another vacationer, might not survive.

And Claire knew life would never seem the same to her. How could she have fallen so hard for a man in a matter of days? Dread filled her at the idea of saying goodbye and going home.

It was like having a huge hollow opening inside her. She might have even made a sound, because Adam said, "What?"

"I... Nothing." His gaze on her face was keen enough, she could tell he wasn't satisfied. "I'm feeling too much. I mean, we started today with your raid on that encampment, we paddled hard in the pouring rain only to face new disaster, we saw the hope of rescue that might not happen because of the bullets flying, and now here we are."

"Yeah," he said gruffly. His arm came around her.

"These last days, you've been a constant in my life I've never had."

"There's the coast guard lifeboat!" a man at the rail called, interrupting them.

A lifeboat? That sounded...puny.

"Finally," Adam murmured.

HALF AN HOUR LATER, the two of them were aboard a ship that might have been fifty feet long. It was painted in an eye-catching bright red and white, which Adam knew to be the Canadian Coast Guard colors. Their kayaks and all their possessions had been transferred, too.

He'd shaken hands with everyone on the sportfishing boat, and a few who leaned across from one of the other boats. Claire hugged everyone, sniffled and then mumbled to him during the transfer, "I probably stink!"

Adam laughed. "I'm sure I do, too. And I can guarantee that nobody cares."

The ship carried a crew of five officers and four others. Six men, three women. Several of them studied the bullet hole in the red kayak before two officers led him and Claire to a cabin to talk.

They listened to his recitation of events, called the number he gave them for confirmation of who and what he said he was and let him speak to his immediate superior.

"We were just starting to get seriously worried about you. I know you expected that tub to turn around and go back to Juneau, but it hasn't docked. Tell me again where you are?"

Adam gave him the bare bones, too, to which the two Canadians listened closely. Then he said, "That freighter *has* to be stopped before it docks or has a chance to transfer cargo. That's got to be a number one priority for both governments. Some or most of the drugs have already been handed off." He gave the identifying details on the yacht. "However, we were interrupted before we were done. That's when the first kayaker, Mike Maguire, was shot and killed, and when I was shot and went overboard." Adam glanced at the two coast guard officers and gave a mental shrug. "They were transporting something else, too. I…overheard the head guy, Dwayne Peterson, talking to his number two man. They'd been paid a lot of money to pass along a little extra."

Everyone in the cabin stayed so quiet, he couldn't hear them breathing. Even Russ Garman, his supervisor, only waited.

"Uranium," Adam said.

Even Claire blinked at the urgency of ensuing conversations. What she took for an oceangoing version of the order, be on the lookout, went out to other coast guard vehicles as well as Canadian ferries and, who knew, Canadian naval vessels? She sat, quiet and forgotten, as US naval and coast guard people were patched into conversations with their Canadian counterparts.

One of the officers left the cabin, and minutes later she realized that the small ship was underway. Taking her and maybe Adam to a drop-off point? Or searching for the freighter that had—what?—an hour head start on them?

Searching, apparently, although it eventually occurred to somebody to feed her and Adam, after which she was escorted to pick up her toiletries and clothes from her kayak before being left in what she felt sure was one of the senior officers' cabins. The shower was tiny but functional. Washing her hair and shaving made her feel amazing. Finally, she dressed in clothes she always held back for the days she and Mike planned to spend a night in civilization—i.e. someplace with showers and real beds.

Then she wiped the steam from the mirror and eyed herself. What she saw wasn't as heartening as she'd hoped. Her sunburn was cycling through a couple of stages at the same time: fiery red and peeling. Her lips were cracked. As she'd seen with Adam, her face looked almost…gaunt.

She slathered her face with cream, rubbed her lips with an ointment and called it good. At least she *felt* better.

When she reappeared on the deck, she didn't find Adam. A female crew member smiled at her and said, "Your partner is showering. He should be out soon."

Claire wandered to the rail. The small ship was moving fast, and when she scanned the closest land, she thought they might be heading north toward Princess Royal Island. Was the plan to leave her off at Klemtu instead of Bella Bella or Shearwater? But she suspected no one was thinking about her. They were searching for the rusty, decades-old freighter she'd really, really prefer never to see again.

Wind whipped through her hair. Trying to corral it with one hand, she shivered and decided to go back to the borrowed cabin and add another layer or two for warmth. And maybe braid her hair.

But just as she started to turn, an arm came around her. Startled, she looked up at Adam's face.

"You shaved," she blurted.

He laughed. "I do that now and again." He studied her. "You're still sunburned."

Scrunching up her nose hurt the tender skin, but she did it anyway. "Gee, I didn't notice."

A smile lingered at the corners of his lips, but he didn't say anything else, only tucking her close to him for warmth, serving as a wind block.

After a few minutes, she couldn't resist asking. "What did I miss?"

"Not much. We've spread our net along the US border both to the north and south. Coast guard and other vessels are watching for the freighter out here in Queen Charlotte Sound and Hecate Strait, and in the passages and channels that make up the inside passage. Some helicopters and small planes are in the air, too."

"And we're out here looking for it, too."

"Yeah," he said slowly. "Part of me doesn't want to hand over the hunt, but the other part…" He hesitated.

She made sure he held her gaze when she asked the question that had been bothering her from the minute she realized the coast guard lifeboat wasn't puttering back to dock in Shearwater again.

"What if we *do* see it? I mean, except for us there are only nine people aboard. And…this is Canada. How well armed are their coast guard personnel? What kind of weapons do your former shipmates carry?" She bit her lip. "If we see the freighter and try to stop it, isn't that kind of suicidal?"

Chapter Seventeen

Adam admitted to sharing her reservations. That said, he doubted they'd be the ones to find the freighter. He hoped not; he'd be a lot happier if Dwayne and company were taken into custody by US authorities, rather than him having to take on the extradition hassle, or allow the Canadians to prosecute the traffickers.

In fact, the coast guard lifeboat had been underway not much over an hour when he was told it was turning around, thanks to a desperate call from a capsized sailboat. They were the closest help to hand.

This was going to be a seriously crowded vessel by the time they reached a port.

He and Claire were allowed to join the captain to listen in on radio discussions concerning his target. The second officer was handling their response to the immediate crisis.

There was a time when Adam would have itched to be part of the boarding operation. Personally slapping the cuffs on Dwayne. Strangely, he felt a sense of distance instead. He was interested, and intensely focused on finding out whether the uranium was still on board and could be seized. But he'd been changed by the events of this week. By the remarkable woman to whom he owed his life.

He'd wanted her from the first night. Now that the desperate need to protect her had relented, he was free to concentrate on how he'd ask her to share a bed tonight.

Surely, wherever they were, there would be a bed.

But he wanted more than that, and hated not knowing whether she felt the same. Sometime in the past forty-eight hours, he'd been slammed with the full understanding of what he was prepared to do to keep her. Would she even consider committing herself to a man like him, a man who had no experience with family or long-term promises made on a personal level?

Feeling a little sick, missing whatever was being said over the radio, he asked himself why she *would* pick someone like him. Underneath the sunburn was a sweet face. Combine that with her curvy body, she must frequently have men hitting on her. Adam liked her pretty blue eyes, her smile and light blond hair, too, but he especially liked her smarts, her competence and the empathy that had her hurting after the two deaths they'd seen directly. What made him think the word *love* for the first time in his life, though, was her courage and her sheer grittiness. He could trust her never to let him down—if she loved him in turn.

Right now, she sat as close beside him as she could without drawing notice. In fact…he reached over under the table for her hand, and felt better right away when she returned his clasp.

Once they located the sailboat, lying on its side in increasingly rough water, Adam and Claire stayed out of the way but watched the efficiency of this rescue. The man and woman clinging to the boat, mostly staying out of the water but having waves washing over them, were brought aboard. Emergency efforts to warm them were begun immediately.

When one of the rescuers repeatedly asked whether they had been the only two people on the boat, the man managed to nod. The tension level dropped considerably.

The man was in bad shape, clearly dazed and confused about where he was, shuddering, teeth chattering, what few words he summoned slurred. Recognizing all the symptoms, Adam felt as if cold fingers were walking up his spine.

The woman, though, was almost completely unresponsive. He'd been there, too. It was a miracle she'd been able to hold on to the capsized boat as long as she had. The decision was made to call for the helicopter again. In the meantime, the captain let Adam know they were heading for Bella Bella, where there was a small hospital.

"Good cell phone service," he added. "Air field, too," he told Adam. "If you'd prefer to fly out rather than taking the ferry."

"I assume we can find someplace to spend the night?" he asked.

"We'll transfer you to Shearwater once we unload our patient. It's better set up for visitors."

"I don't want to go anywhere until I know that damn freighter has been stopped."

The captain's expression held answering grimness. "That may come before we dock."

Ten minutes later, it did.

A US naval ship closed fast on the freighter from the moment it was spotted from the air. One fear had been that Dwayne would decide to dump the especially incriminating cargo overboard, potentially poisoning the ocean, but that hadn't happened. His crew was so obviously outgunned, they'd surrendered without a fight, although the naval officer reporting said, "First thing out of Peterson's mouth was, *This is all that damn Rick Beckman's fault.*" Humor entered the voice. "He was even unhappier when we informed him that Rick Beckman was an alias for a United States federal law enforcement agent."

Adam leaned forward. "The uranium?"

"Recovered, Agent Taylor. You have done a great service to two countries."

His fingers tightened on Claire's hand when he said honestly, "The one we really owe is the woman who saved my life and kept me a step ahead of Peterson's killers."

"Is she with you, Agent Taylor?"

"Right here." Adam squeezed her hand.

"Ms. Holland, I regret not having the chance to meet you and thank you in person. I would hope you'd be awarded a medal by our government, except—"

Adam was meant to interrupt with a hard truth. "That won't happen. This is the kind of operation that will be buried in a deep, dark hole."

"I assumed as much."

He signed off. The coast guard captain stood, bending his head at her. "I agree entirely, Ms. Holland." Then he quietly left the two of them alone.

Adam turned to face Claire. "You deserve a Presidential Medal of Freedom."

She smiled at him. "Thank you, but I don't want one. I just want—" Looking appalled, she screeched to a stop.

"You want?" he echoed softly.

"For those creeps to all spend a long time in jail." Her

eyes widened even more. "Did you tell them about—what did you say his name is?"

"Curt Gibbons. Yes. I feel sure he's been retrieved by now, assuming he hadn't somehow gotten that boat mended enough to put it in the water." He smiled, and not nicely. "Of course, his mother ship abandoned him, which must have come as a shock."

Claire nodded, but not as if she'd been paying that much attention to what he was saying.

"This really is all over."

"It is."

"I don't suppose anyone has found Mike's body."

"Under the circumstances, I think we'd have been told."

"Yes. Um. Will you head back to San Diego? Or up to Alaska?"

It was hard to say, *I do have to keep doing my job, but I'd like to start something with you, too. See where it goes.* The words stuck in his throat, so he said only, "I'm guessing Alaska for the short term. This is my investigation."

"Then tomorrow will be goodbye." She aimed a smile his direction that looked fake, shot to her feet and was out the door and onto the open deck before he could react.

It was just as well they weren't alone together again until they'd docked first at Bella Bella, where she and Adam had walked to the Royal Canadian Mounted Police station. There, they left Kyle Sheppard's wallet, passport, locked cell phone and a few other items that seemed personal. The officer had been in contact with the coast guard and expected them; the coast guard had the instructions for where to find Kyle's body for recovery. It would be up to some lucky RCMP officer to notify Kyle's family about his death. Both Adam and Claire passed on their phone numbers in case anyone close to Kyle had questions.

It didn't take long to cross the bay to Shearwater, also clinging to the water's edge, where they left their kayaks in a designated area. The goodbyes with the coast guard officers and crew were as heartfelt as those with the sportfishermen had been.

Walking down the dock away from the big boat, carrying a bag with clothes and toiletries, Claire felt dazed anew. So many people who'd become so important to her in such a short time.

The courage and kindness extended to them had renewed some of her lost faith in her fellow humans.

She couldn't tell whether Adam felt the same; he must have had many such experiences during his career. Maybe, after his unrooted upbringing, he lacked any ability to make deep connections with other people. That thought was unutterably depressing.

He'd been on the phone almost nonstop the past hour or two, and Claire had taken some of that time to call Shelby. Only later, when she lifted her head to savor irresistible smells from a nearby restaurant did he tuck the phone in a pocket. They walked into the restaurant, Claire expecting them to draw stares, but they weren't the only outsiders here today. A hot meal she hadn't had to prepare on her tiny, one-burner cookstove might as well have been gourmet, as far as her taste buds went. Adam inhaled his meal, too, and they each had a slice of pie besides.

The waitress gave them directions to a hotel. Even if the sun was still high in the sky, Claire felt as if this day had gone on for an eternity.

Adam looked preoccupied as they walked. They'd almost reached the place when he said suddenly, "We going to share a sleeping bag tonight?"

A quiver deep in her belly shook Claire. She faltered in her next step forward. Hadn't she expected this moment to come? This decision? But it really wasn't one at all.

"I think we can share tonight." Wow, she'd almost sounded faintly amused, even sophisticated.

The tilt of his mouth told her "almost" pretty much said it all.

Adam grabbed her hand and hustled her inside. The smiling proprietor led them to his "best" room, small but adequate and including a private bath with a shower. The moment she left them alone, Adam dropped his bag on the floor, took Claire's from her and tossed it on the only chair and gripped her shoulders.

Voice filled with gravel, he said, "God, I want you."

In answer, she went on tiptoe and flung her arms around his neck.

Then his mouth on hers ended all doubts, all possibility of second thoughts. He ate at her mouth, his tongue insistent, the bite of his fingers part of the fierce need she'd seen in his eyes. He groaned when he tore his mouth from hers to nip her earlobe and move damply down her throat. His teeth closed for a not-quite-painful moment on the muscle that ran from her neck to her shoulder. Then he grabbed the hem of her fleece top and wrenched it up, pulled it over her head.

Claire cooperated fully even as she did battle with *his* clothes. She had a fleeting memory of the one time she'd seen him entirely naked, never imagining they'd get to this point. Photos in celebrity magazines were as close as she'd ever come to seeing a man with his kind of body: broad shoulders, long, powerful muscles in his arms, chest and legs. Dark hair that made the sight even more tempting.

And then there was his erection. That had *zero* resemblance to what she'd so briefly seen when she was trying to bring him back from near death.

They all but fell onto the bed, Adam's weight on her, his penis nudging at her opening already. She was so, so ready…but caution was built into her nature.

"Wait! I'm not on birth control. Did you hold on to those condoms?"

He stayed suspended above her for an instant, gaze hungry and intense, before he made a ragged sound and rolled off her.

"Yeah."

To her dismay, he had to get off the bed and crouch by his bag to dig inside it. When he came back to the bed, he had a handful of packets that he let fall onto the scarred bedside stand. But one he ripped open, and with shocking speed he'd spread her legs and thrust inside her.

The sex was hard and fast. Claire had never felt anything like this. It was like being swept up by a hurricane compared to a mild breeze that might ruffle her hair.

After the shattering finale, she had one glimpse of his face before he removed his weight from her and tucked her close, her head on his shoulder. Unless she was imagining things, he looked as shaken as she felt. Maybe just because their past week had been so intense, she told herself. Both of them had built up so much tension, fear and occasional triumph and, yes, sexual tension, it had to be released somehow.

Letting him go without weighing him down with her feelings and regret would be the single hardest thing she'd ever done.

NOT FIVE MINUTES LATER, Adam's body was already stirring. He had every intention of making love with Claire as many times as they could manage tonight. But first he wanted to revel in how she felt in his arms. The hair he rubbed his cheek against was silky, smelling faintly of some unknown shampoo, but underneath he recognized her scent. She fit perfectly against him, which he had already realized after their nights in a shared sleeping bag. Adam hated knowing they had to part ways tomorrow. He couldn't take her with him, and he couldn't walk out on an operation he hadn't completed. *Fell in love* as an excuse would be on a par with *my dog ate my paperwork*.

Much as he wanted to put off a difficult conversation—what if she said no? Did he get dressed and go out to ask for another room?—he disliked even more the gut-churning fear that had taken up residence in his belly.

So he slid one hand down her back, enjoying the delicate feel of her vertebrae, the inward curve at her waist and the firm feel of her butt, and murmured, "We need to talk."

She stiffened. It was a frightening length of time before she asked, "About what?"

"Us."

He'd never used that word before in this context. Never expected he would.

She pulled away, sat up and grabbed a pillow to cover herself in front. Her eyes searched his. "I need to be able to see you."

Talking about hard stuff to someone who couldn't see you would be easier, Adam felt sure, but he understood why she felt that way. He sat up himself, propping a pillow behind himself so he could lean back against the headboard, and said, "You'll get cold. Wrap the covers around yourself."

She eyed him warily, then did as he'd suggested.

He cleared his throat, although that was unlikely to help. "I want to keep seeing you." That sounded less crazy than, *I want us to spend the rest of our lives together.*

Her lashes fluttered a few times. "How is that even possible, with us separated by a couple of states, and given your job?"

"Once I wrap this operation up, I have plenty of time coming. If you want me to, I'll come to Seattle. I can… get a hotel room if you'd prefer that."

For too long, all she did was study him. Her eyes reminded him of the sea: seemingly clear yet hiding unimaginable depths and currents. "I'd…really like if you came for a visit. Of course you can stay with me."

Visit wasn't quite what he had in mind, but even so, he might have slumped in relief if the headboard hadn't been there for support. "Thank you," he said huskily.

She pressed her lips together. "But…then what?"

He didn't like to hear her sounding timid. That wasn't Claire.

"We haven't known each other a week."

"I know." She smiled weakly. "I shouldn't have even asked that question."

"It was quite a week, though. We got to know each other in a way a lot of people never do."

She waited, her blue eyes fixed on him.

"Then… I'm hoping you might consider relocating,"

he admitted. "I can try for a transfer to Seattle, but we tend to get moved regularly. If necessary, I can leave the DEA. But I think I can get a promotion to more of a desk job. If I have you, I want to come home every night."

He was horrified to see tears clinging to her eyelashes. Before he could grovel for assuming too much, if that's what was wrong, Claire flung herself at him. His arms reached out automatically and pulled her in close.

"I was so afraid—" she wailed.

He nuzzled her temple. Fine strands of her hair caught in his evening beard. "Of what?"

"When you said we had to say goodbye—"

"You thought I meant forever?"

Her head bobbed. He felt some dampness against his throat.

"I've never felt like this before." He had to swallow in hopes of dislodging the lump in his throat. "It's... nothing I expected. But despite what was going on, with you I've had moments of being happier than I've ever been in my life."

She lifted her head from his shoulder, blinking away the last of the tears.

He hoped the last of them.

"Once you find out how *average* I am, I'm afraid you'll change your mind."

Adam laughed. She was afraid *he'd* change his mind?

"Not happening," he said with complete confidence.

A smile trembled on her lips, warming him inside. "Okay."

Adam didn't have much familiarity with exhilaration, but he understood what he was feeling. Cupping her cheek with one hand, he said, "Do we have a deal?"

Now her smile could light the world. "Absolutely."

Too damn close to tears himself, he kissed her. Every time he could make love with her would help him survive the days or weeks he'd have to do without her. But after a moment he lifted his head so he could look at her. Just look. And he realized he'd have expected to anticipate apprehension sitting in his belly like a lump of lead until he could get to Seattle to see her…but he was pretty confident he wouldn't have to suffer that much.

Because he trusted her.

He was laughing when he slid down in the bed and swung her up over him to sit astride. Her lips were curved, too, when they met his.

* * * * *

COLTON K-9
TARGET

JUSTINE DAVIS

Chapter One

Annalise Colton knew how nervous she was because of how much she was talking to herself. Enough that she couldn't even pretend that she was really talking to the dogs at her feet.

"Stop it," she said in her best police K-9 trainer voice. "You're even making them nervous."

And now she was giving herself orders. Out loud.

She sighed and made herself turn away from the mirror. She'd done her best, and it would have to do; if she tweaked her makeup any further, she'd be doing more harm than good. She'd already gone from having her long blond hair up, back, then down three times, before finally giving up and just letting it fall loosely.

After Bennett had unceremoniously dumped her in public, it had taken her months to even think about dating again, despite wishing for a settled life and someone to share it with more than almost anything. But when she had finally steeled herself to try again, she had vowed there would be nothing but nice guys from here on out. They might not have Bennett's flash, but they wouldn't have his cruel streak, either.

"Nope," she said to Jack and Apple, the shaggy canine duo she was fostering, "nothing but Mr. Nice Guy for me from here on out."

The two dogs danced at her feet, tails wagging madly. They'd come a long way in the weeks since she'd brought them home, after some wrangling with her landlord. At first they'd been skittish, afraid of everything and nothing. Their true personalities—Jack goofy and bold, Apple quieter and more sensitive—were emerging. Soon potential adopters would be able to see that, instead of the fearful, cringing creatures they'd been when they'd come into the shelter. She only hoped they would be adopted together; hard times had bonded the two deeply.

That's what I want. That kind of bond. The kind that says I'm there for you, no matter what.

"Dream on," she muttered as she checked their food and water. If it went well tonight, she might be late. And it certainly seemed like it should go well; Sam was exactly what she'd been looking for.

Or at least he seemed to be, online. She'd been a little wary of using the popular Grave Gulch Singles app, but some of her friends swore by it. She'd trod carefully, and for some reason the fact that there were awful profiles as well as interesting and appealing ones made it seem more genuine to her. She'd messaged with a few guys who seemed nice, but then Sam Rivers had popped up.

That he was an ER doctor here in Grave Gulch—along with her sister Desiree's fiancé, Stavros, also a doctor there, and she kept meaning to ask him about Sam—was what had caught her attention initially, and that he was warm, funny and kind had kept her messaging with him. And eventually chatting on the phone, where his nice voice and self-effacing charm had won her over. The man checked all the boxes, even a few she was embarrassed to admit to, like chiseled good looks and an even more chiseled body; that photo of him at the lake had taken her breath away. It was probably just as well hospital rules prevented him from video chatting; she'd probably get tongue-tied just looking at his handsome face.

But for her, it wasn't just his looks. No, the icing on the cake was Charlie. The picture of Sam with his adorable beagle lovingly licking his cheek had melted her heart. Surely anyone dedicated to saving lives, anyone who could make a dog love him, had to be a nice guy, right?

And wouldn't it be funny if she and Desiree both ended up with doctors? They could share experiences, commiserate on the downsides, and laugh at the weird-ness of life together.

She shouldn't have started getting ready so early, be-cause now she had time to kill. Too much time to kill. And she would absolutely not change clothes yet again; this was a very nice—but not too nice—outfit, suitable for the Grill. Not that they'd throw her out if she showed up in rags, given her father owned the place.

Her phone signaled an incoming text, and the dis-tinctive chime, a short riff from her little sister's favor-ite song, told her Grace was checking in. They'd agreed when Annalise had first started using the app that she would always send Grace the details on any actual dates. She thought Grace was being a bit overly cautious, but wrote it off to her sister being a rookie cop. Yet another Colton in the Grave Gulch PD.

Ready?

As I can be.

Still on for the Grill?

Yes. She would have preferred this first face to face
with the yummy Sam Rivers somewhere else, but it
seemed his heart was set on taking her to the most popular restaurant in town.

Just talked to Mom. She's keeping Dad home, as promised.

She smiled at that. I owe her flowers.

Because Sam didn't yet know it was her father's place.
As a Colton in Grave Gulch she knew people sometimes
made assumptions simply based on the name, so she'd
held that back. Just as, while chatting about her work as
a dog trainer, she'd omitted exactly who she trained them
for; time enough to get into that when they were together
in reality instead of cyberspace.

I hope he's everything he seems to be, Grace sent.

I think he will be.

She did think so, although she was mentally prepared
for a certain amount of disappointment. No one was perfect. And dating a doctor would be intense—there would
no doubt be lots of times his work had to take prece-
dence—but she could handle that. She could always ask
Desiree for advice on how she managed.

She gave a shake of her head as she signed off with
Grace. She hadn't even met the guy in person yet, but
here she was fantasizing about a long-term future with
him. Maybe in person there would be no chemistry, no

spark. Maybe he'd hate her on sight; maybe her streak of rotten dating luck was destined to continue.

Desperate for distraction, she called up her work schedule for tomorrow. Frowned at the reminder that progress reports were due this week; she loved working with the dogs, but she could do without the paperwork. But they would have to be done, because Robert Kenwood ran a tight ship. A former police K-9 handler himself, the man many still called "Sarge," even though he'd retired from the actual force to become the director of the training unit some time ago, was pretty by the book. But she could put up with his meticulousness, because he loved the dogs just as she did.

Just as Sam did. The thought made her smile. And she kept smiling, until she noticed what she'd forgotten until now; she had a scheduled session with Ember tomorrow morning. The lovable black Lab seemed to have a knack for scenting explosives in particular, and Sarge wanted to find out how solid it was. Which would so not please her handler.

Brett Shea.

The man who had saved the now-fiancée of her brother Troy by dismantling a bomb. Troy had told her Brett had sworn to leave such skills behind when he'd left the military. Something he'd never, ever wanted to do again, and yet he had. Because someone had to, and he had the knowledge and skill.

She felt a little flutter of nerves when she thought about that. Thought about him. Tried to quash it, but it persisted. She grimaced at herself. What was wrong with her? Readying for the first in-person meeting with the man who could be exactly what she was looking for, and here she was feeling butterflies over another, entirely unsuitable, unattainable, uninterested guy?

Of course, any woman would probably find the tall, rugged, intensely masculine K-9 officer attractive. Any woman with a pulse, anyway. Funny, she wouldn't have thought she'd be attracted to a redhead, but combined with his startlingly blue, sometimes uncomfortably intense, eyes it was a potent combination. And seemed utterly right. Now she couldn't imagine him without that thick shock of auburn hair.

You look Irish.

And what does an Irishman look like?

You.

That silly exchange when they'd first met, shortly after he'd laterally transferred in from Lansing, had ended with him adopting a very exaggerated brogue and speech pattern she suspected was a clichéd version of the real thing. And when he did, she too easily imagined him in green. Something else she had never spent much time thinking about before he'd walked into the training center.

Sure, and I am. And you are a Colton, aren't ye?

I am.

Back to his ordinary—although she couldn't think of the deep, rough timbre of it as ordinary—voice, and a very flat tone, he'd ended it then. *Safe bet around here, it seems.*

She remembered watching him walk off with Ember, thinking he'd sounded unhappy. At the least wary. She supposed she couldn't blame him. There were a lot of Coltons on the force. And when one of them, her cousin Melissa, was the chief, it made it difficult to make real connections with people sometimes. Which was why she'd sworn off ever dating a Grave Gulch cop. A decision she was content with.

Or had been, until Brett Shea had turned that brilliant blue gaze on her. And started her mind down paths she'd sworn never to travel.

And wasn't going to start now. She had a date, with a sexy, handsome, exciting guy, and it was going to go fabulously.

She was sure of it.

Chapter Two

Detective Brett Shea smiled when Ember's tail started to wag. The clever black Lab knew she was on home turf the minute they walked into the sprawling old stone building that housed the Grave Gulch Police Department. She hung on to her beloved knotted rope tug-of-war toy though. And he let her; she'd earned it after finding that missing kid so quickly this morning.

The building felt normal to him now, too. And much more welcoming than the big, multistory glass-and-concrete box he'd been used to in Lansing, where he'd transferred from. And every face he passed in the hallway was familiar, which had been one of his main goals in coming here. He knew each name and something about them and was working on learning enough to judge their reactions in any given situation, because someday his life or someone else's might depend on it.

Brett headed for his desk to finish his report on a recovered child, who had in fact only wandered a bit far from home and fallen—thankfully without injury—into a gully that hid him from the street above. Ember followed happily, and after he gave her a good solid pat of approval for a job well done, she settled down on the flat pad near his chair, contentedly chewing on the toy.

He frowned as he wrote the disposition on the case. There seemed to be a lot of kid-related stuff going on in Grave Gulch lately. He didn't like that. Dealing with adult problems was bad enough. First there'd been Mary Suzuki's wedding, when sketch artist Desiree Colton's toddler had been grabbed, then just last month, Soledad de la Vega, the owner of Dream Bakes downtown, had gotten caught up in that ugly case that resulted in the horrible death of her best friend and her getting custody of that friend's baby.

And ending up engaged to Palmer Colton. Don't forget that part.

It wasn't enough that he was practically surrounded by Coltons here at the department and in Grave Gulch. It also seemed all of them were on a binge, getting engaged one after the other.

He'd left the big PD in Lansing for many reasons, one of which had been the size of the department. It seemed too big to him; he'd wanted to know his colleagues, know who he could trust to have his back. A holdover from his military days, he supposed.

So here he was now at a department with fewer than thirty sworn officers, which he'd wanted. What he hadn't counted on was that every other one of them seemed to be a Colton, from the chief on down. He knew it wasn't true; it just felt like it. And it seemed lately the town wasn't too happy with that either, but right now the town wasn't happy with a lot of things, and with good reason. Randall Bowe chief among them.

By manipulating evidence, the corrupt forensic scientist had ruined many cases and lives, and cast a long shadow over the department in the process. Especially over the Coltons, because of how many of them there were on the force. Brett had seen more than one sign at the organized protests that bore sentiments such as Nepotism Brings Corruption.

He understood the feeling. He'd certainly dealt with certain people getting special treatment enough in Lansing, although he suspected that was endemic to any capital city. And it wasn't that he didn't like the Coltons he worked with. In fact, his frequent partner, Troy Colton, was one of the best cops he'd ever worked with. He was no slacker or stranger to long hours. It was part of the reason they worked well together. And Desiree was really talented at capturing suspects from descriptions, better than any computer program he'd used; her sketches were uncannily accurate. Even rookie officer Grace Colton showed great promise.

Another Colton, CSI Jillian, had been under a dark cloud with the whole forensics and manipulated-evidence mess. But it appeared she'd been exonerated, though he was withholding judgment on that, or on her at least; there were too many unknowns.

But it still worked out that—he did the math in his head—a good percentage of the department carried the Colton name. And that wasn't including Annalise.

The K-9-trainer Colton.

He made the mental correction automatically. That, at least, had become habit. Now if he could only get it to happen *before* her name popped into his head. He needed to think of her as just that, the police K-9 trainer, and nothing more. She was Ember's trainer, that's all. Not a lovely, blue-eyed blonde with dimples that lit up a room. Not a graceful, caring woman whom dogs seemed to love on sight, dogs whose instincts about people he trusted completely. Because thinking about her that way could only lead to trouble, and he'd had enough of that in his life.

No, it would be much—*much*—better to think of her as…as a kid sister. Yeah, right, that'd do it. It had better. Because getting involved with a Colton would be riskier than most of the bombs he'd disarmed, back in the day in a different uniform. Not only because her cousin was the chief, but because every one of the Coltons was like a bulldog in protecting the other Coltons. The last thing he needed was one—or all—of them coming after him.

And he didn't miss the irony that he'd come here to work at a department small enough to know everyone, hoping it would feel more like a law-enforcement family than a government entity tied to the politics of the capitol, and instead had ended up in the middle of an actual family. A family he wasn't and would never be part of. And in the back of his mind was still the thought that if it ever came down to one of them saving his ass or a Colton's, there was only one way it would go.

He finished up the report and leaned back in his chair. It would be nice to go home on an up note for a change. Maybe he'd finish up that bookcase project. If he could wear Ember out with a tennis-ball session in the huge backyard… The outdoor space had been the main reason he'd chosen the older house. To call the house itself dated would be an understatement, but the exterior, with big trees, shrubs that bloomed without much attention and expansive spaces for Ember, was ideal.

A sudden jab from his empty stomach reminded him food was in order. He'd been running a little lean lately, judging by the fact that he'd had to take his belt in a notch. But he'd been so consumed by this damned Bowe case that eating had fallen a bit on the priority list. For him, anyway—Ember, as always, ate heartily and well. And the dog literally glowed in the dark these days, her coat so shiny it caught and reflected even moonlight on a clear night, ever since Annalise had given him a supplement to add to her food.

Trainer. Ember's trainer.

Disgusted with himself, he shut down his computer and stood up. *Focus on food*, he told himself.

He was in certainly no mood for the flash of the Grill tonight. The Grave Gulch Grill, owned by Annalise's— *Ember's trainer's*—father, Geoff Colton. Nor did he want the bustle and required social interaction at Howlin' Eddie's bar, even if the appetizers were a meal in themselves. He could stop at Mae's, except he didn't really want to go into the diner and sit down while Ember waited in the vehicle, although the dog could be very patient when necessary.

Pizza. That was it. He could call Paola's now and it should be almost ready by the time he got there. Besides, they always threw in a little side of sausage for Ember, too, which he carefully rationed out to her. And carefully didn't mention to Annalise.

Trainer!

"Shea!"

The yell came from the doorway, and he turned to see Chief Colton in the doorway. She was in civilian clothes, obviously on her way out of the station. "Chief?" Brett answered.

"Patrol's working a possible Bowe sighting five minutes ago. Probably nothing again, but thought you'd want to know."

The hunger ratcheted down as adrenaline spiked. Technically he was off duty. Technically he should wait until they called him in, if they found anything. Technically, technically, technically...

But damn it, he wanted this guy. Wanted him bad. If there was anything that chapped him, it was a miscarriage of justice. It had about killed him when his buddy and fellow cop Mitch had been arrested and gone through such hell in Lansing. The man he'd served beside, who had been one of those who had always had his back, had sworn he was innocent of taking bribes. Brett had known he was, but he hadn't been able to do a damned thing about it. Had been unable to find enough evidence to convince anyone otherwise, in a city too big to care about one single officer's certainty. Had been unable to get anyone to listen; no one seemed to care that he knew the man down to the bone, with the kind of knowledge gained under fire.

That Mitch had later been exonerated didn't erase either what he'd gone through, or Brett's feeling of utter helplessness. It was not something he cared for, and one he'd do just about anything to avoid experiencing again. And the best way to insure that was to find the slimy Randall Bowe, who had contaminated dozens of cases, perverting justice according to his own twisted views.

Yes, he wanted the guy. So, he'd swing by the location, and just say he'd been in the area. Grave Gulch was small enough that could be true no matter where he was. Well, compared to Lansing, anyway.

And small was what he'd wanted. He just hadn't counted on dealing with a family like the Coltons.

Hadn't counted on one of them being a woman like Annalise.

"Ready for another game, girl?" he said to Ember, needing the distraction.

The dog was on her feet in an instant, the toy abandoned without thought at the prospect of what she seemed to love most: seeking what he wanted her to find.

Chapter Three

When Annalise saw Sam's face light up her phone—she'd picked the shot of him with his dog Charlie for her contacts, because it made her smile—her first thought was she'd somehow lost track of time and was late.

Had she done it again? Had she slipped into silly ruminations about Brett Shea and lost track of time? All because his dog happened to be on her schedule for tomorrow?

Sure, she was attracted; with those eyes, that tall, lean but muscular body, that way of moving that had her picturing him striding across wild Irish hills somewhere, who wouldn't be? And as far as she knew, he was single, uninvolved. But he was also incredibly intense and focused, and that could be a warning sign. Maybe he was single because there was no room in his life for anything but the job. She knew a lot of those types. Heck, she'd dated a few of them.

But Ember adored him. And Ember was a very smart girl. Annalise had worked with enough K-9s and their handlers to recognize a genuine and deep bond when she saw one, and Brett and the slick-coated black Labrador had that. It was easy, for her at least, to see that he was devoted to the dog and she to him. And that spoke volumes, in Annalise's eyes.

But being a cop hadn't stopped Troy from finding the love of his life. Grace had joked that all the Coltons had better stop drinking the water, because they all seemed to be getting locked into permanent relationships. Annalise had laughed, but her heart hadn't really been in it, because it was true. Most of her siblings and her cousins had done just that, and she felt pretty left out.

Poor, pitiful you.

Even thinking about Brett Shea—too much—was better than whining.

She gave herself an inward shake.

You're not getting involved with a GGPD cop. You. Are. Not. You're going on a date with a great guy, it will go wonderfully and your long trek through the dating desert will be over. And you'll no longer be one of the last Coltons without her soul mate. Your mother will stop trying to set you up, and your father will quit asking when you're going to settle down.

She caught the incoming call in the moment before it would have gone to voice mail, and her hello was no doubt embarrassed because she'd done it again, slipped into pondering Brett Shea instead of focusing on the charming, handsome doctor who wanted to be with her tonight. Sam was exactly what she'd been looking for, hoping for, so why was she standing here mooning over another man?

Maybe all your dating problems aren't men, but you!

"Honey," Sam began, giving her a little thrill. He'd slipped into the endearment quickly, shortly after they'd started actually talking a few days ago, telling her he'd known the moment he'd seen her profile photo with her foster dogs that she was the one he'd been waiting for. "I'm so sorry. We're slammed in the ER, and there was a big crash and lots of injuries."

"Oh, no! Do you have enough staff? Is Stavros there?"

"Who's Stav— Look, I don't have time. I just wanted to tell you I'm so disappointed I have to postpone. I've been looking forward to tonight all week."

"Oh." *Well, that sounded lame.* Even as she thought it, she was wondering why he hadn't seemed to know who Stavros was. Maybe because he was new, he only knew him as Dr. Makris. "I'm sorry, too," she said.

She was more than sorry. All her anticipation about tonight drained away, leaving her feeling…she wasn't sure exactly what. She had the sour thought that she'd somehow brought this on by all her meanderings about Brett Shea. She dismissed that silly idea and tried to focus. "But I understand," she said.

After all, hadn't she just acknowledged to herself that dating a doctor, especially an emergency-room doctor, would have its downside? It was things exactly like this that she'd been thinking of. So how could she really complain? The man took care of people who needed him. So dating him would be complicated, just like…dating a cop.

"I'll make it up to you. We'll reschedule. But I don't want you to miss out, so I'm sending dinner to you."

"What?"

"There's a waiter from the Grave Gulch Grill on the way, with the dinner we were supposed to have. He should be there any moment now."

Her brow furrowed. She knew she'd never given him her address, but had she ever even told him where in town she lived? "But how did you—"

"Sorry, honey, I have to run. Two more patients just arrived. Later. Love you."

The silence was undeniable, he was gone. *Love you?*

Dr. Samuel Rivers had just said he loved her.

Of course he'd said it in haste, in that casual way that didn't mean anything. It certainly didn't mean he'd meant it in the way she was thinking. But still—

Jack and Apple burst into a cacophony of barking and raced over to the front door. Her first instinct was to smile; the two were already acting like guard dogs. That told her they were starting to feel comfortable here, which made her feel good. It would make it easier to transition them to another, forever home. And she had the thought that she would just keep them until someone came along who was willing to take the pair, keeping the devoted friends together.

Her second thought was to wonder if the waiter could already—

The doorbell cut off her wondering. Sam hadn't been kidding when he'd said any moment now. She walked over to where the dogs were, setting her phone down on the table by the door as she leaned in to peer through the peephole. Sure enough, the man standing there—or kid, he looked awfully small—was wearing the black-and-silver apron from the Grill, had a cart holding dishes covered with the standard silver lids, and…a bouquet of pink roses in a vase.

She couldn't help smiling happily. Sure, she was disappointed Sam had had to cancel, but she'd been cancelled on before. It was another indication of her lousy dating history. But no one had ever gone to such lengths to make up for it. If he'd intended to blow her away, he'd succeeded.

"Hush, now," she said to the dogs, and scooted them away from the door. "Sit." They sat, their gazes fastened on her, and her smile widened. "Stay," she added. That command, and the subtext of *Until I say otherwise*, wasn't quite ingrained yet, but it should hold long enough to get the door open for the kid.

Except it wasn't a kid at all. To her surprise, once she had the door open and could see clearly, the waiter was not that young, but merely short and very thin. So thin the apron he wore wrapped around his back and nearly came to the front again. She could only see part of the silver lettering across the front, *rave Gulch Gri,* and she had the inane thought the phrase sounded like some underground party site or something. Then she felt bad; it wasn't his fault he was so thin.

"Hello, Annalise," he said.

He sounded oddly familiar, although she didn't remember ever having seen him before, at the Grill or elsewhere. And it seemed odd he'd addressed her by her first name, but maybe Sam had given him instructions.

She said hello, only then realizing he wasn't wearing the usual name tag. Maybe he'd been in a rush and hadn't had time to grab it. She wondered what Sam had said to explain what he'd wanted done. Home delivery wasn't something the Grill normally did, so it must have been good. Maybe she'd ask. She'd like to hear what he'd said.

Then again, if it was something like *I gotta miss a date and she hasn't put out yet, so I need to keep up the charming,* she'd pass. She'd been through that one before, too.

"Come in," she said, backing out of the way.

The stay hold on the dogs broke, and they darted over to the waiter, not quite growling but making the low sounds that indicated they were not totally pleased with the situation. The man looked down at them warily. Funny, they seemed much bigger next to him, because he was so short.

"It's all right," she hastened to assure him. "They don't bite, but they're kind of new here so a little nervous."

He muttered something she couldn't hear and she wondered if she should be glad. He wheeled the cart past her into the living room, pushing it rather awkwardly, almost crookedly, as if he wasn't used to this at all. But this was how meals were brought to larger groups inside the Grill, so he should be familiar with it. Maybe one of the wheels was off, like a wobbly grocery cart. Or the white tablecloth that covered it had slipped and gotten tangled.

Belatedly she realized the reason was that he wasn't gripping the cart's handle fully with his right hand, but only had his thumb and forefinger wrapped around it. His other three fingers were curled back, as if he was holding something else. Her mind took off, wondering if Sam had sent a note or card along with the meal, to be presented to her in his absence. But then why wouldn't it just be on the table? Or on the plastic clip she could see sticking up out of the bouquet?

"Doesn't it smell wonderful?" the waiter said with a smile. "You're going to really love this."

She frowned. In fact, she couldn't smell anything. But, she reasoned, she hadn't been closed up in a car with it, either. As soon as the silver lids came off the plates, she was sure she would.

He wheeled the cart over to where her small dining table sat, she presumed so he could set the plates on it. She followed, curious now about what Sam had ordered up for the meal. Wondered if he had remembered their chat about their favorite foods.

You love shrimp scampi? I knew you were the one for me.

It had been the first time he'd said that, about her being the one. It had startled her, since it had only been the second time they'd messaged each other. But he'd instantly made it a joke by sending, Too fast? plus an adorable, google-eyed emoji.

She stopped as the waiter positioned the cart. She still couldn't smell anything. Surely if it was scampi she would at least smell the garlic. She glanced at him, about to ask. He was letting go of the cart and turning toward her. His right hand moved, and as he took a step toward her she saw what he held.

She knew what it was. She'd seen tranquilizer darts before, in Dr. Foreman's office. The vet who worked with the police K-9s also handled other animals the force encountered on occasion, and more than once when the officers had had to take action, the creatures had come in with this exact thing embedded in their flesh. A very cranky badger she remembered in particular.

It took a split second to get past the incongruity of it. Her first thought was for the dogs, after the way he'd looked at them. Did he carry it because he was afraid of them? Were they in danger of being tranquilized because they were still not-quite-growling at him?

And then he took another step toward her. And he raised that hand with the dart.

Far too late it hit her. The dart wasn't for the dogs.

It was for her.

Chapter Four

Brett trusted that Ember knew what she was doing. But then, he trusted her more than he did anyone these days. And certainly more than he did any other female, of any species. So he followed as silently as he could as the dog moved along, questing, searching, for Randall Bowe.

They were on a quiet residential street, lined with small, neat little cottage-type houses. He couldn't imagine what Bowe would be doing here, unless it was looking for someplace to hide.

They were one house down from the corner when he heard the scream from the next house. A very frightened scream. A woman. Ember's head came up sharply. Dogs were barking furiously, smaller ones judging by the pitch of the sound.

It wasn't a tough call. Given how long he'd been after Bowe he wasn't really optimistic that some random maybe sighting was going to yield anything—and a crisis was in progress now, with a woman possibly in danger. He snapped out the command to Ember and headed for the house.

There was a lit window on the side nearest them. He went for it at a run; he needed an assessment before he charged in there. Wouldn't do to get the woman killed in the process.

Things hit him in rapid succession. He noticed two people. A room away from the front, so he could only see in pieces. Little guy. No sign of a gun in his hand. Woman, blonde, fighting back. With something large, round, silver, metallic. He even heard the sound as she connected.

The guy reeled back a little. Probably hadn't expected the fight. *Good for her.*

Brett ran for the front door. Got there just as it was yanked open. Someone barreled into him, and they both staggered back. He grabbed at the other person. The porch light was dim, but in a split second he registered curves, blonde and a familiar scent. The woman. For an instant he felt something crazy, something that had no place in this scenario. *Heat. A special kind of heat.*

He shook it off. Shifted his hold from containment to support. Ember gave an oddly welcoming bark but he had no time to ponder that. The guy was already out the door behind them and running.

He swore silently, trying to disentangle himself. The woman's back was to him, and Ember was oddly close, unusual for her. He dropped the leash and snapped out the command to track. Labs weren't much on attacking, but he'd pit his girl's nose against any dog's for following a scent.

A scent.

It hit him in that instant, before he'd even gotten a good look at the woman.

It was the same sweet, flowery scent Annalise wore.

He pulled back a little as the woman got her feet under

her. But she was shaking, so he didn't let go. He heard her take in a big gulp of air. And then she turned around.

Crap. It *was* Annalise.

Well, that explained the moment of unexpected physical response. His brain might not have known yet it was her, but his body had known instantly. He wanted to back off, feeling more than a little singed, but she was clearly still very rattled, and almost clinging to him. And he was certain she still hadn't registered who he was; she hadn't even really looked at him.

He heard a car start and the bark of tires on asphalt as it left at high speed. In the distance he could see what looked like a midsize silver sedan racing through the halo of a street light. Great. The most ubiquitous kind of vehicle in the universe. And halfway down the block he could see—barely, since she was the color of the night—Ember sitting at the edge of the street, her signal that the trail had ended. No doubt that was where that sedan had been parked.

He freed one hand and grabbed his phone to call it in. And then he let out a piercing whistle to call Ember back to him. Ember, who, contrary to her idiot handler, had immediately known Annalise. The dog started their way, dragging her lead and looking dejected, as she always did after a fruitless search.

"How could I be so stupid?"

Annalise's words were barely a whisper and clearly distressed. And suddenly he didn't want to back off at all, he wanted to hold, to comfort. And that, even odder, scared him more than the realization of who it was he had his arms around.

And then Ember barked. He looked up, saw her again sitting, but this time on the grassy area next to the sidewalk. And the dejection had vanished. Which meant she'd found something, something connected. That familiar tension of the hunt shot through him, and he wanted to go to the dog, see what she'd found. But he didn't want to leave the victim—*damn, Annalise*—here alone and still shaken. So he called out to Ember to hold.

Then he heard a siren. The sound seemed to shake her out of her distress. Annalise's head came up. And immediately her eyes widened. "Brett."

"Yeah," he said, rather inanely. And belatedly let go of her at last. And felt a sudden chill entirely inexplicable, given it had to still be hovering around seventy degrees after a day that had nearly hit eighty.

She let out a soft sigh. "No wonder I felt—"

She broke off, and even in the faint illumination of the porch light he saw her cheeks darken.

You will not ask her to finish that sentence.

He snapped the order at himself fiercely. Get to business, that was what he needed to do. First things first.

"Are you all right? Did he hurt you?"

"I… Yes. He never really touched me."

One corner of his mouth quirked. "Probably because you startled him, wailing on him with that—what was that?"

"A cloche. A plate cover."

This time his mouth twisted wryly. When he ordered in, it didn't usually involve actual plates, covers and a tablecloth. More like paper bags and ketchup in little containers. "Sometimes you have to use what's handy," he said. "Good job." She'd earned that, at least.

"I… I think he grabbed my purse on the way out. He had something in his hand. And he'd already dropped the dart."

Brett went still. "The what?"

"He had a tranquilizer dart. Like you use for wild animals."

All his bemusement at how he'd happened to end up here, of all places, at this perfect time, vanished. A rather fierce anger started to build. "He was going to tranq you?"

"God, I was so stupid. I let him in because I thought he was—"

She stopped as a marked unit slammed to a halt in the driveway. The siren shut off and two uniforms jumped out.

"You're all right? I need to go see what Ember found."

He could almost feel her gathering her composure. Saw her draw herself up, steady herself. "Go. See what that smart girl of yours found."

Once the officers were there, he left her to explain, now that she was calmer, and headed for his dog. Well trained—mostly by the woman he'd just left—she held position as she watched him come. She was sitting just outside the circle of light from the streetlamp, but just inside that circle was a small, oblong object that caught the beam in an odd way. It wasn't until Brett got closer he realized it was a small purse with beads on it, which explained the sparkle effect.

"Good girl," he told the dog, and she wiggled happily. But he hadn't released her from that last command, and she held. She was amazing, Ember was.

He pulled out his phone and took a couple of photos of where the purse lay from different angles, then got out one of the latex gloves he always carried, pulled it on and picked up the small bag. It apparently closed with a magnet, so he couldn't be sure if the guy had had time to rifle through it. It wasn't empty in any case, so Annalise—just thinking her name made him suck in a breath at how close she'd come to being hurt, or worse—would have to tell them what if anything was missing.

He grabbed up Ember's lead and headed back to the house. The house he'd carefully avoided knowing anything about, not just the address but even the neighborhood. Annalise was in the front yard, her arms wrapped around herself as if it was winter and snow was blowing in.

At his request one of the officers who'd arrived got him an evidence bag out of the trunk of their unit. Then Brett walked over to Annalise, who was clearly startled to see her purse.

"Ember found it."

"Of course she did." She managed a smile and a "Good girl," for the dog. "He dropped it?"

Brett nodded. "Whether accidentally or intentionally, I don't know. But it's not empty, so I need you to look and see if anything's missing. Without taking anything out, if you can."

She nodded. With his gloved hand he held it open for her to look. She leaned in, and he realized there wasn't much light. He pulled the penlight he also always carried out and flicked it on to shine into the bag's interior.

"Thanks," she murmured, still focused on the small purse. "He opened it," she said after a moment. "The cash I had is gone."

"How much?"

"Not a lot. Ride-home money. Just in case." Careful, he thought. Not surprising. "My driver's license is there."

"Phone?"

"I had taken it out to answer…" Her voice broke for a

moment. Then she seemed to steady herself. "To answer the call that started this mess."

He wanted to know more about that, would need to for the report, but for now he stuck to the matter at hand. "Wallet?"

She shook her head. "It's doesn't fit in this bag, so I took the license out. Just for tonight."

"Special night?" he asked neutrally.

"It was supposed to be," she said, sounding more humiliated than anything.

"I gathered," he said, his tone dryer than he'd meant it to be.

She looked up at him then, as if puzzled. Then looked back into the purse. And once more he saw her cheeks redden, and knew she'd realized the edge of a small foil packet was visible. "That's…another just in case."

"Always wise to be prepared," he said, and was proud he'd managed a more neutral tone this time. Especially when he was trying to deny that the idea of Annalise Colton going on a date with a condom in her purse unsettled him.

But he had no more time to think about it, because three vehicles pulled up in rapid succession. And out of them poured… Coltons. Troy didn't surprise him. That he had his sister Desiree with him did, a little, although neither was a problem. He and Troy worked well together, and Desiree never failed to thank him for his part in searching for her little boy when he'd been kidnapped in an effort to force the department to reopen an old case. He supposed Grace's arrival shouldn't surprise him either; he knew the sisters were close. Word had obviously spread through the PD that the incident involved one of their own. He wondered if anything else could have gotten them to respond like this.

And then a tall redhead got out of the last car, and he groaned inwardly. The woman strode toward them with as much command presence as any officer he'd worked with. As well she should.

So even the chief of police rolls out after hours—for another Colton.

He understood, sort of, even though this kind of family closeness wasn't something he'd ever had. The Coltons were a tight-knit bunch, and lately they'd been under siege. It was only natural that they'd pull together, knowing they could trust each other but not sure about anyone else.

Including him. He was still an outsider, even after all these months. And he felt it more than ever as Chief Melissa Colton came to a halt beside them. And in that moment, if she'd ordered him to hand everything over to Troy to investigate, he'd do it without a qualm.

Hell, he'd do it gratefully. And take Ember, the only female in his life at the moment, home for a well-earned treat and a tennis ball session. And forget all about this… whatever it was.

And the way Annalise Colton had felt in his arms.

Chapter Five

"You want this?"

Annalise looked up at Brett's words, but saw he was talking to Troy. Who was looking at Brett rather oddly. Did Troy want *what*? Apparently her brother was puzzled too, because his brows lowered as he answered.

"You want to hand this case off?"

Brett shrugged. "Your call. She's your sister."

Troy looked at Brett as Annalise watched them both, curious. Or maybe in desperate need of distraction.

"Some would say that's exactly why I shouldn't take it," Troy said, his voice inflectionless in that way she knew meant he was testing, that he wanted to know how Brett would answer.

"Some would," Brett agreed.

Something in his expression made Annalise think that Brett would be one who would think exactly that—that Troy would have a conflict of interest. Which didn't surprise her—she'd known he had a solid, ethical core when it came to the job. She suspected that was one of the reasons he'd left the big city department to come here; too many there didn't have the same ethics.

And now he thinks...what? That GGPD is a Colton-

family-run organization? Maybe even worse than the big city?

Sure, there were a lot of them working for the department in various capacities, but it wasn't like that. It wasn't anything like that. No matter what the media and the protesters said.

Another thought hit her. He didn't believe all the awful stories going around, did he? That the Colton family was somehow at fault for Bowe's actions? That the mishandling of evidence that had resulted in wrongful convictions and acquittals was the fault of her family? He'd never said much about it, but then, they didn't have long, involved chats when she was working with Ember, or when they were doing so together. *Because you don't dare.*

But Troy had ethics, just like Brett had. And he proved it now by saying, "Now that we know she's okay, I'll get everybody out of your way." And a moment later he made good on the promise, shooing everyone away, saying, "Let the man do his job."

Annalise saw Brett watching, assessing, as the Coltons backed off. Including the chief. Then, at Brett's suggestion they stay out of the way of the CSIs, she led him—and the three dogs now present—down the hall to the second bedroom that served her as an office.

She realized she'd been focusing on recent troubles to keep from focusing on what had actually happened tonight. And now she was going to have to explain. To the person she least wanted to explain to.

She wasn't sure she understood exactly what was going on in the first place. After she'd told him the details of what had happened tonight and Brett started asking questions and taking notes, she knew she was watching the detective he was at work. It was a strange feeling, to see this side of him.

"You've never seen this guy before?"

"No. But he had on the Grill apron. I thought he must be new."

His mouth quirked. She'd always liked the way he did that. "Your sister Grace already called your father. Nobody new hired in the last three months. And no one matching this description."

"Oh."

"Did you notice anything else about him?"

Her brow furrowed. "His voice seemed familiar, but I couldn't place it. But nothing else other than he was short and thin and had a scraggly sort of beard... I'm afraid when I saw that dart I freaked and struck out."

"That may well have saved you from much worse. We'll have you do a sketch as soon as...your sister can get set up. While the details are fresh."

She nodded. She knew Desiree was very good at what she did, and she'd at least feel comfortable with her. More than she could say for being with Brett Shea.

"What about the date you were supposed to have tonight?"

A little jolt went through her. *Sam.* She'd have to tell Sam what had happened, that the waiter had tried to attack her. And her father, who would be furious that one of his employees—

"You met this guy online? On a dating app?"

When he said it out loud like that it sounded...pitying. Or maybe it was just that it was him saying it. And that made her feel a bit snippy. "Yes. You have a problem with that?"

"Not for me to judge."

She wasn't sure why she felt the need to prod. "But you'd never do it?"

He looked up from his notepad then. "Not an issue. I'm not looking." He glanced downward to where Ember had plopped on the floor to patiently wait. Unlike her two fosters, who were clearly overstimulated by all the excitement. "Ember's the only girl in my life."

She looked down at the sleek black Lab who was one of the easiest dogs she'd ever had to train. Then she looked back at her master and said with the smile the animal always brought to her, "She'll never let you down."

"I know," he said softly.

His love for Ember was so clear in his voice it made the last of the edginess that had made her push at him drain away and she answered him. "My friends were nagging me to try the app, and—"

He waved that off. Obviously he didn't care about the sorry state of her love life. Or the lack thereof.

"Who started it?"

"Contact, you mean?" He nodded in turn. "He texted me first. He loves dogs—he has an adorable beagle named Charlie—and when he saw I was a dog trainer he reached out. I didn't say who I trained for though. Some people get spooked if I say I train for the PD."

"Might have been better if you had." He grimaced, as if he regretted the words. "Never mind. So how long before you actually spoke?"

She thought, although she didn't quite see why it mattered. "It was a while. He's an ER doctor at the hospital here, and always busy, so texts were more convenient for him."

He looked a little puzzled then, as if he didn't quite get what she was saying.

"Did you ever initiate a call to him?"

"No, I couldn't because it might interrupt him in the middle of an urgent case." She gave him a smile. Somehow talking to Brett about the man in her life made her feel…something. She wasn't sure what to call it. "He's very dedicated to his work."

"Right," he muttered. And before she could point out that so was he, he asked, "Did you ever do a video call?"

"No. He can't do that at the hospital, for privacy reasons, and he's there so much…" She shrugged. Surely he must understand, being a cop, a job that was as consuming as being a doctor. "Besides, he said he needed a new phone because the front-facing camera doesn't work well, keeps dropping out."

His expression was unreadable now. And his voice became utterly neutral and businesslike. Somehow that was unsettling. "So you've never actually seen him."

What was he getting at? "Oh, I've seen a ton of photos," she said, pulling the phone she'd grabbed up before they'd come in here. She called up the shot with Charlie first and showed him, then swiped through several others. Sam was a truly handsome man—he looked great in even casual photos—and she felt a little burst of satisfaction as Brett looked; at least he'd know a good-looking, successful guy wanted to date her. Why that mattered she wasn't sure, but it did.

"And tonight was the first time you were going to meet in person?"

She nodded. "But they had a rush at the emergency room and he couldn't leave. He's very dedicated."

His expression never changed, but the questions came faster now. "Did you check his other social media? Does he have a lot of friends there?"

"Look, I don't see what this has to do with—"

"Does he?"

This was definitely Brett the cop. He was acting like Troy who, as their father said, was fierce once he got his teeth into a case. *Just answer, then you can call Sam. He'll make you feel better.*

"Not really," she said. "He doesn't have much of a presence. No time."

"Where does he live?"

"I…don't know, exactly. He's rooming with a fellow doctor until he finds his own place." She was starting to get very uneasy. Somehow all these things she'd accepted as they'd gradually happened, when strung together like this, sounded…wrong.

"Did he ever ask where you lived? Maybe under the guise of looking for that place for himself?"

Under the guise? "Yes, but I only told him the street. But the Grill would have access to my address, too, for the delivery because my father has it."

Brett's jaw tightened. Because she had mentioned her father? Troy had told her once Brett was wary of being surrounded by Coltons. But this was different. Wasn't it?

He excused himself to make a couple of phone calls. She watched him walk away. When she realized she was admiring the way he moved—again—she chastised herself inwardly. Tried to focus on something else. Like being grateful her parents were out of town, or they would have already descended on her. Like what she was going to say to Sam when she called to tell him what had happened. He'd be upset, obviously. He'd probably feel—

Brett came back. And she didn't like his expression. He drew in a deep breath. "We'll need your phone."

"What?"

"We'll need to pull the texts and those photos."

Annalise stared at him. "Of Sam? Why?"

"The Grill didn't send anyone, and no one matching the description you gave works there."

"But Sam—"

"Annalise." Something in the way he said her name made her go silent. And then, rather gently for the usually businesslike detective, he said, "There is no Dr. Sam Rivers at Grave Gulch Hospital."

She gaped at him. "What?"

"In fact, there's no Dr. Sam or Samuel Rivers registered in the state of Michigan."

This was bizarre. Of course there was; she'd been in touch with him dozens of times. "I...don't understand."

"I had Desiree check with her fiancé. Stavros confirmed it. No such person at the hospital."

"What are you saying?"

"I'm saying," he said, his tone even more gentle now, which made her conversely more edgy, "you've been catfished."

Chapter Six

Annalise supposed she could be more embarrassed, although she wasn't quite sure how. What she did know was that she had never felt so stupid, so played in her entire life. And that Brett Shea knew it—knew it all—was just the sour frosting on a bitter cake.

She wanted nothing more than for him to leave, so she could hole up in her room and feel nauseated at her own stupidity. When she walked back out into her living room—at least having the presence of mind to leave Jack and Apple in the office—and saw the cart, this time she really did feel nauseous. She suddenly realized she'd never had quite enough empathy for what crime victims had to go through afterward.

But Brett was like Troy; once he had his teeth in a case, he wouldn't let go until it was done. And that's what she was now. A case.

Sam didn't exist. It wasn't even that he was a player, or a liar, a phony, a faker, maybe an orderly claiming to be a dedicated doctor to gain her interest and trust. He did not exist. He never had.

When Desiree had finished the sketch from Annalise's description plus some input from Brett, Annalise practically recoiled from looking at it. Not only because she knew she'd had a lucky escape, but because mentally she was comparing the decidedly unattractive image with the string of photos "Sam" had sent her. At the beach, in the gym, in hospital scrubs, he'd been beautiful in them all. This man was anything but.

And Brett Shea knew it all. Including how stupid she'd been. In fact, he had her phone right now, although it was now in a plastic evidence bag.

She glanced over at him, standing across the room—she wished they'd move that damned reminder of a cart out of her dining room—on his phone again. She'd watched numbly as he had taken hers—which was now prime evidence—and sent the photos of…whoever it really was, to someone else at the department. But now he was still holding hers up to look at.

Oh, God, what if Brett was reading the texts? He probably was. He probably had to, to see if there were any clues there. He'd see her sappy writings, the silly stuff she'd written when… Sam had texted late at night, saying he'd just gotten home off a rough shift and needed some sunlight in his life. She'd been charmed. She'd been captivated.

She'd been fooled. Utterly and completely. And Brett would now see every facet of her idiocy. She felt color flooding her cheeks again at just the thought, although she was a little amazed she had the energy to even be embarrassed any longer.

One of the CSIs on scene looked up at him and asked if he was on with Ellie and Brett nodded. GGPD's tech expert, Ellie Bloomberg, was probably looking into the app.

Great. I can just imagine how that conversation went. "Hey, Ellie, got an idiot woman here who got herself catfished. Best part? She's a Colton."

She wished she'd never heard of the word. Wished it only applied to rather ugly, bottom-feeding fish.

Only then did it strike her how appropriate the word was. Bottom feeders. And ugly.

She didn't know how long she'd been standing there staring at the delivery cart she'd so blithely let into her house when she sensed a warmth behind her. It felt good, because she was feeling chilly. Which was strange because it had been a typically warm August day and after she was ready she'd turned off the air conditioning because she'd been going out.

She knew how out of it she was when she belatedly realized the warmth behind her was a person.

"Oh!" She managed to keep her balance despite her startled spin, but barely.

Brett. Of course. Prove to him even more you're an oblivious fool.

"You okay?"

Did he have to sound so…gentle? *Of course he did. He thinks he's dealing with an oblivious fool.* But that didn't mean she had to like it. She crossed her arms in front of her and glared at him. "Don't patronize me."

He blinked, drew back. "What?"

"I know I was laughably stupid, a complete fool. I don't need you treating me like a child to remind me."

He was silent for a long moment and she kept hearing, not her words but her tone, echoing in the air. She hadn't meant to sound quite so belligerent. But she was so embarrassed about everything, she couldn't seem to help it.

"Given the circumstances," he said finally, "if I had walked in here and found you dead on the floor it would not have been a surprise. That I didn't is nothing to do with me happening to be here. It was you. You're the one who fought back, with the only weapon you had at hand. That's not something I laugh at. It's something I applaud."

She stared at him. That had been undeniably sincere. And his tone had been the polar opposite of her own: warm, gentle and understanding. It made her feel like a starched shirt on a humid day, suddenly wilted. She reached out blindly for one of the dining table chairs, then recoiled as she realized it would put her sitting right by that damned cart.

"I'm sorry," she said. "I just—" Her voice cracked.

"Hush. I know."

He took her arm then and led her out to the living room. She barely made it to the couch before her knees gave out. He nudged aside her stack of books so he could sit on the edge of the coffee table facing her. Again she felt chilled. And then she realized she was shivering. Actually shivering. In August.

"I can't… I don't know…what's wrong."

"What you're feeling now is the fade," Brett said gently. "Your adrenaline spiked, gave you the power to protect yourself. It hangs around for a while afterward, takes some time to clear your system. Makes you edgy even after the crisis is over. But when your mind and body accept that you're safe again, it fades, and then the crash hits."

"Sounds like you've been there before," she said before she thought, then groaned inwardly. Of course he had; he was a cop. She just hadn't expected him to be so understanding. So gentle. So kind.

So caring.

Stop it! Stop reading things into him just being a good cop.

She pressed her hands together and jammed them between her knees, trying to stop the shaking. Grabbing at the first thing that popped into her mind, which hadn't quite gotten the message it could slow down now, she asked, "Why were you here? In the neighborhood, I mean."

"Got a report on a possible suspect sighting."

Her eyes widened. "Tell me I don't have a serial killer roaming my street along with that…that…" She shook her head sharply.

"No. Not him."

She let out a relieved sigh. The thought of a murderer like Len Davison roaming freely was bad enough without thinking he was in her neighborhood. Then shook her head again, slowly this time. "I don't know what's happening to this town."

"People come to smaller places for lots of reasons. Some to get away from what they hate about big cities. Some because they think the people are nicer. And some think the pickings will be easier."

She wrapped her arms around herself again as the chill continued. "Well, I certainly proved that last one right, didn't I? Stupid me, fantasizing about a real future, wondering if I could handle a life with a very busy, dedicated doctor. Thinking I'd finally found what I was looking for."

He was silent for a long moment, long enough that she looked at him, almost afraid of what she'd see in his face, in his bright blue eyes. Sympathy, sure, she could handle that. But pity? Not so much. Him thinking she was a stupid fool? Even worse.

"Don't say it," she muttered.

"Say what?"

"Whatever you're thinking."

"Just wondering what, exactly, you were looking for."

Her mouth twisted. She hoped it looked cynical rather than what it was, an effort to keep her emotions at bay. If she started crying on top of everything else, she'd never be able to face the man again. She could just imagine her trying to dodge him when he brought Ember into her office, making someone else collect the dog and take her back, so she never had to lay eyes on his tall, well-built, masculine self again. Never had to look into those bottomless blue eyes.

"Annalise?"

She gave a sharp shake of her head. "Looking for? Oh, not much. Just Mr. Right. Just true love. Just happy forever, like almost everybody else in my family seems to have found this year."

She could have sworn he gave the slightest, barely perceptible nod of his head. Understanding? Or because she'd confirmed what he already thought? Or did she just think he'd nodded because a strand of his hair had fallen forward over his forehead? She liked the way it did that. Just as she liked so much else.

And she should not be thinking about those things at all. Especially not now.

"They have been dropping like flies since I've been here," he said.

Is that how he saw people finding the loves of their lives? Dropping like flies? Now there was cynical. And she didn't like the way he'd said it, either. "Is that why you left Lansing? Run through the supply of casual hookups?" She nearly gasped at how completely nasty that had sounded. She didn't do that. "I'm sorry. That was very snarky of me."

He'd never even blinked. "Glad to hear it," he said neutrally.

She did blink. What was he saying? That he was glad she now knew that was all he was interested in, romantically? Why would he care, unless he—

"It means you're reviving a little, after the shock. So maybe we can get to a few more questions."

Of course. He was the consummate cop; all he cared about was the case. This was not at all personal for him. She was the one who was off-kilter. Her mind making silly leaps into forbidden territory.

"Right," she muttered. Then, with an effort, she said as briskly as she could manage, "Ask away."

He began by asking questions she would have expected, what she and the nonexistent "Sam" had talked about in the beginning. And that he'd asked early on if she was related to the police Coltons.

"Did you save all your texts?"

"Yes," she admitted, wondering how silly that sounded, that she'd saved them thinking one day she and… Sam might read back over them and laugh at how their relationship had begun.

When he asked her, handing her the phone now encased in an evidence bag like her purse, she went through her messages. She found the first texts, the beginning of the…luring. The seduction.

The scam. Sam's scam. It rhymed. God, she was descending into lunacy.

She handed the phone back, knowing she had no choice, and that now she would get to sit here and watch this man, of all men, read through her miserable attempt at a love life.

"Well, that will make things interesting," Brett murmured.

"What?"

"That's what he said, when you eventually told him you were related to some of 'those' Coltons. That it would make things interesting."

"So?"

"Kind of an odd thing to say."

"It was…new. I just thought he didn't know what else to say. You must know how some people react when they find out you're a cop or connected to the police somehow." She paused before asking, "Or do you only go out with people who already know?"

He never looked up from the screen. "Told you, I don't."

"So you're what, a monk on the side?"

That made him look up, and she couldn't deny she felt a jab of satisfaction. But he didn't answer. Which didn't surprise her, since she'd slipped into snark again. What was it about this guy that sent her off the rails so easily?

No, it wasn't him. It had to be what had happened tonight. She grabbed for some semblance of composure and asked, "Why was what he said odd?"

"Said a certain way, it could be a response to a challenge."

She frowned. "A challenge?"

"Like when you find out a suspect you didn't know was armed has a weapon. It makes things more interesting."

Annalise nearly gaped at him. "Interesting? It makes

things interesting?" He merely raised his eyebrows at her. "I swear, men," she muttered.

"Guilty," he said, and looked back at the screen.

You certainly are.

She sank back into the couch cushions, wondering just how much more humiliation she would have to endure. Her brain was spinning now, and she closed her eyes. But then she saw his face, that nasty little man with his dart, and they snapped open again.

It was going to be a very, very long night.

Chapter Seven

She was, all things considered, doing fairly well, Brett thought. Obviously embarrassed. Maybe more embarrassed than anything, which he found a little odd, considering what Annalise might well have narrowly escaped. Of course, she was still processing that the guy she'd connected with on that app didn't really exist. And clearly the possibility had never even occurred to her. He understood. As well-known as the phenomenon was, as often as it happened, somehow it was always a shock when it happened to you.

He wasn't sure if the fact that apparently she was that innocent was reason to feel bad for her, or to be admired. That trusting nature had always boggled him. That she seemed to have it surprised him more than most. True, while she wasn't on the department, she worked with a lot of officers, and had a lot of cops or people who worked with them in her immediate family. And then of course there was Chief Colton, her cousin. You'd think she would have been more aware just listening to them talk.

Did it take effort to keep that kind of outlook? He didn't know; he'd never tried. He'd grown up with a man whose biggest lesson had been to expect the worst of people, because you'd rarely be disappointed. He'd also never experienced the kind of big family the Coltons had, more than a dozen of them here in Grave Gulch alone. Not to mention the others, closely and loosely connected across the country. He'd asked Troy, whenever he'd seen the name in the news somewhere, if that was another distant branch of his family. He'd done it jokingly, but then realized the answer was almost always yes. It had gotten so that any time he saw the name, he assumed the connection.

Annalise had lapsed into silence for now, while he made some notes and mentally organized the report he was going to have to write. Which was going to have to be damned near perfect, since it involved a Colton. He foresaw a long night ahead, in more ways than one.

Then he heard her suck in an audible breath. He looked up, saw her expression. And realized the possible endgame had finally hit her.

He grimaced inwardly; he should have thought more about what he was going to say when this inevitably happened. No one was *that* naive.

"What do you think he wanted?" she asked, her voice unsteady and quiet.

"No way to be sure, yet," he said, keeping his tone very level.

"Rape? Murder?"

"Annalise, there's no reason to go there yet."

"Yet. So either is a possibility."

Or both. The grim thought had been in his head ever since she'd mentioned the tranquilizer dart. And the thought of this woman, this kind, warm, dog-loving woman, as that kind of victim did more than unsettle him, it made him feel a chill inside he rarely felt anymore. He'd seen a lot, both in his prior job in Lansing and in the military before that. He'd seen horrible, bloody things he wished he could forget but knew he never would. He'd seen first hand and cleaned up the aftermath of a kind of cold-bloodedness that had forever changed his view of mankind. It was hard to find any kind of trust when you'd seen people butchered and children blown to pieces.

But the thought of Annalise, who hadn't lost that capacity to trust, suffering that kind of fate...

What if she hadn't had the nerve she'd had, to fight back, give herself a chance to escape? What if she hadn't and he'd been even just a minute later? What were the odds of the waiter even being here, on her street at this moment? Brett didn't know, didn't even want to think about it. It had happened the way it had, and she'd had the presence of mind and the nerve to do what she'd done. So in the end, stacked up against that, maybe her naivete didn't really matter.

She was staring down at her hands, fingers knotted together, in her lap. She was no longer shaking, but he suspected that was a conscious effort on her part.

"If you hadn't been here," she began shakily.

"Annalise, you saved yourself."

"He would have caught up with me. Stupid shoes. Impossible to run in."

He glanced at the heels she'd had on, kicked off when she'd sat down on the couch. Strappy, summery things that seemed indeed impossible to run in. Hell, to him they looked impossible to walk in. He didn't know how women did it.

But he knew why. "But sexy," he said, and regretted it the instant the words were out. She gave him a startled look, and that alone told him he'd strayed into inappropriate. What was it about her that had him not just thinking dangerous things, but saying them?

Maybe it was that he rarely saw her out of her element. It was almost always at the training center, a repurposed old jail. She was the main trainer at the facility, the one Sergeant Kenwood said was the best, and the reason why had quickly become obvious once he'd seen her working not just with Ember but the other dogs, as well. The first time he'd seen her put the big sable German shepherd Bear through his paces, he'd been convinced.

At the training center, she was relaxed, confident and happy, working with the animals she clearly loved. Here and now, understandably, she was an entirely different person. Shaken, and probably scared now that she'd realized how this night could have ended.

He'd seen women in similar situations lots of times. His job was to deal with the crime, not the emotions. That's what counselors were for, and he carried around their business cards for just that reason.

So why did seeing Annalise so shaken, and knowing she'd had a narrow escape from what could have been horrific, have him feeling like he should do something, anything, to comfort her?

Finally he said the only positive thing he could think of. "They're almost done." He nodded toward the CSI techs who were starting to wheel out the delivery cart. She merely glanced and nodded. "Shall I call your family back?"

Her gaze shot to his face then. "No!" He blinked at the harsh exclamation. "No," she repeated, more calmly. "Absolutely not. It's embarrassing enough that you have to…know all this."

"I'm a cop, Annalise. I've seen worse. Much worse."

"I know that. That's not what I— Never mind," she said, cutting off whatever she'd been about to say.

Not what she meant? Then what did she mean? That it was embarrassing not that an officer in general knew what had happened, but that he, specifically did?

Do not go there, Shea.

For once he followed his own order. After all, it was obvious what she wanted, judging by what she thought she'd found in the nonexistent Dr. Sam Rivers. The texts had made it quite clear: long term, with an eye toward permanence. The kind of thing he had no interest in at all. He'd tried that once, a time or two, and it had ended in a debacle both times. That it was for completely different reasons both times had seemingly made it clear he was the problem, and so he'd sworn off.

When his phone rang he was almost relieved. Knowing the victim in any case made it more complicated, but this was really getting to him.

It was Ellie. "Excuse me," he said and got up to walk a few feet away. He didn't expect anything that would upset Annalise even more, but at this point he wasn't taking the chance.

He listened to Ellie's report, amazed as always at how much she managed to find out so quickly. And in this case she had a lot. And it put a different cast to this whole incident. He thanked her, then put his phone back in his pocket and walked back to once more sit opposite Annalise.

"It's…different than we thought," he said.

Her head came up. "Better or worse?"

"A little of both. He's very careful, but Ellie dug into the app, traced IP addresses and worked her way back to one. She tracked that one and ran a county-wide search and the provider—" He stopped, shaking his head. "Let's just call it magic, okay?"

To his surprise, Annalise smiled. "Okay. What did she find?"

"Bottom line, he's done this same thing before. At least twice here in the county, and those cases are still open. Ellie's spreading the net wider now."

She went still. "Was anyone hurt?"

"No. He apparently doesn't harm his victims, so you weren't in physical danger." He gave her a crooked smile. "I'd say you did more damage to him. His ears are probably still ringing, the way that lid clanged on his head."

That got him a smile in return. And more steadily now she said, "What else?"

He nodded. "This is going to sting a bit. His MO is to pretend to be a wealthy do-gooder. So far he's presented as an oil magnate, a big-shot lawyer, and in your case a dedicated doctor."

She winced, but said only, "Go ahead." She was definitely getting her feet under her again.

"He lures in his victim, which he's very, very good at, *hits all the right notes*, Ellie said. Then when the hook is set, he gets into his victim's home with his little dart, tranqs her then steals anything of value and portable."

She blinked, drew back slightly. "Wait…all this was to stage a robbery?"

"So it seems. At least, that's what happened in the other two cases we know about. You're the only one who's stopped him in the act."

Even as he said it his brow furrowed. *Stopped him in the act.* He didn't like the thought that had struck him as he'd heard his own words.

"What?" she asked, clearly seeing his change in expression. "Stopping him couldn't be a bad thing."

"Of course not. Is anything else missing, besides your purse?"

She looked as if she was having trouble processing this shift in perspective. "I… I don't—" Then, suddenly, she was on her feet. "Oh, no."

She ran over to the table beside the front door, where she'd said her purse had been. CSI had already dusted for prints there, so he followed but didn't try to stop her. Then she knelt down to search on the floor, clearly hoping something had simply fallen. But tonight she didn't have that kind of luck. When she straightened, there were tears glistening in her eyes.

He had to again resist the urge to comfort. "What?"

"Gran's bracelet. It was here on the table—I was going to wear it tonight."

"Bracelet? Valuable?"

"To a thief…yes, valuable. It was a diamond bracelet, worth quite a bit." She made a low, harsh sound, as if she were fighting breaking into sobs. After a moment she managed to say, with a clearly strained effort, "To me, it's priceless. My grandmother left it to me, specifically."

Somehow it was the attempt at staying calm that tipped him over the edge into doing something he never did: make a promise he couldn't be sure of keeping.

"I'll get it back for you, Annalise. I'll find this scumbag and get your grandmother's bracelet back."

"I…" She sucked in a breath. "Thank you. I hope you can."

Then with an effort that was visible she steadied herself. She reached out again, touched the table, then looked at her fingertip, dusty with fingerprint powder. Crime-scene investigation was by nature a messy process, and he remembered a victim back in the city who had bemoaned that the cleanup afterward was like going through the crime all over again.

"Let's get this cleaned up," he said suddenly. "You've got towels and cleaner of some kind?"

"I… In the pantry. But that's hardly your job."

"It shouldn't be yours, either. Let's just get it done."

She gave him an odd look then, one he couldn't interpret. But she went to the kitchen and pulled open a cabinet door. Then, armed with the cleaning materials, they tackled it.

"Floors last," was all she said.

He nodded. "Where everything we miss ends up."

She gave him a slight smile, probably the best she could manage at the moment. And more than many could.

It was sometime later, after he'd finished cleaning the dust off the chair the suspect had moved—he'd taken that task so she didn't have to go near it—and she had finished with the floor everywhere but there when she spoke again.

"What was it you thought of, before?" Brett asked. "When you said he'd never been stopped before."

He wished she hadn't remembered, didn't want her dwelling on it, but perhaps it was better she be prepared. She'd already proven she didn't dissolve into helplessness at a threat.

"It's just…there are some guys like that," Brett said, "when the scenario they've spent so much time on doesn't go the way it was supposed to, sometimes they can get caught up in trying to…fix it."

"Fix it?"

He held her gaze then. "Make sure it does go right."

She frowned. "How?"

He struggled with how to phrase it. He didn't want to scare her all over again, after the evening she'd had. But he couldn't think of any gentle way to say it, this real reason he'd wanted to stay.

And then he didn't have to. Because Annalise was far, far from stupid, and she got there herself. He saw the moment when it hit her by the way her eyes widened and her breath caught.

She stared at him as she put it into words.

"You think he might come back."

Chapter Eight

She should have realized.

Annalise stood there with a damp cleaning rag in her hand, feeling a fool all over again. This cleanup truly wasn't his job. And he hadn't stayed to do it out of the kindness of his heart. Or—she barely allowed the thought to form—because he was trying to help her, personally.

He was doing it because he thought that scrawny faker, that loser, was going to come back.

"You'll be all right," he said quickly. "There'll be units in the area, and I'll stay just in case."

Stay? Here? In her house, with her? She spent what seemed like a long, silent moment wondering what on earth was wrong with her. After what had happened tonight, how could this idea make her pulse jump? And it took her another moment to realize this had blasted the thought of that scummy little man coming back right out of her mind.

Don't be an idiot all over again. You know it's not personal. None of it is, for him. It's Brett's job. You're a victim. He just wants to catch the guy.

"Well, that would be a feather," she muttered.

"What?"

"In your cap. To catch the guy the same night he strikes."

He looked surprised, almost as if that hadn't actually been his first thought. "Would I like to put him away that fast? Sure, I would. But I want to be sure you stay safe."

He said it as if that was more important. She'd like to believe it was. But believing what she wanted to believe hadn't worked out so well. Not just tonight, with Sam-who-didn't-exist, but ever. And that put a bit of snap in her words.

"Afraid you'll have the big boss to answer to if you let her cousin get hurt?"

His gaze narrowed. And when he answered, his voice was chilly. "Thanks for the reminder."

She groaned inwardly. "I'm sorry. I shouldn't have said that."

"Don't be. I always need to remember."

She felt suddenly as chilled as his voice had been. That he had to deal with Coltons differently? Remember that she was a Colton? Was that why he'd never—

"Brett—"

"It's probably safe to let your dogs out now," he said, his tone as brisk now as it had been cool.

"Oh. Yes. I should. Should have thought…" She stumbled over the words. "About a lot of things," she finished lamely.

The dogs were delighted when she released them from their temporary captivity. They practically leaped into her arms. They, at least, didn't care what she said, as long as it wasn't in that "You're in trouble" voice. And when she spoke their names in that loving tone they squirmed with delight.

If you ever used that tone on Brett, he'd squirm, all right. In discomfort.

She had to stop this. He was popping into her head at the most awkward times and in inappropriate ways.

By the time they were back in the living room she thought she had herself under control. And she was determined to write off all these reeling thoughts to the adrenaline spike he'd talked about. Who could be expected to think normally under these conditions?

Now that things were calmer, Jack and Apple trotted over to where Ember, in the down position just inside the front door, was watching with great interest.

"Can she come off 'stay' now?" Annalise asked without looking at Brett, who was tidily gathering up all the cleaning supplies. She could have given the command herself, and as her trainer the dog probably would have responded, but that was a breach of protocol and the training itself; Ember was on duty and thus her handler was in charge.

He didn't answer her, but said, "Ember, at ease."

The Lab responded to the military command eagerly, quickly jumped to her feet and, tail wagging, greeted the two smaller dogs. Annalise did look then, saw Brett was watching the trio and said, "This is Jack, and the shaggy one is Apple."

"Mmm," he said, then suddenly looked at her. "Apple...and Jack?"

She gave him a half roll of her eyes and a sheepish smile. "They named them at the shelter. After someone's favorite cereal. The company that makes it does come from Michigan, after all."

The three dogs were busy getting acquainted, and Brett went back to watching, rather guardedly.

"They're good with other animals," she assured him. "Warier around people. Especially men."

"But not too afraid to come into the room with me."

He was so good with Ember Annalise couldn't imagine any dog being afraid of him, but that was her emotions talking. Again. As a trainer she knew that, just like with humans, a dog's fears could be almost instinctive, so deeply ingrained that logic couldn't even make a dent.

"No," she answered. "A good sign. I think they'll be fine, if you take it slow."

"Always my motto," he said.

Annalise's head snapped around. He still wasn't looking at her, was neatly putting away the stuff he'd collected. Obviously that agreement about taking it slow hadn't meant...anything.

Okay, she was in worse shape, mentally at least, than she'd thought. And having him in close quarters was going to be hazardous if she couldn't keep her mind in line. And if she kept letting her thoughts make it to her mouth before thinking them through, she was going to be facing a night of potential mortification. As if she hadn't had enough of that already.

Catfished.

God, she was such a fool.

She sank down on the couch again. "Do you really think he'll come back? After nearly being caught?" She hated the way she sounded, shaky still, but she couldn't seem to help it.

Brett didn't answer right away. He finished in the pantry—and why did the fact that he'd noticed where she got the stuff and put it back in the right place get to her?—and came back, pausing to stroke Ember's head and visibly notice how her two backed away from him. But he made no effort to reach out to them. She realized suddenly he was ignoring them with purpose, counting on innate curiosity to bring them around eventually. He couldn't have made a better choice for these two. And somehow that didn't surprise her.

He walked over and this time sat in the chair at a right angle to her seat on the couch, as if he'd decided she didn't need him quite so close this time. Or as if he didn't want to be quite so close.

And she hadn't realized—or at least admitted—that she'd been hoping he'd sit next to her on the couch until she realized it was disappointment she was feeling as he took the chair.

Chastising herself yet again for being a fool as big as Lake Michigan, she watched the two dogs move around the room, clearly engrossed in all the new scents left behind by the chaos.

"So what's their story?" he asked.

She knew he knew of her work fostering homeless dogs, getting them accustomed to living with people, so they were more likely to be permanently adopted. They'd talked about it when he'd met one of her prior fosters at the training center.

"They came in to the shelter together," she said, feeling an unexpected relief at the change in subject. "They'd obviously been together for a while."

Brett looked at the two, who had worked their way over to where Ember had been, still sniffing madly. Apple was smaller, his soft, longer coat in a black-and-white pattern that spoke of some spaniel in his ancestry, while Jack was a solid forty pounds of black-tipped brown mutt.

"Safe bet," Brett said neutrally. He shifted his gaze back to her. "How long have you had them?"

"About six weeks. I got them shortly after they came in. They'd obviously been on their own for a while—they were skinny, dirty and a little wild. Scared. We didn't want to put them up for adoption for fear some dog-fight promoter would come along and interpret their fear and nerves as aggression."

His mouth twisted in distaste when she mentioned dog fights. She found it hard to believe—and appalling—that such things still happened. Apparently so did he.

"Anyway," she went on, shifting her gaze back to the canine pair as they worked their way toward Brett, clearly curious, "another two weeks and they go back for reassessment, to see if they're ready to go into the adoption pool. They're obviously bonded, so we'll be trying to keep them together."

"They calmed down pretty fast after all the excitement. You've done a good job."

There was no reason for her to blush; she'd been told that before, and often. Yet here she was, staring down at the dogs because if she looked up she was afraid he'd look at her and see. But then she realized he was watching the dogs as well, and she knew he'd realized they'd decided he was their next thing to be investigated. He shifted one arm on the arm of the chair, letting his hand hang over the edge fingers extended but not moving or reaching.

"So who's the boss?" he asked.

She smiled at that. "Jack tries to be, and Apple lets him get away with it a lot of the time. But he's got limits, and no problem expressing them. And I think Jack is mostly bravado, because in stressful situations, like tonight, he lets Apple take the lead."

"Sounds like they've found a balance."

As he said it Apple reached out with his nose, stretching his neck so he was still at what he must consider a safe distance. He sniffed Brett's hand. Brett didn't move, not even the fingers the dog's nose was intent on. And she realized his knowledge of dogs wasn't limited to just Ember and her training and tactics. He understood them. Was as patient with these two as he was with the Lab.

On the thought, Ember, who had been lying down now near Brett's feet, rose to a sit.

"Hey, Ember girl, don't get territorial now," he murmured softly, soothingly to his partner. "You've had it easy compared to these two. You've never been homeless or gone hungry. Besides, you're on guard duty."

He reached out with his other hand to scratch Ember's ears. The big dog, leaner and more muscular than a typical family pet, leaned into it with a blissful sigh. And that, apparently, was enough for Apple. He nudged that motionless hand with his nose, almost insistently. Brett did the same with him, scratching behind Apple's floppy ears. The dog wiggled a little. Which made Jack crowd in to get his share.

Annalise sat there staring as he charmed three dogs at once, two of whom he'd never met before tonight, and who an hour ago had been nearly hysterical, and a few weeks ago downright snarly.

And she drew in a very deep breath as she admitted, way down deep, that the animals weren't the only ones being charmed.

Chapter Nine

Annalise had relaxed, finally. Talking about the dogs had done it, as he'd hoped. They were her refuge, as Ember was his.

Brett looked into the two pairs of dark brown eyes staring up at him, and kept talking softly, mostly nonsense, as he stroked and scratched. When, finally, both sets of those eyes went half-closed, he knew he had them. For now, anyway. He admired her patience to take this on, again and again, because he knew enough about rescued and scared creatures to know that he might have to go through it all over again next time.

Next time?

He'd thought that like it was a given there would be a next time, here, alone with them.

With Annalise.

Nope. Not happening. She's a Colton, and that is a pool of problems you do not want to dive into.

No, his job was to get her through tonight, while Ellie and others hunted down what details they could find on their catfisher. Then his job would be to find him.

If he hadn't come back here first.

Yes, staying tonight was definitely the right plan. And it would be fine. He was just feeling…protective. Understandable—she was Ember's trainer, so they had a connection. And speaking of Ember, she was being remarkably patient, while he paid attention to two other dogs. True, he'd given her the watch command, which told her she was on duty, but still.

He'd have to make it up to her later, with a fetch session. Maybe he could last until she tired out this time, instead of the other way around. Although that was unlikely. More than once he'd had a vision of his older self, gimping around with an unworkable right shoulder, victim of endless hours of throwing a tennis ball far enough to keep Ember happy.

He looked up to find her watching him. Intently. No, watching her dogs, he immediately thought, his mind skittering away from that flicker he'd seen in her blue-gray eyes. It had been watchfulness, care for her animals, that's all. An assessment of how her fosters were doing with a stranger. Didn't he already know how much she loved dogs? That was all that had been, not a snap of connection.

Casting about for something to say, he blurted, "How did you end up training dogs?"

She smiled, so maybe it wasn't so stupid after all. "They always responded to me, and I loved them, but I never thought about making a career out of it until my mother suggested it. I was working in an office, but volunteering with a rescue group. She told me she'd never seen me happier than when I was working with the dogs, and that I should go for it."

"Nice. That she saw it and said it." His own mother hadn't cared what he did, as long as he stayed out of any trouble that would embarrass her. He'd overheard her once saying she wished she'd never had him, And it didn't take a math genius to realize his parents' wedding had come months after he'd been conceived.

He supposed that was the answer to why they were the way they were. What he knew for sure was that he'd spent years trying to please them, before he'd realized he couldn't, no matter what he did. So he never expected much from family. Which was probably why the Coltons seemed so…overwhelming.

"She's the best," Annalise said. "And she knows a little something about going after what you love."

He didn't know her mother, Leanne Palmer Colton, except by sight. Troy had told him about how his father had met her sometime after his own mother had been tragically murdered when Troy had been a child. Geoff Colton had apparently been hesitant, not only because of his first wife's awful death, but because she was much younger than he was. But Leanne had fallen hard for the restaurateur, had known what she wanted.

Leanne has been pretty much the only mother I've known. And she raised Desiree and I as if we were hers as much as Annalise and Grace, and Palmer. Heart of gold, that woman. Troy's words echoed in his head as he looked at Annalise, who bore a distinct resemblance to her mother. Did she on the inside as well?

"You mean she wanted your father?" he asked.

She nodded. Then sighed, audibly. "Theirs is a true love story."

He managed not to snort his disbelief in the idea that such a thing existed. Attraction, yes, he'd go for that. Or even a long-term connection. But true love, the kind that had made her eyes grow warm and her mouth go soft? Not a chance.

*And you'd better stop thinking words like that. Warm.
Soft. You're losing focus again.*

"So that's what you're looking for?"

She blinked. "What?"

He realized belatedly that that could have sounded as
if he were asking her for…personal reasons. He scrambled to recover. "The app. Is that what you were hoping
to find there?"

She grimaced then. "You don't need to remind me
how foolish that was."

"Wasn't trying to."

This time the sigh was even more audible. And yet
different. How could she get differing emotions into a
simple exhale of breath? Wistfulness when talking about
her parents, and now…disgust? At him, for asking? Or
herself?

"I," she pronounced firmly, "am never dating again."

"Ever?" he asked, very carefully.

"Ever. I'm clearly too stupid to—"

"Stop it. You're not stupid. These guys are good. Really good."

"Right." She gave him a sideways look. "I'll bet you
never would have been taken in."

He started to say he wouldn't have been on the app
at all, since he wasn't looking. But some belated sense
of caution stopped him. He searched for something else
to say. The words were out before he realized they were
probably worse. "I believed a woman who said she loved
me once. Worst mistake of my life."

She looked at him straight on this time. "That's why
you don't date?"

"I'm not the issue," he said, determined to divert this
right now.

"But just because a couple of women burned you, you shouldn't give up on love altogether."

"You have to believe in love before you can give up on it."

She stared at him. "But you have to believe in it, or at least that it exists. Otherwise life is pointless. And if you cut yourself off because of one bad experience, you'll never find the real thing." He said nothing, just looked at her. And after a moment she started again. "You can't really want to stay alone forever. Once burned, twice shy is one thing, but once burned, forever shy is something else altogether."

He kept looking at her, biting the inside of his lip to keep from smiling. A stifled "Mmm" was all he could allow himself.

"What?" she demanded.

She was irritated now. Good. That meant she wasn't scared. "Just thinking you might want to listen to yourself."

"What?" Her tone was puzzled this time.

"You're the one who said you were never dating again."

"And you said you don't date."

"Not exactly. I said I'm not looking."

Her cheeks flushed. "Oh. I'm sorry. I didn't realize you were…with someone."

Where had that come from? Did she really think the only reason someone wouldn't be in a dating frenzy was because they were in a relationship?

"I'm not." He only wondered after he'd said it why he'd felt compelled to clarify that with her. "I meant I'm not looking…for what you're looking for." *I'm not sure it even exists.* "But since you clearly are, you'll have to take your own advice."

She looked thoughtful, as if she was going over what she'd said in her mind. And then she gave him a wry, almost embarrassed smile. "I guess I did kind of contradict myself there."

"Kind of," he agreed.

She let out a long breath. Then, with a wry grimace, she said, "I'll probably try again. Maybe in a year or two. Or ten."

"Ten? So, when you're thirty?"

He got her third "What?" and this time it was startled. "Just how young do you think I am?"

"Don't all women want to be thought younger?"

"Not when it means you think I'm a…kid, practically."

Oh, believe me, I don't think of you as a kid, in any way. "Not a kid. Young, maybe."

"You mean naive," she accused. This time he couldn't stop his slight smile. And it gave him away. Her expression cleared, to be replaced with realization. "You did this on purpose, didn't you? All of this. To get my mind off what happened."

"People think more clearly when they're not scared," he said.

"How about when they're angry?" She glared at him. Or rather, tried to. The slight twitch at one corner of her mouth—damn, that mouth—gave her away in turn. And after a moment, she actually laughed.

"Okay, it worked," she said, and this time the breath she took looked deep and relaxing.

Brett wondered if she had any idea how amazing it was that she was able to even smile, let alone laugh, after the night she'd had. Annalise Colton had resilience, among a multitude of other qualities. And it struck him that he should have realized that earlier, when despite the night's events, she'd still preached to him about true love. Or the real thing, as she'd called it.

She still believed in it.

He wasn't sure he ever had.

Chapter Ten

She should have known.

Annalise chastised herself silently for her oversight. Brett hadn't gotten where he was, coming from Lansing with a stellar reputation, already establishing himself here in Grave Gulch, and—possibly most important—earning the clearly limitless adoration of a very smart dog, without knowing what he was doing. And clearly he knew how to calm a rattled victim.

Victim.

God, she hated the word. She'd rather be the injured party, even a casualty, but victim implied a helplessness she loathed. She wasn't helpless. Naive? Foolish? Stupid? Maybe.

Stop it. You're not stupid.

His words probably shouldn't have soothed her as much as they had. She was afraid it was because they had come from him. His opinion of her mattered. And telling herself it was only because he was a colleague of sorts, that she had to work with him, wasn't working too well.

She tried to focus on Apple and Jack, who had climbed up to join her on the couch. Ember had settled at Brett's feet, but her head was up, her ears active as she listened and sorted whatever she was hearing so far into the non-threatening category.

Annalise didn't get it. She worked with other cops, consulted with a couple of other departments who wanted a dog fine-tuned in her areas of expertise, even flirted with a handsome K-9 handler who had, sounding sweetly regretful, told her he was engaged.

But none of them made her feel the way this man did. The man who had her thinking about him even as she was getting ready for what was supposed to be the best date of her life and had instead turned into a disaster. What that said about her, she wasn't sure, but—

"—say it's going to break ninety tomorrow."

She snapped out of her reverie. She refused to ask *What?* yet again, so instead she said, "It is?"

He nodded. "Maybe you should take the day off. Head for the beach."

"I can't," she said, almost automatically. "I have three sessions scheduled in the morning."

"Reschedule. Go get some sand in your shoes."

Her mouth quirked. "If only it only got in your shoes."

In an instant, tension snapped between them, as if they were both thinking of all the different places beach sand could get, under varying circumstances. And she found herself wondering if he'd ever had sex on the beach somewhere. Probably. The guy obviously could have his choice of companions for the activity.

But he'd said he wasn't with anyone. And he wasn't looking. Had the women in his past really soured him that much?

And there she was again, wondering, speculating.

"Not a beach lover?" he asked, his voice maybe just a shade too even.

"Oh, I am." She smiled. "Funny isn't it, how things are different depending on where you're from? I went to school with a girl from California, and to her the only real beach was at the ocean. For us, the Great Lakes are our ocean."

He smiled back at that. "I worked with a guy who was startled we had sand dunes. He thought the same thing."

A memory struck, made her smile. "We went to Leelanau State Park one year, when I was a kid. I rolled all the way down the Sleeping Bear Dunes. Talk about sand!" She had herself in hand enough to look at him now. "Have you ever been there?"

He shook his head. "I went for Silver Lake," he said.

She studied him for a moment. Then said teasingly, "Let me guess. The off-road-vehicle section?"

In keeping with all her reactions to him it seemed, the smile he gave her then warmed her more than it should have. "Guilty." He shrugged. "Hey, it's the only place east of the Mississippi you can ride sand dunes."

"I didn't realize. I can see the appeal, but seeing little kids out on those dirt bikes is worrying."

"I wasn't a little kid at the time. My family didn't go in for things like that."

"Beach trips?"

"Family trips."

"Oh." Somehow that seemed very sad to her. "I'm sorry. They were great fun."

"My father never—"

He stopped suddenly, and she wondered what he'd been going to say. Wondered if there was anything to do with this man that she didn't wonder about.

"My dad worked hard," she said. "The Grill has been his life since he started there as a busboy. But he al-

ways made sure he was a hundred percent there for us
on those trips, you know? Of course Mom would have
chewed him out if he hadn't. But he ran down the dunes
right beside us."

His head tilted slightly. "Your father worked at the
Grave Gulch Grill as a busboy?"

She nodded. "When he was eighteen. And now he
owns it. I'm incredibly proud of him."

"You should be. That's quite an accomplishment."

"What does your father do?"

"Now? No idea."

She blinked. "What?"

"We're not in touch much. Last time I talked to him,
he was unemployed."

"When was that?"

He looked as if he was thinking. She couldn't imagine
having to think so hard to remember when the last time
you talked to your father was.

"Don't remember exactly," he finally said. "Couple
of years ago."

She made a mental note to call hers and thank him
for being a real father. And, since this clearly wasn't an
easy subject for Brett, she quickly changed it. "So what
do you do, in your time off?"

He glanced down at the dog arrayed on his feet.
"Throw tennis balls?" he suggested.

She laughed. "She's such a sweetie. She'll work her
heart out for you, so she deserves her play time."

"She is, she does and she does."

"Do you ever wish you'd gone with a 'bite-and-hold'
dog?" From her own experience she knew working with
dogs used mainly for scent work was quite different than
the archetypal police K-9 people first think of. Bear,

Grave Gulch's big sable German shepherd, was an entirely different type of dog, the kind who usually got the glory—and deserved it. But so did the quiet ones like Ember, whose nose had literally saved lives.

"If I ever did, she cured me."

Like your ex cured you of the desire to date?

There was a long, silent moment while Annalise reassured herself that she hadn't said it out loud. He didn't react, so she knew she hadn't. She had to get a handle on her errant thoughts. Thoughts like *Hey, since we're both not dating, maybe we should not date together.*

This was getting to be too much. Although she couldn't deny there was a certain appeal to hanging out with a guy who wasn't interested and therefore it didn't matter what she said, did or looked like. And with Brett, she somehow knew that last, what she looked like, would indeed be the last on his list, if he had a checklist of qualities he was looking for. Except he wasn't looking.

She needed to derail this train of thought in a hurry. She grabbed at the only thing she could think of powerful enough to distract her.

"Do you really think he'll come back?"

To his credit—among the many things to his credit—he didn't dissemble. "I don't know if he'll be back tonight, but I'd bet money he will be back, in some way, at some point."

"Why, now that I know he's a fake, wouldn't he just cut his losses?"

"His plan worked for him at least twice. Given how polished he is at it, probably more than that, elsewhere. He's going to be angry that it didn't work this time."

Well, maybe she would have preferred a little dissembling. "Great. So not only will he be back, but he'll be mad?"

"If he is, he'll have a surprise waiting now."

And what happens if he comes back tomorrow night? Or the night after? It sounded pitiful even in her mind. But worse was the thought of being here alone when that…that *thing* was out there.

And it wasn't like Brett could stay here until the guy was caught.

She sucked in a quick breath, fighting down the feelings that idea stirred in her. She was still off-balance after what had happened, that was all. She simply wasn't thinking straight.

"I'll get him, Annalise," he said. "And we'll get your bracelet back, too."

She nodded, thinking it safer than trying to speak. And in that moment of silence, a wave of exhaustion swept over her. She should just stay silent. That was the best plan.

Because too often her mouth outran her brain around this man.

Chapter Eleven

Brett saw the moment when the crash hit. He'd known it was coming, it had to, it was how things worked. The fight-or-flight response was effective, built-in…and draining, once safety was achieved. The aftereffects of an adrenaline spike were something he was all too familiar with. She'd lasted longer than he would have expected.

"You should try and get some rest, if you're going to work tomorrow," he said, trying to make his tone casual.

He could see the effort she had to make to even respond in a similar tone. "I could say the same to you."

"I'm good for a while yet. I'll sleep a little later."

She sighed, and sat silently for a moment. Then she perked up slightly before asking, "Are you into comfort food?"

He blinked. "That depends," he said carefully. Growing up in his house, that had usually consisted of his mother's attempts at colcannon, the Irish mashed-potato-and-cabbage classic. She'd insisted on kale, which he hated, instead of cabbage, had never quite gotten the hang of the pickled cream and refused to just buy buttermilk. He'd only found out how good it could be when he'd one day had it made by an expert, and the difference was astounding. Her soda bread had been good, though, and a big chunk of it still warm from the oven would indeed be on his list of comfort foods, if he had one.

Somehow he doubted Annalise was thinking of either of those.

"Dream Bakes."

"Oh." Okay, anything from the popular bakery downtown qualified as comfort food, he was sure.

She smiled at his reaction. "My brother Palmer is engaged to the owner. It means I get him dropping off leftovers a lot."

He remembered his earlier thought. "Troy mentioned how they were tangled up in that murder case last month."

She nodded, with a sad expression. "Soledad's best friend. They have custody of the baby now." A smile flashed then. "And Palmer's taking to fatherhood. He had a rough start in life himself, so it's wonderful to see."

"Some people have the knack." *And some don't.*

And he didn't think he mistook the rather wistful look that flashed in her eyes for a moment. She really did want the whole thing, kids and all. Just talking about her brother's new family had seemingly given her a second wind. Judging by the way she was with the dogs, she'd be good at parenting. He hoped she got what she wanted someday. With someone.

He cut off that train of thought before it could stray down a siding that would be utterly pointless.

"So what's their idea of comfort food?"

"Today the options are an excellent cherry pie, made from fresh Michigan cherries, or—" her expression slid into a grin "—a wickedly decadent salted-caramel Irish whiskey cake." He blinked at that. Tried to imagine the taste. Failed utterly. Annalise laughed. "All righty then," she said.

And with a final pat for the two foster dogs, she got up and headed for the kitchen, clearly reenergized. Didn't the woman realize most other people would be broken down weeping or curled up in bed in a fetal position, at this point?

He gave himself a mental slap; the last thing he needed to be doing was thinking about Annalise in bed in any position.

The cake was the most amazing thing he'd ever tasted. He hadn't thought much about the whole salted-caramel frenzy—his notions of food were mostly as fuel, with the exception of a good, rare steak or a quality shepherd's pie—but this made him think he could be convinced. *Decadent* had to be the right word.

"I'll need to be running an extra five miles to offload that," he said as he finished the last bite and resisted scraping the plate clean with his fork.

"Isn't it deliciously evil?" she agreed. She'd taken a smaller slice, but had finished it, as well. "I don't even want to know the calorie count. It's too good to worry about."

"Not like you have to worry about it," he said, unable to stop himself from giving her trim shape a once-over. The instant he realized he was doing it, he forced his gaze back to his empty plate.

"Hah," she said. "I'll be starving for two days to make up for this."

She gathered up the plates and forks. "I can do that," he said.

"I know you could. And probably would. But frankly, I need to…do things."

He understood that. And allowed himself another glimpse as she bent to put the plates and utensils in the dishwasher. As she straightened again, his thoughts slipped the leash once more. She really did have the sweetest—

"There's a police car across the street." She was staring out the kitchen window.

"And there will be, off and on. It won't be 24/7, but they'll be around when they can, for a while at least."

She turned to look at him. "They're…guarding me?"

You're a Colton. The chief's a Colton. What did you expect?

"Not guarding, exactly. If someone's got a report to do, or has downtime between calls, they'll spend it there. And Ember and I will make a few rounds, in case you hear us outside."

She looked as if she couldn't decide if she was glad about this or not. "But…won't that scare him off?"

He stared at her. "That's what you're worried about?"

"I thought you wanted to catch him."

"I want you safe more."

Only when her eyes widened did he realize how that had sounded. Not the words so much, because that was in fact his priority, but the way they'd sounded. As if something happening to her, as if her being hurt or worse, would hit him in a very down-deep way. Not just as a failure of the department and of he himself as a cop, but as…an immeasurable loss. To him. Personally.

He had to move, to stop looking at her. At the way she was looking at him. He got up, figuring he'd do a check of all the windows, although she'd told him they were secured because she'd been going to leave. For her date. The date she'd been going on in her search for true love.

The part of him that snorted inwardly at the idea sparred briefly with the part of him that secretly admired her faith in it. Or envied it. But then apparently she'd grown up with good examples of it, whereas he… hadn't. He'd often wondered why they'd even stayed together, since the most loving emotion he'd ever seen them share was a sort of armed neutrality.

He'd just checked the west-side window when a slight gleam from a shelf beside it caught his eye. He looked, saw a small shiny rock, rounded, smooth, and showing small roughly hexagonal markings.

"My Petoskey stone," she said as she came up behind him. Close behind him. He kept his gaze on the rock.

"I've never seen one like that." He knew the stones were a combination of rock and fossilized coral, moved and deposited by glaciers. He thought they were unique to Michigan, maybe even to the lower part of the state.

"I found it when I was a kid, and Dad polished it up for me."

Such a simple thing, yet he couldn't imagine his father doing it. For that matter he couldn't image the wealthy, successful Geoff Colton doing it. But from what she'd said, he hadn't always been that way. Brett had an innate respect for a self-made man and it seemed that's what her father was.

That, and a man who would do something so simple just to make his little girl happy. The little girl who had not only hung on to the keepsake, but placed it somewhere where she could see it all the time. What must that have been like, to have parents like that? Is that what it took to turn out someone as sharp and dedicated as Troy, as talented as his sister Desiree, to take a troubled kid like Palmer and turn him around and to produce a woman like Annalise, so full of compassion, so—

He cut himself off before he launched on a list of all

the things Annalise was. "You really should try and get some rest," he said abruptly. "This second wind isn't going to last."

"Voice of experience?"

"Yes."

He guessed it was a sign that he was right that she didn't really resist. She got a blanket and pillow from a cabinet in the hall and put them on the couch without comment.

"Good night," she said as she turned to head down the hall. He muttered something, he wasn't even sure what, as he fought off imaginings of what her bedroom might look like.

"Annalise?"

She spun around, a look of…anticipation on her face that rattled him enough that it took him a moment to remember what he'd been going to tell her. "Keep your door open." Her eyes widened. "So I can hear anything that happens," he said quickly.

She blinked. "Oh. Okay."

What had she thought, that he wanted her to leave her bedroom door open…for him?

He stared after her as she walked down the hall. This was irrational; he felt as off-balance as if he'd been the one who had the traumatic night. He'd never personally known a victim before the crime occurred before, but that didn't seem like enough to explain his reaction. He was feeling too drawn, too protective, and that she was Ember's trainer didn't seem enough to explain it.

He turned on his heel and methodically went about getting himself settled. He appreciated that she'd thought of the pillow and blanket, but he had no intention of actually sleeping, not like that anyway. The chair closest to the outside wall would do, with a window open enough for him—and Ember—to hear anything suspicious. He could doze a bit, just enough to keep going. An hour or two would do. Sidearm on the table beside the chair, within instant reach, leave the shoes on in case he had to run, and he was good.

Later, he went on one of those external perimeter checks he'd mentioned to her. Then, a unit pulled up and parked near where the one she'd seen earlier had been. Since Ember had signaled nothing new, he headed that way. The woman in uniform was alert and aware enough that she either saw or sensed him coming from a good distance away. Then she spotted Ember, and Brett saw her snap the safety strap that held her weapon in the holster, indicating she'd been ready to draw if she had to.

"Officer Fulton," he said, reminded once again of why he'd come here; in Lansing it could have been a cop who'd been on the force for years and he might never have spoken with them before. But here, in less than a year, he'd already interacted with everybody on the force at one point or another.

"Detective," she said. "All calm?"

He nodded. "He may be done for the night."

"But not for good?"

"I don't think so." Brett felt his mouth quirk. "But what do I know?"

"More than most, from what I've heard." She said it as if it was as true and real as the lake just to the west, and he felt a burst of satisfaction. Before he had to formulate a response she asked, "How's she doing?"

"Amazingly well," he admitted. "She was worried that marked units hanging around meant we wouldn't catch the guy."

Fulton smiled. "Well, she's made of tough stuff. So's the family, or the boss would have buckled long ago under all this pressure."

He couldn't deny that. The protests were getting louder and rowdier. Chief Colton had withstood it all so far, but he didn't know how much longer she could hold on. "It's getting uglier," he said.

"Yeah." She glanced toward the tidy little house. "You're staying, I hear?"

Well, that hadn't taken long, for that to get around. "Yeah. Just in case."

The officer's gaze shifted to Ember. "Have to keep your dog's trainer safe, huh?"

"Yeah." *Your dog's trainer.* That's what she was, and he'd best remember that.

As he went back to the house, Officer Fulton's words echoed in his head.

He was already an outsider in this seemingly Colton-dominated enclave. He wasn't about to make it worse by getting involved with one of their own.

No matter how much he might want to.

Chapter Twelve

Annalise stared into the darkness, hoping that forcing herself to keep her eyes open would perversely trigger the overwhelming urge to sleep. It was her last resort; she'd been lying here for two hours, unable to find a way to turn off, or at least slow down, her whirling thoughts.

And the fact that a few minutes ago Brett had come to her open doorway and lingered a moment didn't help.

She'd heard the faint creak of a floorboard and felt a spike of that adrenaline rush before she realized it was him. That realization caused a spike of an entirely different kind until she heard him walk away and realized he'd only been checking on her.

What did you expect? That he'd climb into bed with you?

She rolled over and buried her face in her pillow, wondering why these wild thoughts kept careening into her mind. What kind of woman was she, to have been so very excited about her date tonight—never mind that it had all been a scam—yet almost simultaneously so attracted to this man who had no interest at all in her that way? Or in anything like the kind of relationship she was looking for?

I'm not looking for what you're looking for.

He meant it. She didn't doubt that. And she knew she should consider it fair warning. A warning some men would never bother to give. Why had he? She felt her cheeks heat at the thought that maybe he knew, how she reacted to him. Maybe she'd betrayed it somehow. That would be embarrassing. They'd always gotten on well in the joint training sessions with Ember, but her focus had been on the smart, willing dog, not on him.

Well, not any more than usual. Qualified, capable K-9 officers with a record like his weren't thick on the ground, and he'd proven that rep well-earned in their first exercises together. That he was quietly competent and apparently unaware of his own looks were big points in his favor, in her book.

She'd assumed at first he was married, because how could he not be? He didn't wear a ring, but some men didn't. Then Troy had told her a week later he wasn't and had never been.

You have to believe in love before you can give up on it.

She sighed into the darkness. That just might be the saddest thing she'd ever heard. Yet he didn't seem sad to her. Or bitter. Just…closed off. Except with Ember. That alone told Annalise that he wasn't completely closed off.

But that didn't mean she should be lying here thinking about him.

And about what she would have done if he had climbed into bed with her.

"I CAN DRIVE MYSELF—"

"I know you can," Brett said patiently to Annalise the next morning, "but I have to drop Ember off anyway." He didn't mention that he also didn't want her taking off to go get lunch or something. He wanted her under observation at all times, and he'd already called Sergeant Kenwood to let him know to keep an eye on her; the man might be retired from active duty, but his instincts were as sharp as ever.

"But I'll need my car to get home."

"I'll pick you up when I come get her," he said, with a scratch of the Lab's soft ears. "After I talk to the two other women this jerk targeted."

"I want to take Apple and Jack," she said. "I don't want to leave them alone. They were scared, too."

And that was Annalise Colton in a nutshell, he thought. "Fine. There's room. And Ember won't mind."

And so he ended up with a carload of three dogs and the woman adored by them all.

Including you?

He yanked his mind off that fruitless path. He drove, trying to concentrate on mentally organizing his day.

As he dropped her, the two foster dogs and Ember off at the training center, he didn't mention that his first stop was going to be the chief's office. He also didn't mention the early morning text from said chief that had precipitated that visit. The boss was concerned about her cousin, which was only natural. His family might not be close, but he understood—envied?—those who were.

And that was also part of why working here was turning out to be much more complicated than he'd expected. If he'd studied the roster and seen how many times the Colton name popped up, it might have sent up a red flag. But he hadn't. So now here he was, dodging Coltons at every turn.

As he walked down the hallway to the chief's office, he remembered the first time he'd made this trek. The day of his final interview for this job. He'd been impressed with Chief Colton when she'd met with him personally to ask him to take the position, because they both needed and wanted people like him on the job. And when she'd promised he could slide right into an available K-9 position because he already had the knowledge, it had been the lure that had had him agreeing.

Her office hadn't changed since he'd been here, and yet it felt different. He could only imagine what it must be like to be the holder of this position, with the Bowe case ongoing, and the integrity of one of the most crucial parts of the department under such intense scrutiny. He knew many in the mobs outside had made up their minds already, some before any, let alone all of the evidence was in, but he supposed that was to be expected given that it was evidence itself that had been brought into question in a very public way.

If it was starting to have the air of a bunker, it was only to be expected.

Chief Colton rose the moment he opened the door to her office after her aide had cleared him through. The tall, fit redhead—they'd joked about that in that interview, that she was all for hiring more redheads—did look a bit more harried than she had during his final interview. But something else had changed with her, something it took him a moment to put his finger on. He finally realized that under all the tension, both the kind that naturally came with the job and that caused by a serial killer on the loose, not to mention the whole tainted-evidence scandal, she was…not happy, but not as stressed as she had been.

That things must be going well at home was his first thought. He knew she and the owner of the Grave Gulch Hotel, Antonio Ruiz, had connected during the whole fiasco at Mary Suzuki's wedding, when Desiree's little boy had been grabbed as leverage to get Grave Gulch PD to reopen an old case. And they'd fallen in love and gotten engaged; Troy had mentioned they would likely be seeing a wedding as soon as things resolved and Melissa and Antonio both wanted a family.

Just like her cousin. She wants the whole thing, love, family and probably the damn white picket fence, too.

He shook it off and proceeded to assure the chief that her cousin was fine.

"She actually dealt with it very well, considering she had no idea he doesn't generally injure his victims."

"I'm just glad you were there," Melissa said, and it was clearly heartfelt.

"She would have been okay anyway, I think. She used what was at hand and got away from him, before I was close enough to help."

"And after?"

He shrugged. "The crash was a little rough, but she recovered quickly. Much more quickly than I expected."

"You stayed with her?"

He hesitated a moment. "I did, with my dog, just to be sure," he finally said. "And any units in the area who had downtime or reports to write in the field, did it on her block."

"Thank you," she said, and again there was no questioning the true feeling behind it. "You're sure it's the same guy from those two other cases in the county?"

"Fairly. MO's the same. Tailors the profile to their tastes, initiates the contact, can't or won't video chat, cancels out on the first in-person meet for some dramatic reason, it's all there. I'll know more after I interview the other two victims."

"And you're headed there now?"

He nodded. "I just dropped An—Ms. Colton off at the training center. Sergeant Kenwood knows what happened and will keep a close eye on her." He decided not to mention that he'd be going back to pick her up this afternoon. He was avoiding thinking about it himself, because he didn't want to think about dropping her at home and then leaving her there. Alone. But he'd deal with that later.

Something had shifted in the chief's eyes—bluer than Annalise's blue-gray, he noted—when she changed to the more formal *Ms. Colton* midsentence. But all she said was, "I'd like you to take—"

She didn't finish because a tone came from the cell phone on her desk, the sound enhanced by the vibration of the device. She glanced down at it, frowned, tapped the screen and called up a messaging app. Brett would have left while she handled whatever this was if she hadn't begun an order before the interruption. Because that's what an "I'd like you to" was when it came from the occupant of this office.

Barely a second after the message appeared, Chief Colton stiffened, staring. And under her breath muttered something he decided quickly he was probably glad not to be able to hear. She stared at the screen a moment longer, then looked up at him.

"It's Bowe," she said.

Chapter Thirteen

Brett stared at her. "Randall Bowe just texted you?"

She nodded. "It says he wants to make a deal."

For a long, wire-taut moment neither of them said anything more. He could almost feel her mind racing. Then she gestured him over to her and gave him a look that was almost apologetic.

"I'm sorry, but with the current state of things, I might need a witness to this conversation."

He understood what she was saying. The department had been under the microscope for months now, and she had to tread very carefully. He would not want to be in her shoes. He remembered talking to the chief in Lansing shortly after he'd started as a cop, and how the man had assumed everyone aspired to his position. Brett had laughed, saying he should get his feet under him in the job first. But in less than six months of watching what the man had to deal with, his answer was *no way*. He couldn't imagine a job he'd want less. His former partner had joked that that was why he should get the gig, because he didn't want it.

She held out the phone and he read the message. Let's make a deal. Cute. He noted the number it had come from. "Not his known cell number, I presume." The chief nodded, still staring at the screen. "Your provider back up your texts so Ellie can get the data?" She nodded again.

"I think for the moment we have to go on the assumption this is really him."

He nodded in turn. "Agreed."

She looked up at him then. "Troy tells me you're deep into finding Bowe."

"I want him, yes."

"Then you've studied him?"

"Read every case file."

Her eyebrows rose. "That's a lot of cases."

"Tell me about it."

"Did you find out anything?"

"He's good. Very good." He grimaced. "And he knows it."

"My take, as well. So...do we want to take Bowe down a peg or stroke his ego to lure him in?" He thought she was just thinking out loud, but then realized she was looking at him, waiting. She'd been asking him his opinion on how to proceed with the case? "Troy told me he sometimes feels like when we earn your trust, we'll be on our way to earning back the trust of those protesters."

He blinked at the seeming non sequitur. But then had the thought maybe it wasn't a non sequitur at all. "Troy said that?"

"He did. He thinks a lot of you. And he's a good judge."

He had no idea what to say to that, so went back to her original question. "My gut says it's too early to try and get in his face. Bowe needs to think he's going to get what he wants, because of course this is his plan, and he's the best."

"Belief in his own infallibility," she said.

"Yes. And if we try to play him now, he's liable to decide he needs to prove to us just how in control of this he is. And I don't like thinking about what he might come up with to try and do that."

"Agreed. So no telling him he's in no position to deal."

"Because sadly, he is."

She let out a long breath, and then tapped out a short reply.

What are you offering?

Nothing came back. They waited. Still nothing. "Did I take too long?" she finally asked aloud.

"I'm betting we'll wait almost exactly as long as we made him wait."

She drew back slightly. "You think he timed it?"

"One way or another. If I'm right, he'll answer… right…about…now."

The chime went off a split second after he said the last word. The chief gave him a wide smile. "Points to you, Detective."

Everything you want to know.

The chief sighed. Brett raised a brow at her. "I really, really want to be a smart ass back at him, I'm so angry," she said. "But I know you're right. Not yet."

The chief typed, then sent, I'm listening.

First, don't bother trying to trace this phone—it'll be dead the instant we're done.

Still listening.

I'll give you all the cases I had my fun with.

The price?

You find my brother.

The chief's brow furrowed. "His brother," she murmured.

"We've been looking for him for months, just for an interview," Brett said, frowning. "Troy even had me check with a contact of mine from the marshal's office, to see if he was in witness protection, but there was nothing."

We've been looking. No luck.

Look harder. If you want that info. When you find him, set up a call. I have a burner phone just waiting.

Puzzled, Brett said, "Bowe's wife said she doesn't know Baldwin's location. They've been estranged for years."

"I wonder why he wants to talk to him now?"

Brett shrugged. "Ask him."

She typed it out. Why? You haven't spoken in years.

I have a score to settle with dear Baldwin.

"A score to settle?" the chief asked. "After all this time?"

"He's obviously not rational to begin with," Brett answered. "Who knows what idea he's got in his head about his brother."

"And he's on edge anyway," she agreed. She let out an

audible breath. Brett could only imagine the pressure she must be under. Yet she was handling it well. He wondered if any of that composure came out of the newfound love in her life. Then he laughed inwardly at himself. *When the hell did you become a romantic, Shea?*

He pushed away an image of Annalise, cuddled up with her dogs. That was the last thing he needed to distract him right now, when they had a major suspect reaching out, and he was standing here with Annalise's cousin, who also happened to be his boss.

I'm waiting, dear chief. Is it a deal?

"Impatient," Brett said.

"I suppose it's too much to wish he's on edge enough to make a mistake," the chief mused aloud.

We'll keep looking, she sent. And find him ASAP.

After a moment Bowe answered with an emoji of a skull with burning eyes.

"Well that's charming," the chief said sourly.

You'd better, he sent then.

Three minutes ticked by and the screen remained unchanged. They looked at each other, and Brett knew they were thinking the same thing.

Bowe was gone.

And the phone he'd called from was probably already in pieces somewhere.

Chapter Fourteen

"Well," the chief said as she dropped her phone back on her desk, "that was...interesting."

"It was."

She turned to look at him. "I'm glad you were here when that happened." His brows rose in question. She grimaced, and a touch of bitterness came into her voice as she explained, "These days having a non-Colton witness seems crucial."

He'd never thought about it from that angle before all this had happened, that having half your family on or working with the department could have a serious downside. And she looked tense enough he decided that the comment about him being a non-Colton hadn't been a jab.

And then she was all business, the command-and-control side of her jumping to the fore. "I'll call Troy in and give him this info. You need to get back to this catfish case."

He'd never really left Annalise's case, merely been distracted for the moment. But at her words it came rushing back. He did need to continue with the active investigation. Not only to clear the case and catch the guy, and to get back Annalise's precious bracelet, but so he could put her out of his mind again, thinking of her only when Ember had a training session.

Yeah, right. Just put her right out of your mind. No problem. You do it all the time with cases, once they're over.

Over. Done with. No need to ever see her again, except at the training center. That's what he wanted. Wasn't it? Wasn't that—

"—take someone along with you to these interviews, if you don't mind."

He snapped back to reality. Ran the words back through his mind, including the last ones, which hadn't been in the tone of a question. No, that had been the chief speaking, and it was an order despite the polite wording.

"I… Sure." Not much else he could say, really.

"She's a rookie, so we're trying to get her as much varied experience as we can. And watching a veteran like you tackle a case like this could teach her a lot."

As she walked past him to the door—which he noted because he'd known a supervisor or five who would be above it, instead using the intercom to order someone else to do it, wanting that sense of being a superior—a touch of trepidation hit him. *She. A rookie.*

He groaned inwardly when the newcomer appeared in the doorway. He'd been right. Grace Colton.

Normally he wouldn't mind at all having a rookie tag along; it only helped him later if the beat cops had an idea what he did and how he did it. He tried to shake off the feeling, but it was difficult as he stood there with the two Coltons.

Did it have to be Annalise's sister?

Of course it did.

And if he didn't get moving, Troy would probably

show up for the news on Bowe's contact. Then he could be in the middle of a freaking Colton family reunion.

"Let's get moving," he said gruffly.

She looked a little startled, probably at his tone, of maybe the fact that he hadn't even said hello, but he was feeling a bit surrounded at the moment. Absurd, given there were only two of them, but then they were Coltons and that was, as always, different. He'd heard that Grace was smart and capable, from people he respected, so that's what he needed to focus on. Not her last name.

Somewhat to his surprise her first question when they got into his unit wasn't about her sister. Instead, she glanced in the back of the SUV and then asked, "Where's your dog?"

"Training."

"Oh. Annalise didn't mention she had Ember today."

Belatedly it hit him. She didn't need to ask about her sister, because she'd probably already talked to her. This was different territory for him, these close family ties.

A memory of the look on Annalise's face when he'd said he had no idea what his father was doing these days, and that he hadn't talked to him in a couple of years, shot through his mind. She'd been truly shocked. He took it as a matter of course. Maybe that's why they made him nervous, all these Coltons. It was just nerves, wasn't it?

He pondered that as he drove—leaving out the back way to avoid the cluster of protesters out front; they seemed to have a schedule set up so there were always a few around—hoping his edginess around anyone named Colton stemmed only from sheer numbers and the close ties, and not out of some subconscious feeling that they were guilty of everything those people with the signs and placards were claiming.

He couldn't believe it. He'd swear an oath that Troy wasn't; the man was one of the best cops he'd ever worked with. For that matter, none of the Coltons seemed the type to him. He'd seen enough of them now to recognize the genuineness of their family bond, and he was honest enough to admit his unease at being surrounded by them was in large part due to his own lack of those same bonds with his own family. It was simply foreign to him.

Yet he felt a secret small bit of relief that Annalise wasn't as closely connected to the department as the others, and not likely to get sucked into whatever happened in the end.

No, she had her own troubles. And that's what he needed to be focused on right now.

"—for being there for my sister last night."

Yet again he snapped out of a reverie. Daydreaming something he was normally prone to, but since last night he couldn't seem to stop. He glanced at the woman in the passenger seat.

"Lucky coincidence," he said.

"But she told me this morning that you stayed, took care of her. Thank you for that. She was so shaken."

He shrugged. Tried not to read anything into that *took care of her*. Tried not to remember those long hours when he'd wanted more than that. And waited until he could speak evenly to say, "That's to be expected. And she recovered pretty quickly. Handled it well, overall."

She dropped the subject then, not saying another word about her sister. He should be grateful, he supposed. And would have been if he hadn't suspected it was because he wasn't a member of the club.

Instead she focused on the interviews ahead, asking him what he would do, how he would handle them, what

he would ask. Good, intelligent questions. She had potential, he thought.

They spent the rest of the drive—north to a neighbor-
ing hamlet for this first one—talking about the forth-
coming interviews. While he drove she read him what
information they had on the first woman who'd been catfished by this man, including the actual crime report. He
liked to know as much as he could about a victim before
talking with them, because it helped guide his approach.

"She's owned Lively Gifts—that's their last name,
Lively—for three years. It was the family business,
started by her mother ten years ago."

"She inherited it when her mother died, right?"

"Yes."

"Kids?"

She drew back slightly. "Does that matter?"

"Might. Some parents, thinking you might have put
your kids at risk is the worst part of what happened."

With his peripheral vision he saw her study him for a
moment. Finally she said, "Some parents?"

He shrugged. A gesture that had become quite useful when dealing with this family who seemed to have
invaded his life. "Some wouldn't care. Or even think
about it."

"My mother," she said flatly, "would have wanted him
dead."

She said it with flat confidence, and he wondered what
it must have been like, to have grown up with that kind
of feeling, that kind of certainty of a parent's love. He'd
mostly felt he was a nuisance they'd be glad to be rid of,
if he survived to eighteen.

And her mother was Annalise's. And the woman who
had raised her to believe in true love. The real thing.

Whatever. The thing that had her searching for it, which had gotten her into this mess.

Elizabeth Lively was small, with dark shoulder-length hair and medium brown eyes. He paused outside, looking through the window. She was a quick mover; he watched her flit around the store, straightening a display on the middle row, speaking briefly to a customer looking at a little ceramic thing like those some people apparently liked to dust, tidying a card rack over near the register, then walking behind the counter to fiddle with something underneath.

"Think she's nervous?" Grace asked from beside him.

"Or looking to restore order. Her incident was the most recent prior to Annalise. She might still be dealing."

"I'm not sure you ever stop dealing with something like this," she said, surprising him. "After you've been fooled like that."

He soon discovered Elizabeth Lively was, above all else, embarrassed as she recounted the tale of her "heart-felt" connection—she'd thought—with a man who had the same passion for art that she had. She'd planned to meet at a drawing class in a local park. And how he had had to cancel last minute, but had—so sweetly, she'd thought—arranged for the teacher of that class to come to her home and give her a personal lesson.

"He gave me a lesson, all right," she said bitterly. "Nothing like waking up in the ER—thank goodness my sister came over and found me—and finding out you've been drugged and everything of value you own stolen."

And she turned bright red when shown the sketch of Annalise's catfish, and nodded before she closed her eyes in obvious humiliation.

"That's him," she said.

He tried to tell her what he'd told Annalise. "Don't feel so bad. The guy is very good, very smooth, very practiced at this."

"While I'm too stupid to live. I give up. I'm never dating again."

Exactly what Annalise had said. "That would just please him," he said. "Don't let him win."

The woman gave him a thoughtful look, then said quietly, "Thank you. That was nice of you to say." Nice? Maybe. He didn't know. Because he had no idea what had made him say it all in the first place. "But for now I'm just going to focus on making this the best and most popular gift shop in the county."

"You go, girl," Grace said with a wide smile.

Elizabeth smiled back. "I intend to."

"That *was* nice of you to say," Grace said when they were back in the car.

He shrugged. Again.

They headed the opposite direction this time, drove through Grave Gulch to the south, to a small shopping center just outside the city limits. This time the goal was a small hair salon, not a place where he would feel in the least comfortable.

"You look like you're about to get off a plane in Afghanistan or something," Grace said teasingly.

He gave her a sharp look. "Trust me," he said coolly, "this is nothing like that."

She looked sufficiently abashed and stayed quiet as they went in. He had no idea what happened in these places, but guessed what he could smell was some kind of hair dye or treatment. Someone in the back was apparently getting a manicure, from what little he knew about that process.

A woman approached them, and he recognized Natasha Tracy from the file photo. Tall, curvy, with long hair that was about ten different shades of blond that somehow all seemed to blend.

"Wow," Grace said, sounding as if it was almost involuntary. "Whoever does your hair, I want them."

Natasha looked startled, then smiled. And seemed to relax a little, so Brett gave Grace an approving nod. "My partner does it. She's here on weekends, if you want to make an appointment. I'm Natasha." Her gaze shifted to Brett, lingered. "Let me guess. Detective Shea?"

He nodded. But looked at Grace and whispered, "All yours."

Grace's eyes widened but she recovered quickly and asked if there was someplace they could talk. The woman led them to the small room at the back of the salon, where there was a table just big enough for the two chairs around it. When Brett told them to take the seats, Ms. Tracy sighed.

"A real gentleman. Unlike the imposter I got duped by."

Grace worked the encounter carefully, slowly, taking her time and asking good questions even as she exhibited full compassion for the victim's roiled emotions. Clearly she'd separated her personal connection; she was a cop now, not the latest victim's sister.

Annalise's sister.

The story that came out was very similar to the others. A carefully crafted luring, a slow build and a final cancellation with an excuse and an impressive action to make up for it—in this case a delivery from Dream Bakes, a sampler of luscious treats and a pitcher of their famous cherry lemonade. Then the dart, oblivion, and waking to the aftermath.

And when the sketch came out again, she winced visibly.

"Yes, that's him. God, I am so stupid. That's what I get for trusting him. For trusting anyone," she ended, rather vehemently. "Never again. I'm done, with all of it."

A string of thoughts tumbled through Brett's mind. Elizabeth Lively, running the family business; this woman had started her own, clearly neither weak nor foolish people. And Annalise, warm, caring and confident in her work and her love for the dogs she trained. This was more than just a scam to steal; it was an undermining of faith and hope, and it turned his stomach.

"Stop blaming yourself," he found himself saying. "None of this is on you. He's a scumbag, a weak, pathetic excuse for a man who has to trick people because he's incapable of doing anything worthwhile. Don't let him steal that...light from you." He faltered a little at the end, wondering where the hell all that had come from. Both women were staring at him. He ended it awkwardly, retreating to what he'd said before. "I'm just saying don't let him win. There are plenty of good guys out there."

Ms. Tracy's expression changed then. And the smile she gave him made him feel even more awkward. "Obviously," she said, looking him up and down. "Question is, are you single?"

"I...uh..." *Well that's articulate, Shea.* With the feeling he'd just walked himself into a mine field, because after what she'd been through a quick rebuff could be a harsh blow, he scrambled for a tactful answer. "Thanks. And if I was in the market, I'd...be interested." He tried a smile. "But I'm not the only good guy around. Might want to pass on the dating app thing though."

She didn't seem to take offense, only grimaced and said, "I deleted it the instant I got my phone back."

They were back in his unit when Grace said, "That was a good thing you did. Again."

He shrugged, not knowing what to say since he had no idea what had brought on the outburst. "You did well with her. Just the right balance."

"Thank you." Grace sighed. "She looked cool and calm on the outside, but she's still hurting."

"Yeah. She's had her foundation rocked."

"Just like the woman at the gift shop. And my sister."

"Yes."

There was a moment of silence in the car before Grace added quietly, "No wonder Annalise felt safe with you."

He had no idea what to say to that, so he said nothing, just drove. And thought. About the twisted mentality of a man who made his way in life by duping innocent women. He thought of everything he'd learned over the years about men like that, characteristics, how they thought, the kinds of things they did and where they went. He was building a picture in his mind, a picture that he hoped would lead him down the right path.

You're going down, catfish.

It was both promise and vow, to himself and the victims.

Especially Annalise.

Chapter Fifteen

Back at the station, Brett made a call and found out the person he wanted to see, the psychologist they sometimes consulted, wasn't due back for another hour, so instead of going inside he dropped Grace off and headed over to the training center. He arrived just as Annalise was finishing her session with Ember in the big arena. He could tell that by the praise she was lavishing on the delighted Lab. Even as he watched she dropped down to her knees, not caring about the dirt, not when it came to stroking and hugging and petting the dog, who looked utterly ecstatic.

Like you wouldn't be if she was doing that to you?

A blast of heat rocketed through him as the image formed in his mind, and he was glad he'd stayed in the car, because he had no doubts his thoughts would be reflected in his face. Not to mention another body part she seemed able to wake up simply by existing.

He had the sudden thought that the dog would be delighted to have Annalise around all the time. And a fantasy of them all together rose in his mind as fully formed as if he'd been thinking about it every day.

But he hadn't been. Had he?

And then Ember, ever alert even at this distance,

whirled around, ears up and nose in the air. He heard her let out a happy bark and she broke away and headed for him at a run. Annalise stood, but made no move to call her back. Instead she followed—at a much slower pace—and reached them after Brett had had a chance to properly greet the loyal animal.

"She did well. We're really pushing the envelope on older scents and complicated ones. And I worked a bit more with her on air scenting," she added, referring to the knack of tracking airborne odors as well as those on the ground. "I think she's really getting it."

"She's the best."

"I would not argue that," Annalise said with a smile.

He hesitated, but decided it was part of his job and asked, "How are you doing?"

"All right." Her effort at a smile was almost believable. "You told Sergeant Kenwood to keep an eye on me, didn't you?"

It wasn't really a question, so he only shrugged and said, "He was already here."

"But not usually hovering the way he did today."

"You needed to feel safe."

"Yes. I did. I wasn't complaining." She gave him a sideways look and a small smile that sent his insides tumbling as his earlier thoughts had.

He had to get out of here. Get away from her. She did too many things to him. He was too drawn to her, and the pull was getting harder to resist. He'd managed to keep it at bay before, but somehow last night, holding her, seeing her scared, vulnerable and self-condemning, had crumbled the walls he hid behind around her.

He hated that she felt any part of what had happened was her fault. It had been bad enough with the two other

victims today, but with her it was magnified, amplified…
personal. And wound him up until he wanted to find this
catfish and pound him into the ground.

"I need to get to the station and tie up some things.
You get off at five, right?" At her nod he went on. "I'll
be back to pick you up then."

He didn't wait for her to acknowledge, not when what
he really wanted to do was grab her and hold her until
she was her bright, happy self again. He turned on his
heel and headed back to his vehicle, Ember at his side.

*Ember, the only female you should be thinking about
sharing a house—and a life—with.*

WELL, THAT HAD been a little abrupt.

"Goodbye to you, too," Annalise muttered as she
watched him go without even giving her a hint about
how the interviews had gone. Then she felt bad. She
should cut him some slack; he was obviously focused on
the case. And that's what she wanted, right? She wanted
that guy found and put away for what he'd done. Preferably for a very, very long time.

Yet some small part of her, a tiny voice she tried to
smother, was saying something quite different. It was
saying what she really wanted was more of last night's
time with Brett—specifically that time when he'd simply held her until all the stress, all the worry, all the humiliation had seemed to leech out of her. When she'd
abandoned her efforts at being strong, and let the reaction take hold and work its way through, as he'd said it
would whether she fought it or not.

He'd been so kind, so gentle…and yet she'd never felt
as if it was because he thought her weak.

You're the one who fought back, with the only weapon

you had at hand. That's not something I laugh at. It's something I applaud.

The words echoed in her mind, in the same obviously sincere tone in which he'd said them. He'd meant it. While she'd been thinking the worst of herself, he'd been thinking the best. And he had the experience to know, didn't he? He must have seen people in bad situations countless times, seen how they reacted, what they did or didn't do. So surely—

Her phone cut off her thoughts with the tone she had assigned to family. It was the theme of an old movie her father had so loved they had all ended up seeing it countless times growing up.

She pulled it out and glanced at the screen. Grace. She automatically reached to swipe up to answer, then froze.

Grace. Who had just spent the entire morning with Brett.

She had to fortify herself with the knowledge her little sister wasn't a gossip about family. But she could chatter when nervous, and Annalise already knew she had been nervous about the chance to go on an investigation with the quietly effective and efficient detective. So it was a moment before she could make herself complete the swiping motion.

"How'd the interviews go?" she asked, before Grace could ask how she was; she didn't want to go through that again.

"Great! I learned so much. Br—Detective Shea even let me do the second one myself."

"Congratulations," Annalise said. "That's his kind of high praise."

"I know. I was so excited he trusted me, but I had to

hide it. Wouldn't do to show I was thrilled in front of a victim." She caught herself. "Except I just did, didn't I?"

Annalise laughed, for the most part because she was relieved that *victim* hadn't been the first thing in her sister's mind when it came to her. She let Grace go on with what she could reveal—which wasn't much, even though Annalise was a victim herself, since it was an ongoing investigation—the bottom line of which was both women had positively identified Desiree's sketch as the man who had shown up at their door after a canceled date.

Annalise didn't know if this news made her feel better, knowing that she wasn't alone in her foolishness, or worse because after working with the police for this long, she should have been the one to realize something was off with... Sam-who-doesn't-exist.

"But you know what impressed me the most?" Grace asked. "About him, I mean?"

Annalise was almost afraid to ask. Her sister sounded a bit awed, and she wasn't sure she liked that. "I assume you don't mean his big blue eyes," she said dryly.

"No," Grace said, in that teasing tone she'd heard from the time her sister had been old enough to talk. "That's your department." *What's that supposed to mean?* "But both women, they're smart, they run businesses, but they still felt like you did, like they'd been stupid and would never trust anyone again, and never, ever date again."

Annalise was wondering where Grace was heading with this. True, it made her feel...something, not comfort really, but more a sense of a burden shared, to know others felt the same.

"Anyway," Grace went on, "Brett was great with the first woman, but he really stepped up with the second, told her not to feel that way, not to let him steal that light from her, because that would mean this guy had won."

"He…said that?"

"Yes. And he reminded her there were plenty of good guys out there. Of course then she tried to flirt with him, but—"

"She flirted with Brett?" Okay, that had come out a little sharp.

"He wasn't having any of it, but he was very kind about it. Just said he wasn't on the market, but there were lots of other good guys out there."

At least he's consistent. "He told me that, too, that he wasn't…looking."

"Oh." Grace sounded disappointed. "I was hoping it was because of you."

"What?"

"That he wasn't looking because you and he—"

"Don't be silly!" That had come out even more sharply. And she could just picture the expression on her little sister's face. The one she always wore when attacking a puzzle of any kind.

And Annalise was fairly sure she'd just given her a very big clue.

BRETT HAD BEEN about to text the chief the interview results when he remembered she probably didn't have her phone, that Ellie was probably going through it with her deep-reaching, fine-byte comb. He changed direction and headed for the tech whiz's desk instead, Ember at his heels. The dog was used to coming in here, because Brett always brought her inside if he was going to be a while. She was popular among the troops, and especially liked to visit the records section, where the clerks cooed over her and gave her treats from the jar they had hidden in a drawer.

Ellie's domain was one the rest of the department regarded with wary awe. Brett was reasonably competent with tech, but even he treated it—and her—with the respect she'd earned by being able to find things it would take him five times as long to find, or things he never would have found at all.

"I matched the photos of the guy on Annalise's phone," Ellie greeted him without preamble. He liked that, too, that she didn't require a lot of niceties, not when she was hot on a trail. "They're from a stock photo site. The real model does everything from fitness shoots to—surprise, surprise—medical stuff, complete with the stereotypical stethoscope around his neck."

"Watermarked?"

She nodded. "Wouldn't be that hard to mask that, if you had some basic skills. Do you think he'd actually buy the pics to use?"

Brett shrugged. "No idea. You'd think he wouldn't want to leave a trail, but I can't say he didn't. He might think he's clever enough to hide it."

"Don't they all think they are?" Ellie said wryly.

"Point taken," Brett agreed. "Give me the numbers on the images you matched and I'll look into getting a warrant for their records on who's purchased those particular shots."

Ellie nodded and moved on in her usual, rapid-fire manner. "I think I have at least three other cases, maybe four. I'm comparing the texts now and finding definite similarities."

"Where?"

"None here in Grave Gulch," she said, "but all in the county, and within the last year."

"I'll need copies of their reports," he began. "I—"

"Already in the works."

Brett turned quickly, recognizing Melissa's voice from behind him. He nodded to her. "Chief." She smiled back. It was a better smile these days, no doubt thanks to her fiancé.

"Thank you for taking Grace with you," she said.

"She did a good job taking lead on the second interview. Built a rapport with the victim right away."

The smile widened, but only for a moment before she turned serious again. "And they both made a positive ID on the sketch?"

"Positively. No hesitation, it was him."

He gave her what other details they had, although he guessed Grace had probably given her a full report already. And that she listened intently to his told him she valued all input. That mattered to him and was one of the reasons he didn't bail on this Colton-dominated department. That and the fact that if he did, it could be used against the GGPD by the media and the mob, and he wasn't about to throw gas on that fire.

"What's your next step?"

He liked that, too, that she made it clear he was to proceed as he saw fit, not as she ordered. Again he remembered his final interview with her before he'd taken the job, when she'd said, *I try to hire the best, then let them do their best.* That had been a deciding factor, although he hadn't told her that. Mainly because he'd known he wouldn't find out for a while if that was a real, guiding philosophy, or just talk.

"A talk with Dr. Masters," he said.

Somewhat to his surprise, he'd ended up liking the department's consulting forensic psychologist, Dr. Matthew Masters. They didn't use him often, but he'd been very helpful when they had.

"Good idea," the chief agreed. "And he is back from court—I just saw him outside his office."

Although he was only fifty, Dr. Matthew Masters looked like everyone's ideal of the sweet old grandfather. Or maybe Santa Claus, Brett thought as the man opened the office door to his knock, with his silver hair and a tidy little beard, roundish face and a wide, genuine-seeming smile.

"Been expecting you," he said, ushering him inside. "I saw the report on poor Ms. Colton this morning. She trains your pup, doesn't she?" he asked as he bent to pet the dog's head. Brett liked that the man had no problem with Ember's presence; in fact they had once had a discussion about therapy animals, in which the man was a firm believer. "Once you've seen someone so desperate they've attempted suicide respond to the simple presence of a loving dog, you'll never dismiss it again," he'd said.

"Yes," Brett answered, "she does train Ember. She's brilliant with her."

Dr. Masters didn't go to his desk but took a seat in one of the chairs opposite it, and gestured Brett to the other. As he sat, Brett wondered if there was some reason for that, some messaging that he wasn't looking at him as a patient or something like that. Then he wondered why he was wondering that, and if everybody who dealt with a shrink in some form or another had similar thoughts every time.

And if his wandering thoughts were more of his strenuous efforts to stop thinking about Annalise, he didn't admit it even to himself.

Chapter Sixteen

"How's Annalise doing with this?" Dr. Masters asked.

"Rattled. Uncertain," Brett answered. *And no longer really trusting herself or anyone else.*

"To be expected."

Brett nodded. "But she did great during the incident," he felt compelled to add.

"Clobbered him with a plate cover, I believe the re- port said."

Brett found himself smiling as he nodded again. "She did. Bought herself enough time to get away."

"Good for her."

"Yes." He only hoped she would eventually get that, how rare it was that she had the presence of mind and the nerve to do anything but freeze in horror, as most people would when confronted with such a situation.

Even as he thought it, Dr. Masters verbalized a similar thought. "That should help her accept, later, when she has more perspective. She'll see she wasn't a helpless victim."

"She—they all feel—like fools." He had to stop doing that. Annalise wasn't the only crime victim here, even if she was the one he thought about most. And that wasn't right.

"Also to be expected. It will take time for them to realize he's at fault, not them." Dr. Masters leaned back in the chair and steepled his fingers. "What's your take on him?"

Brett had an answer ready, since it had been the only thing able to keep his thoughts off paths he should not follow. And he'd spent a long time studying Desiree's sketch, as if it was a pathway into this predator's mind. He'd studied the narrow, rather pointy face, thought about the size and lack of body mass of the man he'd seen running; if he didn't know, Brett would have thought him a kid. And he couldn't help thinking that all played into this, that his size was part of what had made this con artist into what he was.

"I think this is a case where the suspect wouldn't be able to do what he does without the internet and mobile technology, and the ability to fake. His appearance would sink him if he tried to scam anyone in person."

"We're such a shallow society," the doctor said, and Brett couldn't tell if he was being dramatic or serious with the pronouncement. "But he does look a bit…shady."

"Yes," Brett agreed. Personally, he thought the man looked like a ferret, but that wasn't something he was about to say. "You're the expert, not me, so correct me if I've gone wrong. My guess is he resents that people see him that way and has worked that up into a 'the world owes me' mindset. And that he chooses women to victimize because he feels they in particular owe him, because they've likely ignored him or turned him away. He probably doesn't feel guilty at all, because he doesn't think of his victims at all, only himself."

Dr. Masters raised his eyebrows. "Been reading up?"

"A little. I like to know what I'm dealing with." But Brett well knew he didn't have the training and experience the psychologist had. And he'd seen him testify in court, and knew he made no idle arguments and could back them up if questioned. "But I'm not assuming I'm right," he added, out of respect for the man's position and title.

"I think you probably are, for the most part. His approach and method are the classic catfish. Showing up himself is a blip, but I don't know how serious."

"How will being interrupted and almost caught affect him?"

"A very good question I'm afraid I can't answer without further knowledge of him."

"Would the history of his interactions on the dating app help?"

"It would."

"I'll see that you get them." He'd need them himself anyway, because he'd had an idea.

Dr. Masters pondered for a moment. "In a way," he said finally, "Ms. Colton is fortunate."

Brett didn't think the man meant simply that she hadn't been physically hurt. "To have had the nerve to fight back?" he asked.

Dr. Masters smiled. "Yes, that, most definitely. But I meant the fact that this was clearly a catfish with the intent of theft, not solely a social one."

Brett wondered when the law would catch up with tech and make such impersonations and scams prosecutable. Considering the relative speed—or lack thereof—of both, he wasn't optimistic. But in this case, at least, the catfish had violated laws already on the books. He nodded then. "So it's a crime, and she has recourse."

"And you on her side," the man said.

Brett started to speak then stopped himself, certain

Dr. Masters hadn't meant that the way he had first taken it, with a far-too-personal interpretation. "We can pursue it, yes."

"But there's also another aspect. Most people find such an elaborate scam for the purpose of stealing more…understandable than those who do it merely because they can, or like to toy cruelly with other people, or require the attention they believe they aren't getting any other way."

Brett hadn't thought of it in that way, but it made sense. One was simple, a crime he could understand. The other was more twisted, malevolent in a way he understood only logically even as it made his stomach churn and sparked the kind of outrage he rarely felt. In part, he suspected, because he was helpless even as a cop to do anything about it.

"Not a crime," he muttered.

"Yes," Dr. Masters said, his tone echoing some of Brett's own feelings, "but with victims nevertheless."

Victims who would perhaps never be the same. Like Elizabeth Lively and Natasha Tracy. And Annalise.

"Will she—" He caught himself and changed his words. "Will they ever be able to trust again?"

If Dr. Masters caught the break and change, he didn't say so, for which Brett was thankful. "Trust? To some extent, yes. As wholeheartedly or as easily as they once did? Not for a long time, if ever. At the least, they will have a sense of wariness they did not have before." He smiled then. "And perhaps, as painful as the lesson is, that's not a bad thing."

As he and Ember headed back out to the unit he pondered that. If it would help keep her safe, he supposed it was true the lesson might be worth it. Even if it was painful to think of Annalise's normally sunny nature curbed

by mistrust, that was a lot better than a couple of alternatives he could think of. There was a lot less evil to deal
with here in this small town—even if a big chunk of it
had been under their own roof apparently, in the person
of Randall Bowe—but that didn't mean it didn't exist.

So in that way, yes, she had been lucky. This fake
suitor had been after money, property, not herself. It truly
could have been much, much worse. In ways that made
his stomach churn far more than the simpler crime did.

In ways he was having more and more trouble denying were personal.

Annalise settled Apple and Jack in the cushy bed beside her desk, at this point in their progress fairly satisfied they would stay there until she was finished. They
were quiet and seemingly happy—they'd had a busy day,
and she'd been able to work with them a lot between her
other clients.

She made her final notation on the training session
with Bear the German shepherd. She smiled as she did so,
because she had just finished writing up Ember's session,
and the differences between the two dogs were quite evi-
dent. In large part it was the intrinsic differences in the
two breeds, and she spent some time musing about that
as she often did, that the shepherds were bred to protect
and control, the Labs to retrieve, and how that played into
their skills in police work and the military. Bear was an
absolute terror to criminals—there was a reason cops
were required to give a suspect the chance to surrender
before unleashing him—and skilled in tracking, but he
didn't have the nose Ember did. Ember was not an apprehension dog, but could find just about anything under
conditions most would think impossible.

But Annalise always said the biggest factor was their hearts, and the need and drive to please their pack leader. Their beloved human. That she had no doubts about.

As she went to close the files she saw again the photo of the black Lab. And as if sparked by the picture the memories of last night flooded her again. She supposed the fact that her thoughts of the catfish, the images of the skinny little man who had stolen not just her grandmother's bracelet but big chunks of her trust and self-esteem, were quickly pushed aside by warmer memories, of Brett Shea's efficient investigating, his quiet understanding, his warm compassion, was a sign of progress.

The memories of his arms around her, and what that had made her feel, were something else altogether.

"Stupid," she said aloud. "That's the word for it, stupid."

"Who you calling stupid?" Sergeant Kenwood's voice from the doorway was full of clearly mock belligerence.

Annalise looked up and smiled. "Not you, ever."

The man smiled, his teasing expression turning to one of understanding. "Don't call yourself that, either," he said. "Those slimy guys are cunning in a way good, honest people never see coming."

She managed a smile, touched that the sometimes gruff veteran had made the effort at comfort.

He turned to go, but then looked back over his shoulder. "Oh, and your ride home just pulled in."

Brett. He was here. Early. Her pulse leaped, and she could only hope nothing of her inner reaction showed on the outside. Judging by the sudden narrowing of Sergeant Kenwood's gaze, she doubted she had that much luck.

Chapter Seventeen

Focus.

That was his problem, Brett decided as he sat in his unit after turning the engine off. He needed to keep his focus on the case, the crime, the suspect, as he normally did. His ability to exclude distraction had been a large part of his success as a detective, and it was irritating that he was having trouble at the moment doing what usually came easily.

It was beyond irritating that he knew perfectly well the distraction he couldn't seem to exclude on this case had a name, beautiful blue-gray eyes, a mane of silky blond hair and curves that made his fingers curl. It was downright frustrating, and in more ways than one. He hadn't wrestled with the urges of his body this much in years.

She's a coworker. Something you swore off the day you got the badge.

Except she wasn't, really. Not in the sense that they were on the job together. She was a few steps back. Which actually worked well sometimes—she had enough knowledge from her work with the department K-9s to understand what he did, but she wasn't directly involved in it. Several of his fellow cops in Lansing had ended up marrying emergency-room nurses or physicians, because they understood the high-stakes, high-tension life that came with their jobs.

So, scratch that reasoning.

He sat there, tapping his fingers on the steering wheel. He glanced at the clock in the dash. Four fifty-four. *Six minutes to get your head together, Shea.*

She's Ember's trainer. You don't want to mess that up.

Right. As if she'd ever let anything affect how she felt about the sweet Lab. Not Annalise. Her love for the dog, for all the dogs, both the ones she worked with and the ones she fostered, was heartfelt and pure, and nothing would ever change it. He knew that as surely as he knew his eyes were blue.

And the fact that that acknowledgment of this embedded aspect of her made him wonder if her love for a man, if she ever gave it, would be the same, only tangled him up more.

He let out a disgusted breath. He wasn't having much luck here. He watched the clock roll over to four fifty-eight. If he got out now, he'd hit the office right at five, as promised.

But he'd still be in this quandary.

In desperation he fell back on the only thing he had left.

She's a Colton.

And yet hadn't every Colton he'd dealt with so far, from the chief down to rookie Grace, been completely accepting of him? Hadn't he found them all competent and then some, each in their own job? Yes, they were under fire right now, and maybe that was part of the reason they seemed to be such a solid unit; they'd had to pull together. Which was more than his own family would have done, or ever had done.

Or was it really only the idea that there were so many of them, and that they were a family—and a family so unlike his own—that had made him feel the outsider? And was that feeling not their problem, but his?

He didn't know anymore.

With a sharp movement he yanked the door handle and got out, willing his body to calm down. On impulse he also let Ember out, thinking the dog would be a good buffer. He could always focus on her, no matter who else was around. She seemed a bit puzzled to be back at the training center, but she trotted along amiably.

Coward. Hiding behind a dog.

Brett sighed inwardly, getting with the distinct feeling he was losing it as he walked toward the building.

And toward the woman who was the cause of it all.

SHE HAD WORRIED for nothing.

Annalise sighed inwardly as she fastened the seat belt in his car. She'd gotten herself all worked up in expectation of Brett's arrival, her pulse kicking up at the thought of seeing him again, of him taking her home. She'd even been trying to decide if she dared ask him to stay for a while. She'd offer to fix dinner for them, just as a thank-you, of course, for his kindness the night before. Nothing more than that, of course. It wasn't like she would ask him to spend the night. Again.

But her imagination had run riot with that scenario, and what might happen, and she'd ended up in a tangle of emotions ranging from keen anticipation to self-condemnation, because just last night she'd been committed to starting a relationship with another man. And yet had spent a great deal of that night thinking about Brett

Shea instead of the man she'd planned to be with. And she didn't like the way that made her feel.

That that man didn't and never had existed didn't change that. All it did was prove that she was a fool. But Brett had never made her feel that way, had in fact gone a long way toward easing that uncomfortable assessment of herself.

At least, the Brett who had been with her last night had. The one who was here now was a different creature altogether. The one who was here now was brisk to the point of brusque, businesslike and utterly impersonal. There was not a trace of the connection she'd felt last night. Not even the connection she usually felt when they worked with Ember. It was as if he'd put a wall up between them.

Can you blame him?

It wasn't personal, she tried to tell herself. He was simply being what he was, a professional. He'd helped her through last night, but now that was over. Maybe he did that with every victim he dealt with, helped them.

Spent the night with them?

Well, it wasn't like he'd really spent the night with her; he'd merely spent it under her roof. To keep her safe. But why? She doubted he did that with every victim. Was it simply because he knew her? Because she was Ember's trainer?

Or…because she was a Colton?

That thought gave her pause. Had he only gone out of his way because she was related to his boss? Was it that simple? She didn't want to think so, but it was something she couldn't be sure didn't factor in.

God, being a Colton was so darn complicated sometimes.

The silence in the unit as they headed toward her

house began to seem like a physical thing. It wore on her, dug at her, until she finally blurted out, "Grace told me how good you were with those other victims."

He glanced at her, his expression unreadable. "She talked to you about the interviews?"

"Not about the case. She never would," she said hastily. She breathed again when his gaze went back to the road ahead. "She just told me how...supportive you were to them. Telling them it wasn't their fault." She bit the inside of her lip but the next words came out anyway. "Like you were with me."

There was a pause, so brief it could have been a search for words or merely a registering the vehicle approaching on the left at the intersection, before he said in that same businesslike tone he'd greeted her with back at the training center, "All in a day's work."

That stung as if it had been a slap. Which told her how far out of line she'd gotten. She was obviously only that: part of a day's work. He was making it clear where she stood, what she was to him.

And what she wasn't.

As they turned into her driveway she reached for the seat belt so she could be ready to get out—and get away—the moment they stopped.

"Hold on," Brett said. Startled, she glanced at him. He wasn't looking at her, but obviously he'd seen or sensed her move. "Just wait a minute."

He'd put down his window and was studying the house. Her pulse kicked up for an entirely different reason than it usually did around him. "Is there something—"

She stopped when he held up a hand. He was listening intently. All she could hear was the occasional slight snap of the engine cooling. Finally he put the window back up and looked at her.

"What?" she asked, unable to hold it back any longer. "Did you see something? Hear something?"

"No." He said it flatly, and his brow was furrowed in a way that didn't fit the denial. In a way that seemed familiar to her.

"Then what?" she asked.

"I don't know. Just...never mind. Let's go."

She gathered up her dogs from where they'd ridden in the back with Ember, gave the Lab a goodbye pat and headed for the house. Her dogs squirmed as if eager to make their usual circuit of the little yard when they came back from anywhere, so she let them loose once they were safely inside the fence.

She and Brett were nearly to the door when it hit her what had seemed familiar to her about his expression. It was the same look she'd seen on Troy's face when he'd been trying to explain the gut feeling he sometimes got on a case to Grace, back when she'd been considering joining the department.

I can't explain it. It's just a feeling. Sometimes it's that I'm missing something. Or that there's something wrong I can't see. Sometimes it's that I'm going down a wrong path. But it's strongest when I'm on the right track.

Something wrong I can't see...

The words were still ringing in her mind when, after she'd unlocked it, Brett pushed the front door open. They stepped inside.

All seemed quiet, calm. The living room, which faced west, was getting the full force of the summer evening sun. It looked pleasant and peaceful, and she liked the way the sun caught and gleamed through the blue glass bottles she'd arranged on the window ledge.

She breathed more easily. Brett was walking around, checking all the windows. Annalise headed toward the kitchen and dining room, already thinking about what she could fix for dinner that he might like, if he would stay if she asked, if she could even work up the nerve to do it. She'd made extra spaghetti sauce the last time she'd fixed it, and there was a tub of it in the freezer. Or there was the—

She was two steps into the dining and kitchen space when she stopped dead. A shriek rose in her throat, and she couldn't stop it.

Because there, there in nearly the exact spot as before, was a near duplicate of the delivery cart from last night.

He was back.

Chapter Eighteen

"Don't move." Brett snapped out the order. Annalise didn't seem to hear and took a step toward the cart. He grabbed her and pulled her back. "Don't," he repeated. He felt the shivers going through her and, unable to stop himself he pulled her against him.

She was sucking in quick, shaky breaths, and he hated the sound of it. Hated the thought that she was being terrorized in her own home. He wanted to get her out of here, take her someplace where she would feel safe again. Where she would be able to simply smile again, coo over her lucky dogs, use that amazing connection she had to push Ember to even greater success.

He wanted it more than he wanted to get this guy, and that realization sent up not just a red flag but a warning signal as loud as a klaxon. He never, ever put the personal side ahead of the job, not on an active case. At least, he never had before. And that thought sent up another warning; he had no business even thinking about a personal side here.

Still, he kept one arm around her as he pulled out his phone and called it in, all the while staring at the food cart. The same pristine white tablecloth, but that's where the similarities ended. This time the table held, most noticeably, a large bouquet of white roses in a gold vase. The platters under the covers appeared to be gold, as well. Stepping up the game? Announcing she was a valuable target he wasn't about to give up on?

"Two," he murmured as he finished the call and put the phone away. There were two platters on the table this time. He didn't like the implications of that, which were that somehow the catfish knew he'd stayed here last night, after the first abortive attempt.

He pulled out the key ring that held the fob for the unit and pressed the button combination that would open the back hatch. Ember would be here in seconds. Annalise murmured something against his chest, where her face was pressed against him. It was unbelievable, that in the middle of all this all he could think in that moment was how much he liked holding her like this. And that realization snapped him back to the job at hand.

"Annalise," he said firmly, "Ember has to do a search. I need you to wait in the unit while she—"

"No!" Her head came up sharply, and he heard her quick intake of breath. "I can't. I need to get my dogs. What if he's still outside? I should have thought of that first, before I let them loose in the yard—what if he was still there and he hurt them? I—"

"I'll get them," he promised, hoping she was wrong, because he wouldn't put it past the guy to take the animals out however he could. But how like her that this was her first thought, her main worry.

"But—"

"Annalise, please." As he heard Ember's sharp bark from the front porch, he went for a temporary stall. "Just stay here—right here, don't move an inch—while I let her in. We have to let her do her job."

As he knew it would, putting the focus on the dog settled her. He went to the front door and let the eager animal in. He walked Ember over to the cart, saw the quiver that went through her as her nose filled with the remembered scent. For Brett, that was as good as a sworn statement that it was the ferret again. Not that he'd had any doubts.

"Find," he ordered.

The dog practically snapped to attention and began to hunt. The animal was so well trained, she went right past the person who had helped make her that keen searcher without a glance; she was working now, and that was all she was focused on.

Brett let her do it, only moving when the steady black Lab moved from the cart to the kitchen. He guessed her goal by the time she'd gone the first three feet: the back door. Clearly the guy had come in that way this time. Vehicle in the alley, and through the back gate no doubt. Which would explain why he hadn't been seen—back door, no dogs home to raise a ruckus. Brett knew that the watch over her house wouldn't have been as intense since Annalise was safely at work, and the guy probably waited for his moment, when whoever had been watching was sent on another call.

He looked back at Annalise, who was standing in place, watching. "You locked it, right?"

"Yes. Of course."

For all the good it does. He looked at the door with the window in the upper half. Within easy reach of the doorknob and the lock. If he had his way, that kind of door would never be installed anywhere. "Ember, hold." The dog stopped instantly, although obviously not happy about it. But if what Brett suspected was true, he didn't want her over there yet.

Ember sat, practically vibrating, staring at the back door, clearly wanting to go on. Brett reached into his pocket and pulled out a glove; he didn't want to mess up any prints that might be salvageable. He walked over, his gaze on the floor just inside the door. There was no sign of the broken glass he'd feared having Ember step on. So did they have a lock picker on their hands? That took some skill, and his gut was saying *not this guy*. He relied on his scam to get him inside.

He nudged aside the blind that covered the window. Not a lock picker. He'd been right. A tidy, nearly perfect circle was cut out of the glass at the bottom corner of the window, near the knob. It was just big enough for a hand, and clearly done with a glass cutter.

A chorus of barks and yaps came from outside as Jack and Apple charged up onto the small back porch. He wasn't worried about contamination there; neither the CSI nor Ember would mistake the dogs' trails for their suspect's. But he did want them contained when the troops arrived.

"Annalise, can you come over here and get the dogs, without touching anything else?"

"Of course."

"And try to keep them from running around and messing up any evidence inside."

"I can put them in their crates," she suggested. "We crate train our fosters, for the feeling of safety it gives them."

"Great," he said.

She did it quickly and efficiently, and he guessed she was glad to have them to focus on instead of what she'd come home to. He could hardly blame her for that. He wondered if she realized yet all the implications of the catfish's return.

He opened the door, and almost immediately spotted the glint from the intact circle of glass lying on the ground a foot away. He let Ember out, gave her the command to track. The dog sniffed at the glass, but then followed the exact path he'd expected, straight to the back gate that led out to the alley behind the house. He followed her, careful to take a route to one side of the path she'd followed; he couldn't see any footprints, but he didn't want to take the chance.

When he got there he opened the gate and looked, holding Ember back for a moment. It was empty except for a dirty brown sedan that looked as if it hadn't moved since last summer, parked several houses down. He sent Ember through, and after some intent snuffling around about six feet north of the gate she sat, giving the signal the scent ended here.

So now they knew where he'd likely been parked.

He had to, as always after a fruitless search, convince Ember not finding the quarry was not her fault; the dog seemed to take any unsuccessful search as a personal affront. They'd have to do a door-to-door to see if anyone had seen the vehicle—maybe the same van—or the "delivery."

Or the ferret.

He went back, and found Annalise standing next to the cart. Staring at the array. "I can't tell you how much I hate that he was in my house, again."

"I know," he said quietly.

He heard the sound of at least two vehicles out front. The cavalry had arrived. But he wanted a look before they moved in and took over. He reached out with his gloved hand and lifted the lid over the closest platter. And went still.

On the rather ornate china plate lay a scrawny rat, very dead. Tented over the body was a note card, bearing a word in large block letters.

COP.

Annalise moved. He tried to stop her, but she got her head turned around enough to see. For a moment she just stared, her eyes wide with shock. He tightened his arm around her, hating once more that she was going through this. But then the shocked expression faded and he saw her gaze shift to the second platter.

"Let me look. You don't need to see…whatever's there."

Her chin came up, and she straightened. Pulled back. He let go of her, with a reluctance he didn't want to acknowledge even to himself.

"Yes, I do." She said it with surprising firmness. "This is my life he's screwing with, Brett. He's scared me into near panic twice now. He's not going to do it a third time."

He looked at her, at the determined expression on her face. And couldn't help but smile. "I think the phrase, according to Grace anyway, is *You go, girl.* Not sure a guy can say that though."

"You can," she said quietly. "To me, anyway."

He wasn't sure how to take that, so instead he turned back to the task at hand. He could hear voices outside now, close, so he moved quickly, lifting the second lid.

By comparison, what was on the platter was lovely. An elaborately decorated chocolate heart. But the note was more ominous, not just promise but threat, in the sort of way that made him think of old-time villains cackling.

Soon enough, my sweet. I'll be coming for you.

And with that gut-level cop instinct that he didn't need Dr. Masters to confirm, he knew this had just shifted to an entirely new level. He'd wondered how the catfish would react to being found out in the act, to having one of his victims see through him and fight back.

Now he knew.

And Annalise was in danger of more than just smashed expectations.

Chapter Nineteen

"Grab what you need for a few days. You're coming back to my place."

"What?" Annalise knew she was probably not reacting normally after everything that had happened, but she was not used to feeling totally blank after hearing such a simple statement.

"You can't stay here," Brett said flatly. He wasn't looking at her, instead watching the CSIs work.

"I...don't want to, but..."

"It's after eight. Too late to go hunting down someplace else for you to go. It's the easiest thing to do."

She focused on his first words. She'd never realized before how long a thorough crime-scene investigation really took, especially when there was more evidence. She knew a couple of uniformed officers were going door-to-door talking to her neighbors, on the chance one of them might have been both home and looking into the alley when the guy had been here. It didn't seem likely to her, but she'd overheard enough tales of pure luck in investigations that she didn't discount it entirely.

But the rest of what he'd said hammered at her. Easiest? There was absolutely nothing easy about the thought of...going home with him.

He finally looked at her. His expression was unreadable to her, and his tone a little too neutral for her comfort when he said, "Unless you want to call Grace, or Troy or maybe the chief?"

She shuddered inwardly. They would descend on her, loving but smothering. They'd hover, and worry, and they already had enough to worry about. Especially Melissa.

Besides, she didn't like the way he'd said that. As if he'd forgotten but then suddenly remembered she was a Colton. And it made a difference to him.

"No," she said hastily. "No, I don't. It'll be bad enough when they find out. But the dogs. I—"

"There's plenty of room. Ember will enjoy having them there to play, once she knows she's off duty."

"What about you?" The words were out before she could stop them.

She thought she saw something flicker in his gaze before he turned it back to the investigators again. "I'll be able to focus on what I need to, once you're safely out of here," he said, back to that very neutral tone again.

Well, that was…businesslike enough. Clearly he wasn't feeling any of the internal tumult she was. But then, his house hadn't been broken into. Twice, essentially, once by subterfuge, once by flat-out burglary.

She wasn't sure she'd consciously made the decision, but she found herself in her bedroom dragging out the backpack she used for hikes through the forest. She began gathering necessities.

Necessities. Which for a hike in the woods would be quite different than a night spent at Brett's.

A shiver went through her, and this time it was not of the horrified, my-life-has-been-invaded kind. No, this was entirely different, and if she had to put a name to it, it would be…anticipation. And no amount of telling herself it wasn't like that could completely quash the sensation. And in the end for her clothes she went for her bigger bag and tried not to call herself a fool as she added her favorite perfume. Just in case.

In case of what? He's overwhelmed by your charms?

She grimaced at her own foolishness. And that got her through to zipping up the bag and going back to the living room, where he was talking to the last CSI to pack up. He turned to look at her, nodded at the sight of the bag, but said only, "Do you want to take the dog's crates? Are they nervous in a new place?"

She liked—maybe too much—that he'd even thought of that. "It wouldn't hurt," she said. And so she, Apple and Jack, their crates and Ember were all loaded into his K-9 unit. He got in, connected his phone to the in-vehicle system and started the engine.

He didn't speak as he drove, and she decided it would be wisest not to force a conversation. They were at the intersection with Grave Gulch Boulevard when there was the chime of an incoming call. She instinctively glanced at the screen and saw Ellie Bloomberg's name. He tapped a button.

"Ellie?"

"Brett, I just heard. Is Annalise okay?"

"We arrived after the fact. She's with me, and you're on the car system."

"Annalise, I'm so sorry! You've had a horrible couple of days."

"I'm fine. But thank you," Annalise said.

"Brett will get this guy," Ellie promised. "He's the best."

Annalise glanced at the man behind the wheel, just

in time to see one corner of his mouth quirk. But all he said was, "Did you have something for me?"

"Oh, yeah. I just wanted to let you know that I did a little hunting in the outlying areas, outside town. And over near the gift shop you were at, I found a burglary report from a veterinarian's office."

"The dart!" Annalise almost yelped it.

"Exactly," Ellie said. "Usually it's drugs, but this time their entire stock of tranquilizer darts was all that was taken."

"I'll need the report," Brett said.

"Already on its way. Take care of Annalise, Brett."

"I intend to," he said, and Annalise couldn't read anything into his tone. *As well you shouldn't.*

It wasn't until the call had ended and they were through downtown that it occurred to her that the tech whiz assumed she and Brett would be physically together for him to take care of her.

She had just decided she was reading too much into Ellie's no doubt casual words—she must have meant the instruction in the "she's one of us" sense that the entire GGPD seemed to have, even for those who, like her, were on the periphery—when they turned away from the lake on a residential street that looked quiet and peaceful, shaded from the summer sun by large trees. The houses were large family-sized, and angled for, she guessed, a glimpse of the water. They went on until the houses got smaller but the lots much bigger, then made a turn onto a short cul-de-sac.

He drove to the end, to the last house on the right. It was set far back from the road, a cottage-style one story with a single garage attached, small but well-kept, painted a medium blue with crisp white trim. He pulled off the road into the long driveway. This time of year there was still plenty of light even well after nine o'clock, and she caught a glimpse of the area behind the house.

"Wow," she said. "Judging by the fence, you weren't kidding—you've got a lot of room."

"The lot is nearly two acres."

"Lots of upkeep."

He glanced at her. "I've surrendered about half of it. Not enough time, and Ember likes romping through the tall grass."

She managed a smile, the first real one since they'd walked back into her worsening nightmare. "I'll bet she does."

They pulled into the garage. It, like the outside of the house, was tidy, with a workbench along one wall, a few tools, including an intimidating-looking chain saw. He opened the hatch to release Ember, who hopped out easily and trotted toward the door into the house. Brett glanced at Annalise, and she shook her head.

"They can stay in the car a few minutes, until I bring the crates in for them."

He merely nodded and closed the hatch again. The two smaller dogs weren't happy but didn't fuss. They truly had come a long way in the weeks she'd had them.

The inner door opened into what appeared to be a combination mud/laundry room. A laundry room he apparently used, because there was a basket with a few items of clothing—including a blue shirt she recognized—on the floor beside the washer.

She followed him into the next room, an open space with a kitchen area along the closest wall, an island with stools and on the end of the counter what looked to have been set up as a charging station for various devices. Next to that on the counter was an odd-looking box with what looked like a fingerprint reader.

Ember walked over to a raised set of bowls near a door that clearly led out to the back—and had a doggie door big enough for her in it, although it appeared currently latched—drank some water, nosed at the dry food, then ambled off into the large living area beyond. Annalise could see there was a hallway on the far side she supposed led to whatever bedrooms there were. Including his. In the back, with all that open space behind it. Quiet. Private. Very private.

Her mind skittered away from the thought of his bedroom and she focused on the room they were in. She didn't know what she'd expected. Denied to herself that she'd spent as much time as she had wondering what his home would look like. Trying to imagine what would suit a man like Brett Shea.

What suited him apparently were cool colors, mostly the blue and green of the lake and trees, a sectional couch that looked infinitely rearrangable, with a side table on the far end that held another of those odd boxes, and a stack of books. Actual books. That seemed significant somehow. And they apparently weren't for show, because behind the table was a torchère-style lamp with a reading light attached.

There was a flat-screen TV on the wall opposite the couch, but while big enough it wasn't huge. In front of the end table and against the wall was a dog bed, adorned with some toys and a half-finished chew that Ember picked up before she plopped on the bed and went to work on it. That made her smile; Ember was obviously not relegated to a kennel or crate when at home.

Not that she would have expected that. No, Brett loved his furry partner.

Ember's the only girl in my life.

"Welcome to Chez Shea," he rhymed, tossing his keys down next to the charging station in what was obviously a familiar habit.

She laughed. Actually laughed. Which after tonight on top of last night was no small miracle. And when she did, Brett smiled back.

"Now that was a nice sound," he said.

"It felt good," she admitted. "Thank you."

"For a silly rhyme?"

"For bothering."

He shrugged. "Just an old joke."

She wondered how many times he'd used it. And on who. *Ember's the only girl in my life.* The words ran through her mind again.

She doubted that meant he never…indulged. And a guy who looked like him would surely have no trouble finding a casual hookup when he wanted one. Had there been a parade of women through this place? Somehow she doubted that, but at the moment she had so little faith in her own judgment she didn't trust her assessments on anything with fewer than four legs.

Especially that damned catfish.

Chapter Twenty

Once they were all settled in, Brett found himself wondering why he'd thought this a good idea. He didn't mind the two dog crates taking up a chunk of the kitchen, didn't mind their nonstop racing around, and he even enjoyed watching what they were doing now, Ember playing hostess as the two smaller dogs explored the expansive space out back.

No, he didn't mind the dogs at all. It was Annalise who was getting under his skin. Not because of anything she was doing, because she was exquisitely polite, the perfect guest, looking for things to do and arrange so that she and the dogs had as little impact on his home as possible, clearing everything she did with him first.

But then, the impact on his home wasn't the issue. It was her impact on him.

He'd reacted from the gut, wanting her in a safe place where he could protect her if necessary. He'd thought they'd come here, he would settle in to work while she did…something. Anything. And she was trying to fit into that image, even without knowing it.

No, he was the problem. He was the one who stood stock still watching her, trying to ignore how…right it felt to have her in his home. He'd never brought a woman here. In fact, except for an unexpected, one-night encounter with a blatantly sexy brunette who was just passing through, he'd pretty much ignored that aspect of his life since he'd gotten to Grave Gulch.

That had to be it. It had just been too long. This constant ache was just pent-up need, that was all. And that was not something he could or would slake with Annalise Colton, even if she was willing. But she wouldn't be, not for what he needed. Because she was looking for more.

Because even after the betrayal of this stinking catfish, she still believed in love.

You shouldn't give up on love altogether.

You have to believe in love before you can give up on it.

But you have to believe in it, or at least that it exists. Otherwise life is pointless.

The remembered exchange echoed in his mind, and it was warning enough for him to tamp down his response to her. A little, anyway.

"They're having such fun," she exclaimed suddenly, snapping him out of this frantic reverie. "They've never been able to run free like this. They pulled them out of a hoarding situation where they were never outside a cage." She sighed. "It's so wonderful to see them like this."

He dared to glance at her, now that he had himself under control. Sort of. She was watching the three animals bounding through Ember's beloved tall grass.

"Just don't let them out on their own. Once they figure it out we'll have to keep the doggie door latched if we or Ember aren't with them. There's at least one coyote in the neighborhood, and they're just small enough to be tempting." Her eyes widened, and he hastened to reassure her. "With Ember they'll be fine. She and that wild one have reached a respectful accord."

At his words her expression changed, and she smiled. "I love the way you put that."

He couldn't say why her words pleased him so much, but they did.

It wasn't until they called the dogs back—with Ember carefully making sure her new companions were coming, too—that a slight growl from his belly reminded him he'd usually have had dinner by now. And he hadn't even thought about feeding her. Them. He usually went for something simple like grilling a steak, or frozen meals, or takeout, but that was when it was only him.

"Let me get her fed," he said, "and then we can figure out dinner for us."

"I'm not really hungry," she said.

"Not surprising. But you need the fuel, especially now." He tried a slight smile. "And so do I, frankly."

She let out an audible breath. "Of course."

"Afraid I'm not really prepared. We can scrounge or order in."

She grimaced. "As long as it doesn't come on a fancy cart."

He couldn't help it; he chuckled. She gave him a slightly startled look and then, to his surprise, she was laughing. Again. And again it was one of the most wonderful sounds he'd ever heard.

"How about in a box? Paola's delivers. Or if you'd prefer to avoid delivery people altogether, we can go get it." He badly wanted to get to work on that idea he'd had earlier, but right now food—whether she wanted it or not—was paramount. Besides, he could work and eat pizza at the same time.

"I love their Hawaiian pizza, sacrilegious though it may be to some," she said, still smiling.

He gave a very exaggerated sigh. "I suppose, under the circumstances, I can allow that. We can do it half and half."

She laughed yet again, and he let the sound of it wash over him and allowed himself a little satisfaction that he'd made it happen. "I'll be okay. With delivery, I mean. As long as you go to the door."

"I will." He gave a mock eye roll. "And the delivery kid knows me, a bit too well."

Another sweet laugh, this time with a grin that had him thinking he'd even eat her silly Hawaiian pizza to keep it on her face.

They were waiting on the delivery when a text notification sounded on his phone. A very particular one, that had him going for it quickly.

Annalise? the chief asked. She must have gotten her phone back already. Ellie would move fast, not only because the text she'd gotten when he'd been in her office was from Bowe, but because it was the chief. Or maybe she just got a new message.

Safe. With me for the moment, he sent back.

For the night?

Well, this had sure turned into a minefield in a freaking hurry. He considered his words as he'd once considered his next step in one of those minefields. And ended up answering without really answering.

She needed to be out of there.

Yes. Thank you for seeing to her. Status report in the morning, please. That, he noted, was not a request.

Affirmative. I have an idea.

Share?

I want to set up a profile on that dating app. See if I can lure him.

Good idea. Annalise can help, since she'll know what makes him bite.

I can give her access?

Fine. Ellie's already been compiling info from the other profiles he interacted with, for commonalities, to see if we can head off other victims.

That info might help. I'll contact her.

Hang on... He waited a moment, then read, She'll be sending it to you.

And again he noted the chief didn't hold herself above such basic tasks. Not if it would help get the job done. He sent back a response.

Thx.

Give Annalise my love.

Brett tried to ignore the ideas and images that routine phrase brought on. It was harder to ignore the rush of heat that flooded him. Heat he couldn't write off simply to it being an August evening.

They both signed off—thankfully—and Brett put down the phone. He tried to think of words again, wondered why it was so darned hard with Annalise, and finally just said "Your cousin sends her love."

"My cousin the chief?"

He nodded. "Her main reason for texting was she wanted to know how you were." She was staring at him now, and oddly, her expression seemed amused. "What?" he finally asked.

"Your notification tone for her is *'Hail to the Chief'*?"

"I...yes." He shrugged, and knew his expression was a little sheepish. Hers was definitely amused. "What can I say—I like a little warning."

"Does she know this?"

"By now? Probably. I'm sure it's gone off in front of one Colton or another at some point."

The amusement faded. "So you assume that a Colton told her? Which one do you think it was who ratted you out? Troy? Desiree? Grace? Maybe Jillian, she's got nothing else on her mind right now."

Brett felt a jab of remorse. When she put it like that, named the names, he realized he wouldn't really suspect any of them of doing such a small thing. Troy would never betray him like that, Desiree would just find it funny, Grace was too mindful of her rookie status and he'd never spent much time around Jillian.

"Sorry," he muttered. He ran a hand over his face, feeling a little weary. The stubble on his jaw didn't help, but shaving had fallen by the wayside a bit lately. As had haircuts—he shoved back an errant strand that was tickling his forehead. "I don't..." He stopped, but the thought that he owed her at least an explanation prodded him. "My family's not like yours. Connected. Protective."

Her brow furrowed in that thoughtful way. "To me, that's what family is."

She sounded so puzzled it made him say something he rarely talked about. "My parents kicked my sister and me out when we were eighteen, saying their job was done and it was up to us now."

Her eyes widened then, in something that looked a bit like horror. "Just…kicked you out?"

He nodded. "Her first, then me. She's six years older, so we lost contact after she left."

"Desiree's seven years older than me, and we'd never…"

"Like I said, connected."

She was gaping at him now. "No wonder you don't get us. We're totally outside your life experience."

He grimaced. "A rather shrink-y way to put it, but yes."

"I'm sorry. I can't imagine growing up that way. We've had our problems and we don't all always get along, but when the chips are down…"

"The Coltons pull together," he finished for her.

"Yes." The look she gave him then was very different, and he couldn't put a name to it. "And that's why you always assume we'll pull together, even if it's against you?"

Sad. That was the word for her expression. She was sad, sorry that he felt that way. And something tickled at the edge of his mind, something important, but at the moment, with her looking right at him, he couldn't put his finger on it.

"That doesn't matter, not right now," he said briskly. "What does is catching this guy. So I need to get to work."

She blinked. "A little late, isn't it?"

"In more ways than one," he muttered. Because he

wanted this guy, wanted him bad. And he told himself firmly he would feel just as strongly even if Annalise hadn't been one of the victims.

He even almost believed it.

Chapter Twenty-One

Annalise looked around the room Brett clearly used mostly as an office. He'd said the house had only the two bedrooms, that he seriously considered using the master as his office because it was bigger, and he only slept in the other.

Only slept? She firmly directed her mind out of the gutter it leaped into at that, and said merely, "What was the deciding factor?"

He gave her a half shrug. "There wasn't really enough room for Ember to sprawl out in here."

Annalise's heart melted a little. He said it as if it were a given decision, and anyone would make it that way. When in truth she knew too many who wouldn't even consider that.

"Do you mind if I stay? I'll be quiet, promise."

He looked at her for a moment, and she wondered if he was trying to think of a tactful way to say no. But in the end he just shrugged and said, "Make yourself at home."

She knew it was just a saying, but it still sent her pulse racing a little.

He sat down at the L-shaped desk in the corner. It was clearly well used, and likely often, judging by the size of the monitor hooked up to the laptop, the array of notes on the desk and pinned to a corkboard on the wall and note-books on the shelves above. Ember had followed them in, and promptly hopped up on the small sofa on the opposite wall. Her two furry ones were sound asleep in their open crates, where they'd gone to den up happily, exhausted after their explorations outside. She really needed to look into a place with land like this.

She sat down next to Ember, who shifted a bit to look at her, then plopped her chin on Annalise's leg. That made her smile, and she began to stroke the dog's head and soft, silken ears.

It felt cozy here in this smaller room, as he sat reading an email and she snuggled with the sweet, willing Lab. It felt comfortable.

It felt right.

And she wasn't having much luck keeping thoughts like that out of her head.

She saw him nodding to himself as he read. He picked up a pen and made some handwritten notes as he went. And then tapped the end of the pen on the notepad a few times before swiveling halfway around in the office chair.

"You want to help?" he asked.

"Of course," she said, not really caring what he meant, specifically. "With what?"

"I need to set up a profile on that dating app."

She blinked. "You do?"

"You can walk me through it, since you've done it before."

"I…of course," she repeated, feeling a little rattled. "But why?"

"Ellie put together a list of commonalities across all the profiles our catfish interacted with. I'm going to set one up with as many of them as I think I can without him getting suspicious."

She stared at him. "You're going to use the app to... lure him?"

He nodded. "The chief recommended I do it. I want to get that started while we're waiting for the info on who bought the photos from the stock site. Although I doubt he used his real name there, either."

She fought down the hideous embarrassment she felt every time she thought about mooning over those pictures. "Do you think he actually did buy them, and not just lift them from their website?"

"Ellie does. She said she couldn't see any trace of the watermark being removed or fudged from the profile images."

The embarrassment won out when she belatedly realized just how many people were going to know about her folly by the time this was over.

"Annalise?" he asked with a slight frown, and she realized she'd been sitting there silently for a bit too long.

"Sorry," she said sourly. "Just realizing how far my humiliation has and will spread."

He tossed down the pen. Turned around the rest of the way on the chair, leaned forward to rest his elbows on his knees, so he was at eye level with her. "You're neither the first, nor will you be the last, to get fooled. And no one thinks any the less of you because of it."

"I wish I could believe that."

His gaze shifted to the floor for a moment, and she heard him let out a breath. Then he looked back at her face. "Some of us don't even have the excuse of being fooled by a perfectly manufactured online profile. Some of us get fooled with the real person right there in front of us."

Her breath stopped in her throat. What he'd said that first night rang in her head. *I believed a woman who said she loved me once. Worst mistake of my life.*

She stared at the steady, dedicated man before her. She knew what it felt like to care—and worry—about someone in law enforcement. She'd often wondered how anyone who fell in love with a cop stood it. But that wondering had suddenly become much more personal. And specific.

And finally she said the only truth she could think of at the moment. "She was the fool, not you."

He drew back slightly. But he didn't look away. In fact, he was looking at her so intently she felt as if she guessed a suspect must feel under that piercing, utterly focused gaze.

Then, so low she was fairly sure it wasn't aimed at her, he muttered "Not going there," and straightened up again.

Annalise had only a moment to wonder if that had meant he wanted to go "there" but wouldn't. Or if he simply was trying to keep this professional because that's what he was, a professional.

Or if he simply didn't want to go there with her.

Okay, so bringing her into his home was one of his stupider moves. It was done, and he couldn't change it now. Brett gave himself an inward shake.

Focus. It's what you're good at, right? What you're known for?

The image of a long-ago day with his very first training officer shot through his mind. A day when he'd walked right past a crucial bit of evidence in pursuit of another bit of evidence. That evening's debriefing had been a rough one.

You've got great focus, Shea. But you're going to have to learn that sometimes focus becomes tunnel vision.

Well, he could use a little tunnel vision just now. Then maybe he could concentrate on this case instead of…the victim. *This* victim.

She was the fool, not you.

She'd said it so softly, looking right at him, and it had been a tremendous effort not to read more into it than was there. She'd just meant what he'd meant, that it hadn't been his fault. She was just being kind, supportive. Trying to pay him back a little, he supposed.

This was getting…muddy. He usually had no trouble thinking big picture, and he would usually be determined to take this guy down for the sake of all of the victims. But this time his usually disciplined mind seemed to have stubbornly decided this one, this woman, was who he was doing it for. As if he had some personal stake in this. As if he wanted to do it just for her, because…because…

Because what? Because she was, in a way, a colleague? Because she was so good with Ember? Because she was in many ways an innocent, who'd been taken advantage of? Because she'd looked at him with tears in those big eyes? Because he wanted to see her smile again, see those dimples flash?

Or was it because—he might as well admit it—he had the hots for her? But then, what man wouldn't? What man could look into those eyes and not want to jump?

He swore silently. He sounded like some hormonal teenager with a crush. He hadn't spent so much time in useless mental meanderings since high school.

"Let's get this set up," he said, not quite gruffly, as

he turned back to the computer. "Just the basics now. I want to see what's involved in setting up a profile. Ellie's working on some details and photos, then I can actually start setting it up."

They began, and more than once when an app question popped up that seemed very personal and private to him, he glanced at her and asked, "People really answer all these…questions? Share all this, with people they've never even met?" At her expression he added hastily, "I'm not accusing, just asking."

Still, it was a moment before she answered. "You don't have to answer everything, to set up your profile. But I answered most of it. It seemed the best way to find a good match." She sighed audibly, and he knew she was about to say something self-condemning again, so he held up a hand.

"Don't. Try and make this…clinical. Not personal." *Good advice, Shea. Take it yourself.*

"Right."

"Walk me through the ones you did answer." Something had just occurred to him. "I want to compare it to the other profiles he interacted with."

"Why?"

"In case that's a factor in his choices."

"Oh." He knew she was thinking, not just reacting now. "You mean…if he went for those who answered most or all?" Her mouth quirked wryly. "The oversharers, so to speak?"

He nodded. "They might seem, to him anyway, more…" He stopped himself, but she supplied the exact word he'd almost used.

"Desperate?" Her tone was dry, but better than the pained, hurt tone that stabbed at him.

"Yes," he agreed. Then, more thinking out loud than anything, added, "He's not used to your kind of plain honesty and openness. He isn't himself, so he doesn't look for it or expect it in others."

Her expression changed again. He'd always been, by necessity, fairly decent at reading people. He'd had to be, growing up with his parents. But since then it had always been business, part of the job. Looking for reactions, for tells, that would lead him down the right path in an investigation. This was different. Everything with this case—with her—was different.

When she spoke, there was a change in her voice, as well. "Was that a veiled compliment, Detective Shea? Or was it a warning, not to be that way?"

He couldn't hold her gaze, and that was a rarity. He turned back to the form on the screen and said merely, "Yes." Even as he thought how much he would hate to see her close herself off, and no longer be the honest and sweetly open woman he'd known.

And that might be the biggest reason to take this scum down. He had no right to do that. Not to anyone.

Especially not to Annalise.

Chapter Twenty-Two

"Now what?" Annalise asked when—between bites of the pizza that had arrived, neatly divided between her pineapple-adorned Hawaiian and his more traditional sausage and cheese—he'd finally seen all the queries on the profile questionnaire.

"We already know he doesn't go for just one physical type. Because that's not what he's after. He's looking for a certain…mental state."

"Desperation again?" she asked, making sure she sounded more sour than hurt.

"More like…hopeful. I think—and this is just gut instinct on my part—he likes destroying that."

Something in his expression when he said it made Annalise feel, unexpectedly, almost sorry for this twisted human being when Brett caught up with him. And Brett would.

She looked at the array of information they'd compiled. "So we answer the ones everybody he interacted with answered?" They'd found nine questions every victim or potential victim had answered. Including her.

Brett nodded. "In a similar way. Then we'll go through and see if we can find anything in the other answers each one gave that might have steered him to them. With an eye out for any strong answers."

"Strong?"

"Like not just *I don't like olives* but *I hate them*. Not just *I prefer classical music* but *I hate everything else*."

Her brow furrowed. "But…wouldn't that maybe scare him off? Strong feelings like that?"

He gave her an approving smile. "Exactly. That's why I want to see if those correlate with profiles he interacted with but didn't pursue."

Feeling absurdly pleased at his words and tone, she went back to going through the profiles. But the feeling faded as the similarities she saw gradually got through to her.

They all loved animals.

They all liked spending time at the lake.

They all worked hard, hoping for a better future.

They all hoped for a lasting relationship.

Hope. Exactly what Brett had said. He liked to destroy hope.

She didn't know how long they'd been working on it when she heard Brett say, very quietly.

"I've got the gist of it now. Take a break."

"But you want to get this done fast, right?"

"Yes, but once it's done, it's going to take time for him to bite, if he's going to. He's going to be warier now. There'll be enough for you to do if he does bite."

She wrested her mind out of the rut it had slipped into, going through the profiles. "There will?"

"I'm reasonably sure I suck at sounding like a woman, even on an app." To her shock, she laughed, at both his words and his wry smile.

"I would imagine so," she said.

"So that's when I'll need help. Why don't you get some rest?"

While you keep working, because that's the kind of guy you are?

She smothered a sigh. "I'm not tired," she said. "Just…"

"Just what?"

She gestured at the profiles they'd been poring over, in essence taking an answer here and an answer there to build an image they hoped the catfish wouldn't be able to resist, even after his narrow escape.

"They're all so…so…familiar." She couldn't seem to help the forlorn note that crept into her voice. "They sound like me."

It was a moment before he said softly, "You mean, like kind, giving, caring people you'd be lucky to have in your life? Yeah, they do."

She stared at him. Probably gaping again. And for a moment that seemed to spin out forever, yet at the same time seemed far too short, he held her gaze. And when he turned back to his laptop, she felt stunningly bereft.

Kind, giving, caring… He meant it in a friend way. Not in an attractive, sexy, I'm-going-to-die-if-I-don't-kiss-this-person kind of way.

Not the way she felt about him.

The truth hit her with a thud she felt must have been audible. But he didn't react, so it must have been just in her mind.

And that's where it needs to stay. Haven't you made a big enough fool out of yourself?

"I'm going to go check on the kids," she said, giving Ember a final pat and getting to her feet.

Only when his head came around sharply did she realize that her usual, affectionate term for her two fosters could be taken in a very different way under different circumstances. And she couldn't get out of that suddenly far too small room fast enough.

Kids. Talking about kids in front of the guy you just finally admitted to yourself you're totally hot for. Could you be more stupid?

She answered her own internal question with a stern reminder of just how stupid she could be. Stupid enough to fall for a guy who didn't even exist, to think he was finally *the* one, just a couple of days ago.

And now she'd switched to poor Brett, who not only was in essence a coworker, but who didn't trust her because of her name.

That's carrying rebounding a bit far, isn't it?

That thought seemed to steady her. She saw Jack and Apple were restless, signaling a trip outside was required. She was about to let them out into the spacious backyard when she remembered the coyote. So told them to sit and stay—they'd progressed to where they were good for a couple of minutes—and headed back to the office.

"The dogs need to go out," she said without preamble. "Will the coyote be around?"

Brett, intent on something on screen now, barely glanced at her. "Take Ember," he said. The Lab's head came up. "Go," he told her. "Watchdog."

Without hesitation the dog scrambled off the couch and trotted over to Annalise. "Thank you," she said, and left it for Brett to decide if that was aimed at him or the dog.

Ember clearly understood and took her duty seriously, just as Annalise would have expected. She ushered the two smaller dogs as if she'd been born to herd instead of retrieve, and as Annalise watched, Ember made sure neither of them strayed too far from the other. It would be a foolish coyote to take her on when she was in guardian mode.

Motion-sensing floodlights had come on the moment the dogs had left the small back deck, illuminating a large portion of the space. When the canine trio started to near the demarcation between light and night—she'd been surprised to see by the clock on the microwave that it was nearly eleven—she tensed a little, but as if Ember understood this was the limit in this mode, she nudged them back. She truly was a remarkable dog.

But then, her handler—and clearly her chosen master—was a remarkable guy.

When they got back inside and the dogs were once more settled, she followed Ember back to the office, where Brett was still focused on the screen before him. For a moment she thought he wasn't even aware, until he spoke without looking around.

"Go okay?"

"Fine. Yes. She was the perfect shepherd." Brett's head turned then. "In the literal sense, not the breed sense," she added hastily.

"Don't tell me—tell her," he said, nodding at Ember. "She's the one you insulted."

"I didn't mean—" She stopped when she saw the corner of his mouth twitch. "Cute," she said wryly.

There was the briefest hesitation, just long enough to register, before he said, "Thanks." And turned back to his work before she could even react.

She'd meant, of course, his joke. But he'd reacted as if she'd meant it as a personal compliment. As if she'd been saying he was cute. Which he was, of course. Along with a host of other things. None of which she was about to say.

In fact, it would probably be best right now to say nothing at all. That way she couldn't get in trouble. Any more trouble, anyway.

She resumed her seat on the couch, watching as he wrote what appeared to be an email. Ember hopped up beside her and settled in. It was a long email, and several minutes passed before he finally sent it. Then he stood up out of the chair and stretched.

Annalise yanked her gaze away when she realized how avidly she was watching the way he moved, the way his shoulders flexed and his back arched as he raised his arms over his head, fingers interlaced as he stretched. The man was really put together, no getting around it. But she focused on petting Ember, lest he catch her gaping at him yet again.

"You're spoiling her," he said when he relaxed and turned to face her.

"A little spoiling won't hurt her," she said, without looking up at him. "Besides, it's me, not the boss."

"You're her boss, too."

"Not like you are." There was no missing that after a few minutes of observing them together. She did look at him then. "She'd die to protect you, you know."

"I know. That's why it's part of my job to be sure she's never put in that position."

She wasn't sure why that answer made her tear up, but she couldn't deny the moisture gathering in her eyes. Before he could see—she hoped—she grasped at something else to say. "Was that email about the case?"

He nodded. "To Ellie. She's going to set our fictitious woman up as a teacher. She'll contact somebody at the school district to plant records and photos. Then she's going to do a search for an empty house and get with the county to dummy up records on it in our teacher's name."

"That's a lot of work."

"Knowing Ellie, she'll have it done by lunch tomorrow. Which is good, because I want it in place for the weekend."

"You think he'll bite that soon?"

"No. I'm guessing it'll take a while. But I want the bait in place ASAP."

She nodded; that made sense. At this point she welcomed doing anything, as long as it was something. That it made sense was gravy.

"It's late—you need to get some rest after all you've been through."

She knew she was tired. She could feel a crash hovering. More making sense, she thought rather inanely.

But then he knocked all sense out of her.

"My bed will be better for you."

Yes. Oh, yes, it would. Her mind practically shouted the words. But all she managed to say out loud was a faint, "What?"

"Come on. We'll move your stuff in there."

"I…" She couldn't say another word because he'd stolen her breath away. The images racing through her mind were tempting, vivid and impossibly hot. From visualizing him naked to imagining what it would feel like to have his hands on her, everywhere, and to be able to touch him in turn, they swamped her. And suddenly tired was the last thing she was feeling.

Belatedly he seemed to realize where her mind had gone. For a moment an answering heat seemed to flare in those blue eyes, but she knew she had to be mistaken, because gently—too gently, as if he was trying not to embarrass her for her silly thoughts—he said, "I'll crash on the couch. I've still got some things to do, but you need to get some sleep."

Her suddenly busy mind wanted to read something into even those innocent words.

Something like, if he went with her, they wouldn't be sleeping.

Chapter Twenty-Three

Brett realized he'd been staring at the computer screen without really seeing anything, for…well, for way too long. But then, he hadn't been running on all cylinders since that moment he'd seen that flash of searing, tempting heat in Annalise's eyes when he'd told her to use his bed. As if she'd thought he'd meant to join her. As if he'd meant for her to use him, too.

Use him.

And the instant those words formed in his mind he almost lost it, thinking of all the ways he'd want that to happen. Thinking of Annalise touching him, stroking him, kissing him…riding him. He tossed down the pen he'd been tapping against the desk, shook his head in silent disgust.

He spent a few minutes in denial. Telling himself that this wasn't a sudden case of unexpected lust for someone he knew, worked with, had known for months. It was simply his usual feeling of concern for a victim, and it had somehow gotten distorted by the fact that he knew her, worked with her. And that Ember liked her, trusted her. He had a lot of faith in the dog's judgment, and maybe that was coloring his feelings.

It had nothing to do with his suddenly awakened libido. It had just been too long since he'd indulged. It was only natural that being in close quarters with a beautiful woman would cause…something.

But this? This overwhelming sense of longing, wanting, need? This aching for something he'd never had, had never quite believed in?

You shouldn't give up on love altogether…you have to believe in it, or at least that it exists. Otherwise life is pointless.

His life wasn't pointless. Far from it. He had a calling, something he was good at, something worthwhile. Something that kept the roof from falling in on the innocent, or found them justice when it did. He'd always been proud of his work and had convinced himself—or so he'd thought—that that was enough, all he needed from life. It was more than a lot of people got, after all. So why was he thinking like this? Why did he have to keep fighting his mind heading down pathways he didn't want—didn't dare—take?

Maybe it was simpler. Maybe it was the whole family thing. He'd never known the kind of closeness the Coltons had, where even if you were on the outs on the inside, if a threat came from outside, they all stood together. Maybe he was just…envious. He could admit that much.

Of course, that didn't explain why he was sitting here, overheating at the thought of Annalise in his bed.

I should have told her to lock the damned door.

No, an invitation from her would shatter every defense he had, and that was a position he was not used to being in.

It was a good thing that invitation would never come.

He rubbed at eyes that had had about enough of staring at a computer screen. He'd set up everything he could think of to lure this jerk in. It had been a fine line to walk, getting enough of his temptations in, but not so many he got suspicious. He'd carefully constructed a persona, a rather quiet, shy schoolteacher who found using the dating app awkward, but was somewhat new to the area and didn't have a lot of friends yet. That had been Annalise's idea, and he thought it a good one.

Especially after he'd tried messing with a Colton.

Something you might do well to remember yourself, Shea.

He'd had the idea to add another kind of lure and sent off another email to Ellie asking if she could find a photo of their "bait" wearing an expensive-looking piece of jewelry. Not as the focus of the shot, like an advertisement, but just visible—he was certain the slimeball wouldn't miss something like that. And as he thought again of Annalise's precious bracelet, from her grandmother, the determination to get it back for her rose in him again.

Once that email was gone, he leaned back in the chair he'd been sitting in for far too long. He could do no more until he got the details from Ellie, that she had the cover employment records and location setup. Then they would take it live, and wait. Not that he would stop hunting, this was just a baited hook, a lure his quarry might or might not take. It didn't mean he'd stop looking in other ways. No, he wanted this guy, wanted to toss him in a cell personally, and he'd do whatever that took.

He went quietly down the hall, resolutely not looking at the closed door to his bedroom. He let Ember out, after checking on Apple and Jack, who seemed content in their little dens. Why they hadn't demanded to be snuggled up in bed with Annalise he didn't know.

Just because that's where you'd rather be...

He swore under his breath at himself. Gave himself a severe self-lecture ending with a rather fierce order to his unruly mind to knock it off.

Ember gave him a puzzled look when he hit the couch, grabbing one of the throw pillows and shoving it under his head.

"We're here for now," he told the dog. "Settle."

With a low, quiet whuff that sounded like the canine equivalent of *If you say so*, she went over to her bed, circled once and plopped.

It was going to be a long night.

ANNALISE DREW IN yet another deep, savoring breath. How could something be so unsettling and comforting at the same time? Yet here she was, wearing her comfortable shorts and T-shirt as pajamas—she wouldn't have dared bring the sexy nightgown she'd bought on a stupid whim, with visions of a certain nonexistent doctor in her mind— catching the faint lingering piney scent on the pillow that told her this was the one he used, and trying not to think about what it would be like if he'd joined her.

Not like you're sleeping, anyway.

She smothered a sigh and rolled over onto her other side. There was more than enough room, given it was a king-size bed. Something he probably needed, given his height. And thinking about that, and that while tall and lean he was also as well-muscled as any good hunting dog she'd ever seen, made her thoughts about him joining her linger, and when she finally slid into sleep it was restless. Not simply because she was in a strange place, but because her revved-up brain kept spinning out heated dreams in which Brett actually had joined her. Dreams of them sharing his bed, and each other, in all the ways two people could share.

When she opened her eyes, gritty and resistant, the room was faintly lighter, telling her the early summertime dawn was approaching. Somewhere between five-thirty and six o'clock, she guessed, not wanting to reach for her phone to confirm the time. Too early to get up and start making noise—Brett hadn't left his office until well after midnight. She'd still been wide awake, wrestling with tangled emotions, when she'd at last heard him walking quietly down the hall.

She tried to go back to sleep, but she'd gotten just enough, and had made the mistake of letting her brain click on. Her thoughts were already humming, and the possibility of more sleep retreated quickly. A night of racy dreams, followed by awakening to the reality of her life at the moment, was a dichotomy that shattered any lingering sleepiness.

She didn't know how long she had been lying there contemplating her pitiful situation when she heard the sound of running water, and realized he was up. And the sound triggered a sudden need for the bathroom, so she quickly decided she should do it while she knew he was already awake. She sat up, rubbed at eyes that would like more rest if only the mind would cooperate, then swung her legs over the side of the bed. She yawned as she stood up. Glimpsed herself in the dresser mirror and realized her body would betray her in an instant; her nipples were still rigidly tight from her dreams, and poked at the cloth of the T-shirt.

Feeling her cheeks heat, she grabbed at the blouse she'd been wearing yesterday and threw it on over the too-thin T-shirt. Then she cautiously opened the door and, hearing nothing for a moment and thinking he must be done, she tiptoed down the hall toward the bathroom door.

The bathroom door that opened just as she got there. And suddenly she was face to chest with Brett. Face to bare, broad, delightfully sculpted chest. And abs. And navel, with the slight trail of hair leading downward. And jeans that were only half-zipped and riding low, leaving far too much naked to her hungry eyes.

His voice was low, rough, and sexy as hell as he rumbled, "See anything you like?"

Yes. Oh, yes...

She felt her hand twitch and fought the urge to reach up and touch him, run her fingers over that smooth skin. When she found herself wondering if his nipples were sensitive she had to curl her fingers so that her nails dug into her palm to stop herself from finding out.

She tried for some calm, some cool, some semblance of not being stupid. "I've always thought you were... nicely put together."

His mouth quirked. "I seem to remember you saying that about a dog once."

"Probably," she admitted. "I admire beauty, wherever it is."

He snorted. "Beauty? Hardly. I'm just a hardheaded Irishman."

He wasn't kidding, Annalise realized. He didn't know how beautiful he was. To her, anyway. "Luckily," she said quietly, "you don't get to decide what I think is beautiful."

He looked disconcerted then, and she lost her battle with the need to touch. She lifted a hand, extended just her index finger where it was directly in her line of sight and realized with a sharp little prod of need that she didn't want to just touch, she wanted to see her hands on him. She'd never felt anything like that before, and it made it suddenly hard to breathe. And when she did touch, the feel of him, of solid, powerful muscle, of hot, sleek skin, breathing became impossible.

Only the fact that his abs visibly tightened at her touch, as if he were feeling the same way, kept her from pulling back in embarrassed shock. Who was this woman she became with him?

And then Brett's fingers were around her wrist, gently but firmly. "You need to stop." Heat flooded her cheeks. Humiliation, a too familiar sensation of late, began to build inside her. And then he dashed that too by adding, "You need to stop because I don't want to."

The heat that flooded her then was of an entirely different kind. And when she lifted her gaze to meet his, she saw the same kind of heat reflected there, as if he, too, was fighting a very primal urge.

When he pulled back and edged past her, headed back out to the couch where he'd spent the night so she could spend restless hours in his bed, Annalise stood there, wondering if she could or would ever move from this spot.

It had been an innocent, maybe flirting at most, encounter by some standards. And yet she'd felt more in these brief moments than she'd ever felt in her life.

And she'd done it herself. She'd been the first to reach out, to touch.

An odd idea struck her, about all the guys she'd dated, about her sisters teasing her about her penchant for bad boys before she'd sworn them off, asking her why she went for them. Was it this? Was it that simple, that with the "bad boys" she never had to make the first move?

This was an aspect of her vow to give them up for nice guys she hadn't thought of before. But then, she'd never really wanted to make the first move. Until now. With Brett. But that need to touch him, to watch herself touch him, had been overwhelming, irresistible.

You need to stop because I don't want to. And if she hadn't stopped? Would he have…given in?

When she could finally move again she darted into the bathroom and closed the door. It shouldn't be that stunning a realization, but it was.

With Brett, she would have to make the first move. And knowing her stubborn Irishman, maybe the second and third, too.

And she didn't even realize until she was staring at her tired eyes in the mirror that she'd thought of him as hers.

Chapter Twenty-Four

Brett threw his pen down in disgust. He'd been staring unseeingly at the computer screen for so long the screen saver had popped up. And if asked what had been on the screen before that, he wouldn't have been able to answer. He was truly losing it.

He rubbed at his eyes. He'd tried going back to sleep after they'd…collided outside the bathroom, but had failed utterly. His body seemed to have a mind of its own and was fixated on that moment when he'd felt her touch on his skin, and his mind couldn't seem to find the strength to divert from the memory. Or the sudden, fierce craving for more of the same.

Much more.

He'd slept on that couch before, usually inadvertently, falling asleep while reading or watching something that hadn't held his attention, so it wasn't that it was too uncomfortable to sleep on. No, the reason for his restless and nearly sleepless night was now just down the hall. In the shower, God help him. Hence his staring at the screen unseeingly. Because his mind was full of images of Annalise, naked, with lucky, lucky water sluicing over her body, finding and sliding over every sweet curve, every delightful inch of her.

And all while his body was still aching, even a couple of hours later, from his own swift, fierce response the instant she'd touched him.

I admire beauty, wherever it is.

He'd been called many things in his life. Rugged, he'd been told. Masculine, which hopefully was a given, although he'd had the feeling they might mean it in a different way. Even, now and then, sexy. And a few less complimentary things on occasion. But beautiful? Never.

Luckily, you don't get to decide what I think is beautiful.

He let out a low groan. Tried to recite to himself all the reasons this would be wrong. She was a colleague.

She was Ember's trainer. If it went sour, what about Ember?

She was a Colton.

She was looking for forever.

And he was not a forever guy. He'd grown up with parents who'd stayed together, but with all the fighting it seemed to him it was in spite of each other, not because of each other. He wasn't even sure the latter existed. At the same time he looked at Troy and Evangeline, or even the chief and her fiancé, and he'd swear they were together for life. So was it he just didn't believe it was possible for him? Because of what he'd grown up with?

But that made no sense either. Troy had had to deal with much worse, a loving mother who had died in the ugliest of ways, murdered during a home invasion, when he'd been a toddler. It was, Brett knew, the reason Troy and probably all of the GGPD Coltons had gone into police work; the case had never been solved, the murderer never caught. Sometimes he thought the reason Troy in particular was so dogged, dedicated and determined was to bring as much justice to the world as he could, to make up for what they hadn't been able to do for his mother.

But Troy wasn't letting the past tragedy hold him back. He was going for it, for the big prize, with Evangeline. Full out, no holds barred.

Maybe that's it. Troy is just braver than I am. Give me a bomb to disarm any day.

Brett froze at his own thought. No wonder he never spent much time in this kind of introspection, if this was the kind of thing he came up with. Give him a bomb? He'd never been happier to walk away from anything than he had dealing with every kind of explosive device a human mind could devise. And some of those minds so twisted it had left him with nightmares for a long time? Was he really thinking *that* was preferable to taking the kind of risk Troy was taking, with his heart?

"Is that Big Sable?"

It was all he could do not to jump when her voice came from mere steps behind him. As it was he jerked around sharply. Half-afraid she'd be standing there wrapped in a towel from her shower or something. Thankfully for his grip on sanity, she'd dressed. Not so good for that grip was that she was in a pair of jeans that were tight enough to tempt, and a plain blue T-shirt that had found every damp spot to cling to. Her hair was pulled up into some kind of knot atop her head, but loose tendrils fell around her face, and his fingers curled against the need to reach out and brush them back. And stroke her cheek in the process.

He gave himself an inward shake and said, a bit too sharply, "What?"

She nodded toward the desk. "The picture. On Lake Michigan."

He was so surprised he'd been caught off guard by

her appearance so close behind him without him being aware—something he was not used to at all—that it took him a moment to realize she meant the computer. He glanced at it and saw the screen saver image was indeed the Big Sable Point lighthouse. It was a beautiful shot, of the sun just touching the waters of the lake, casting a golden glow over the water, the sandy beach, and the grassy, rolling land behind it. He liked lighthouses, so that was why he'd picked the series of images for the slideshow.

"Yes. Yes, it is."

She came in then, and he noticed her feet were bare. Small, delicate looking feet, arched and tempting.

Feet? When the hell had he developed a thing for feet?

"I love that place. We went there a couple of times when I was a kid." She smiled at an apparent memory. "I always remember Desiree and Troy arguing about it."

He blinked. "Them arguing makes you smile?"

"Because it was funny. You have to pay to climb the tower, and they were arguing because Desiree called it a donation since that's what the sign said, but Troy said it can't be a donation if they make you pay it. Dad just laughed at them both and said, *Welcome to real life, kids.*"

"I'm inclined to agree with Troy on that one," Brett said.

Annalise smiled, and Brett felt a bit of wistful—and silly—wondering what it must have been like to be in a family that did things like that, together. A family with a father who laughed so easily.

"What did you do on weekends when you were a kid? On vacations?"

"Nothing."

Something in his tone must have registered, because

she was immediately apologetic. "I'm sorry. I shouldn't have assumed every family is as lucky as mine, to be able to afford to—"

"My family could have afforded it fine. My parents just didn't want to spend any more time with us than they had to." She stared at him, looking stunned. And he wasn't sure why that made him go on. "They didn't want to spend any more time with each other than they had to."

"Then why on earth did they stay married?"

He shrugged. "Hell if I know. Maybe they didn't want to have to learn how to fight with someone new."

"I…can't imagine. My parents disagree sometimes, but never for long. They love each other too much."

"So you've said."

"No wonder you looked like you didn't believe it."

He was on the edge of saying something even stupider, like *I believe it for some, but not for me.* There was no question he sucked at mornings after, and now he knew he sucked at them even when nothing had happened.

Nothing? That's what you call going into overdrive with one simple touch?

He was saved from further fumbling by her changing the subject.

"Do you need to get into the station? I don't have a client until noon, but I can always catch up on other things at the training center."

Say yes. Anything to get some distance between you.

But when he answered, it was with a shake of his head. "No rush. I'm waiting for Ellie to get the backing records set up, then I'll go live with the profile."

"And then we wait," she said, a bit glumly.

"That's a big part of what we do, sad to say." He tried for a smile. "It's not all action and excitement."

"And that," she said, in an entirely different tone, "is fine with me. I don't want you to—anyone to get hurt."

He didn't miss the midsentence change. Tried not to read anything into it. Was aware—and annoyed—that it was an effort. An effort he wasn't used to having to make.

He stood up abruptly. "I hope you like eggs for breakfast. That and bread for toast is about all I've got. Maybe some bacon, I think."

A supply run would be required. His brain leaped ahead to logistics. Make her make a list of what she wanted and leave her here, locked up in the house just in case? Alone, with no protection? He could leave Ember with her, knowing the dog would do what she could, but if the catfish had escalated to weaponry, even the dog couldn't stop him.

So take her with him? On something as...domestic as a grocery-shopping trip? How much that unexpectedly appealed rattled him. But from a safety standpoint, he'd be happier if she was with him, where he could take action if something happened. Leaving her here and going himself, he'd spend the whole time worrying. Not that he really thought the catfish would find her at his place, but he couldn't declare it impossible, and that was a risk he wasn't willing to take. Not with Annalise.

It was just his normal cop instinct, right? That gut feeling he'd learned to trust, just as he'd been able to spot booby traps overseas? He would have felt the same way about any victim of such a crime in his care. Wouldn't he? It wasn't—

"Will you let me fix breakfast? It's the least I can do."

He snapped out of his reverie, something he seemed

to slip into around her far too often. He normally wasn't given to such constant introspection, and he didn't like it.

"Sure," he said, not quite sourly. "I need to go shave anyway."

Her gaze flicked to his chin, and he wondered if she was thinking, *About time*. He certainly was. But then her gaze met his again, and all he could think was how her eyes looked more blue than gray this morning, and he wondered if it was the blue shirt. If the reflected color of the cloth was what made them look like the lake on a sunny day. Or if they just somehow changed hue on their own, and how. Or—

"How do you like them?"

They're beautiful.

He sucked in a sharp breath. He hadn't said that out loud, had he? And then, belatedly—as he seemed to be reacting far too often around her—he realized she'd meant eggs, not her eyes.

"I...sunny-side up is fine," he said hastily.

He was surprised he didn't cut his throat while shaving, he was so...distracted. So distracted he shouldn't be trusted with anything as sharp as a razor. He'd already nicked his jawline. At least it hadn't bled much.

He had to steel himself to head back out to the kitchen. And when he did, he ended up pausing at the end of the hallway anyway.

She was singing.

Well, humming and singing, a light, lilting thing he didn't recognize. And she had a lovely voice, the kind that sort of brushed over you and made you smile. He stood there listening to the airy tune for a moment—okay, longer than a moment—and only when the smell of bacon make his stomach growl so loudly he was sure she must hear it did he move into the room.

"Just in time," she said with a smile. As if her life hadn't been upended completely, as if she didn't have a scummy catfish after her, one he was afraid might have taken her escape very personally. And if that had shifted this from theft to a more personal thing, as the latest offering had indicated, she could be in some serious danger.

She slid a plate across the counter toward him. He sat down on the stool in front of it as she turned to pour a cup of the fresh coffee she'd apparently also made. He doubted it was as strong as his usual brew, but he wasn't about to say anything about something he hadn't had to make himself.

Then he looked down at the plate. Stared. Then lifted his gaze to her.

"Seriously?" he asked.

She looked back over her shoulder at him. "Why not? We could use some cheer."

He looked back at the arrangement of two sunny-side up eggs—perfectly done, he noticed—and the strips of bacon, all arranged in the undeniable shape of a happy face. And he couldn't help it; he laughed.

"And that," Annalise said with obvious satisfaction, "was worth the effort."

Chapter Twenty-Five

This was, Annalise thought, a far, far more pleasant morning than she would have expected. Not simply because she was away from the scene of the crime—although she hated thinking of her home that way, she couldn't deny that at the moment that's what it was—but because Brett seemed willing to pretend that moment in the hallway in the predawn hour hadn't happened.

He sat over his empty plate and sipped at his coffee, saying nothing, as he had throughout the meal.

He is probably too embarrassed to bring it up. You should never have touched him.

Even thinking about it brought on a wave of remembered heat that rippled through her from head to toe, with a few interesting stops along the way. And once more she wondered what was wrong with her. How could she have gone so quickly from thinking she might have found "the one" in her nonexistent doctor, to lusting over—because she could no longer deny that was exactly what she was doing—Brett Shea?

Yes, it was true she'd always found him attractive, and that she loved the way he worked with Ember, and how much he obviously cared for the dog and thought of her welfare before his own. But why had it only now burst into something more? Circumstances, like her being terrified and angry and ashamed all at once? Proximity? Or, as she'd thought earlier, a fickleness she'd never recognized in herself before?

Or—her breath caught as another thought struck her—had it simply been that it had taken this illusion-shattering situation for her to wake up to what had been in front of her all along?

"This is a bit strong for you, isn't it?"

She snapped back to reality in an instant. Realized he was gesturing with the coffee mug. "Oh. Yes." She pulled herself together; not for the world did she want to betray what she'd been thinking just now. "I noticed that you always hit Sergeant Kenwood's coffeepot when you come into the training center, and I know his brew can melt spoons."

"That it can," he agreed, with that crooked smile she'd always liked, but that now made her pulse kick up. "What about you, how are you drinking it?"

She tried to return the smile. "I stole a lot of milk," she admitted. "Which I'll replace, of course."

He gave a one-shouldered shrug that was familiar to her too; it was what people got who tried to thank him, for just about anything. "Help yourself," he said. "Although we'll need a shopping trip soon, to stock up. I was kind of down to the bare bones anyway."

She'd started to smile again, better this time, when the full sense of what he was implying hit her. Stock up? Just how long was he assuming she'd be staying here? With him? Until…when? The catfish was caught? That could take weeks. Months even.

Or maybe they'd never catch him, then what?

She opened her mouth to ask, couldn't think of a single way to phrase it that wouldn't embarrass her further, and closed it again. Thankfully he was focused on draining the last of his coffee and didn't see her. And then his phone, on the counter beside him, sounded. He looked, and his entire demeanor changed.

"Ellie," he said without looking up. "She's got a location in place."

"Already?"

He did look at her then and nodded. "I asked her to put a rush on it." He grimaced slightly. "What can I say— I'm impatient. I want this guy."

And to be rid of your houseguest? One who tries to... fondle you in the dark?

"I'll clean up," she said as he started to gather up his dishes, her voice a little tight. "So you can get on this." She reached out to take his plate as she added a bit more vehemently, "I want this guy caught, too."

He reached out and put a hand over hers. She froze, staring down at his fingers, curled around hers, imbuing warmth and steadiness. "I'll get him, Annalise. I swear it."

"I know you will." Her voice was at least steadier now. As if he'd somehow given her some of his strength through that touch.

And then he was all business, glancing at his watch. "Let me go through what she set up, plug the details into the profile. Then you can look it over and...feminize it."

She somehow found the composure to smile at that. "Make it sound girly, you mean?"

"Sort of," he answered, sounding a bit uncomfortable. "You know, put the emphasis on... I don't know, the garden instead of the tool shed. The flowers, not having to mow the grass."

To her own surprise, Annalise found herself smiling, then grinning at him. "Sexist much?"

There had never been a trace of that from him, so it was supposed to utterly be a joke. But his expression shifted and he said quietly, "I try not to be. But I think he is. The worst kind."

Her smile faded. The seriousness of what she was dealing with flooded back. "Excellent point," she said. "I'll be in as soon as I finish here."

BRETT OPENED THE email and smiled. Ellie had, as usual, done a stellar job. She'd not only found an empty house that had been rehabbed and not yet put on the market, but the renovator had some loose connection to the Coltons and had been willing to cooperate. He'd even offered to stage the place to make it look more real, since he was going to do it anyway.

He studied the photos she'd sent of the location, then opened his map program to look at the aerial view. A quiet-looking neighborhood, with only a couple of vehicles parked on the street. A switch to the street view showed neat, tidy houses, well-kept and homey.

He went back to the aerial view, zoomed in on the house Ellie had found. He noted what looked like a dog-house next door, and a children's play set in the back-yard on the other side. That would help with details for the profile; dog barking on one side, kids yelling on the other. Nothing like complaining about your neighbors to make you seem real...

He signed into the department system remotely and

began a stat check on the surrounding area, looking for any reports on file about anything someone living in that house would be aware of. While he was waiting for the results he would go back to the photos, note things like colors of the walls and the way the walkway to the front door bent around that big tree, the one he thought was a red oak.

Just as he sent the query, Annalise came in.

"Is that the house?" He nodded. And tensed despite himself when she leaned in to look. She was so close, and he could smell that sweet, rich, flowery kind of scent. He'd never cared much about women's perfume before, but this stuff practically made his fingers itch to—

Not going there.

"It's actually very nice," she said.

"It was just remodeled, but not on the market yet." He gave her a sideways look. "The flipper knows your uncle, so he was willing to help out."

"Oh." She drew back slightly, looking at him. "Another Colton connection, huh?" she asked, in a tone suggesting she knew what his reaction had been.

"Hard to avoid around here." He thought he'd said it neutrally, but apparently not neutrally enough.

"I can't help that. Any more than you can help your family being…not so connected. And if it makes you feel any better, we're not that close to my uncle Frank. Aunt Verity keeps trying to pull us all together."

"Verity?"

"She's Jillian's mom."

"Oh. That's got to be rough."

"Yes. She's always wished we were all closer." She let out a sad-sounding sigh. "I suppose she wants us to be close because she misses Richard so much, even after all these years."

"Richard?"

"Her kids' dad. He was killed when Jillian was only three."

"Sorry," he muttered, not knowing what else to say to her. So instead he went on with the matter at hand. "Once I go over the location check and pick out some details, you can go through that, too."

"And feminize it?"

He shot her a sideways glance, but she didn't seem to be jabbing at him. "Yes. All of the profile."

"You mean that our fictional target likes rom-com movies and roses and such."

"Yeah. And some other things from the list we have of commonalities."

"Okay." She gave him a look then he couldn't put a name to. But said, lightly, "But just for the record? Personally I prefer action flicks."

He blinked. "What?"

"I love watching the stunts and trying to figure out how they did them."

He couldn't help it, he laughed. "You didn't say that in your profile."

"I didn't answer that one. The same taste in movies isn't a criterion I think is all that important." Then she sighed. "But then, look where my choices got me."

"Get over it," he advised briskly. "Now, how about we go restock my pitiful kitchen?"

That seemed to perk her up. And as it turned out, he didn't mind at all; her enthusiasm over a task he usually found boring at best, annoying the rest of the time was…entertaining. Once he'd picked up his version of staples—coffee, more eggs and bacon, milk, bread and a couple of steaks and some chicken—he spent the rest of the expedition trying to figure out what her plans were for the collection she put together.

"Do you like lasagna?" she asked.

"Is there a human alive who doesn't?"

She grinned. Damn, that looked good on her. "While we're on Italian, what about a frittata?"

"I'm not even sure what that is."

"It's got eggs, veggies and lots of cheese. Any deal breaker there?"

He found himself smiling at the way she put it. "No."

"How about pancakes for breakfast?"

"Yes. But you don't have to—"

"I know. I want to." She wanted to…what? Cook? Or was it specifically cook for him? She went on cheerily. "I get the feeling you stick pretty much to grill-and-eat meals?"

"Interspersed with frozen packages of stuff," he said dryly.

"We'll fix that," she said.

"We?" He ignored that he liked the sound of that.

"Well, I will."

"Isn't that a bit sexist, the woman doing the cooking?" he asked, his tone ultrainnocent.

She turned to face him then, a carton of a dozen eggs in her hand. "Not if she likes to do it. It's the assumption she'll do it just because she's the woman that's—" She stopped abruptly, and he knew she'd gotten it. "You're using my own joke on me," she accused. She sounded as if she was trying for anger, but coming closer to laughter.

"What gave me away?"

"Oh, maybe that little twitch at the corner of your mouth?"

She said that with a smile, and he was glad enough that she wasn't really upset, that he managed not to focus—too much—on the admission that she'd been looking at his mouth. Especially given what raced through his mind when he looked at hers.

The rest of the expedition was…nice. An absurd word to use, in his mind, for something as mundane and usually annoying for him as grocery shopping. But it was. And when in the checkout line the woman behind them in line, who was buying a stack of the frozen dinners he had an even bigger stack of in his freezer, looked at the lasagna makings and said to the checker with a smile and an exaggerated sigh, "I want to have dinner at *their* house," he couldn't help grinning at her.

Their house.

It was only the woman's joke that had made him react that way. Not that phrase.

When they arrived back at the house they were greeted by the canine trio: Ember happily, going to Brett first, then Annalise. Jack and Apple went to Annalise first, much more frenzied, as if they still weren't sure she'd come back to them. But he got a greeting too, and it was nearly as bouncy. As if they'd accepted him into their lives, or at least trusted he wouldn't hurt them. He counted that as a win, even as he told himself the fact that her dogs liked him didn't really mean anything.

As they were putting away the supplies his phone sounded a work email notification. He checked, saw it was from Ellie and labeled *photos*.

"We've got our bait," he told Annalise, and headed for the office.

"That was fast," she said as she followed him down the hall.

"Ellie's got the bit in her teeth. I found out she used that dating app, before she met her boyfriend, Mick. I think she's taking this a bit personally, thinking it could have been her."

He walked into the office. Sat down, trying not to notice Annalise standing right behind him. He booted up the laptop and called up the email from Ellie. As usual, it was short and to the point.

I was going to do it myself, but got an insistent volunteer. And if our suspect wants voice contact, she can do that, too. I think these pics are perfect. She went by the house location and the park up the street and took the selfies, and we just went to lunch together and took the rest. Note the necklace!

Brett's brow furrowed. It hadn't occurred to him that Ellie might use a real person for the bait photos. But instead it was someone she knew? He opened the first image file. Blinked as Annalise cried out.

"Grace! No!"

Chapter Twenty-Six

"No," Annalise said firmly. "No, Grace."

"Anna—"

Annalise's grip on the phone tightened as she paced the small office. "I don't want you to do this."

"It's already done. It'll be fine, sis."

"But what if—"

"There's no way he could know who I am or find me. And if we end up talking live, he won't recognize my voice, either."

"You're not going to talk to him!"

"Only if it comes to that. That's Brett's call."

"But if he figures out you're a Colton—"

"He'll have no idea. I erased all my social media accounts recently, so I'm just an anonymous face, and as far as he knows Miss Brittany Hale, schoolteacher." She heard her little sister laugh. "I haven't cracked my big case and gotten my picture in the news yet."

"Grace—"

"Hey, you haven't even mentioned that gorgeous necklace! Isn't it outrageous?"

She had, of course, noticed the jewelry in the shot showing Grace in formal wear. She thought it was the dress her sister had worn to Mary Suzuki's wedding back in January. But Annalise knew she hadn't been wearing the elegant—and expensive looking—diamond necklace that sparkled at her throat in the image on that day. And she knew her little sister didn't own a piece like that. That extravagant.

"You didn't steal it, did you?" she asked dryly.

Grace laughed. "Actually, it is stolen. We borrowed it out of the evidence room. With permission, of course. It was about to be released back to the store it was taken from anyway. But the owner of the store liked the idea of using it to help catch another jewelry thief."

"Don't think I didn't notice that you're changing the subject."

"Not changing, that subject is closed."

Her tone was flat, uncompromising and final. Annalise blinked. When had her little sister become so...resolute? Having grown up with Grace, she wasn't fooled by her waiflike appearance, and it took some toughness to get through the police academy, but this was new.

"I'm a cop now, sister mine," Grace said quietly. "This is what I do." Then, briskly, she went on. "And I called Madison."

Annalise blinked. "Our cousin, Madison?" What on earth did she have to do with—

"She's going to send some pictures of her student's drawings she's saved over the years, to add to the whole teacher vibe. Oops, gotta run, my TO's waiting. Later!"

And that quickly she was listening to silence. Her mouth quirked. "Well," she muttered, "don't keep your training officer waiting."

"I know her TO," Brett said as she handed him back his phone. "I wouldn't keep him waiting either."

Her gaze shot to his face. He looked utterly serious. "Oh."

"She'll be fine, Annalise. Grace may be a rookie, but she's got good instincts." He smiled. "That idea about the kid's drawings was great, given we're setting up our bait as an elementary school teacher."

They spent the next couple of hours doing just that, setting up the bait. Fleshing out details, adding in the photos, each one of which gave Annalise a qualm. It was one thing to accept that her strong, capable big brother Troy was a cop, another thing altogether to think of her little sister that way. What that said about herself, Annalise wasn't sure. Maybe she was the one who was sexist. Or maybe just overprotective, as Grace had always said she was.

I love my sister, and I worry about her. That's all it is.

It took her a few minutes to process this development. And only when she accepted that she couldn't do a darn thing about it was she able to focus on the task at hand.

She studied the photos of the house, found a couple of things to mention in the profile. Brett chose what seemed most likely to have attracted the catfish to the other profiles he'd interacted with and added them in, reworded or tweaked to be different yet similar, with Annalise adding the female spin he'd asked for. It took a surprisingly long time. Much longer than she had ever spent entering her real profile.

Which may explain a lot about the disaster that turned into.

Finally they retreated from the office, both weary of staring at the facade they were building. Brett put on a fresh pot of coffee while Annalise got down mugs. She was trying hard to put her head in that place, where their imaginary woman would be. But her mind kept straying into wondering if the catfish had done the same, put this much effort into building the imaginary Dr. Sam Rivers.

"I wonder if he tried to put himself into an imagined mindset, like this. Or did he concentrate on what would be the best lure for the victim he was hunting for?"

She only realized she'd been musing out loud when Brett looked up from watching the coffee drip and said, "You mean did he just build his trap and wait for whoever's attention he caught, or study profiles and build his fake one from there specifically to draw them in? I don't know. I suspect the latter. Or a combination of both. He's obviously been at this a while, so I'm guessing he's developed a system."

Clearly, he'd been thinking about that, too. She put the two mugs down next to the coffee maker, then stood there looking at him. She looked at the set of his jaw and the glint in his blue eyes; she realized how down-to-the-bone determined he was to catch this guy. He was going to take down this catfish no matter what it took.

Or what risks he had to take.

Her breath caught, and it must have been audible because his gaze narrowed suddenly. And her thoughts must have shown in her face because he asked, with some concern, "What?"

"I… I just…be careful, Brett."

"Always." His voice was steady, reassuring.

"But if anything happened to you—"

"It won't. But even if it did, it's not on you, it's on him." He smiled rather wryly. "Well, and on me, if I let him get the upper hand."

"Still. I'd never forgive myself."

"Annalise," he said, and then stopped.

She stared at him, wide-eyed, unable to hide the fear she was feeling. And in that moment she felt something shift inside her, some final change in the slot he occupied in her mind, in her life. This wasn't just Ember's handler, a colleague, a man she liked and respected.

This was a man who made her breath catch, her pulse pound and her flesh heat, in a way no man ever had. And unlike the phantom they were trying to catch, she knew who and what this man was. Knew it down deep, with the kind of certainty she'd rarely felt about anyone.

"Don't." His voice was taut, almost strained.

"Don't what?" she whispered.

"Look at me like that."

"Like...what?"

"Like you want—"

He broke it off abruptly, started to look away. She could feel him withdrawing as if it was a physical pain. Something knotted up inside her and she reached out and put a hand over his. She needed to know. She had to know.

"I do want," she whispered. "Do you?"

His head snapped around and he stared at her. In those blue eyes she saw all the heat she could ever have imagined, and a need, a wanting that matched her own. And then he was holding her shoulders again, and for a moment she couldn't tell if he wanted to keep her away or pull her close. In the end, he did neither. He just moved, crossing the last distance between them in barely a single second. She knew the instant she saw his head move, lower, what was coming. And she tilted her head back, almost afraid to breathe, afraid if she did anything, even that, he would stop.

He didn't stop.

His mouth came down on hers hungrily. She gasped at the feel of it, and the pressure instantly eased. He didn't break the kiss, merely lightened it, shifted to a slow, intense exploration that sent ripples of chill and heat through her at the same time, something she would have thought impossible were she not experiencing it firsthand.

She kissed him back just as hungrily. He tasted of warmth, a hint of coffee, but most of all just… Brett. And he was delicious. She wanted more, much more, and when his tongue lightly traced the line of her lips, she met it with her own. She heard him make a low, deep sound, and thrilled to the realization that he was feeling this as strongly as she was.

In the instant she wished he would, he pulled her closer. She felt the heat of his tall, strong body pressed against her, and wondered if her knees could hold out against the tide of sensation. He deepened the kiss, probing, tasting, and she clung to him as her knees indeed gave way. From head to knee they were pressed together, and Annalise felt a hum from somewhere deep inside, a feeling of rightness that took what little breath she had left away.

This, this was what she'd been looking for.

And it had been right in front of her all the time.

Chapter Twenty-Seven

The last thing Brett wanted to do was let go of her.

The first thing he had to do was let go of her.

It took more resolve than he ever would have imagined to do. He felt suddenly chilled when her warmth was no longer pressed against him. And the moment he looked down into her face, the moment he saw the look in her eyes as they slowly opened to look back at him, he knew just letting go wasn't going to be enough.

He took a step back. Put more space between them. He was hearing an odd, rhythmic sound that he abruptly realized was his own breath coming in audible pants. She had literally taken his breath away.

And now she was just staring at him. Staring at him with those big, blue-gray eyes. Eyes that held a look of... wonder. A look that echoed what he was feeling, a bit of shock and awe right here in his kitchen.

And it suddenly descended upon him, the true size of the mistake he'd just made.

"That...shouldn't have happened," he said, unable to make his voice anything less than gruff, so tight was his throat.

"But it did," Annalise said softly, and the same wonder he'd seen in her eyes echoed in her voice. "And I'm glad."

He swallowed. Hard. "Glad?"

"Now I don't have to imagine what it would be like anymore."

He nearly groaned aloud. "I don't have that much imagination."

He regretted the words as soon as they were out. Somehow acknowledging the conflagration they'd nearly started made it even harder to think about stopping it right here and now. But he had to stop it. For all the reasons it never should have started in the first place.

"We're not doing this," he said, and this time his tone was sharp. "It's inappropriate, unwise and…and—"

"Unprofessional?" she suggested, and her tone was cooler now.

"That, too."

"I can see why you wouldn't want to…get involved with someone foolish enough to get sucked in by a—"

"That has nothing to do with this!" He snapped the words out, tired of her blaming herself for being the sweet, trusting soul she was. His hands came up as if to grab her shoulders again, and he had to stop himself. His fingers curled into fists as he forced them back down to his sides.

"You're not foolish. You're smart and kind and beautiful and sexy, and if your Dr. Rivers had been for real, he'd be a damned lucky guy to have you. Any man would be."

"Except you?" she asked quietly.

Brett realized abruptly that she had done this on purpose, maneuvered him into defending her in a way that betrayed what he thought of her. "Did I mention smart?" he muttered.

"First thing," she said.

Then she smiled. And there was something different about this smile. Something old and deep and very feminine. Warily he had the thought that she'd learned what she wanted, and now all he had to do was wait and see how she'd use it. Against him? Or should that be, for them? He didn't know anymore.

All he knew for sure was that kissing Annalise Colton had been a watershed moment for him, and that when this case was finally over, when she was safe—and she would be, he vowed silently—he would be looking at a very momentous decision.

Annalise sat on the edge of the bed. She'd retreated here because she had to think. And she couldn't seem to do that if she was in the same room with Brett. At least not in a rational way—her thoughts tended to stray in just one direction when he was anywhere in her line of sight. And if he was close…if he was close, her thoughts went haywire. Careened into imaginings like she'd never had before in her life. And she couldn't help wondering if this had been here all along, but had only been unleashed because of the circumstances and their enforced togetherness.

Which made her wonder again what would happen when this was over. And it would be over; Brett hadn't built his reputation and his clearance rate by giving up. He'd said he would get this catfish, and he meant it. And then what? If what had just happened was any indication, it was obvious. He was trying to friend-zone her. There wasn't any other answer for the way he kept retreating. And yet when she'd used his seemingly instinctive urge to defend her, to deny she was as big a fool as she felt over falling for the catfish, to prod out of him that declaration of what he really thought of her, his words had been balm to her battered ego.

The moment when they'd been talking about the other victims came back to her.

They sound like me.

You mean, like kind, giving, caring people you'd be lucky to have in your life?

That sounded quite like what he'd said just now. *You're smart and kind and beautiful...*

Kind. Why else would he keep emphasizing how kind she was? Kind was a generic sort of compliment, the kind of thing you said to or about a friend. And he probably didn't want to alienate Ember's trainer, knowing they'd have to continue to work together with the dog when this was over.

But he'd also said sexy. And that any man would be lucky to have her. Did a guy say that kind of thing if he was trying to push you away?

The other side of her, the side that seemed to heat up whenever she got close to the man, was hammering on her mind, demanding that she deal with the most obvious piece of evidence.

That kiss.

There was absolutely nothing friend-zone-ish about that kiss.

At least, there hadn't been for her. Had it not been that way for him?

Now I don't have to imagine what it would be like anymore.

I don't have that much imagination.

Oh, yes, it had been. And yet he was still pulling back.

And here she sat, in his bedroom, on his bed. The bed he'd insisted she take. Alone.

And if he'd wanted to share it? If that kiss had led to where it obviously could have? Right here to this bed?

The very thought took her breath away. And all the lecturing—telling herself that she was just on the re-bound, that she'd been humiliated and wanted proof she was truly a desirable woman, that she was reacting and responding to him this way because of what had happened to her—didn't seem to be working.

Because that kiss had been real. Very, very real.

She jumped to her feet because she simply had to move. She started to pace for the same reason. The room wasn't huge, but there was some space despite the king-size bed. *His* bed.

She spun on her heel and started back the other way. Looked around rather desperately for something else, anything else to fixate on. The room was tidy, with only a shirt she thought she recognized tossed over a bedpost. She wondered if she picked it up, if she would get a touch of that piney scent she associated with him. Whether it was aftershave or just that he spent a lot of time out in the woods with Ember, she didn't know.

And you're not going to pick it up.

That demand made of herself, she looked around some more. Noticed the utilitarian-looking box attached to the side of the nightstand, realized it was a gun safe. She stared at that for a moment. It wasn't that she wasn't used to weapons. She'd been a teenager when Troy had become a cop, and it had seemed exciting. When she worked with officers and their K-9s it was her job and she mainly focused on the dogs. So somehow the sight of that safe brought home to her the daily reality of being a police officer; when something bad happened, you ran toward it, not away from it.

She turned away from it to look at the rest of the room. Found herself smiling now when she realized the messiest thing here was Ember's bed, with her toys strewn in the vicinity. That seemed right, somehow.

There were a couple of things on the dresser, what looked like a tray for things probably pulled out of his pockets at night, and a framed picture. A photo of him, down on one knee beside Ember, both posing nicely.

It made her smile. And then it made her breath catch. Because this photograph was very, very familiar.

She had taken this shot. She remembered the day; it had been after the clever dog had run a long, complex obstacle course, one that had thrown others off on a wrong track, perfectly. The Lab had never wavered, never lost track of her goal no matter what distractions, masking or camouflaging had been put in her way. She'd set a new record for success on that course, and Brett had been delighted. In fact, she realized as she stared at the image, he'd been happier than she'd ever seen him, before or since.

And it was familiar because it was one of her screen savers. One she rarely failed to pause and appreciate when it popped up. The others, other clients and trainees, made her smile, but this was the only one that made her stop what she was doing and simply look until it rotated off the screen.

Dear heaven, maybe she really had been lusting after him all this time and had just never acknowledged it—or been forced to acknowledge it—until now. Maybe this heat had always been there, maybe—

Something tickled the edge of her awareness, and she realized she could hear Brett talking, muffled by the closed door. It was late for some kind of friendly call, so maybe it was something official. Something she should know about.

She pulled the door open and stepped through.

"—know he's due to hit again any day now," she heard him say. "I think a sting's the best way to get a shot at him." A pause, then, "I know that, Troy, but I don't think the guy would ever go for someone walking a dog like Bear. He practically screams police K-9. Ember's a Lab, like a million goofy pets. And I can fake his preferred target type."

What? As he paused again, clearly listening, she walked quietly down the hall. Then he spoke again. Rather sourly.

"If for no other reason than if it goes south and Davison gets away, I'll take less heat because my last name's not Colton. I'll do it."

Annalise stopped dead. Forgot to breathe.

Davison. It had to be Len Davison.

A chill rippled through her, unlike anything she'd ever felt before. Even when she'd seen that dart in the catfish's hand and realized she was in danger, she hadn't felt like this. No, this was an entirely different kind of fear. And the power of it made one thing perfectly and undeniably obvious.

She had fallen hard for Brett Shea.

She loved him, and he was going out there after a serial killer.

Chapter Twenty-Eight

"What are you planning?"

Brett shoved his phone back into his pocket and turned around. His brow was slightly furrowed, as if he was thinking about all the ways that question could be answered just now. And she saw a trace of a grimace before he said, very neutrally, "Dinner. I thought I'd grill the chicken we bought—"

"So you do think I'm stupid." He'd no more been planning dinner than she'd been planning to swim across an entire lake.

He sighed, closing his eyes. Odd, she thought, that she was able to think a bit more clearly when he wasn't looking at her. At least, she was until her imagination took off again, and she found herself staring at him and... wondering. Wondering what it would be like to kiss him again, and this time let it proceed.

Then he was looking at her again. "As important as your case is, it's not the only one we have."

Well, that was nice and impersonal, in both words and tone. And she guessed he'd used that *we* intentionally, to drag the entire department into it. But the mere fact that he was doing that told her it was all deflection. She just wasn't sure if it was from what she'd overheard, or something else.

Something like us? The very personal us?

She shoved the idea out of her head. "Len Davison," she said flatly.

"Annalise—"

"You're going after him."

"We've been after him for—"

"I don't want the *we* obfuscation. Troy's obviously in on it—"

"And Bryce," he said, as if adding the name of her cousin, the FBI agent, made it all right.

"And whoever," she snapped, "but you're going to be the lure, aren't you?" She didn't really make it a question because she already knew the answer. "You're going to be bait, just like our fake schoolteacher. Did that inspire the idea?"

"Maybe," he said, sounding more than a little wary. "Same principle, anyway."

Great. So if anything happened to him, she was going to feel responsible. "Except the big difference is you're putting yourself in the path of a killer, not a thief."

He drew in a deep breath and said gently, "It's my job, Annalise."

The obvious effort to placate her had the opposite effect. "Your job? To try and get yourself killed?" Her tone was becoming strident but she couldn't seem to help it.

"Calm down. I'm not going to—"

"Don't tell me to calm down." She could see she wasn't reaching him, so she changed tacks slightly. "You're going to use Ember as part of the trap?"

He seemed to relax a little. As if he thought her reaction was only because of the possible risk to a dog she loved. "It's part of his profile. But he never hurts the dogs. So it'll be fine. And Desiree is going to use aging makeup to make me look like I'm in my fifties, like his other targets."

Except for you trying to get a serial killer to attack you. She wanted to scream at him for his obtuseness. And it made her blurt out, "Are you even thinking about what that would do to…us?"

Brett went very still at her last word. He was looking at her with a sudden intensity that was almost unnerving. "You mean the Coltons having to deal with the death of a cop on top of everything else?" he suggested, giving it an interpretation she hadn't thought of. Giving her an out.

She didn't take it. Instead she exclaimed, "I mean me having to deal with your death!"

He was looking at her as if he'd heard everything she hadn't said, everything that had pushed her into making that undeniably passionate declaration. "Annalise," he whispered.

"Don't make me do that, Brett. Don't make me do that," she whispered back, not even caring how broken her voice sounded. "Not when I only just realized…how I feel about you."

He went rigidly still. Stared at her. Opened his mouth—parted those lips that kept drawing her gaze— then closed it. She just looked at him. She'd thrown her heart out there in what her grandfather had called a *damn the torpedoes* moment. She couldn't take the words back, and her gut was screaming that if she said anything more, she would only make it worse. He couldn't have made it any clearer that he didn't want this, didn't want her, and here she was forcing him into a situation that had to be beyond uncomfortable for him. She had to say something, do something. Pretend she hadn't said it? Turn it into something less, say that she'd meant it as a friend? Or that she didn't want Ember to lose him?

You're a good friend, Brett, and I don't want to lose you.

There, that could work. And had the advantage of also being true. It just wasn't the whole truth. But then, she'd just blurted out the whole truth, hadn't she? She'd just—

He kissed her.

HE HADN'T MEANT to do it.

He'd practically screamed at himself not to do it.

But as those words, those sweet, innocent, clearly genuine words had hung in the air between them, as he looked at her watching him with her heart in her eyes, he was lost. That she could still have that sweetness after what had happened to her wasn't just surprising to him it was…overwhelming. And he had moved before he thought, was probably beyond thought, pulling her to him and doing what he'd been aching to do again every hour since the first time.

He wouldn't have thought it possible, but she tasted sweeter, hotter than he'd even remembered. He stroked his tongue over her lips, and they parted willingly, even eagerly. And when the tip of her tongue brushed over his own, pure, hot fire sizzled through him. He nearly lost control right then, and plunged deeper, craving more. Craving everything.

The soft moan she let out against his mouth, a sound that echoed his own need, slammed into him. His body responded instantly, hardening in a rush that nearly left him dizzy. He could feel her name wanting to burst from him, but it was all he could do to simply keep breathing.

But finally he had to breathe, and lifted his head. Not away, just enough to catch some air.

"Brett…"

She murmured it as she held on to him, tightly, as if he were her anchor in a spinning world. Ironic, considering his own world—and his head—were spinning, and he felt as if she was the only solid thing left in it.

"Nothing can happen to you," she whispered. He wasn't sure if it was pronouncement or prayer, but either way the words clawed at him.

"It'll be all right," he said softly against her hair. "Troy will be there, and Grace, Bryce… I'll have Coltons at my back, so I'll be fine."

She pulled back just enough to look up at him. "You mean that? You really mean it? You trust them? You trust us?"

He looked into her eyes, although it was hard to drag his gaze away from her kiss-swollen mouth. And he realized with a little shock that he did mean it. "I do. Bryce is a good agent, Grace is already sharp as can be and Troy…there's no one I'd rather have as backup."

Her arms tightened fiercely around him and she laid her head against his chest, making his pulse kick up all over again. "Thank you," she whispered, as if he had given her some wonderful gift.

He marveled at that. It was so different from the way he'd grown up, he could only guess at what it must have been like to grow up as a Colton, and know that when the chips were down all of them would be there for you.

And then she stretched up and kissed him, tentatively at first, but the fire apparently lit as quickly for her as it did for him and in mere seconds it was again that fierce, burning thing. He felt her fingers digging into his shoulders, pulling at him as if she wanted him closer. That he understood, because more than anything at this moment he wanted her as close as he could get her. Preferably without the barrier of clothing between them.

He wasn't quite sure how his hands had slid down to her hips, but since they had he pulled her tightly against him. And again his body had reacted as it had even before that first kiss, in a way he hadn't experienced in a long time.

Ever, you mean.

Yeah. *Ever.* He nearly groaned aloud at the feel of her pressed to his hardened flesh, and in that moment he thought if they didn't pursue this to the inevitable end he would regret it for the rest of his life. And he practically groaned her name against her lips.

She broke the kiss and his every sense cried out in protest, but then she looked up at him and said simply, "Yes."

He went rigidly still. Yes? Yes to what? Because yes to everything he wanted right now was a very big yes. The biggest. He tried to find the words to ask, to make sure, because he had to be sure, he had to know she wanted this as much as he did, he had to—

A too familiar ringtone sounded from the phone in his back pocket. He'd forgotten, in that list of Coltons he trusted, that there was one more, one more he needed to be wary about, one who could easily hold any hurt he caused Annalise against him, both personally and professionally.

Hail to the Chief.

He couldn't do this. He shouldn't do this. He shouldn't even be thinking about going there, no matter how Annalise made him feel.

He let go of her and stepped back.

And it was likely the hardest thing he'd ever done in his life.

Chapter Twenty-Nine

"How's my sister?"

Brett shot a sideways look at Annalise's sister Desiree, who had turned her considerable artistic skills to making him look twenty-five years older than he was.

Which would be younger than I feel at the moment.

He mentally brushed aside the thought. When Troy had mentioned this operation, she had volunteered to make him believably look in the target age range. She was proving as deft a hand with makeup and temporary hair dye as she was with her charcoal and pencils.

"I…she's fine," he finally said, rather lamely. When Desiree simply looked at him, waiting, he added, "A little rattled, still, but that's to be expected. All in all she's handled things amazingly well."

"Of course. She's a Colton."

His mouth twisted wryly. "Yeah. I noticed."

"She really likes your place."

He blinked. "What?"

"She said she loves all the outdoor space, the yard, and wants to see the coyote."

"Oh."

"And that your bedroom is nice and quiet, with all that open space behind it."

"It is," he said. Then, as she continued to stare at him, belatedly realized what she was getting at. "If you're asking if we're…sharing that room, we're not."

Not that I wouldn't in an instant, if not for…so many things.

"Why not?"

He blinked again, truly startled this time. And almost answered a blank *What?* again. He suddenly felt like he was back overseas, about to step into what he knew was a minefield.

"Are you really asking me why I'm not sleeping with your sister?"

Desiree smiled. "Aside from my little boy, she's been the most adorable, loving thing I've ever seen since the day she was born. I'm asking how, being in such close quarters, you can keep from falling head over heels for her."

He stared at the woman. The mention of her son reminded him of everything she had been through in the past few months, and he found himself marveling at her self-possession.

"You Coltons," he said, his tone a bit awed.

"We're a strong bunch," she agreed. Then, with a rather impish grin added, "Especially we women. So is that it? She's too strong for you?" He gave her the eye roll that deserved. "So it's that she's a Colton? That's what's holding you back?"

Strong. Yeah, that's the word. So give her the truth. "She's related to you, our guest FBI agent, one of our CSIs, my frequent partner, a rookie I'm helping train and my boss," he said flatly. "What do you think?"

"Well, when you put it that way," she said wryly. "But

I have to admit, I thought you had more nerve than to let that stop you."

"Sorry," he muttered, "all my nerves right now are focused on being a target."

"Point taken," she said, and thankfully dropped the subject.

And far too belatedly it occurred to him that he'd never contested her only half-teasing inquisition with the most effective answer. He'd never said he wasn't interested in Annalise.

He'd never said he wasn't sharing that bedroom—and bed—with her because he didn't want to.

When Desiree was done and he at last got the chance to look in a mirror before they headed out, he felt a jolt. He stared at his reflection, wondering if he was truly seeing himself in twenty-five years. Graying hair, more lined face, features succumbing a bit more to gravity. He tried to focus on her artwork—because there was no doubt that's what it was—but all he could do in that moment was wonder where he would be, what his life would be, when this really was the reflection he saw in the mirror.

And that his first thought was Annalise—simply because of those close quarters Desiree had mentioned. Not because he thought she might still be in his life by then. Nobody lasted in his life that long. And he'd never really cared about that.

But the thought of, when this was all over, going home every night to a house empty again except for Ember, seemed…crushingly depressing.

He shook it off. He had a job to do, and it was a job that required his head be fully in the game. Because if he missed a cue, a clue, he could end up dead.

"Hey, Pops! You ready to roll?"

He snapped out of the bleak thoughts and turned to look at Troy, who was grinning at him.

Brett did his best old-voice imitation of one of his father's dressing downs. Troy laughed, and they headed for the unmarked van that held the communications equipment necessary for tonight's sting.

As it turned out, it wasn't necessary at all. Brett and Ember made several circuits through the park, carefully timed, Brett taking care to walk more slowly than he normally would, with nothing more happening than an occasional friendly wave from strangers passing by, and a couple of compliments for Ember. But none of them had expected to strike gold the first night of the sting, which he explained to Annalise when, makeup washed away, he got back well after midnight. And found her waiting up for him. As if she couldn't rest until he was home safe.

Home.

That's what it was. This was no longer just the place he lived, chosen for its functionality for Ember. It felt like home, in a way nowhere he'd lived before ever had. And there was only one reason for that. The woman who looked him up and down as if she needed to be sure he was truly all right.

I'm asking how, being in such close quarters, you can keep from falling head over heels for her.

Good question.

"No problems here?" he asked, trying for a diversion.

"No," she said. "And no action on the profile yet, either." He'd told her it would be okay for her to monitor it, while he was working the Davison case, but not to respond to anything.

"I didn't expect anything this fast. We only went live this morning."

Those few moments were difficult. Mostly because Brett didn't dare say much. And that was because his conversation with Desiree kept playing back in his mind.

If you're asking if we're sharing that room, we're not.
Why not?

And it was playing in his mind again when he told her to get some rest and watched her as she retreated back into that very room. And no amount of telling himself that going out as bait again when exhausted would be borderline suicidal seemed to work. He lay sleepless on the couch he was getting mightily tired of.

But adrenaline kicked in and did its job and he was awake and alert the next night when he and Ember strolled through the park again. He was glad it had cooled a bit tonight, maybe even dropped below sixty, given he had to wear a jacket to hide his sidearm. Ember was again having a great time, sniffing the wind, the ground, leaves, and not for the first time Brett smiled at the catalog of scents that must reside in her mind. Or nose. Wherever she kept it, it was a skill he both respected and admired.

And it was Ember who warned him. The dog's head came up rather sharply, and she swiveled around to face into the very slight breeze. Then she gave a low whuff of sound as she sat, looking up at him.

He spoke very quietly into the mic concealed under the collar of his jacket. "She's on a known scent."

"Copy." Troy's voice came back instantly through the nearly invisible earbud. "I'm on your six."

And he would be, Brett knew. *There's no one I'd rather have as backup.* He'd meant those words he'd said to Annalise. And it occurred to him that he should probably say them to Troy, too. He knew the man knew he had had reservations about the Colton presence on the department, but Troy had never pushed, had only said that made it their job to earn his trust.

Brett saw and heard movement in the trees to his left. It was too dark to discern much else, but he was still certain. Relayed it through the mic as he bent to pat Ember's head as if she were simply a recalcitrant pet who was tired of walking. And he turned slightly as he did it, so that he was almost facing the direction where he'd seen the movement.

And then a man stepped out onto the path. He was casually dressed, and wore a Tigers baseball cap, pulled low over his brow, casting his face into pure darkness.

Fitting.

Because it was Davison. He knew it, even if he couldn't fully see the murderer's face. He thought he would have sensed that himself, even if Ember hadn't told him in her own eloquent way. "Stay," he whispered to the dog.

The sting had worked. They had Grave Gulch's infamous serial killer within reach. And he wanted to end this now, toss the plan they'd all worked out and just take the guy down himself right here and now.

But that wasn't how it worked. He had to trust Troy and the others. *Trust.* The one thing that was hardest for him. But he had to do it, trust the team that was even now closing in for the capture and arrest.

All he had to do was stay alive until then.

Chapter Thirty

"Sorry if I startled you," the man said pleasantly, conversationally, "but I was wondering if you had the time."

"For what?" Brett asked, pretending to misunderstand, stalling as his backup moved in.

It was a second before the other person responded, "Pretty dog." He said it as if he'd never asked the first question, and Brett knew he'd disconcerted him.

"She is," Brett said, taking advantage of the situation to give Ember, who was quivering with recognition of the scent she'd been set to track so many times filling her nose, a steadying pat. They were pushing the boundaries of her training, but all the work Annalise had done with her was paying off; she wasn't happy, but she was doing as ordered.

"She doesn't like strangers?" the man—Davison, he was sure now, shadowed face or not—asked with a note of wariness.

You're no stranger to her. "Do you like dogs?" Brett countered.

"Sometimes."

Brett heard a sound from behind him, the merest rustle of a branch. But it was enough to set Davison off, because in the next instant he spun around and was running. Back into the dark shadows of the trees.

"Rabbit!" Brett yelled into his mic as he started after the man at a dead run.

Troy's answering shout echoed in his ear, and the team abandoned any effort at stealth. They were all running now, following the fleeing suspect. Brett heard Bryce's voice in his ear acknowledging Troy's directions.

The terrain, the trees and the darkness were making it impossible to see, and the suspect was making no noise at all. Which seemed impossible, given the spreading branches and the underbrush. Unless Davison knew these woods well, Brett thought. Very, very well. That was worth remembering.

Ember tugged at the leash, wanting loose, but Brett held her back. He didn't want her in the line of fire during a foot pursuit of a killer. Black dog and black night were an invitation to a nasty accident. She could follow the scent easily enough later, if necessary, so he kept her close. And hoped that her prodigious tracking abilities wouldn't be necessary. This needed to be over, for the sake of possible future victims and the entire town of Grave Gulch. And the department that served it, but now was taking so much heat on so many fronts.

Not for the first time he had the thought that if he'd wanted a quieter, slower pace than the sometimes ugly big city, he hadn't gotten it. Not yet, anyway. But he was still happier here than he'd ever been in the capital. Hell, he'd been happier in the last few days than he'd been in his entire life. And that was a realization that slammed him in the gut like a sucker punch. Because there was only one reason he could think of why that was possible.

And it was the same reason every moment of those last few days.

Annalise.

He gave a sharp shake of his head. If he went down that path, even in his mind, he could practically step on Davison before he tuned back in to reality. And that was not a good place for a cop to be. Ever. But most especially when on the hunt for a serial killer.

He heard the chatter over the radio. Heard Grace's voice, higher than normal, clearly excited, and sent a silent warning to her to stay safe; he did not want to have to tell Annalise her little sister had been hurt. Moments later another exchange, this time Troy and Bryce, Troy sounding a bit fierce as he called a halt, for everyone to just stop, and listen.

Brett sat Ember as he halted. Listened. Barely breathed. Heard nothing. He was no woodsman, but it seemed too quiet. Not even the hoot of an owl broke the silence. As if even the wild things knew a wilder, much eviller thing had passed through their world.

"He slipped past us," Bryce said over the radio, his agitation clear.

Brett swore under his breath. This was the closest they'd ever gotten to Davison, and he'd somehow vanished?

"How'd he freaking do that?" Troy was not happy either.

"Dog in play," Brett said shortly, "hold fire." Ember knew those words, although as the well-trained K-9 she was, she waited for the order. Once the team had acknowledged his transmission, he gave her the full length of the heavy leash and said, "Ember, track."

The jolt to his arm and shoulder as the eager canine

took off never ceased to amaze him. His girl was on the job, and she would track that scent to the ends of the earth if he asked it of her.

I'll settle for to Davison's door, wherever it may be.

It was going to be a long night.

ANNALISE MADE ANOTHER circuit of the living room floor. She'd given up trying to stop herself from pacing. She couldn't stop, not until Brett was safely back home. Apple and Jack were already convinced she was losing it, she was sure. She'd had them outside at least a half-dozen times in the last three hours. She had tired them out with games and fetch and anything else she could think of, never truly acknowledging even to herself that it wasn't the dogs she was trying to wear out.

If she could have done something stupider than fall in love with a cop, she couldn't think of it at the moment. Nor could she deny any longer that that was exactly what she'd done. Despite the stress and strain and worry she'd seen her family endure for loving someone in this intense but crucial profession, she'd gone and fallen for one.

The dogs didn't even lift their heads anymore as she turned on her heel in front of them and started back across the room. In fact, they barely twitched an ear. She tried to focus on the pair, and how much they'd progressed. Even being uprooted from her place to here, they'd settled in nicely. In fact, they were happier here than she'd ever seen them. Whether it was the huge yard, Ember's companionship or that there were two people here to provide them attention, she didn't know.

Or maybe they fell for Brett the same way you did.

Yeah, there was always that. And if that was true, then

she was dreading the moment when the pups would have to go back to her place.

But then, she was dreading that herself.

As another hour rolled by on her phone's screen, she stared at it. Contemplated calling the station, to see what the status was. Told herself they had better things to do than answer her worried question. Not to mention she might as well run up a flag that declared she was in love with Brett Shea. She was not ready for that.

And she was certain he was not. Because she wasn't certain he felt the same way about her. She gave a shake of her head at the way her thoughts kept echoing each other, chasing each other, stirring up continuing chaos in her mind. And the longer this went on, the more chaotic her thoughts got. She started imagining all sorts of horrible scenarios, and she was close enough to the department to know just how horrible the scenarios could get in reality.

She'd worried about officers involved in dangerous situations before, especially those she worked with directly.

It had never been anything like this.

As dawn crept closer she dozed fitfully on the couch. The couch where Brett had been sleeping since she'd invaded his space. It was somehow comforting.

It was the dogs who stirred her to alertness with a couple of happy yips. The kind they reserved for their new buddy. Whether that was Ember or Brett, she wasn't sure. And since they were practically a unit, it didn't really matter. What mattered to her was they were home.

She was on her feet and had the door open before they even hit the porch. The only one who looked more dejected than Brett was Ember, who appeared beyond sad.

Then Brett realized she was there, and his expression shifted to surprise.

"You're all right?" she asked anxiously. "Both of you?"

"Fine," he said. "Fuming, but fine. Why are you up?"

"I couldn't sleep." She didn't add *Because I love you and I was worried.*

"Everybody's fine," he assured her. "Troy, Bryce—"

"And Grace?" Annalise asked. He hesitated, as if wondering if he should answer that one. "It's safe to tell me, as long as she's all right."

"She is," he said, and headed inside.

She studied his face as they came in. He looked exhausted, but his jaw was set as if he was fighting anger. Still, he saw to Ember first, checking her bowls for water and kibble.

"I made sure they were ready," she said, and this time when he looked at her his expression was a little milder. She wasn't sure she should ask, but she needed to know. "Fuming?"

He ran his hand over his stubbled jaw, then through his hair. Then he let out a frustrated sigh. "We almost had him."

She nearly gasped. "Davison? He...took the bait?"

He nodded. "But he heard or sensed...something and took off running. Ember lost the scent deep into the woods." He frowned then. "It was weird. She sat like she does when the scent just ends, like when someone gets into a vehicle."

Annalise had to force herself to focus on what he was saying, even though she was hating every word of it. "In the middle of the park?"

"Yes." He gave a weary shake of his head. "We've

been searching since midnight. No trace. Ember went over the trail three times, and it always ends right there."

"Could he have had a vehicle there?"

"Nothing bigger than a bicycle," he muttered. "Which is possible, I suppose. But if he was able to do that in the dark, then he knows the park inside and out. He certainly knows it well enough to get away from us." He rubbed his hand over his face again. "They'll go over the scene again in daylight—maybe something will turn up. They'll try again, with someone else, different dog. Maybe Ember's just too big and scared him. The others have been smaller. And patrol will be focusing on the area, especially at night, but…"

He gave a half shrug and shook his head at the same time. She could only imagine how it must feel to have been that close only to have the killer slip away. And poor Ember—she knew the animal well enough to realize she felt as if she'd failed somehow. She'd done her job, tracked the scent to the end of the trail, but Brett's demeanor had to be telling her it wasn't enough.

"She's taking it hard," she said, bending to stroke Ember's head.

"My fault," Brett said instantly, warming her. "She did her part."

"She's a sensitive girl."

"I know. She reads my frustration." He rammed his fingers through his hair. "I could have grabbed him. He was that close."

Annalise's heart gave a funny little leap. And not a happy one. Brett had been within arm's length of a serial killer. She had spent a long time tonight thinking about it, repeatedly telling herself she could deal, that she'd grown up in a police-connected family, but this was different.

This was the man she loved. Not matter what his feelings were—or weren't—she couldn't deny her own.

"I'm not sure we'll-ever have a better chance than we had tonight," Brett said. "And we blew it. I blew it."

"You didn't blow it. And you came home alive," she pointed out, a little shakily.

"That's not my job. My job was to catch this guy. Before he kills someone else."

And suddenly she was face-to-face with the reality of his work. The simple fact that part of his job was to put himself in harm's way. To risk injury, even death, so that someone he didn't even know, some citizen, did not have to. He obviously accepted that.

But now, as she stood there looking at him, she wasn't sure anymore if she was tough enough to accept it herself.

Chapter Thirty-One

His house was too damned empty. And that was a thought Brett had never had before; it had never bothered him to live alone, and with Ember, he'd never really felt that way.

Until now.

When Annalise had insisted she needed to go home, he'd understood. Even though he felt better with her here, where he could keep her safe, she had her own life, her home, her routines, and wanted to get back to them. He would have preferred she stay until they had reeled in this catfish, but he understood.

What he hadn't understood was how could one woman and two dogs, who had only been here for three days, leave such a hole? Such an aching, empty place, not just in this house, but…in him?

He shoved aside the memory of coming home to this empty place and tried to concentrate on the laptop screen before him. Ellie had assured him she'd set things up so no matter where he checked the dating app from, it would appear the same. That that also made it possible for Annalise to do the same he was trying not to think about. It only made sense, after all, for her to have access, because she would probably be quicker than anyone to recognize the real catfish. He had the record of their text communications, and he'd read them several times—several because he'd had trouble staying objective, reading her excited and, face it, innocently optimistic posts—but that wasn't the same of having done it yourself in real time. Plus, it wasn't burned into his memory the way it no doubt was in hers. She still hadn't forgiven herself for falling for the guy's facade.

Which brought him back full circle again, thinking about Annalise and…missing her presence. And the dogs.

It was just too quiet. But how could he have gotten so used to the bustle and noise of the three of them so quickly? And why couldn't he shake the thought that it wasn't just wanting to go home that had made her insist on leaving? That it was, somehow…him?

He would have physically slapped himself upside the head, as his father had always said, if he thought it would do any good. He'd never had a problem with focus before, yet now he couldn't seem to go five minutes before his mind slid back into what was getting to be a rut.

It was simply that he was concerned for her safety. The catfish knew where she lived, and his gut was still telling him the guy wasn't going to take her catching him out lightly. Sure, patrol was keeping a close eye on her and her house but that wasn't the same as her being here, in a place the criminal didn't know about, and with him to watch over her.

But he hadn't been able to convince her to stay. And it was the way she'd looked at him when she'd doggedly insisted she needed to leave that had him thinking he was at least part of the reason.

Because he'd kissed her? Twice?

No, because she'd kissed him back. Eagerly. She'd wanted that.

So, because he'd wanted more, so much more, and it had been obvious?

Face it, you wanted everything. You wanted her mouth, her hands, her body, everything.

He threw down the pen he'd been toying with. Trying to hang on to that past tense was so much work he knew that proved it a lie. Proved he hadn't just wanted, he still did. Everything.

And what about her heart? That sweet, giving heart?

He didn't want that. He'd never wanted that from any woman. Hell, maybe that was what Annalise knew; maybe that was why she wanted out. Because to her, all the heat, all the need, all the wanting in the world didn't matter if it didn't come with the kind of love she was after. The forever kind. The kind he'd never known in his life.

The kind he didn't even believe in.

Or did he?

Ember nudged his elbow, startling him. Which told him how out of it he'd been, when the dog managed to sneak up on him. She didn't give him the "outside" signal, but instead simply leaned into him, encouraging him to pet her. He stroked her head, her impossibly soft ears, wondering what it was about dogs that enabled them to sense when their people were…what? Distracted? Unsettled? Confused?

He let out a long, audible sigh. He'd admit to all of those. It was the other ones he didn't want to admit to. The ones like empty. Lonely.

Hurting.

What you should be obsessing about is that you had Len Davison within reach and let him get away.

The fact that it wasn't anything he'd done that had set

Davison off didn't matter; he was the one who had been close enough to grab him. That it had been the plan that he'd hold off until the others closed in didn't matter, either; he should have scrapped the plan the instant the guy was close enough. Except that he'd agreed to the plan.

All of which reduced him to wondering which was worse, obsessing about his empty house and Annalise's absence or the Davison fiasco. That he couldn't decide was just further evidence of how screwed up his mind was right now. He needed to concentrate. Their fictional schoolteacher had attracted a few hits on her profile, and he needed to go through them—

His phone signaled an incoming text. It was the generic tone, not work, so he finished calling up the profile to look at the hits before he looked.

When he did look, he froze for an instant.

I should have assigned her a ringtone. Then at least I'd have some warning.

Before he could veer off into trying to decide what tone would be suitable for her, he picked up the phone and opened his texting app. And denied that some part of him was hoping she was feeling a bit of what he was feeling. Maybe even that she wanted to come back.

I looked at the profile. I think he bit.

That blasted all else out of his mind.

Just opened it now. Which one?

The guy named Colin Stetler. Or calling himself that.

Checking.

He hit the icon to call her. He'd been resisting doing just that all evening, but this was business.

When she answered, he started as she had, no preamble, no niceties. "What makes you think it's him?"

She answered the same way, all business. "To start with, it's the same opening line, almost word for word. And has the same feel."

"The bit about her dog being cute, and how he's a fellow dog lover who wouldn't trust anyone who didn't love them?"

"Yes."

He remembered the catfish had done the same with her without having to look up the transcript. He practically had the interchanges they'd had memorized. How the catfish couldn't, because of his very busy schedule at the hospital, spend as much time with his dog as he wanted to, how much he missed little Charlie the beagle while at work, and on and on. The guy had played on her love for dogs perfectly.

And counted on her warm, kind heart.

He shoved the emotion aside, into that room in his mind it kept stubbornly breaking out of. He scanned the profile, noted the same sort of perfect, polished images of a good-looking, outdoorsy kind of guy with a big grin he supposed most women would like. The kind of images you might find in an ad campaign for some outdoor equipment store.

"This guy is even claiming he broke up with his last girlfriend because she and his dog didn't get along," she said.

"Search-and-rescue dog at that," Brett muttered as he looked at the profile.

"Yes. Nice and heroic. Just the type some women fall for."

The tiniest of edges had crept into her voice, making the words a bit too pointed. Was that aimed at herself? Falling for her fake doctor.

Or you?

He immediately tried to quash how that made him feel. Besides, that would mean she saw him as…heroic. Which he wasn't. He was just a cop, trying to do the best job he could.

He shoved the thoughts back in that room again, and this time he mentally locked the damned door.

"Anything else jump out at you?"

"Yes." Her voice seemed back to normal now. Or at least brisk and businesslike. "Look at the way he talks about his mother in the family section. Not that it might not be true, but it's another similarity."

He paged down. *She's the greatest.* He remembered the catfish profile. *Best mom in the world.*

"Dr. Masters thinks he probably has mommy issues," he murmured.

"And some guys know women look at how they treat their mothers to get a hint of how they might treat their wives."

He couldn't help it—the exchange made him smile despite what it told him about how she must look at him. "Guess I strike out on both counts, since I didn't know that, and my mother and I only talk on Mother's Day and her birthday."

"I call mine on my birthday. To thank her for having me, and for loving me."

For some reason that tore at him. And he barely

stopped himself from blurting out something stupid like how easy it would be to love her.

"That's nice," he said instead, and it sounded incredibly lame even to him. "Anything else?" he asked, back to the matter at hand.

"I…"

"Annalise?"

"It just…feels the same. The way he uses words, the short sentences but big words."

"Like he's smart enough to have a big vocabulary, but too busy to spin out a long tale."

"Exactly," she said, sounding relieved. "And the pictures have the same feel, too. A bit too posed, too expert, no selfies, and the one he posted about a search-and-rescue mission he was involved in could be anyone at that distance."

He called up the image, which was indeed a distance shot of people combing through a thick stand of trees, one man in the background with a dog on a leash, obviously searching. "You're right. I'll have Ellie run an image match first thing, see if those other shots turn up on a stock photo site anywhere. And see if she can dig up a news story this photo might have gone with."

For a moment she didn't answer. Then, "Brett?"

"What?"

"I just noticed something. Look at that first picture of his dog."

He scrolled back up to the shot of a happy German shepherd with a tongue-lolling grin. "Yeah? Nice dog."

"Now look at the shot of the search again."

He went back to the other photo. There was something about the markings, the coloring of the German shepherd in the action shot… Then he sucked in a breath. "That's not the same dog."

"No. It's not. I know he doesn't say specifically that's him and his dog, but he certainly implies it."

"So it's either obfuscation, or…he's a fake."

"And if he's a fake…"

"He sure sounds like our fake."

Chapter Thirty-Two

Our fake.

How far gone was she that even him saying it like that, using those words, made her pulse kick up? *We. Our. Us.* Such simple, short words and yet they could have enough impact to change an entire life.

He didn't mean it like that.

And for one of the few times in her life she wished her last name wasn't Colton, since that seemed to be a big part of the barrier between them. But she immediately felt guilty and silently apologized to her parents. Besides, he had seemed to be getting past that. Just in time for her to realize she couldn't deal with him putting his life on the line, every day.

"I'll send this on to Ellie right now," he said, jolting her out of the recurring maelstrom of her thoughts. "Then a text to give her a heads-up. If I know her, she won't wait until morning to start searching."

"No wonder she and Mick barely see each other." But apparently the tech genius and her boyfriend made it work. Somehow.

"So now we need an answer for this guy."

She frowned instinctively, even though he couldn't see her. "Shouldn't we wait until Ellie finishes? To be sure?"

"I figured you'd be in a hurry."

"But what if he's a real person? It would sort of be like what the catfish does in reverse, wouldn't it? I'd hate to do that to some basically nice guy."

It was a moment before he said, sounding strangely bemused, "At least you think nice guys are still out there," he said.

"I do," she said. *I'm talking to one, even if he doesn't believe it.*

"All right. Why don't we make up a response now, but only send it if Ellie's able to prove our suspicions?"

So they spent a few minutes working up a casual yet friendly response to the man's query, with Brett agreeing to her additions and suggestions without hesitation. "It needs your touch," he told her. "I'm too down to business. You know, too get to the point and do it now."

"Too much a guy, you mean," she said, making sure her tone was teasing.

And she could almost see him smiling when he answered, "Exactly."

So the final version had the essentials Brett wanted, but with her own feminine touch. Then there was a long pause, and she wondered if he was trying to think of a way to just end the call. He'd been so...not quite brusque, but close. But then he spoke, softly, almost awkwardly.

"It's...really quiet here."

"I imagine you're enjoying the peace," she said, keeping her voice even with an effort.

"Not as much as I would have expected. The place feels empty." She suddenly couldn't speak. Found herself holding her breath. Then, his voice back to normal, he said, "Ember misses her friends."

"Do you?"

It was out before she could stop it. And when he answered, his voice had gone quiet again.

"Yes. I miss all of you."

Annalise clung to those words, and how he'd sounded saying them, long after the call ended. For Brett Shea, that was quite an admission.

It wasn't long before Ellie confirmed the photos on the account were faked; they were from a modeling agency. Which was a change from the stock photo sites, but they figured the catfish was being careful, switching things up a little. Otherwise he was following the script, with a few minor variations; he clearly wasn't stupid enough to just copy pictures. At least, not from himself; Ellie, being Ellie, had dug even deeper and found the guy sometimes did cut and paste sentences from other men's profiles.

"It's like he kept a file," she'd told them on a group call, "then tracked what he'd saved back to which guys took themselves off the app because they'd found 'the one.' Then he used the things they'd said."

"A real success model," Brett had said sourly.

And when Ellie had disconnected from the call, Annalise had said just as sourly, "So he uses real nice guys to pretend to be one himself. Charming."

"Yeah. But also a reminder. He's not stupid."

Brett sent the response they'd prepared. They had an answer within an hour, one full of enthusiasm and a charming humbleness that she'd answered. The same sort of feel she'd had from the catfish. She buried the humiliation that wanted to surge to the surface again and helped Brett craft an answer. And so it went over the next couple of days, back and forth between the predator and the bait, a slow, tantalizing game that would have

seemed full of hope and promise, if she hadn't known
how fake it all was.

On the work front, those couple of days were almost
normal. Except for the time she spent looking at her session calendar and lingering on Ember's name, a full week
away. Would she not see the sweet Lab before then?

Would she not see Brett before then?

True, she talked to him daily, usually more than once
as they strung along the catfish. But it wasn't the same
as being under the same roof. That had felt so... She
wasn't sure what the word was. Wasn't sure there even
was a word for that odd combination of unsettling and
yet comfortable. Natural. Right.

But now his approach was all business. Their conversation was all business. His tone made that clear, and he
never veered away from the case at hand. And that, she
supposed, told her she was wasting her time wishing it
was otherwise.

She tried to stay busy, to not think about it. She was
grateful for the training sessions with her other clients.
Each animal had its own personality, each handler their
own way of working, and she adapted to each. The purpose of these eight-hour sessions was to keep the dog's
skills sharp. Every two weeks they worked hard at it.
Or every week in the case of a couple of dual-purpose
canines she worked with, like Bear, the ones who were
trained in not just tracking and searching, but protection
and criminal apprehension.

But always in the back of her mind Brett lingered,
Brett and the black Lab she'd come to love. She missed
them, darn it. She missed them, she missed his cozy
house with all the space for the dogs, she missed watching Jack and Apple play with Ember, she missed sharing

the kitchen tasks, missed cooking for them or watching him cook for them.

He'd said he missed them. All of them. Had he meant that, or was it just the dogs underfoot he missed?

Take him at his word, her heart said. *He meant all of us. He missed all of us; he liked the time you'd spent under his roof as much as you had. And he kissed you, like you've never been kissed before. He wanted more. He wanted everything you wanted. It was obvious when he had you pressed against him.*

Don't be stupid again, her brain said. *That was just a physical reaction. He's never said anything to indicate it's anything more than that for him. So yeah, he kissed you, but then he slammed the door. What does that tell you? And the last time, when it seemed like he'd opened that door again, his job came calling. And maybe that was a good thing, because do you really want to live in constant fear that one day he won't come back? Isn't that why you had to get out of his house? You know you're not tough enough for that.*

And right now that was the only thing she was truly certain of.

By THURSDAY OF that week Brett was convinced he'd lost his mind. It was all he could do not to show up at Annalise's house and have it out with her. Make her tell him exactly why she'd bailed in such a hurry. The real reason.

And for the hundredth, maybe thousandth time, he wondered what would have happened if the chief hadn't called to give the go-ahead on the Davison op at that precise moment the other night. Would he have found out that breathy yes hadn't meant what he thought it had? Or would they have wound up in his bed, finding out just how fierce this need really was?

Like you don't already know...

But now that she was gone, now that his house echoed as if hollow, he was beginning to realize it wasn't just his house that was empty. He felt her absence like an entirely different kind of physical ache, one centered in his chest. A kind of ache he'd never felt before, one that could only be eased by her presence.

And he realized with a jolt that he wanted that presence, not just in his bed but in his life. He wanted the days to go on with them together, because it made him feel complete. He'd never realized what that would be like, and now that he had, it was gone.

She was gone.

And he didn't like it. He didn't like his life without her. Even though—or maybe because—she'd turned it upside down.

He didn't know what to call it. The only word that came to mind—love—scared the hell out of him.

But it was the only word that fit.

When a new message arrived, he didn't know whether to be glad of the distraction, or groan that it was from the dating app, which meant another return-message session with Annalise. At a moment when his thoughts were in chaos.

Almost reluctantly he looked. And went still, staring.

Not even a minute later his phone rang. And this time he knew without picking it up, because he'd finally assigned it a ringtone that fit. The pulse-pounding theme from one of those action movies she'd told him she loved. Although the music wasn't the only pulse pounding.

He took a breath, connected the call and before she

could speak—and maybe say something he wasn't ready for—he said, "I got it."

"This is too fast, isn't it? He's never gone this fast before, gotten to asking to meet so quickly, with me or with the others. Maybe it's not him after all."

She sounded distressed, and from what she'd said before he knew it was as much because she was afraid they'd strung along some nice, innocent guy as thinking they'd wasted time while the real catfish had maybe landed someone else. She really was one of the best people he'd ever met.

"Take it easy," he said reassuringly. "Don't forget the photos, and the thing with the dogs. Even if it wasn't him, he's still lying."

"Oh. Yeah."

"But I think it's him."

"But why so fast? It was a month before he pushed me to meet in person."

"Because that went south on him. He wouldn't take that well." He'd had another long talk with Dr. Masters, and they were in agreement on this.

"So you think he's hurrying to…what, make up for that?"

"I do."

He didn't elaborate, didn't tell her she'd humiliated the catfish more than he ever could have humiliated her, because his ego was fragile, much more fragile, and he would go to extremes to repair it, to be able to tell himself he'd gotten even. He didn't tell her because he didn't want to scare her, because he had a bad feeling about just how far this jerk would go.

Bottom line, this ruse had better work.

"So…do we say yes?" she asked.

"I think we say yes, but not for his day. He wants tomorrow night. Maybe for a reason, Friday, lots of people out and about he won't stand out as much."

"Not because it's *Friday the Thirteenth*?" she asked, her tone dry. He smiled, glad she could joke.

"Maybe that too. But let's offer him Saturday night instead."

"But that would mean you're working another weekend. You deserve a break."

He couldn't quite put a word on how it made him feel that that was her first thought.

"We're all sometimes working weekends until Davison is caught anyway," he said. Then, because he had to, added, "But thanks."

"Maybe we should make it Sunday afternoon, middle of the day, out in the sunlight. That way we can recognize him easily, because he'll be the worm drying out in the sun."

He laughed. And then, because she'd earned it, he said, "You're amazing, you know that?"

There was a moment of silence—a too long moment— before she said quietly, "I wish I could believe you believe that."

"I do believe it."

"Even though my name is Colton?"

Brett hesitated, then went for it, hoping he could get the real reason why she'd suddenly decided she had to go back home. He still didn't buy the routine explanation she'd given him. But he didn't know if it was something he'd said or done, or that what had nearly happened between them had scared her.

"The name doesn't trigger me as much as it used to."

"I'm glad of that," she said, in a tone so neutral he

suspected it had to be purposeful. But before he could push the issue, she said, "So how shall we word her acceptance and alternate day?"

They worked it out and sent the response. Grave Gulch Coffee and Treats, Saturday night.

When the call ended, it was Brett sitting there not liking her all-business approach. The irony of that did not escape him.

If this is how she felt with you, no wonder she left.

Later, lying in the bed she had lain in, a fact that was more unsettling—and arousing—than he ever would have thought, he wondered if he'd ever be able to sleep here again.

And he was still restlessly and almost painfully awake when, just after closing time when the patrol officers would be on the lookout for drunk drivers leaving the bars, his phone rang. With the work ringtone.

He rolled over and grabbed the phone off the nightstand. Troy. Something was up. He grimaced at the date that glowed at the top of the screen; it was officially Friday the thirteenth.

"Go," he answered without preamble.

Troy answered the same way, but fury echoed in his voice. "It's Davison. Bastard hit again."

Brett smothered a vicious oath. He had no doubts Davison had chosen the day on purpose.

Friday the thirteenth, indeed.

Chapter Thirty-Three

"In the park?" Brett asked, although he suspected he already knew.

"Yes. But nowhere near where we were working the sting."

Place was too damned big. "Victim?"

"ID'd as Terence Parks, fifty-six-year-old male, married, no kids."

"Dog?"

"Yes. Little furball thing, unharmed. Belongs to the wife."

The widow, Brett thought grimly. "On the way," he said.

He rolled out of bed, flipping on a light as he did so. Ember looked at him curiously.

"We're on," he told her, and the dog leaped to her feet.

They were in the car and rolling five minutes later. Five hours of searching later, exhausted and far beyond frustrated, he was standing with Troy next to a marked unit parked at the entrance to one of the many hiking trails that meandered through Grave Gulch Park. The officer sitting inside, who had been the first one on the scene, was working on what would end up a very lengthy report.

The only clue they'd gained was from Ember. She had once more led them, although via a different path, to the same spot as the other night. The same place, up against the mossy rocks. And yet again she stopped, signaling the trail ended there, impossibly, amid the trees and underbrush.

They watched as the coroner's van left the scene, Brett thinking he was glad not to be the one who got to deliver the news to the man's wife. He'd done enough death notifications to never want to do another.

"This guy," Troy said, "is really, truly ticking me off."

"Amen," Brett agreed. "I want his ass on a platter, preferably skewered."

The radio in the marked unit crackled, and all heads swiveled toward the dispatcher's voice saying "All units, be advised…"

Brett sighed inwardly as the report he'd hoped he wouldn't hear quite yet came over the air; the protesters had arrived. It didn't even matter at this point how the word had gotten out; what mattered was the large crowd already gathered—and growing—in front of the station.

"At least they're not here, screwing up the crime scene," he muttered.

"Yet," Troy said sourly.

"Good point. Let's get it wound up, then," Brett agreed.

A couple of hours later, after the beleaguered CSI team had gone over every blade of grass and speck of dirt one last time, Troy and Brett finally cleared the scene. By then the report was not only that the crowd of protesters had grown, they were getting nastier, so Brett decided to drop Ember off at the training center. She wasn't trained for crowd control, nor did she have the intimidating appearance and demeanor that would make people think twice before approaching her. He didn't want her hurt, so she'd be better off there.

With Annalise.

He braced himself to see her again, for the first time in more than four days. Decided to monitor the radio as distraction, and heard the crowd was getting more and more unruly, becoming more of a mob than concerned citizens.

Sergeant Kenwood met him near the entrance. "Sounding pretty bad over there," he said as Ember padded over to greet him familiarly.

Brett nodded. "Why I'm leaving her here before I head over."

Kenwood took the leash with an answering nod. "Good call. Was thinking of heading there myself."

Brett shook his head. "You've got civilians and animals here, and if that mob gets a wild hair to go after anything police related, they'll need you."

Kenwood sighed. "You're right. It just goes against the grain."

"I know, Sarge. I know."

Brett heard the door behind him open and knew who it was instantly. A sort of tingle hit the back of his neck and shivered down his spine.

"Hell of a mess," Kenwood said. "You take care over there."

"I will." He heard quick, light steps, headed toward them and tried to brace.

"I just saw a news report. You're going to the station?" Annalise almost demanded. He finally turned to look at her, and the worry in her expression, in eyes more gray then blue today, quashed the tension he was feeling.

"Yes."

"I'm coming with you."

"No. There's no—"

"They're screaming for my cousin's blood, my family's blood. I'm going," she insisted, "with or without you. I just thought one less car in the mess might be better."

She meant it. He could see that. She was afraid, but for her family she would stand in the face of potential danger. And when it came down to having her go there by herself, or with him so he could watch out for her, there was no contest. No contest at all.

"All right," he said. "But you do what I say when I say it." He practically snapped it out, because the thought of her being hurt made him shiver inside.

"Yes, sir," she answered, with nearly as much snap.

The mob was even bigger than he'd expected. It filled Grave Gulch Boulevard, and in fact had two fronts. One side was facing the police department, shouting about incompetence and how many more people had to die, while the other half was aiming at city hall across the street, demanding Chief Colton resign.

He turned off the boulevard well before they reached the angry crowd and headed for the back entrance. He was counting on the fact that the media was out front to keep the protesters there, who sometimes measured success, or at least the impact they were having, by the number of reporters present. But even behind the big stone building the sounds, the yelling, the chants, all the ugliness was clearly audible. The refrain "Chief Colton has got to go!" was repeated over and over, and in one moment a single yell about getting rid of every Colton like the rats they were rang out.

Annalise was shaking by the time they got inside, her

bravado fading in the face of such hatred for her cousin, her entire family.

"Try not to let it get to you," he said once they were safely inside.

"They hate her so much. They hate all of us, and all we've ever done was try to protect them, keep them safe."

"They're scared and angry," he said as they walked down the hallway toward the chief's office. "People do unusual things under either of those conditions. Both together is a recipe for...what's happening out there."

She stopped dead and looked up at him. "This is my *family* they're threatening!"

He didn't know what to say so said nothing, although his jaw tightened. And as if she'd noticed, her expression changed, softened. And to his shock she reached up and cupped his face with a slender hand.

"And I wish you knew what it feels like, to at least have a family you love and who love you."

He stared at her, stunned that in the middle of all this she could even think of that. And suddenly everything seemed to shift, and the crowd outside, the antagonism and downright hate, felt very, very personal. As it must to her. He'd never felt anything quite like this sensation, and it was both startling and disconcerting. And he realized that he was feeling as if the threat to the Coltons was a threat to him.

Because it was a threat to the woman he loved.

Heat flashed through him, not the heat of need but of shock as he realized what it was he was feeling, as he finally admitted it in so many words.

He loved her.

He loved Annalise Colton.

He was still a bit shaken when the door to the chief's

office opened and a man came out. Brett glanced over and went still as he recognized him. Camden Kingsley, internal-affairs investigator for the county. This wasn't the first time he'd seen the tall, deadly serious man nosing around; he'd spotted him here in the station a few times over the last couple of days. And while the man himself might be okay, Brett didn't know him well enough to say otherwise, just his position and the job he did was enough to set any cop's teeth on edge. Thankfully the guy kept going.

Then the chief, her top aide and the department PIO—not a job Brett would wish on anyone right now, not that public information officer had ever been a position he'd envied—stepped out. They were clearly finishing whatever conversation had been going on inside, but Brett saw Chief Colton register their presence and gesture them toward her. The two other officers left with silent nods as they approached, and Brett thought he'd seen expressions less grim at murder scenes. And as she turned toward them he saw that the chief herself looked exhausted.

Once the others were out of sight Annalise ran the last few steps to her cousin and hugged her fiercely.

"Thanks," Melissa Colton said. "I needed that."

She wasn't joking, and again Brett marveled at the strength this family took from each other. What must it be like, to be part of a unit like that? He'd always figured it was sort of like being a cop, but connected by blood instead of uniform. But this was different. This was more. And he felt a powerful jab of something it took him a moment to recognize as longing.

When the chief looked at him, he wasn't sure what to say. Settled on "I'm sorry, Chief." He nodded toward the

front of the building and by inference the crowd outside.
"You don't deserve any of that."

"But maybe I do." She sighed. "I'm thinking it might
be best all around if I step down, for the good of the department. And Grave Gulch."

"No!" He startled himself with his own vehemence.
"No way. You're the best I've ever worked for. This'll
calm down once we get Len Davison and Randall Bowe,
and in the meantime we've got your back."

He meant it. He hadn't really crystallized it into words
until this moment, but he meant it. It was a rather startling realization after all his wariness about the pack
of Coltons threaded throughout the department, but he
couldn't deny he'd meant every word.

Annalise was staring at him. Then she smiled, so
warm and sweet it was all he could do not to grab her
and kiss right there in front of her cousin, his boss.

The chief asked for an update on the catfish. Brett was
surprised she'd even thought of it, given what was going
on outside. But it only proved what he'd said was true;
she was the best he'd ever worked for.

And he'd do anything he could to see that the mob
outside didn't get their way.

Chapter Thirty-Four

"Who was that guy, the one who walked out first?" Annalise asked as she came to a halt beside Brett's desk, where he'd gone to check in while she stayed with Melissa to give moral support. "Melissa just waved me off when I asked."

She knew she hadn't been wrong about his reaction to that man and hoped he didn't try to deny it. Or brush it off as nothing, as Melissa had.

He didn't.

"Internal Affairs," he said shortly.

She felt a chill. "Oh."

"Yeah."

"He's investigating—"

"Everything," Brett said, in a tone that matched his dour expression. "They're watching us, all of us, like a hawk. One foot wrong, and they'll come down on us hard."

"You mean about Bowe?"

"Yes." He reached out and shut down his computer, grabbed up his phone and stood up. "Asking did we know what he was doing with evidence and look the other way, like some of that mob outside claim? Can any of us be trusted?"

"That's so unfair. It was Bowe, no one else. Especially not Jillian!"

"I...admire how you all stick together."

That was a change, and her breath caught, because she understood so much better now. "Because you've never had family like that."

It wasn't really a question, but he answered anyway. "Never."

"Well, you do now. Melissa told me you have the complete respect of everybody on the department, starting with her."

Her cousin had also told her, with a too-knowing look, that she couldn't do any better if she was looking for a man to build a life with.

I'm not tough enough to be with a cop.

You're a Colton. You'll cope.

But he's not looking for that.

Her cousin had smiled softly then; for a moment her troubled expression was replaced with something much softer, a look Annalise had only seen on her face since she'd met her fiancé, Antonio. *Sometimes men don't know exactly what they're looking for until you show them.*

Brett was staring at her now, as if he'd had to process what she'd told him. "She said that?"

"An exact quote." He looked almost embarrassed. But he also looked pleased, which pleased her in turn. "Do you have to stay here?"

He shook his head. "I just needed to check in on some things. Troy's handling the Davison case for the moment, so I can prep for the catfish tomorrow night."

"We're really sure this is him?"

"My gut says it is."

"All right."

He gave her a sideways look. "That's it? No doubts?"

She had complete faith in him, and she let it ring in her voice. "Not if you say it is."

"Annalise," he said.

He stopped, but something had changed in his voice, something that reminded her of how he'd said her name before he kissed her the first time. Her pulse kicked up a little and stayed there. But it wasn't until they were back outside in his car that he really looked at her.

"Tell me why you left."

That caught her off guard and she stalled. "You want a list?"

"Fine."

"It was time."

"Try again."

That pricked her temper. He wanted honesty? She'd give him honesty. "All right. I was starting to care about you. And you made it quite clear you don't want what I want—"

"Annalise—"

"Don't interrupt me. You're the one who wanted a list. As I said, you made it clear, so staying hoping you'd change your mind would be stupid. And I've had enough of being stupid about men."

"You're not—"

"I'm not finished." He was looking at her rather oddly now, but she was on a roll and wanted it all out in the open before she lost her nerve. Which thought brought her to the final, most compelling reason. "Most importantly, I was afraid," she said honestly. "That I'm not tough enough to be with a cop."

Even as she said it, her cousin's voice rang in her head. *You're a Colton. You'll cope.*

And as she said it, something flared in his eyes. "Does that mean...you wanted to be?"

"Does it matter? You don't want the same thing I want. I'm not looking for a fling, and you don't want anything else."

"Maybe I've changed my mind."

"You're going to have to be more definite about that."

He drew in a deep breath. "Come home with me," he said abruptly.

She stared at him, her heart truly beginning to race. The heart that wanted her to jump at the hope in those words. But for once her common sense, still a bit battered by the catfish, reined her in.

"Why?"

"That house is too damned empty without you." His mouth twisted at one corner, into a wry half smile. "All of you."

"So, it's my dogs you want?" she asked, determined to make him say it. And as if he'd understood the intent, he turned in the driver's seat to face her.

"Cut me some slack. I've never been here before. I've never fallen for anybody like this before. But it's you I want. Any way I can have you. Any way you'll give me." He took in a deep breath and added, "For as long as you want."

For Brett Shea, for Mr. I'm-Not-Looking-For-What-You're-Looking-For, Mr. You-Have-To-Believe-In-Love-Before-You-Can-Give-Up-On-It, that was quite a declaration.

And for stars-in-her-eyes, believes-in-the-fairy-tale Annalise Colton, it was enough for now.

APPLE AND JACK scampered around in delight, clearly glad to be back. Ember seemed happy as well, to have her new canine friends back with her. Brett was letting the excited dogs out back, and as he watched them go Annalise saw him grin and say, "Let the romping begin."

She felt her cheeks heat as she thought of the other ways those words could be interpreted. She knew perfectly well what that brief stop at the drug store in town had been for. She appreciated the precaution, and not having to deal with it herself. Especially right now. She was not quite in the same state of mind as the dogs. It wasn't that she was having second thoughts, but now that they were here, she felt a bit awkward. On the few occasions she'd spent the night with someone, it had been a spontaneous sort of thing. This was not that. This was planned, intentional, a conscious decision.

And exactly what you wanted. What you've wanted long before you ever realized it.

And shouldn't it be a conscious decision? More often than not, she regretted impulse moves she'd made in her life.

He bent down to unlatch the doggie door so the trio could get back in on their own. And her cheeks heated all over again as she admired how his backside curved those back pockets.

"Brett?"

He turned around, still smiling. And she realized she'd never seen him look quite this way. Lighter. Happier. Despite everything going on around him and the department, happier. And as she looked at him she felt herself start to smile, because it seemed impossible not to.

It's you I want. Any way I can have you. Any way you'll give me. For as long as you want.

All her doubts, her awkwardness vanished. And she decided to voice that other interpretation of his words.

"Speaking of romping," she said. "Maybe we should take advantage of their absence."

Instantly heat flared in his eyes, and his entire demeanor changed. He crossed the space between them in two long strides, and when he pulled her into his arms she felt as if she was coming home after a long, stormy journey.

He kissed her, long, deep and hot, and for the first time in her life she truly realized how intimate a kiss could be. With others it had been a testing, an experiment. With Brett, there was no testing necessary; she already knew the effect he had on her, the places in her he reached that had never been awakened before.

I don't know if this is love because I've never been there before.

His words had seemed almost sad to her when he'd said them, but she suddenly realized that part of them was true for her, too. Because she had never been here before. But she knew what it was, because unlike him, she'd grown up with it, seeing it every day between her parents.

Love.

And it made her realize how amazing it was that the child, the boy who had never known what she had, had become the man he had. It told her more than anything else could about the heart, the core of Brett Shea.

And suddenly she wanted to make it all up to him, to show him what it could and should really be like.

She kissed him back, more than eager, more than hungry. She kissed him with all the longing, all the need she'd ever felt, probing, tasting, savoring. She heard him groan, low and deep in his chest, in fact she thought she felt the sound of it. His hands slid up over her rib cage and she felt a light caress over the sides of her breasts. Tentative, as if asking permission.

Speaking would require breaking the kiss and she didn't want that. So she instead slid her own hands down and pulled at his shirt, yanking it free of his belt. Then she slipped underneath it and stroked bare, sleek skin over his taut abdomen, loving the way that he sucked in his breath, the way she could feel that reaction under her fingers.

She wanted to whimper when he broke the kiss, but then she heard him suck in a breath so deep she thought he had, as she had, forgotten to breathe. Or perhaps forgotten how. And then he whispered her name, and the way he said it made her forget how to think. This was a time for feeling, and new and exhilarating sensations were flooding her.

"Now?" he asked, in that same shaky voice.

"Right now," she answered, sounding much the same.

He swept her up into his arms and carried her to the bedroom, to the bed he'd surrendered to her before. The only surrender she was interested in now was to the sensations overtaking her, awakening every nerve, every muscle, every inch of skin. She moved to help him when he started to tug at her clothes, or maybe it was her tugging at his; she wasn't sure anymore, and it didn't matter anyway. She wanted him naked, and she wanted to be naked with him. More new territory.

Clothes shed, they went down to the bed together, his hands on her and hers on him, stroking, searching, finding, memorizing. She wanted to know everything about him, everything he liked, so she could lure him to these moments again and again, prove to him it could last, even forever. At the same time he seemed to somehow know her, intimately, already. He trailed his hands, his mouth over her, waking up every nerve until she was nearly crying out with the feel of it. He rubbed, flicked, then suckled her nipples until she did cry out, her body practically rippling with fierce sensation.

His hands slipped over her, lingering a moment at the curve of her hip, then moving downward to stroke the very core of her. She didn't need the way his fingers slid over that knot of nerves to know that she was slick and ready, because she already knew it. But the bright, hot flash of fire that shot through her was new, breath-stealing, and again her body rippled under his touch.

He paused only to grab one of the newly bought condoms, but once he had it open she took it from him. He stared at her. "Let me," she whispered, wanting to touch him more than she wanted her next breath. She savored the look on his face at her words, the way his jaw clenched, as if he was assessing whether he would survive. Then he closed his eyes and she reached out. The groan that broke from him as she sheathed him was the most wonderful sound she'd ever heard.

He truly was beautiful. Tall, lean, powerful and purely male. She was certain he would laugh again if she said it, so she didn't. But later she would tell him, in no uncertain terms, just how beautiful she found him. And she wouldn't let him deny it.

And then she had no time to think. Or any desire to. Her desires had narrowed down to one thing. She wanted him, now, hot and hard and inside her. And when he moved to slide into her she welcomed him with a cry of his name. He groaned out her name in turn, and it was the most beautiful sound she'd ever heard.

And as if a dam had broken, all the months of denying how much he appealed to her, all the stolen glances, the telling herself it couldn't be, burst through. And as her body gathered itself, the impossible sensations building, she felt an unusual kind of gratitude for the circumstances that had brought them here. And then all thought was blasted out of her mind as her every nerve seemed to convulse at once, sending heat searing through her as her body clenched around him, and the only thing she heard was him saying her name like an oath, and her own voice moaning his over and over.

Chapter Thirty-Five

"Ember's not going to like you three going home," Brett said as he dished up the scrambled eggs he'd just finished cooking.

Annalise looked at him as he slid her plate across to her. "Oh?"

"Neither am I."

"They do like it here." She met his gaze, held it steadily. "I like it here."

Memories raced through his mind of all the times they'd come together. It had been the most astonishing, incredible, damned-near miraculous night of his life. Of any life, even one he could only have imagined. And the times in between, when he simply held her, when she snuggled up against him in utter contentment, had made him feel something he'd never felt before. An urge, a need, a demand entirely apart from the physical wonder he'd found with her.

He'd meant it when he'd told her he'd never been here before. And because of that, he'd had no idea. No idea what it would feel like to want, to need someone so compulsively it was almost unbearable not to have them. Not just sexually, but always, quiet moments like now, together, a unit, stronger together than the sum of the parts…

And he realized this was what his parents had never had, had never known. And he felt suddenly sorry for them, because this…this was the most amazing thing ever. And he smiled as he thought of all the time ahead, time he wanted to spend learning about her, every bit of her heart and mind.

The smile she gave him now, as if she knew exactly what he'd been thinking and felt the same way, gave him the nerve. He leaned forward, planted both palms on the cool stone of the counter and said it, the words he'd never expected to say.

"Then stay."

She stared at him. "What?"

"I know it's a little farther from the training center, but the extra room is worth it, isn't it? For the dogs, I mean? I know this house is smaller than yours, but we can expand, there's plenty of room, and we can update a few things—"

"Brett Shea, are you asking me—us—to move in with you?"

He'd thought that was obvious. "I… Yeah."

"One night together and you want us to move in."

"Actually, it's been several nights," he pointed out. "And we've known each other for nearly a year. This is just the first night we…" He trailed off, not sure how to describe it. His mornings after had never really mattered before.

"Had mind-blowing sex? Screwed our brains out? Nearly set the house on fire?"

By the time she got to *fire*, he was grinning despite himself. He walked around the counter to her and took her hands. "All of that." But then, with one of the greatest efforts of his life, he made himself add, "But something even more important happened last night."

"It did?"

"You made a guy who never has and never thought he would, believe in love."

She stared at him. Waited, silently. And he realized she wanted the words. Maybe needed the words. Deserved them, for sure. And suddenly he wanted to give them to her.

"I have to believe in it now," he said softly, "because I love you."

She threw her arms around him and gave him a kiss that had an effect on him that, until about ten days ago, he would have denied was even possible.

The eggs were cold by the time they got to them, but neither of them cared.

Late that morning Brett took her back to the training center to pick up her car. Then he would head to the station for the final briefing on the operation tonight, date night for the catfish and the schoolteacher. They wanted everything and everyone in place well before the appointed time, just in case the guy was watching.

As he drove, Brett was pondering how he could expand the garage so there would be room for her car as well as his unit and gear, listening to the rustling in the back as her dogs scrambled for the best position to look out the windows, while a glance back showed Ember looking on with what he'd swear was amusement.

"She's like an elder sibling, watching the younger ones be silly," Annalise said when she saw his look.

He laughed. He'd thought he'd laughed more since he'd been with her than he ever had in his life. "And she will be, soon." He reached out and put a hand over hers. "If you're sure?" he asked.

"I am. I'll start packing the minute I get home." She turned her hand over so she could grasp his. "Now you have to really, truly be careful tonight."

"Assuming it all happens as planned. He's a pretty smart guy, or he wouldn't have gotten away with this for so long."

She smiled at him. "You don't have to keep saying that anymore. Yes, I was foolish, but I know I'm not really stupid. I fell for you, didn't I?"

He had no words for how that made him feel, so he didn't even try. And at the station he carried those words around in his mind as they ran through the plan once more, then began to put it into action. One by one so they wouldn't draw attention, his backup team headed for the staged house. They would take up predetermined positions around the house, up and down the street, most in civilian clothes and vehicles. Two, in uniform and fully armed and armored, would be the actual takedown team if necessary.

Brett was determined it would not be, because he wanted to take down this scrawny little imposter of a man himself. More now than ever.

In place inside the house, Brett secured Ember with commands to stay and for silence; he'd considered not bringing her for this, but she was his partner and he might need her. Then he again inspected all the possible points of entry, did a final test on communications with the team, made sure the phone they'd rigged as the teacher's was charged and on, then settled in to wait.

He supposed it was a measure of how things had changed—how he had changed—that instead of the usual calm, patient attitude he usually managed on a stakeout, he was edgy, pacing and forever thinking. And not about what he should be thinking about. He was personalizing this. Because, damn it, it *was* personal now. He was antsy to have this done, to take down this clown who had hurt Annalise, to put an end to this unpleasant event in her life. He wanted it over and done with and in the past, so they could start into the future.

Their future. Something he'd never had before or never expected to look forward to in this way.

He was just glad the rest of the team was outside, so he didn't have to explain the silly grin that broke loose far too often. Which led him down another path—what he was going to do when, as it inevitably would, news got out about them.

Them.

Annalise and him.

Him and Annalise.

A couple.

A long-term couple.

Forever? He hoped so. For the first time in his life, he hoped so. No, not just hope, he was determined it would be. He'd have to make that clear up front, to…all of them.

The chief. Troy. Desiree. Grace. Jillian. FBI Bryce. The other Coltons he'd never met. The list was incredibly daunting for a guy used to being alone, on his own, for nearly fifteen years, since he'd been eighteen and his parents had pronounced their duty done.

Those Coltons would never do that. For better or worse, they are a unit and stand together. Have each other's backs.

Driven by an urge that was as new to him as the rest, he called up the website for the K-9 training center on his own phone, just so he could look at her picture. He should take a better one, so he could have it with him. The official portrait was fine, but she looked so formal and…well, official. He wanted a picture of the smiling Annalise, the laughing one, the soft one. Hell, he wanted the angry one, too, with her chin set as she faced down whatever it was. When the chips were down, she was as tough as she had to be. And despite her doubts—*I'm not tough enough to be with a cop*—he knew she would always be.

The text came in as expected, just before the teacher would have had to leave to meet at the coffee shop. Brett read it, a sour grimace on his face. *Figures.* Of course that would be the excuse, something dramatic, laudable. A search and rescue for a missing little boy was his excuse. *I'm so sorry.*

Brett typed in the response he and Annalise had prepared, expressing the teacher's disappointment but understanding, and a compliment on his heroic vocation. And then came the rest of it, the vow to make up for it later, and in the meantime for her to expect something to make up for the forced cancellation. The delivery of her favorite drink—and some special treats—from Grave Gulch Coffee and Treats would arrive shortly.

Brett sent out the signal that it was a go, putting the team on high alert. They all reported back, in position and ready. And Brett was back to pacing again. And all his self-lecturing that it wasn't good to be this edgy, that that was when you made mistakes, wasn't helping. He wanted this over, wanted Annalise out from under this cloud, and he wanted it now.

"Incoming white van. Southbound from Hilltop. Slow."

The announcement came through loud and clear. Officer Fulton, he thought, the quiet but dogged patrol cop who had volunteered for this because she'd been at Annalise's the night the catfish had struck.

"Copy," he returned.

It was a minute later before the southern lookout spoke. "Got him under obs. He's slowing. Looking at houses. Or addresses."

"Copy," Brett repeated. "All units?"

Each reported in turn. They were as ready as they could be.

Come on, come on, come on...

"Heading for the driveway!"

A split second after he heard the words Brett saw the sweep of light across the front windows as the headlights of the van raked the house. He moved to where he could see through the big front window but would be far enough back not to be seen by the suspect. They'd agreed on radio silence starting the moment the suspect got out of the vehicle until Brett gave the signal to move in by turning on the porch light.

The man who got out of the white van looked right. Short, thin, at least, it was impossible to see more from here in the dark. He walked to the back of the van and unloaded a cart. This time it was a more casual affair, no linen tablecloth, but what Brett guessed from his visits to the place for morning coffee was a festively colored paper mat. The suspect then set several items on the cart, including some sort of machine like Brett had seen in the shop, he guessed to make the cappuccino as promised.

The catfish spared no detail, obviously. And Brett felt a twitch of misgiving, wondering if they really had covered all the bases. Once more he reminded himself this guy was not stupid. But he was here, and in moments he'd be cuffed and on his way to where he belonged.

The man wheeled the cart up to the front door and knocked. Brett waited a three count, then walked over. Weapon drawn now, he stood with his left shoulder to the wall, keeping his gun arm free. He reached with his left hand to open the door while in the same motion he flipped the light switch beside it with his elbow. Light flooded the porch from the high-power bulb he'd installed the first day he'd come here to check the site.

"Don't move. You're covered on four sides."

The shorter man's head came up. His face was now as clear as if spotlighted. And wide-eyed fear was just as clear in his expression. "What?" he practically squeaked.

Brett swore violently as the team closed in. "Stand down!" he snapped out.

"What's up?" Officer Fulton asked as she neared the front door.

"It's not him," Brett said disgustedly.

"What?" the young cop asked. "But he's got the van, the cart—"

"I saw him that night. This isn't him."

The former suspect realized he'd been absolved, although he likely had no idea for what.

"But…does that mean some regular guy just happened to use the same MO?" Fulton asked, sounding bewildered.

"I don't know." But he doubted it. The catfish had to be connected to this, somehow.

"I wonder where he really is," Fulton said, looking around as if she expected the real criminal to just walk out of the dark and into their hands.

"So do—"

Realization slammed into Brett as hard as if that van in the driveway had hit him at sixty. The little differences, the rush, the photos—he'd written them off to the catfish changing things up so he wouldn't get caught... But they weren't for that. They were because, for the catfish, this *was* different. This was to make up for the last time, to salve his ego, to show no one, but no one foiled him. Especially not his target, his mark.

Soon enough, my sweet. I'll be coming for you.

Annalise.

Annalise, at home alone, with just her dogs, because they'd assumed she'd be safe tonight.

He'd assumed.

And now he ran.

Chapter Thirty-Six

Apple and Jack barked and howled in an odd sort of accompaniment that made Annalise laugh. She'd been working since the moment she and the dogs had gotten home, packing, organizing, and probably ridiculously, singing the entire time. But she couldn't help it, her heart was soaring, so full of happiness it couldn't be contained.

She was going to have the future she'd always dreamed of. Well, minus the loving a cop part. That, with all its accompanying stress and danger had never been part of her dreams, but she would simply have to deal. She would talk to Evangeline, and they could compare notes, coping strategies. Her future sister-in-law was tougher than she was to begin with, and her time as a prosecutor had honed that, but Annalise was certain she could learn. She had to learn, because there was no way she was giving up Brett.

She was using the opportunity to set aside some things she no longer used or wore—and a couple of bad choices that had never been off the hanger or out of the box—to be donated. It was making a bit of a mess, but that was okay. Because she wasn't going to be here much longer.

She was going to need boxes. There was a moving company in the next town that sold them, she knew, and mentally added that to the list of chores that was growing rapidly.

And then there was the other list. The people list. People she would have to tell she was moving. Where she was moving. And why. Starting with her parents. And she had no idea how they were going to take it.

Maybe she'd start with her siblings. Grace and Desiree, they'd understand. Heck, they'd practically already guessed anyway, at least that she was attracted to him. And Troy would be okay with it, she knew, because she knew he liked and respected Brett. Or would he? Sometimes liking and respecting a colleague was different than accepting them as the lover and boyfriend of your sister. She hoped—

The sound of the doorbell startled her off the merry-go-round of thoughts and sent the dogs into a cacophony of noise.

"A little late, guys," she teased them as she started that way. "Did my glorious singing drown out the sound of someone coming to the door?"

She'd been in the bedroom at the back of the house. So aside from a bit of barking at a car that had parked in the alley a little while ago, she hadn't heard anything but the dogs. They had been more interested in what she was doing and—apparently, from their dancing around—her wonderful mood.

Not so long ago she would have just opened the door, but no longer, sadly. She felt a little pang as she realized she might never feel that safe again. But she smiled as she remembered soon she would both feel and be safer than she had ever been, because Brett would be there for her.

She stopped at the door and leaned forward.

"Pizza?" Annalise stared through the peephole at the

box from Paola's the delivery man was holding up. "I didn't order any pizza."

That wasn't to say it didn't sound wonderful.

"It says it's a gift," the voice came through the door. "So somebody thought you need it."

Brett. She grinned sillily. It had to be Brett. Even while he was working, he was thinking of her.

She unlocked the door and pulled it open.

And gasped in horror.

BRETT'S PLAN WAS to come in from the alley, so he'd slowed to a crawl before making the turn off the street. His mind was racing so fast he was surprised he couldn't hear it whir. They'd have to be careful, startle the guy and who knew what he might do? Have to assume he was armed in some way. Knife, maybe. Because this was personal. She'd scared the catfish, so he wanted her scared. He wanted to make her pay.

The thought of her hurt, cut, bleeding, made a cool, calculating sort of anger rise in him. The bastard would not get away with this. Not with Annalise.

His SUV edged forward, and he looked down the alley. The first thing he saw was the white van, which had stood out by size alone even at this distance.

Two people behind it.

A man, short, thin, wearing a shirt as white as the paint job.

A woman.

Wrestling with him. Fighting.

Annalise.

He couldn't really see the woman from the far end of the alley, but he knew.

A jolt of pure fear shot through him, spiking his

adrenaline level. It was all he could do to keep himself from ramming his foot on the accelerator, making a tire-screeching turn and giving away the game.

He registered everything, assessing in split seconds. She was fighting him, so she was conscious. But even as he thought it, she went limp. Which answered the dart question. The man shoved her into the van. Jumped in after her. And the door slammed shut.

He knew it had only been a couple of seconds, but it felt like a lifetime. He put out the info, not caring if what he was feeling was obvious in his voice.

"He's got her. In the alley. White panel van. Fulton, take the north end."

"Copy. I'm less than a minute out."

The sound of the van's engine cut through the night. Less than a minute wasn't going to be fast enough. Brett yanked the wheel around and jammed the accelerator to the floor. His SUV leaped forward, just as the van pulled away. The other driver realized quickly he was in trouble, and both van and police vehicle headed through the alley at far too high a speed.

The chase through the night was harrowing. For the first time since he'd left the city Brett missed something: the ability to call for air support. He could use a helicopter with a nice, bright spotlight. It was clear the catfish knew the area. He made turns down narrow streets that looked as if they should be dead ends but weren't. Cut through the parking lot of a small local grocery to come out on a bigger street. Increased his speed, dodging through Saturday-night traffic. And twice not dodging quite enough. Brett managed to avoid the collisions himself. Barely. And that gave the van a few precious seconds to pull ahead.

And to make a last instant turn. Brett followed. Ember let out a yelp as the SUV careened around the corner.

The van was nowhere in sight. Gone.

Annalise was gone.

HE WOULD FIND HER. If he had to cover every inch of Grave Gulch on foot, he would find her. He would walk his feet bloody if he had to.

He'd been driving up and down every street, not just looking for the van but for anyplace it could hide. But there were houses with garages everywhere, and if the catfish had rented one, he could be out of sight altogether.

Fine. So we do a damned door-to-door.

His jaw tightened even more. He should have known. He never should have let her stay at her place, but he'd been so happy she wanted to move in as quickly as possible he hadn't protested. And now she was caught, trapped, in the hands of a piece of human debris who, in his way, was as bad as Bowe. Always blaming everything on someone else, in Bowe's case his wife, in the catfish's probably every woman who'd ever turned him down.

He was not going to lose her. Not when he'd only just found her, when he'd only just found out what it was all about, not just love but life itself. He'd finally—

His foot hit the brake almost before his conscious mind registered what his peripheral vision had caught. A block of white. He backed up to look. And saw a sliver of the back of a white van, barely visible behind a tall fence.

He stopped his SUV on the cross street, out of sight. Leashed Ember, who was already at a high pitch, feeding off his fierce state. They started toward the spot, using the fence hiding the van to hide themselves and proceeding a few feet off the sidewalk.

Ember told him several feet before they got there that she had the scent. Her head came up, and even in the dark he could see her nose working, pulsing as she sorted the smells. Annalise, he thought. Wouldn't it be something if that work she'd been putting in with his dog ended up saving her?

He put the location and call for backup out in a whisper. He barely noticed the responses and didn't care. This was his to do. He'd made the monumental screwup of not realizing what the catfish would do.

Ember paused, clearly uncertain. She was onto something, but looked at him in puzzlement. Yet her tail was wagging slightly. She was getting both her quarry and Annalise.

"Track," Brett ordered quietly.

Ember led him to the back of the run-down cottage. Not to the door of the cottage itself, but to a separate shed behind it, a small building with a door and a broken window beside it. Ember danced, still not sure if she should be proud she'd found Annalise or worried about The Other.

Then her head came up and turned, as if she'd scented something—or someone—new. Her signal wasn't alarm, so Brett figured it had to be someone she knew. A yell came out of the darkness to his right.

"Duck!"

Instinctively he dropped. Heard something go over his head and land with a metallic clatter behind him. A glance told him it was a lethal, curved blade that looked like nothing less than a machete. Flung full force through the broken window in the moment when he'd been checking Ember's reactions. And it could easily have hit him and done some serious damage. If not for the warning.

He spun to his right and Troy Colton materialized out of the darkness.

"Heard your backup call," his fellow detective whispered.

"It's the catfish. He's got Annalise."

Troy went very still. "Then let's take his ass."

No questions, no doubts, no hesitation and full confidence. They really did have his back. Not just Grave Gulch PD, but the Coltons.

"I saw a door on the back side. You want to try talking him out, while I go in from there?" Troy whispered. At Brett's look, his grin flashed. The grin that had become so frequent since Troy and Evangeline had connected. Which Brett finally understood. "Hey, I blend in at night better than your pasty Irish face, bro."

"Can't argue that. I practically glow in the dark." And he felt the kind of connection he'd only felt with compatriots he literally trusted with his life.

"Let's do this," Troy said.

Brett called up every hostage-negotiation tactic he'd ever been taught. Pretended he was reluctant to take lethal action. Pretended he was perfectly willing to wait out here until the catfish decided, as if ceding control to him. And pretended—to himself, because he had to—that he was certain the man wouldn't kill Annalise because he wanted to torment her for insulting him.

The first time the guy called out an answer, demanding he leave, Brett knew they were on. Troy would know the suspect's attention was on Brett and make his move. And staying here, letting it happen that way, was the hardest thing he'd ever done. But it was the best chance for Annalise, and right now that was all that mattered. And Troy would see that it went down right, that she stayed safe. Because that's what Colton cops did. And in a way, he was one of them now. They didn't know it yet, but he'd make sure they did. He wouldn't accept any less, for Annalise's sake.

Brett started to move when he heard a shout from inside. Then the door on this side burst open and the catfish bolted out, looking back over his shoulder as if terrified.

Brett reached out with his right foot and caught him on his next stride, right above the ankle. The guy went down like the flailing bag of scum he was. Flushed out like a quivering quail and tripped up like a graceless freak.

And Brett couldn't think of a more appropriate ending for him.

Chapter Thirty-Seven

Annalise listened for a moment before she opened her eyes. The last image in her mind, so vivid, so ugly, was that slimy monster with his hands on her, trying to force her into that van. He had to have used one of his stolen darts on her.

But now she was lying on a bed, in a place where there were other people, because she could hear distant voices and footsteps. And someone was here, because she could feel the warmth of a hand wrapped around hers. And that scent... Like the forest, like the pine trees she loved.

Like Brett.

Her eyes snapped open. Hospital? She was in a hospital? But in the next instant even that didn't matter. Because Brett was there, he was the one holding her hand, and looking at her with as much love as she ever could have hoped for in his bright blue eyes.

"Welcome back," he said softly.

"You figured it out," she said. "You found me. Saved me."

"With some help from Ember. And Troy." Her brows rose. "He was there when I needed him," was all he said, but she read much more in his eyes.

"You caught him though?"

He nodded. "Name's Ben Toomey. He played along several women on the app, hoping we'd be on one of them, instead of you."

"So it wasn't your fault."

"Less my fault than I first thought," he amended. "I was afraid I'd done something to tip him off."

"Of course you didn't."

"Turns out he lost most of what he had in a nasty divorce. Dr. Masters thinks he's stealing from women as payback."

"Better than some things he could have done, I guess." She frowned. "But I don't remember—"

He squeezed her hand gently. "They said you'll probably remember most of it, once the drug's completely out of your system."

"I do remember that when everything went blank I was in hell, but—" she squeezed his fingers and smiled at him "—now I wake up in heaven."

He actually blushed. Which pleased her to no end. And when he lifted her hand to his lips and kissed it, she felt her pulse leap. Curious, she glanced at the monitor near the bed and laughed. He looked up, appearing a bit startled. She pointed with her other hand to the screen, to the suddenly higher number that was slowly decreasing.

"I guess there's no denying what you do to me now, is there?" she teased.

His gaze locked with hers. "If I was hooked up to one of those, mine would do the same thing. Every time you look at me."

She drew in a deep breath. She could have died last night, if Brett was a little less brave, a little less determined. She could have died without ever saying it. And so she said it now.

"I love you."

The expression of wonder and relief that came over his face then said more than even his words did. "I never really knew what love was. I do now. It's what I feel for you."

Warmth flooded her, but she had a single reservation left. "I should never have opened the door to him. But I thought you'd sent him."

"It doesn't matter. He's locked up, and he's going to stay there for a long time."

"But I was fooled again. I should have learned by now never to trust—"

"No," he said, stopping her. "Please, Annalise, don't ever lose that sweetness, that warmth." He took an audible breath before adding softly, "Sometimes it may be the only thing that keeps me going, knowing that there are people in the world like you. And your family. I won't deny I had my doubts, but I see now who the Coltons really are. And I know they'll have my back if I need it."

She held those words close to her for the next few days. They helped her get through giving her statement to the patrol officer who came to her room. Once she was released from the hospital she returned to packing, feeling a shiver of relief that she would be leaving this place that had once been a home but was now simply the place where the worst things in her life had happened. Brett had taken a couple of days off to help, and it was a joy to hear him telling her recklessly to bring everything she wanted, and they'd figure out where it all would go later.

He even talked about his plans to expand the house, in such detail she knew he had to have been thinking about it for a while. Which removed her last fear that he might have just said those wonderful words because she'd been lying in a hospital bed. The dogs were deliriously happy, which she completely understood since she was, too. They'd be even more happy if they knew Brett had suggested they just adopt them themselves, so they would always stay together.

And her joy bubbled over when he took her on an elaborate, elegant weekend date at the historic Grand Hotel up on Mackinac Island, an elaborate meal and two nights alone in a luxury room. When she asked why, it was so expensive, he'd said simply, "I want you to remember this date, not the bad ones."

But two weeks later it hit a peak she'd never thought possible when he came home—a phrase she loved, saying it or thinking it—with a rather tentative expression on his face.

"What?" she asked immediately.

"This is only so you can see it," he said, almost warningly. "It has to go back. I had to get the chief's and the prosecutor's permission to take it. But I wanted you to know I kept my promise."

"You always keep your promises, Brett Shea."

The smile he gave her then sent her pulse flying all over again. Then he pulled a small plastic bag out of his pocket. She frowned, recognizing an evidence bag. But then she saw what was in it.

Her grandmother's bracelet.

Moisture gathered in her eyes, and she flung her arms around him. She couldn't find a single word to say, so she just hugged him, holding on as if...well, as if she was holding on to the rest of her life. And he hugged her back in the same way.

"I was thinking," he said against her hair, his voice sounding oddly thick, "that since you can't really have this back until the trial's over that maybe we should get you…something else with diamonds."

She went very still. Became aware of his heart hammering in his chest, almost in time with her own.

"Brett?" she whispered.

"A ring. Would you wear my ring, Annalise? Will you marry me?"

She stared up at him. Was vaguely aware there were three dogs sitting near their feet, the clever Ember, who realized something important was up, keeping the smaller two in line. Their family. For now. Swallowed tightly, found her voice.

"I'll want kids," she warned.

For the first time doubt flashed in his expression. "I don't mind but I don't know how to be—"

She lifted a hand, put a finger to his lips. "Sure you do. Just do the opposite of what yours did."

He laughed, and she felt his tension ease. Then his brow furrowed slightly. "Does that mean…yes?"

"Yes, yes, a thousand times yes."

And Annalise Colton looked up into the blue, blue eyes of her future husband, and realized she truly had been holding on to the rest of her life.

* * * * *

COMING SOON!

We really hope you enjoyed reading this book.
If you're looking for more romance, be sure to
head to the shops when new books are
available on

Thursday 2nd
September

To see which titles are coming soon, please visit

millsandboon.co.uk/nextmonth

LET'S TALK
Romance

For exclusive extracts, competitions and special offers, find us online:

- **f** facebook.com/millsandboon
- 🐦 @MillsandBoon
- 📷 @MillsandBoonUK

Get in touch on 01413 063232

For all the latest titles coming soon, visit

millsandboon.co.uk/nextmonth

JOIN US ON SOCIAL MEDIA!

Stay up to date with our latest releases, author news and gossip, special offers and discounts, and all the behind-the-scenes action from Mills & Boon...

 millsandboon

 millsandboonuk

 millsandboon

't might just be true love...

MILLS & BOON
True Love
Romance from the Heart

Celebrate true love with tender stories of heartfelt romance, from the rush of falling in love to the joy a new baby can bring, and a focus on the emotional heart of a relationship.

MILLS & BOON
MODERN
Power and Passion

Prepare to be swept off your feet by sophisticated, sexy and seductive heroes, in some of the world's most glamourous and romantic locations, where power and passion collide.

MILLS & BOON
MEDICAL
Pulse-Racing Passion

Set your pulse racing with dedicated, delectable doctors in the high-pressure world of medicine, where emotions run high and passion, comfort and love are the best medicine.